sins of the brother

mike stewart

G. P. PUTNAM'S SONS   NEW YOR

sins of the brother

"Not Waving But Drowning" by Stevie Smith,
from *Collected Poems of Stevie Smith.*
Copyright © 1972 by Stevie Smith. Reprinted by
permission of New Directions Publishing Corp.

G. P. Putnam's Sons
Publishers Since 1838
a member of
Penguin Putnam Inc.
375 Hudson Street
New York, NY 10014

Library of Congress Cataloging-in-Publication Data

Stewart, Mike, date.
Sins of the brother / Mike Stewart.
p.   cm.
ISBN 0-399-14537-0
I. Title.
PS3569.T46544S5   1999   99-24672 CIP
813'.54—dc21

Printed in the United States of America
10 9 8 7 6 5 4 3 2 1

This book is printed on acid-free paper. ∞

BOOK DESIGN BY LYNNE AMFT

For the girls

Nobody heard him, the dead man,
But still he lay moaning:
I was much further out than you thought
And not waving but drowning.

Poor chap, he always loved larking
And now he's dead
It must have been too cold for him his
   heart gave way,
They said.

Oh, no no no, it was too cold always
(Still the dead one lay moaning)
I was much too far out all my life
And not waving but drowning.

STEVIE SMITH

sins of the brother

prologue

M OVING ACROSS THE current, the boat slid through black water as streaks of reflected moonlight angled away from the bow. An electric hum pushed the men quietly toward the far bank. They watched for a break in the jagged line of treetops against the night sky. In a bend, the men saw clouds interrupt the tree line to form a "U" where the riverbank recedes into a slew. The older, heavy man in the stern pointed the bow toward a place just north of the dip in the moonlit clouds to compensate for the current and bring the boat into the mouth of the inlet. Once inside, the motor was cut, and its warm hum was replaced by the sounds of crickets, bullfrogs, night birds, and the occasional splash of a bass taking a dragonfly off the shimmering surface.

Out of the current of the main river, even the hum of the electric trolling motor was an unnecessary risk. The younger man leaned out over the bow to pull the boat farther into the slew with a short paddle, steering carefully among rotting tree trunks that pierced the water's surface and rendered the slew almost unnavigable. When the skiff was well inside the narrow inlet, he dropped a nylon cord weighted with scrap iron to anchor the boat near a thick trunk that split into twin prongs six feet above the water. The older man removed a square of paper from his pocket, unfolded it, and switched on a penlight with his thumbnail. Placing the miniature flashlight in his teeth, he studied a map of the slew sketched next to a list of numbers and letters set out next to numeric dates. The bulb cast a moving circle of light on the paper as the man scribbled new notations.

"Who's there?" An unexpected voice startled the men. The older man killed the penlight, and the younger one reached for a short rifle in the boat's bottom just as the voice on the riverbank came again. "I said who are you. What are you doing out here this time of night?"

The older man whispered, "Put the gun down. You don't shoot somebody just 'cause you don't expect them to be there. And you can't shoot somebody you can't see anyhow. Calm down."

"Calm down my ass," the younger man said too loudly, then lowered his voice to a whisper. "Somebody's watching us. They've seen where we put down anchor, and they spotted us because you like to play with that stupid list."

"Hall, just stand up like we got nothing to hide and tell him we're night fishing."

"The hell with that. You stand up and talk to him."

"Look, you sound like a good old boy and I don't. Now just stand up and answer him real friendly."

The boat rocked gently as the young man stood slowly, bracing his knee against the metal seat for balance. Before he could answer, a disk of light illuminated his face. His head appeared to float above the water—a pure white apparition against the black river. He saw a flash of fire among the trees just before the explosion dropped him out of the light and into the dark water. The older man lay quietly in the floor of the boat, listening to the gunshot echo across the river.

chapter one

F ALL LIGHT ANGLED low through the office window overlooking Mobile Bay, laying a bright trapezoid of sunlight across
the floor. I had separated from Higgins & Thompson some six months
before to get away from the billable-hour marathon. I succeeded
admirably. I hadn't worked more than twenty hours any week since
leaving the firm. It had begun to dawn on me that I was a lawyer, not
a rainmaker.

This was not an original thought.

Last spring when I told Wilbur Thompson III, the managing partner, I was leaving, he smiled and said, "You won't make it. You're one
of the smartest lawyers I've ever seen, but you're also a prick. Clients
don't hire pricks. They hire nice guys who can supply them with
pricks."

He paused to reach inside his coat and casually remove a black
and gold fountain pen the size and shape of a cheap cigar and to ad-
mire the luster of the black barrel which, as he had mentioned on a
dozen occasions, was made of "space-age polymers." He played with
his three-hundred-dollar pen for a few seconds—a true thespian emot-
ing disinterest—before he continued. "This firm has been your keeper.
We give you cases, and our firm's reputation gets you clients. We stand
on the golf course and tell CEOs what a smart, tough lawyer you are.

We supply the meals. All you do is feed. All you do, Tom, is out-prick all the baby pricks."

Wilbur sat there looking at me over half glasses like he had just handed me the key to wisdom. I said, "Fuck you," and left.

On the way out, his secretary gave me an empathetic, I-guess-you-got-fired kind of look. I said, "Do you think we should tell him that space-age polymer is plastic?"

She didn't smile.

It was six months later, the last Thursday morning in September, when Kelly buzzed me. "Your mother is on line one. She sounds awful."

"Have you met my father?"

"Line one."

I picked up the receiver and punched a blinking acrylic button. "Hi there."

"Hello, Tom."

"Is something wrong?"

"It's your brother. They found him in the river near the lake house. He's dead, Tom."

"What happened?"

"I don't know everything. Your father won't tell me."

"Let me talk to him. Is he at work?"

"I don't know where he's gone. You know how he is. Sam is probably out cussing the rescue squad for waiting till Hall was dead to find him."

When I didn't respond, she added in her soft mother's voice, "I'm sorry. That came out bad. Dr. Pearson has given me something, and I'm a little fuzzy. I want you here. I know you're busy starting your own firm, but I think I need you here as soon as you can."

"Mom, I'm on my own. I'm not starting a firm, and if I were you know I'd still come. Hall's been jerking all of us around for ten years, but I love him as much as you do."

Silence.

I said, "Are you okay? I mean, I know you're not, but—"

She interrupted. "Tom, I'll be okay. Like I said, Dr. Pearson has given me something to help, and Mabel's here to look after me." She paused before going on. "Sam won't say it, but we both need you here. There's a lot that's wrong about all this. Even more wrong, I mean, than it looks like now."

"What do you mean?"

"I don't know exactly. As I said, Sam hasn't told me everything."

"When is the funeral?"

"Saturday."

"I'll be there tomorrow morning. Goodbye, Mom. I love you."

My lips and cheekbones started to go numb as I lifted my suit coat from the door hook and left the office. On the way by Kelly's desk, she asked if something was wrong.

"Call Dan Smitherman and tell him my brother just died and the Scrimscher case won't try next week. Call Judge Varner and tell him the same thing, then draft a motion for a continuance and sign my name to it."

"That's not funny, Tom."

"I know."

In the elevator, the numbness seemed to spread to my hands and feet. I found my Jeep in the parking deck, got in, and wondered momentarily where to go. Outside, I found my way through town, crossed Polecat Bay, and took I-10 to the coast highway, where I rolled down the windows, and headed south toward Point Clear.

The autumn wind felt cool. Ocean smell filled the world, and in less than an hour I pulled onto the familiar crunch of the white gravel drive at home. Inside the beach house, I left my suit, shirt, and boxers on the bedroom floor, pulled on canvas shorts, and walked across the sand to feel cold waves on my feet before running a few steps and diving into a rolling swell. It was late in the year, and the sudden cold made my stomach tighten. I began to pull through the water, raising my head to the left every fourth stroke to inhale before blowing out into water. After fifty yards the numbness gave way to warm blood, and

I slowed to a steady rhythm. Two hundred yards out, I stopped moving and floated upright like a fishing cork. The swell gently lifted and lowered me as waves rolled in from somewhere out in the Gulf of Mexico and lost momentum inside the bay.

In my memory, Hall and I had half grown up in the water. Not in the Gulf, but in swirling river water the color of rust. We swam in it, pulled bass, crappie, and catfish out of it, skied on it, and now Hall, somehow, had been killed by it. Even clearer in my mind than the gray and green swells around me, I could see Hall at seven or eight years old, bobbing in muddy water behind Sam's gold and white ski boat. Hall had turned as dark as our mother's Creek ancestors, as he always did in summer. Early afternoon sun glinted off the small hard muscles in his shoulders and off the knuckles of his small fists as he clenched the plastic handles of the nylon rope. Invisible beneath the dirty water, a white strip of foam rubber circled his waist and kept him afloat. Hall was always more strong than agile until he stopped growing in high school, and that afternoon he was having trouble learning to ski. He was having more trouble than Sam thought any son of his should have, and Sam had been dragging Hall behind the boat, through one failed attempt after another, for the better part of an hour. I could see Hall trying not to cry, trying not to let our father down. I wanted to help him. I told Sam that Hall looked too tired to get up. Sam looked disgusted. "Look at him, Tom. See his eyes? Big as saucers. He's scared. He'll get over it. He quits being scared, he'll get up."

I wanted to defend my brother, who had been tougher that afternoon than I thought he could be. All I could think of to say was, "Hall isn't scared." Sam ignored me. I watched as Hall braced himself to be dragged through another hundred feet of water. I was only ten or eleven, and I could see that nobody, not even someone who could already ski, could pull up after being repeatedly snatched through the river for an hour. Sam was right about one thing, though. Hall's eyes were big. White showed all around his dark irises. I knew the look. Hall wasn't scared, except maybe of Sam. He was trying not to cry, and I was mad. "He's not scared. He's tired. He needs to get in the boat."

Sam said something about us acting like a couple of little girls all day. Like a child, I threw something across the stern of the boat. Sam turned sideways in the vinyl captain's chair to lock eyes with me. He just said, "Fine," and turned the boat hard to head back toward Hall, who was too tired to pull himself out of the river. I grabbed a small, slick arm and pulled. Hall was halfway in when he slipped and fell back. Sam stepped out of the captain's chair and walked back to the side where Hall bobbed in the current. Hall was worn out, and he was looking up into Sam's face for something—for approval or encouragement or just about anything to not feel like he had let him down. Sam reached over the side and picked Hall up in one hand, grabbing him by his forearm and lifting him into the boat like a hooked fish.

We waited for Sam to say something. He didn't. He left Hall alone, and we headed back to the dock. Hall sat cross-legged on the seat next to the outboard motor and shivered inside a light blue towel. Finally, unable to hold on any longer, tears began to roll down his sunburned cheeks. Sam didn't speak to either of us again that afternoon. He dropped us off at home and drove away, probably to check on his sawmill.

I shook off the memory.

To the south, cumulus clouds met the horizon and stood out in perfect contrast to the sky like a Steve Graber charcoal. I watched the shore, the horizon, the clouds for a long time before turning toward shore. As always, the gentle crosscurrent brought me out a couple of hundred yards south of my piece of beach. I sat there for an hour on someone else's sand. The wind grew cold and the sky gray before I stood to go home.

A hot shower washed away the salt and cold. Wrapped in a terry cloth robe, I sat on the deck eating cold grilled shrimp out of a Ziploc bag and drinking warm Glenfiddich. By nine o'clock I was filled with an overwhelming sense of relief and joy. Two hours later a dark weight began to lower.

It had been almost two years since I had seen Hall, when Mom had been able to talk through all our excuses, wear us down, and bring the family together for Thanksgiving. And it started out pretty bearable. We watched football and had drinks and everything was fine until the big meal when Sam decided to motivate Hall by comparing his life to mine. Thinking back, even then, there seemed to have been undercurrents that I was unaware of.

Sam began by teasing Hall about his girlfriend, who lived with Hall but had not been invited to dinner, and then worked his way into Hall's "academic career." Sam sarcastically asked, "How many quarters were you at Patrick Henry Junior College, Hall?" Hall didn't answer. I ignored Sam, and Mom tried to talk about something else. Sam had a few drinks in him. He went on. "Managed to maintain a C-minus average at that institution of higher learning for two quarters. Isn't that about right?"

Sam couldn't get anyone to play. A cloud of silence settled over the table, and Sam decided on another tack. "I'm sorry. I don't mean to pick on you, son. But sooner or later, you're going to have to get your act together. Got to quit chasing trailer-park girls and trying to make a living betting on football games."

Enough was enough. I pushed back from the table and looked at Sam. I said something the whole family had heard Sam say all our lives about foolish drunks. "If a man can't hold his liquor, he shouldn't be drinking." Sam flushed red, stood up, and walked out of the room. Mom followed. I could hear them arguing on the front porch. I looked at Hall and said, "Don't worry about him."

Hall stretched to reach across the table for a basket of rolls. He said, "I don't."

It dawned on me that Hall seemed to be the only one at the table who had not been bothered by what Sam had said. During Sam's diatribe, Hall had never stopped eating, and his expression had never changed. Hall hadn't been hiding his feelings about Sam. *He didn't have any.* The realization scared me. I wanted to talk to my brother about it, but Hall had gone to a very cold place. And I didn't know what to say about that.

Now he was gone. I looked out across the black expanse of Mobile Bay and cried for my little brother until I passed out in a deck chair.

At daybreak the sun brought me around. I walked carefully into the kitchen with each step sending echoes of pain from neck to temples. Following the remedy we used in college, I washed down three aspirins with a sixteen-ounce Coke and went to bed. At nine, the phone rang. Kelly told my machine that Judge Varner's law clerk called to extend condolences and let me know the continuance had been granted. I got up a few minutes later and forced down a quart of water to replace fluids taken by salt water and Scotland's oldest distillery, then fell back into bed. I lay there for another hour in an uncomfortable tangle of terry cloth bathrobe until I heard tires on the gravel driveway. A few seconds later the front door opened and closed, and I headed downstairs, finally wide awake. I found Kelly in the kitchen standing on tiptoe trying to reach a couple of glasses on the top shelf of the cabinet next to the sink.

I said, "Good morning," and she turned to look at me. Kelly stands about five-two in bare feet and might weigh a hundred pounds with sand in her pockets. She has black hair, cut too short for my taste, bright blue eyes, and a complexion that has never seen a freckle, much less a blemish or wrinkle. Kelly is a few years younger than I am. She runs five miles a day—considerably more in the fall when she trains for the New York Marathon—and she looks it. On the counter next to her left hip sat two plates of pancakes, each garnished with twin sausage patties. Next to the plates lay three Styrofoam breakfast trays from McDonald's.

She said, "Can you hand me down a couple of those juice glasses?"

I smiled. "You know, we could just drink out of the paper cups from McDonaldland."

"No way. I came out here to do something nice for you. I can't cook, so we're going for presentation."

I walked over and handed the short glasses to Kelly. She stood there with her elbows resting on slender hips, holding an empty glass in each small hand. She searched my face with her eyes, then asked, "Are you okay?"

"It wasn't a great night."

"I know. It's a stupid question."

"It's the same one I asked my mother when she called yesterday."

Kelly stepped forward and, still clutching the empty juice glasses, hugged me hard around my rib cage. When she let go, she said, "Grab the plates and sit down. I've just got to pour the juice. I put on a pot of real coffee after I got here, by the way."

"I'm impressed."

"You were meant to be. Go. And do something about that robe."

I picked up the breakfast plates. "I always thought I looked pretty cute in this robe."

She turned toward the counter and said, "Yeah, but if it falls open another two inches, I'm going to find out some things that a secretary just doesn't need to know about her boss."

I turned and walked very quickly out of the kitchen.

Over breakfast, I told Kelly as much as I knew about Hall's death. She agreed that it was going to take more than a weekend to settle things, and she said she'd clear my calendar for the next few days. I promised to call as soon as I knew when I'd be able to get back to my life in Mobile.

Less than an hour after she left, I was showered, packed, and driving north on I-65 to attend my only brother's funeral.

Thirty miles north of the Gulf of Mexico I pulled onto an off ramp, turned left under the four lane, and headed due north along a narrow stretch of blacktop as the interstate pulled away to the northeast toward Montgomery and Atlanta. Soon the flat coastal plains began to roll, and the road curved more and more often to move over and around the land. Creeks large enough to be called rivers in New England cut back and forth across the road, requiring a bridge every few miles. Soybean fields, cow pastures sprinkled with brown and white Herefords, and dense stands of timber passed by. Occasionally, an anachronistic field of cotton floated past as the road descended into bottomland. Almost a hundred miles from my beach house in Point Clear, I passed a wooden sign cluttered with the seals and insignias of the Civitans, the Kiwanis Club, the American Legion, and the Fighting Wildcats. All of them officially joined in extending a civic-minded welcome to anyone who stumbled across the city limits of Coopers Bend, Alabama.

I took a few minutes to drive around the courthouse square and along Magnolia, the main drive, before turning toward the house where Hall and I grew up. My father's house sprawls across a hilltop overlooking the town and, more important, overlooking his sawmill. Out of twelve thousand residents, a thousand make their livings, one way or another, from the mill. I pulled the Jeep around the circular driveway and onto a cement pad next to the carport where I had parked my old Chevy in high school. Inside, my mother was sitting in the atrium surrounded by greenery and smelling of bourbon and cigarettes. A copy of *Redbook* fell from her lap as she rose to kiss me, smearing my neck and cheek with tears.

"Thank God."

"How are you, Mom?"

"I'm not too good."

"Where's Sam?"

"He's at the mill. He wanted you to come down there as soon as you got here."

"I'll stay with you. He can see me when he gets home."

"No, Tom. It's okay. I'm fine as long as I know you're here to take care of things. You know how he is."

"Yeah, I know how he is. He's a bastard. I came here to be with you. I'll stay with you, and he can see me when he sees me."

Her eyes focused on my face for the first time. "I don't need to hear that now. And we both know he's not the only bastard in this family." She emphasized the word *bastard*, which seemed as foreign to her tongue as Serbo-Croatian would have been to mine. "I've got all I can handle. Just go down and talk to him. You're Hall's big brother. We all need you to act like it." She was being brave. Obviously and pointedly brave, but brave nonetheless. And she made her point that I was not.

"I'm sorry."

"Don't be sorry." Her voice was soft but firm. "Just go meet with your father. I'll be here when you get back."

There's something about being in the house where you were a child, where your parents were gods, where adolescence and hormones later made it a territorial imperative to challenge those gods and to make temporary enemies of the people who gave you life and as much love as they were capable of feeling. It is odd that grown men, and I suppose women, revert to egocentric children in the place where they learned to be independent and self-sufficient by challenging and denying the love and authority of the flesh and souls that produced them.

I thought these completely unoriginal thoughts as I drove away feeling about thirteen years old.

The sawmill was not in the city limits. It lay on a rail spur about five miles from downtown. As I bumped over the railroad crossing and turned into the mill yard, the dirty, human beauty of the place struck me the way a littered, graffiti-covered strip of urban playground must strike those who have innocent memories of such places. Even the soot exhaled from triple smokestacks seemed picturesque and somehow graceful. Tall bundles of freshly cut yellow pine lumber stood in perfect order on a football-field-sized landing; men and women with kerchiefs and hard hats covering their heads slowly and deliberately operated large, loud, hand-crushing machinery so they could make payments on tract houses and pickup trucks; and stray dogs with razor ribs and rheumy eyes delicately sniffed bits of trash for scraps of ham sandwiches and Vienna sausage among greasy lunch sacks. The workers and the dogs always looked the same. They had looked the same since I was a little boy. The men and women who ran the machines, who hauled logs and lumber and trash, were powdered from head to toe with sawdust that clung to sweat-soaked clothes and salty faces and hair, with wooden dust that seemed the deadening opposite of the stuff that kept Peter Pan young and lighter than air. The dogs that dodged kicks throughout the day to search for scraps looked like the same part bird dog, part coonhound, part God-knows-what that had lived on the yard for as long as I could remember.

Lying along the town side of the property, in contrast to the dirty, sweat-drenched beauty of the mill, was an out-of-place strip of manicured green lawn separating a small asphalt parking area from the wooden building that housed my father's office. The afternoon was warm and humid. I parked in a space near the brick walk, left the Jeep unlocked, and walked into a wall of cold, artificial air as the front door swung open. I found myself facing a twenty-year-old girl with permed, straw-colored hair that had been sprayed and locked into a cresting wave above her tiny forehead.

"Mr. Tom. How you doing?" She used the Southern habit of putting Mr. in front of a first name to show respect coupled with familiarity. It's the way I addressed my father's friends as a child. Now the children of my married friends in Mobile call me by my first name, which always seems disrespectful until I try to think of why any particular respect is due. Social customs from childhood die hard.

"I'm fine. Is my father here?"

"I sure am sorry about your little brother. We all loved Hall."

"Thank you. I'm sorry, do I know you?"

"Naw. I was a baby when you left here. I just knew you were coming, and you look like your daddy."

"Thanks a lot."

"Mr. Sam's a good-looking old guy. I always thought he must have been a hunk when he was younger. Now I know."

"How about telling my father the hunk that I'm here."

"That's not what I meant. I meant—"

"This is a bad day. Please just tell him I'm here."

Her lower lip puckered like a child's as she picked up the phone. "Mr. Sam. He's here."

The office door opened and Sam filled the doorway. He was as tall as I, but much broader. The years had progressively softened and widened the shoulders that had made him an all-state fullback in high school. He had even played a little ball at Auburn. By the time I got to the same college, high school stars who were six feet and weighed one eighty sat in the stands and watched guys half again their size ram each other.

"Good to see you, Tom. Come in."

As much as I disliked hearing that I looked like the old man, I knew I was looking at exactly what I would look like in twenty-five years. I have the same sandy hair, the same copper eyes, and the same physical attitude.

We shook hands briefly. He walked behind his desk and sat down. "Want a Coke or a beer or something?"

"No. I'm fine."

He left me sitting there in silence for some time while he studied my face. The next thing he said was, "Let's go for a ride."

"I didn't come here to go for a ride. I want to know what happened to Hall. Mom doesn't know, which I think is pretty shitty, and I don't even know why, or if, he drowned. I know he liked to scuba dive in the river, which is beyond me since you can't see a goddamn thing three feet down in that muddy water. I just want to know, did he get caught in fishing line on the bottom, or did he run out of air at the wrong time, or did he just get drunk fishing with Zollie and fall in the river? It shouldn't be too complicated. Hall fucked up and drowned. I just want to know how he fucked up this time." I realized I was rambling and trying to act like a tough lawyer to impress my father and taking out my anger on a man who had just lost a son. And I didn't care.

Sam said, "Are you through?"

"If you tell me what happened to Hall we'll both be through."

"Tom, Hall didn't drown. He didn't live long enough. Somebody blew away part of his neck with a deer rifle. Looks like he was on the river when it happened, but he never drew another lungful of air or water after he was hit. Apparently some of his friends knew where he liked to go fishing. Once he'd gone missing, the rescue squad dragged the area for three days before they hooked him."

"Somebody shot him?"

"That's what I said."

"Do they think somebody was shooting at a deer on the bank?"

"No."

I could feel my face grow hot and flushed in the air-conditioned room. "Sam, this cryptic shit is getting old. Tell me what happened."

He did not respond. Once again, he just sat there studying my face. I was rising to leave when he finally said, "Hall was mixed up in some things that would kill your mother. I knew some of it before. Since we found out he was dead, I've found out a lot more. Looks like he was breaking the law in about a dozen different ways, got crossways with someone, and they killed him." He paused for a moment. "This is my place of business, and I'm not going to talk about it any more here. Now, do you want to go for a ride and talk about this like a grown man and figure out what to do about it, or do you want to go home to your mother?"

With that, he got up and walked out of the office and through the front door. I stood there for a moment trying to control my anger before I went out and got into his Blazer. We drove about ten minutes before I realized he was headed for the lake house. A few minutes after that, he began to calmly tell me about the man my little brother had become, and, for the first time, I began to listen.

chapter two

EVEN IN LATE September the temperature had been in the low eighties at noon, and Sam had been running the Blazer's air conditioner full blast since before I walked out and climbed in beside him. Two horizontal half-moons of warm frost arched across the bottom of the windshield as hot wind from the pavement pushed against the glass, reacting with the untouchable cold inside.

Sam began, "I don't want your mother to know what I'm about to tell you. If I ever hear you told her, I'll make you sorry. Do you understand?"

I said, "I'm a lawyer. I know how to keep a confidence. But I'll tell you right now that I think Mom has a right to know why Hall died."

"You're not the one to decide about Elizabeth's rights. I asked you if you understood, and I want to know your answer," he said. "When I said it would kill your mother to learn what Hall has been up to, I was not trying to be dramatic. Elizabeth had a minor stroke about four months ago. She cannot be involved in what I'm going to tell you about your brother."

I was stunned. "Why didn't you tell me about the stroke before now?"

"Because Elizabeth didn't want you to worry about her. She knows you left your firm under questionable circumstances, and she didn't want to add to your worries."

"The circumstances weren't very questionable. I told the managing partner to fuck off and left."

"So I heard. I still pay some pretty fat retainers to a couple of lawyers in Mobile. I know what happened. You could have handled it better, but I really don't much blame you. I never could stomach working for anybody else myself. People at the top always want you to eat as much shit as they did to get there. Never could work up the appetite."

I just sat there. It was bad enough the old man seemed to understand me. I didn't have to make polite conversation about my problems.

He said, "Do we have an understanding about your mother?"

I touched my index finger to water droplets on the windshield and tried to draw the letter T before realizing the condensation was outside. Sam's eyes flicked over to notice what I had done, and my mind flashed across childhood memories of a hundred cold mornings when I drew my name on the frosted windows of Sam's old step-side pickup as we bumped along dark roads that led to creeks and rivers and beaver ponds where we would shoot ducks over the water at sunrise. When I saw Sam look, I tried, without thinking, to wipe off the initial that wasn't there, or maybe I tried to wipe away the lingering memory of frost on a child's small fingertip.

My mind came back to thoughts of my mother sitting alone in her sun room, drinking and chain-smoking the things that would, sooner or later, end her life. I said, "We have an understanding."

I noticed Sam's knuckles change from white to tan as he relaxed his grip on the steering wheel. He said, "You know Hall liked to smoke a little marijuana every now and then?"

"Yeah, I knew. I just didn't know you knew."

"I know a lot more than that. I also know he'd started selling it again. You remember when y'all had that fight one time when you came home from college?"

"Yes."

"Well, between what Hall told me and rumors around the mill, I figured out that you found out Hall was selling marijuana or cocaine or something and you kicked his butt."

I didn't say anything.

He said, "That is what happened, isn't it?"

I said, "Everybody under twenty-five in America since the seventies smoked a little dope, and about half of those sold some at one time or another. Hall was doing something stupid. I tried to talk to him. He wouldn't listen, and I ended up popping him a few times. I could have handled it better." I thought that would probably be on my tombstone: *Here Lies Thomas McInnes—He Could Have Handled It Better.*

Sam said, "Well, whatever you did and whatever I did didn't work because it looks like Hall moved from selling a little dope on the weekend to supplying half the county. I figured something was wrong because he always had too much money. Said he got it gambling on football and baseball, and I have no doubt that he gambled a hell of a lot of money. But you don't make money on sports gambling unless you're the one taking the bets. I know now he was betting a couple of thousand a weekend with some bookie in Birmingham. Sheriff Nixon says he still owes this bookie a few thousand."

"How would the sheriff know how much Hall owed some bookie in Birmingham?"

"He knows because he has investigated Hall's death. Sheriff talked to Hall's friends, and he put together some pretty good information. I also suspect he knows 'cause he's not above taking a little money under the table from the bookie's local man. Sheriff figures no one gets hurt. Everyone bets sports. He'd have to arrest half the men in the county if he wanted to do anything about it. And the bookie buys pretty cheap insurance that he won't even run into minimal problems from local law enforcement."

I said, "So Sheriff Nixon is on the take, and he just freely tells you information that proves he has connections with organized crime? Not only that, he implicates a bookmaker he has accepted bribes from and who could turn around and implicate him if the investigation goes any further." I stopped and looked at him in disbelief. "Either Sheriff Nixon is feeding you a load of crap to keep you off his back or he's lost contact with reality."

Sam leaned his head back against the headrest and took a deep breath. "Tom, we're all going to be asked a lot of questions about this murder before it's over." It was the first time the word *murder* had been used, and it surprised me how impersonal it sounded when Sam said it. "I want everything I tell you now to be considered privileged. You're a lawyer, and I never want this to go any further." He didn't wait for me to agree or disagree. "Every sheriff for the past fifty years in this county has been on the take. There's no way for a man to make a living in the job otherwise. Twenty years ago, when Billy Sadler was sheriff, he made a damn good living on the bootleggers. The dirt road juke joints and black whorehouses would each pay a few hundred dollars a month just so he would look the other way and let people do what they have been doing for a thousand years and will keep on doing for a few thousand more. Everybody except the Baptist preacher and Billy's wife knew it, and everybody figured it gave the sheriff some control over some bad stuff that was going to happen whether he was involved or not."

I interrupted, "Sam, I grew up here. I know how things worked. Believe me, you don't need the protection of attorney-client privilege to tell me this."

"I know I don't need the privilege for what I've told you so far, but it may come in handy after I tell you I paid Billy four hundred dollars a month when he was sheriff, and I pay Sheriff Nixon a thousand a month now."

Sam paused. I couldn't think of anything to say.

Sam said, "I'm not running whores or liquor, but I am trying to run a sawmill. Every couple of weeks, one of my men gets drunk and beats up his wife or cuts up his poker buddies on Saturday night. If I need him at work on Monday morning, I make a phone call and he's back at work with no questions asked. Our trucks also get cut a little slack on the county roads as long as the drivers don't get reckless. If they do, Sheriff Nixon calls me and I deal with them."

Here's an enlightened guy. Some redneck beats the hell out of his wife and Sam just makes a call and puts him back on the street because he needs a forklift driver.

He said, "All of this is to explain why Sheriff Nixon may tell me a little more than you'd find in his official file. Nixon may take a little protection money, but he's not going to protect some asshole who killed my son. If it comes to it, he'll talk with some friends at the Capitol in Montgomery, and the bastard will be arrested so fast he won't know what hit him."

We pulled off the last of the blacktop and turned onto a mile of red gravel road that leads to the lake house. Along the roadside, loblolly pine had given way to water oak and cypress webbed with Spanish moss. As the weathered frame house came into view, I saw Sheriff Nixon's unmarked cream Caprice parked under a stand of young oaks. Sam said, "I thought you would want to hear as much as you could firsthand. You and I don't much like each other, but you're smart and you can help on this. And I figure lawyers are used to working out problems without worrying too much about going through normal channels."

As Sam pulled in next to the sheriff's car, I said, "Most attorneys aren't as sleazy as people think."

He opened the door and got out, giving me the courtesy of not responding to a comment that was less a defense of professional ethics than a need to form some response to the sting of my father saying calmly and without emotion that he didn't much like me. I always thought I was the one who didn't like him. And, I thought, he probably meant most of what he said as a compliment. To men like Sam, it's a virtue to handle problems in a practical, results-oriented way without the bother of a lot of soul-searching or paper shuffling. In his view, his estimation that I could be trusted to meet with serious people about sensitive and marginally illegal matters, and to later forget whatever was necessary, was immeasurably more important than whether we liked each other. But whatever he meant or didn't mean, Sam was right.

Some lawyers become enamored of flawless briefs and intellectual arguments. Others solve problems with no fuss and very little paperwork at meetings that never happened. The latter are more effective and, if my business or reputation were on the line, I would choose the less honest lawyer, the shark . . . the prick.

I stepped down out of the passenger door and followed.

What we have always called "the lake house" is actually more of an old two-story hunting cabin that squats on a high bank overlooking the Alabama River, incidentally, without a lake in sight. Early on, Mom insisted on calling it a lake house. She said "cabin" sounded like it was a shack and "river house" sounded like we were operating a house of ill repute in some short story by Faulkner. As with most of the few things in life that Mom insisted on, we all fell into line and began to call it the lake house, and pretty soon it would have seemed wrong to call it anything else.

A porch runs around three sides of the bottom floor. We found Sheriff Nixon sitting in a straight-backed rocking chair on the porch overlooking the river. He was drinking a can of Coke, and the outside door to the kitchen was standing open. Sam didn't seem to mind, and I figured the sheriff had his own key or knew where Sam kept an extra.

Nixon was in the Marines when I was a kid, so I never really knew him growing up. Before he came home to run for sheriff, the only reason I even knew he existed was because the newspaper ran two or three articles in the early seventies about some decoration or medal or honor of some kind he received in Vietnam. I had gotten to know him better at a couple of Sam's dove shoots over the years. As far as I could tell, Nixon was like most of the ex-Marines I had known—not exactly a fount of human kindness, but competent and just smart enough to do what he needed to do without losing sleep over life's gray areas. He is the antithesis of the fat, sweaty Southern sheriff imagined by skittish travelers and bad writers. For starters, he's black, which is more the rule than the exception in Southern towns these days. He also has a short, wide frame of angular, useful muscles, and he somehow manages never to cough or scratch or do anything to look less than solid and hard and in control. Nixon rose out of his chair and shook Sam's hand, then took mine and, in that clipped, metallic accent peculiar to career military men, said, "Tom, I'm sorry for your loss." He said it like he'd said the same words a hundred times, but like he still meant them.

Sam walked through the open door to the kitchen and came out with two more cans of Coke and handed one to me. We pulled up more chairs and sat in a half circle facing the river. Sam said, "I filled Tom in on some of what you found out. I told him about the gambling and some of the business with the drugs. We both appreciate what you've done. You don't know Tom well, but he can help us work through this. I want you to tell him everything you know."

Sheriff Nixon sat completely still, just looking at the water. After a few seconds, he said, "Sam, I want to help you, but this is an official investigation. I met you here because you are a friend and you asked me to, but intervention by family members may not be productive." He was choosing his words carefully, feeling his way along. Something was wrong. Sam's expression clearly showed this was not what he expected.

I said, "Sam, will you excuse us for a few minutes?" To my surprise, he immediately got up and walked inside. I turned to Nixon and said, "What do you know about me?"

Again, he paused, seeming to order his thoughts before speaking. "I know Sam, and I knew your brother. Sam is hard. He has a temper. But if he gives you his word, then that's it. He will go to his grave and there won't be a word, a scrap of paper, even an offhand comment that betrays what he told you he would do." He paused again. "Your brother was a lot like Sam. You could have beat him to death and he wouldn't have told you something he didn't want to tell. But—and I mean no disrespect—if he lost his temper or got some chemicals in him, he was likely to say things that would have been better kept to himself."

"And you're wondering which one I'm like."

"Look, Tom, we've met a few times, but I don't know you. I've heard you're a lot like your daddy, and, like I said, Sam's got a temper but he controls it when he needs to. I do know that half the county was scared of Hall, and I heard you could whip his ass without breaking a sweat."

"I was ten years younger the last time I had to whip anyone, and, as far as Hall goes, most of the edge there was about being his big brother. He expected me to come out on top, so I did."

"Yeah, it works that way with brothers. But that's not really the point, is it?"

"No, it's not. You want to know if I'm as crazy as Hall. You want to know if I can control my mouth and not try to get tough at the wrong time."

Nixon waited a few seconds before he spoke. "This thing with Hall involves some bad people. I don't plan to be the next one to swallow a bullet because some hotshot lawyer from Mobile couldn't keep his mouth shut. And I don't plan to face charges because you messed up." I noticed he was measuring his words less, which meant either he was irritated or he was pressing to gauge my response. He didn't look irritated, but I'd never seen him when he did.

I said, "I'm not a drug runner, and I'm not some small-town hardass. I am a lawyer who makes a living finding solutions to problems without leaving anyone's ass in the crack. I'm like you. I'm good at what I do, and I'm not a Boy Scout. Now, we've talked this to death. Are we going to quit playing games, or do I just start from scratch? If you're willing to work with me, I could use the help. If you don't trust me, I'll find out what happened anyway, and I won't have to worry about protecting anybody except myself and my family."

The sheriff and I locked eyes, and I could almost see some trace of emotion moving behind his black irises. He suddenly stood and walked to the kitchen door. I figured I had blown it. He stayed inside for two or three minutes, then walked quickly past my chair and said, "I told your father you and I were going for a ride."

I thought, *Well, he's either going to help me or kill me.* I stood and followed him to his patrol car. As he pulled open the driver's-side door, I said, "Everyone wants to go for a ride today."

"What?"

"Nothing."

Nixon's unmarked Caprice looked more like the company car of a mid-level executive than a patrol car. The only signs of its official use were the blue bubble on the dash and the police radio unceremoniously bolted to the instrument panel. As we drove back to town, Nixon checked with the base unit operator, then spoke with a deputy whose nervous, high-pitched report of a domestic knifing sifted into the car through the grit of static. Not until we were parked outside his office did Nixon finally acknowledge my presence in the car.

He said, "I'm going to give you a copy of my report. It's complete, which means it contains details of investigations into your brother's other activities in the county, and it contains some materials about a murder from last July that we thought for a while might have something to do with what happened to Hall. Complete also means I'm giving you a copy of the coroner's report, including pictures of the body."

When I didn't respond, he said, "I can take out the coroner's report if you want. Hall was in the river three days before we got him up, and there was an autopsy. The report and the pictures probably won't do you much good anyway. I know if I was you I wouldn't want to see them. But they're there if you want them."

I said, "Sheriff, I don't want to look at any of it, but I've seen too many lawsuits turn on a handwritten note in the margin of a supposedly unimportant document to feel comfortable about leaving anything out."

Nixon just stared straight ahead as if he were constructing or dissecting something in his mind. He was the kind of man who dominates conversations not by being loud or aggressive, but through long pauses that force you to sit in uncomfortable silence or fill the gaps with noise. It was probably a useful device in interrogations. I had used it in depositions to get witnesses talking, but he was getting on my nerves.

After a ten-second eternity, Nixon said, "Wait here." He unbuckled his shoulder harness and snapped off the radio before stepping out of the car and shutting the door in one movement. I watched him disappear into the red brick building that housed his office. No more than a half minute passed before he slid back into the driver's seat, methodically buckled up, and flipped a knob on his radio that revived the hum of low-level static and lighted a small green circle on the unit. He handed me a thick manila envelope. A small white label was centered on the front of the package, and my name was, in turn, typed precisely in the center of the label.

He said, "Where do you need to go?"

"I left my Jeep at Sam's office."

Nixon nodded and pointed the Caprice in that direction. I said, "I'm going to need to talk with you at some point. I assume all the facts you've been able to put together are in the file, but I also need to know what you think. And, if you have anything that for some reason couldn't go in the file, from what Sam tells me that may be the most important information you can give."

Nixon said, "We'll talk later. No need asking questions already answered in the report. Once you've got a handle on things, spent some time on the report and the autopsy, I can fill you in on some background about Hall's problems."

"Tell me one thing now, though. Who is the bookie in Birmingham who took Hall's money?"

"Bookies don't take money. People give it to them."

"You're not answering the question."

"You're right. I don't know who the bookie is."

"Don't know or won't say?"

"Amounts to the same thing."

"Sam told me you know a lot about this particular bookmaker."

For the second time that day, I saw a quiet anger pass across his face. "It would be better if you kept your conversation with Sam to yourself." We sat and listened to each other's breathing for a couple of minutes before Nixon said, "Some things you will have to find out on your own. You can ask questions, talk with people, maybe pressure people to give you more than they might give to a law enforcement officer, and you can follow up on things that I can't."

We rode the last few minutes in silence. He pulled into the parking lot next to my Jeep, and I stepped out onto pavement. The office was closed. The mill droned on, waving smoke into the air. Nixon said, "Call me next week," then backed out of the parking space and started out. At the exit onto the service road, he put the unmarked patrol car in reverse and backed up. I walked over to the car and watched my reflection disappear into his door as he lowered the electric window. He said, "I'll be at the funeral tomorrow." Pause. "Talk to Zollie Willingham. He can point you the right way." The window closed as he pulled away.

I opened the driver's-side door of the Jeep, walked around and opened the passenger door to air out the interior and let the heat escape, and started to toss the thick manila envelope on the seat. Instead, I held onto the package. Most of the sun had moved behind trees, leaving a deep red smudge across the horizon that made the mill black in silhouette and turned the smoke blue and yellow against the darkening sky. As I gently laid the envelope on the seat and turned the key in the ignition, light-sensitive bulbs across the mill began to pop on and illuminate smokestacks, outbuildings, water tanks, and open-air workstations. I rolled down the windows and drove home slowly with the scents of pine and thick undergrowth filling the coming darkness.

Silhouetted pines and black kudzu spun by, and I pushed away thoughts of the autopsy pictures sealed inside Nixon's envelope. There was another murder—one that might or might not be connected to what happened to Hall, and one that, it seemed to me, Sam should have mentioned before he left me to deal with Nixon.

I pulled onto the parking pad next to Sam's garage and walked toward the front door with the thick envelope tucked under my arm.

chapter three

Sam was home ahead of me. I told him I had nothing to report.

At dinner, Mom found something else to talk about every time I steered the conversation to her health. She seemed to be growing more uncomfortable with each question, and Sam was getting exasperated with my feeble efforts to find out from Mom things I already knew but was not supposed to know. I gave up and retreated to the room Hall and I had shared as children, where I began to work through the thick sheath of materials handed over by Sheriff Nixon.

The contents of the envelope could be divided into four basic groups: the official report outlining how and where the body had been found; several interviews conducted by Nixon with the last people to see Hall before the murder; a coroner's report, with pictures attached; and a Sheriff's Department file dedicated to my little brother's questionable activities over the past few years.

I was surprised and a little confused that there was no separate file regarding a second, possibly related murder in the county. Either Nixon had inadvertently left it out, or the "material" he mentioned was buried somewhere in one of the other files. There was nothing to do but start somewhere and work through the jumble of reports page by page.

Nixon had sealed the coroner's photos in a separate white envelope. I returned the photos to the larger manila envelope without breaking the tape that held the images of my brother's final horrors inside. I had been maybe an inch taller and ten pounds lighter than Hall, but he and I had looked very much alike. Hall inherited Mom's dark hair and olive complexion while I had my father's sandy coloring, but we clearly swam from the same gene pool. I wanted my memories of Hall to be of that smiling, dark reflection. I would never look at pictures of the bloated and dissected corpse photographed for the coroner's report. I insisted on copies of the photos precisely because Nixon had suggested that he could leave them out. If necessary, there were experts who could review the coroner's reports and photos to determine if the coroner had done an honest and competent job.

After putting the envelope containing the photos out of sight, I started on the coroner's report. My doctoral education allowed me to understand almost nothing of the physician's notes and conclusions. I could tell only that Hall had been shot in the neck and that he had died almost immediately. I should have stopped reading after the section headed "Cause of Death." Under the last section of the report, simply entitled "Comments," the coroner noted with apparent professional pride that, although Hall's body was badly decomposed, he could clearly ascertain that Hall had been fed upon by turtles and scavenger fish as he rolled about on the muddy floor of the river.

I stopped and went to the bathroom to be sick, but felt only numb. After splashing cold water on my face, I walked down to the dining room and poured a lot of bourbon and very little water into a tea glass filled with ice from the kitchen. The bourbon and I went into the atrium. I sat in the dark surrounded by a hexagon of glass walls and by unnaturally healthy vegetation, black against moonlit windowpanes. In late September, the trees outside had not yet shed summer growth, and the wind pulled and turned leaves and branches, changing the shape of the willow oak in the side yard as thousands of slender leaves alternately reflected the moonlight with silver undersides then fluttered to blackness as the dark green tops turned toward the blank stares of the atrium's windowpanes.

Houses have a different feel in darkness, at once eerie and comfortable. Adults tend to turn on lights, read, watch television when sleep refuses to come. Children learn to sit and watch the night unless they want to be lectured or fed warm milk or bundled back off to bed. I spent countless midnights in this room away from everyone, especially away from the little brother who slept in my bedroom. Now, as a grown man, the solitude and the bourbon helped ease the shock induced by a pathologist who never knew his observations would find their way to the corpse's family. Walking with easy familiarity through the dark house, I headed back into the bedroom to finish the first, and I hoped most disturbing, step in this god-awful process of uncovering details of Hall's life that I did not wish to know.

Around one in the morning, I gave up, stumbled out to my Jeep, and came back in with a laptop computer and a portable scanner I used for copying discovery documents, pleadings, and briefs onto a collection of research disks. I planned to build files that could be organized and supplemented as I learned more in the course of my research into Hall's death. I wanted to be able to link theories to specific facts without covering the reports with scribbled notes, and I wanted the ability to password-protect other information learned along the way.

In truth, the immediate benefit of all the copying and cataloging was avoidance. It let me concentrate on the mechanics of operating the scanner and the computer, rather than continue to drink in the filth and pain that filled the reports scattered across the desk where, twenty-five years earlier, I had often done my homework and Hall had sometimes pretended to do his.

It took more than an hour to scan all the reports and files onto a three-and-a-half-inch floppy disk. I then copied the files onto a second disk, converted the files into ASCII and then into WordPerfect, and finally assigned passwords to protect the data from examination by anyone but a determined expert. Just before three A.M., I dropped the disks into the bottom drawer of the desk and fell into a fitful sleep that became a virtual coma.

Saturday morning passed in a haze of dark clothing and sobbing, flowers and fresh earth. I cannot recall, and seem not to have heard, the words of any prayer or eulogy. The only really clear memories I have are of bright green artificial turf draped over the edges of a freshly dug grave and the frayed nylon straps that squeaked as Hall was lowered into the dark.

When we returned to my parents' house after the funeral, a back window had been broken. A snub-nosed Smith & Wesson .38 Police Special was missing from Sam's desk. Sheriff Nixon's file was missing, and my computer keyboard and screen had been kicked in. The backup disks were in the drawer where I had left them, undamaged and apparently unnoticed. Before anyone else entered the bedroom, I carefully slipped the disks into the side pocket of my suit coat.

chapter four

WHILE WE WAITED for Sheriff Nixon to arrive, Sam and I searched the house to see if anything else was missing. Mom sat in the living room, surrounded by friends and a few vaguely familiar relatives from Atlanta. Business and family friends milled around discussing, in hushed tones but with great enthusiasm, the fate that had befallen the black sheep of the McInnes family, leaving paper plates stained with dollops of half-eaten casseroles on the furniture, and thoroughly enjoying the hum of speculation about the burglar who had invaded "a grieving family's home during a murdered child's funeral service," as one flushed, white-haired lady opined again and again as she wandered from one conversational group to the next, savoring her rendition of the facts surrounding the break-in, which changed a bit with each telling, and relishing the shocked reactions and comments offered by each new audience, which changed not at all from one group to the next. By her fourth or fifth telling, the peach-shaped, white-haired oracle had developed quite a little speech about Hall's life and death and the burglary and how each reflected the breakdown of Republican values. I was thinking of bopping her on the head with a heavy, metallic implement of some kind when Sheriff Nixon walked in the front door looking thoroughly pissed off.

Without any greeting, Nixon said, "Tom, we need to talk. Come in Sam's study." He led me and Sam into the study as if he owned the place. "Am I correct in my understanding that you left my official investigative file lying around for some dickhead to come in and wander off with?"

"Actually, I left *my* file lying around for some dickhead to wander off with. I assume your file is still in your office."

"Don't give me any shit, Tom. You screwed up. If it gets out that I gave you a copy of the official file, there is going to be hell to pay."

I said, "Calm down."

Nixon said, "Who the hell do you think you're talking to? Do you know what kind of people are involved in this thing? You messed up. You messed up the investigation. You messed up any chance of keeping a tight lid on this thing, and you messed up your ability to get any more goddamn help from me."

"I'm getting the impression that you think I messed up." No one smiled. "Let's be logical. The file contained an autopsy report which, as far as I could tell, only said he was shot in the neck and died immediately. That was in yesterday's paper. There was a report saying where the body was found and a report on Hall's criminal record, both of which are public knowledge all over the county. The last thing in the file was the interviews you did with Hall's girlfriend, Christy Shores, and with Zollie Willingham. No offense, Sheriff, but the bottom line on the interviews was that both Christy and Zollie saw Hall alive the day he was killed. Period. Christy, who was a virtual fountain of information compared to Zollie, added that she got worried and called your office late the next day. In other words, while I appreciate your giving me the file, it really didn't have shit in it that will do anybody any good, including us."

Nixon said, "Fine. Then you won't be brokenhearted when I tell you that there's no way in hell I'm giving you another copy." He turned and walked through the gathering and out the front door, along the way reigniting the criminal justice theme of the party.

Sam said, "What was that supposed to prove? You screwed up. You should have just taken the dressing down and apologized. We've got to start from scratch without him."

"I'll go see him Monday and smooth things over."

Sam said, "Try to get a second look at the file while you're there. You could have missed something. You were up there reading it in the middle of the night. Maybe you were too sleepy to see what was in it that got him so upset."

"I saw enough."

"Well, I would have liked to see it. See if maybe I could come up with something."

"Trust me, Sam, you don't want to see it." I touched my coat pocket and felt the outline of the computer disks. "And, believe me, I got everything I need from Sheriff Nixon's files." I tried very hard to sound confident.

The gathering had started to thin out a couple of hours later when a bent-over little man in a double-knit suit told me I had a phone call. I found the phone in the entry hall off the hook.

"This is Tom McInnes."

"Tom McInnes, this is Christy Shores."

"Christy, how are you? I thought you'd be here."

"Oh, I was at the funeral. I spoke to you, but you looked like you were kind of dazed."

"Why didn't you come by? I would love to see you, and I need to talk to you about Hall."

"I need to talk to you too, but your mother and father wouldn't be too happy about me coming around over there. They never got used to me and Hall living together."

"I'm glad he had somebody. Look, I really do appreciate your call-ing. I'm drowning in insincerity over here. Can we get together tonight? Like I said, I really need to talk to someone who knows what Hall has been up to for the last few months."

"I'm not sure how much I can help you. I don't think anyone knew everything Hall was doing. He didn't like me in his business stuff, and that was fine with me."

"Maybe we can talk later, then."

"No. I didn't mean to blow you off for tonight. I just don't know if I can help, but I would love to see you and talk with somebody else today who loved Hall. Come get me at seven o'clock. We'll get some dinner and talk."

"Where are you?"

"That's right. You never came to see me and Hall, did you? I still live in our place on the water. Just come out Whiskey Run Road till it hits Cedar. Turn left. My cabin is two and four-tenths miles down on the left. I'll leave the light on beside the driveway."

I said goodbye and hung up. Strange feelings.

I still had about three and a half hours to kill before my dinner date with Christy. I trotted upstairs, threw my suit on the desk chair, and pulled on chinos, a houndstooth shirt, and Timberland shoes. Downstairs, I kissed Mom and told her I was going out. As I passed through the entry hall for the tenth time that day, one of my generic Atlanta relatives commented that I was "the spitting image of Sam. My goodness, you even dress like him."

I briefly thought about buying some Italian loafers and designer shirts when I got back to Mobile.

Zollie Willingham raised Hall and me. It's just about that simple. Sam more or less hired Zollie to be a father to us. Zollie took us hunting and to ball games and even drove us on our first dates. I could drive to his house with my eyes closed. It never occurred to me to call. It never occurred to me that Zollie might not be there waiting to talk with me on the day of my brother's funeral. And I was right.

Zollie's place was just outside the city limits, down a curving gravel road lined on either side by a pine plantation. The grid of the plantation dissolved into natural growth about a quarter mile before the steel mailbox that marked the turn into the circular dirt drive in front of Zollie's white, sort-of-Victorian house that had, like many old homes, gained character and confusion as a new addition had been added every ten years or so. He must have expected the visit, because by the time I had parked he had descended the tall steps from the covered porch and was standing in his front yard, wide and strong and black as coal. The afternoon sun glinted off pure white tufts sprinkled through his close-cropped hair; and his pupils had contracted into pinpoints in the afternoon glare, highlighting the unusual amber, almost green, color of his eyes. He was wearing the same kind of khakis and woods boots he had worn every day I had known him, but had on a starched white shirt with long collar points. I guessed from the shirt that he had been at the funeral, even though I couldn't remember seeing him there.

Zollie gave me a bear hug and ushered me up the steps with one thick arm around my shoulders. We dropped into wrought-iron chairs on the front porch. He had already placed a plastic cooler filled with Red Mountain Ale between the chairs, leaving no question that he anticipated my visit.

Zollie said, "I heard your daddy's house got broken into when you was at the funeral."

"How the hell did you hear that? It only happened a couple of hours ago."

"Small town."

"It's not that small."

Zollie just shrugged, fished two bottles out of the cooler, and handed one to me. "I'm real happy to see you, Tom. Hall getting hisself killed has been hard."

Zollie was turned sideways looking intently into my eyes. I looked back, trying to see or understand what he was looking for in me. I said, "I'm going to find out what happened to him." I thought Zollie would have something to say about that, but he just shifted in his chair and looked out at the yard. "I've talked with Sheriff Nixon. I'm not his favorite person right now, but it looks like he's doing everything he can to figure out what happened. He told me you know something about Hall."

Zollie kept his eyes focused on the front yard. "I reckon I know just about everything about Hall, except who shot him."

"What he said was that you could 'point me the right way.' I know Hall was gambling a lot. And Sam thinks Hall has gotten into real problems in maybe the last year or so. Who's he been betting with recently?"

"Last few months, Hall was betting with Toby Miller. A walking piece of shit."

"I'm going to need to talk to him."

"He ain't going to like that." Zollie paused to think. "We'll both go have a little talk with Toby. He's working the juke joints tonight taking bets for Sunday pro games. Give me to around lunch hour tomorrow. I'll poke around, find out where he'll be."

"I appreciate it."

Zollie turned again to look hard into my eyes. "With due respect to Mr. Sam, Hall's really only got you and me. We'll tend to Toby Miller."

"He may not know anything."

Zollie nodded his head as he spoke. "Well, whatever he know, we going to know by tomorrow night."

We sat on the porch drinking ale until after sunset, replaying old conversations and old times, the way people talk who have a past but nothing in common in the present. Around 6:30, I climbed into the Jeep and headed for Christy's cabin. Living in Mobile, I had forgotten how close together a small town can be. After getting turned around in the dusk trying to find Cedar Lane and then missing the turnoff into her driveway, I pulled up next to her house at 6:45.

I walked down to look out over the river, figuring Christy might not be ready. Muddy black water flowed like oil between the wooded banks, reflecting the last colors of sunset on each ripple.

"Hello."

I turned and saw Christy standing just outside a pair of open glass doors overlooking the water. I thought it was impossible for her to look better than she had at eighteen. It had been that long—about seven or eight years—since I'd seen her. Her auburn hair was darker and shorter, just below the shoulders now, and she seemed taller somehow, maybe five-eight or five-nine, but those dangerous green eyes looked out with the same jaded amusement that had been there since she was a pesky little kid running wild under the stands at summer softball games. Even as a child, she always looked like she had seen too much life too early and had decided the whole thing was more ridiculous than sad. Later, in high school, she had turned into the most sensual, if not the most classically beautiful, woman I have ever seen.

Sam never approved of Christy because she had sprung from a trailer park that popped up overnight when I was twelve and the lock and dam was under construction fifteen miles upriver. The migrant construction families came and went in two years, depositing Christy and her newly divorced mother in our midst. She and Hall had been together for a few years, and, as far as I knew, she had made him happy.

"Christy, you look wonderful."

She walked out and met me on the deck and hugged me hard. She smelled wonderful, but didn't seem to be wearing perfume. She felt wonderful and clearly was not wearing anything under her blouse.

"Thanks for coming," she said. "Let's go eat."

chapter five

DURING THE SHORT time I had gazed at the river, the last haze of dusk had faded from the treetops, and night had swallowed the world in a tangible blanket of blackness that framed and polished every star and planet. For most people these days, for people who live in or near large cities, the glow of ground light washes out and muddies the night sky. Even the air above my beach house holds a fine, almost invisible mist of light cast across the bay from Mobile. But here in the Alabama woods, above the flow of the river and the canopy of oak and cypress and pine, thousands of stars and a silver moon dominated the landscape.

Christy and I climbed into the Jeep, and I started out of her long driveway toward the carriage light that marked the turn onto Cedar Lane. Red gravel passing beneath the Jeep's tires made soothing, crunching noises in the dark.

After Christy's initial greeting, an uncomfortable silence had filled the air between us—one of those first-date silences when you know the night is going to go badly. I switched on high beams to watch for deer. Outside, gray tree trunks rolled by as the headlights swept through turns ahead of us.

I tried to be cheerful. "I haven't eaten out in Coopers Bend in ten years. Where should we go?"

"You remember Jimmy Carpenter?"

"Yeah. He was a year behind me in school."

"I forgot how old you are."

"Thank you."

"Jimmy and his wife inherited his grandfather's old plantation home and turned it into a restaurant. You can't get seafood, but you probably get enough of that on the coast. It's mostly steaks and a few Italian dishes, and it really is good. And they have Glenfiddich at the bar."

We headed east through town. Dusk-to-dawn lights hung from creosote telephone poles at hundred-yard intervals. Side streets rolled by and disappeared into the dark. Lots of white sideboard and latticework, occasionally punctuated by newer, red brick pseudo-Colonials, lined both sides of the street as we passed through the original residential section. We passed in front of the old courthouse, turned south, and cruised past the Baptist church before leaving town behind as we moved through pastureland along the road back toward Mobile.

The Carpenter family home, a classic, white, two-story antebellum mansion, sat on a rise on the eastern side of the road about three miles from downtown and maybe two miles outside the city limits.

Christy and I parked in an unpaved lot graded off to the right of the house, then walked up the brick pathway, between thick columns, and across the veranda. As I reached for the front door, a kid opened it and welcomed us to "Carpenter's Bluff." We walked in and had just given our names to Jimmy's wife when Jimmy spotted us. He came over, introduced me to his wife, and immediately ushered us to a table in the corner of a book-lined room that used to be his grandfather's study. I noticed that every male eye in the place followed Christy through the restaurant. She seemed not to notice.

As he seated us, Jimmy said, "We are all so sorry about Hall. I lost Dad a little over a year ago. It's tough." He went to the bar in the old dining room and brought us our drinks before turning us over to the waitress, with instructions to "take good care of these people. They're my guests. No charge."

I said, "Jimmy, you don't have to do that."

He said, "Be quiet," and left the room.

I looked at Christy and said, "You move away to a big city and start thinking convenience and diversity and, I don't know, access to different people and different ideas makes a good life. But there's not a soul in Mobile, except my secretary, Kelly, who would take the time to do what Jimmy just did."

"You don't let people get close enough to care about you."

"People here care."

"Yeah, but they've known you your whole life. They saw you grow up, and it's a small place where we all get to know each other whether we want to or not. Folks around here have known you long enough to know that underneath all that macho bullshit you got from your daddy you're a pretty good guy."

"I was just having an epiphany here and you bashed the whole thing to pieces."

"I don't know what an epiphany is. But if it means you can't blame the place you live for not being happy and that most people will be as decent as you let them be, then you're right."

Christy was wearing a white cotton blouse that had pulled tight across her breasts when she sat down, and it had become obvious that I had been right about the absence of a bra when I hugged her at the cabin. Also, her top two buttons were undone, revealing the beginning swell of cleavage.

A crooked little man shuffled through on his way to the restroom, and Christy turned to flash a smile and said, "Hi, Mr. Simpkins." When she turned back, I was looking at the front of her blouse, not, it seemed to me, in a disrespectful or lascivious way, but the way most of us can't help but look at beautiful things and beautiful people. I looked up quickly, and Christy laughed out loud.

"Tom, you seem preoccupied. Why don't I just go ahead and unbutton this so you can have a good look?" I turned red, and she actually started unbuttoning her blouse.

She had unbuttoned two buttons when I said, "For God's sake, Christy. I'm embarrassed enough. You don't have to make it worse."

"You're a hoot. Hall would have just said, 'Let's see 'em,' and I would have been the one who ended up embarrassed."

"I'm not Hall," I said with more emotion than I intended.

"I'm sorry, Tom. That was stupid. I'm just trying to cheer you up."

I tried to smile. "Well, you can start by buttoning your shirt; one more button and I could see your navel."

"Do you want to see my navel?" She was laughing again.

"No! Now please button your shirt before someone sees you."

"Say please." She was having a wonderful time.

A tall waitress with orange hair approached the table. After she jotted down our orders, she leaned down to Christy, held up the menus to shield her mouth, and, in a stage whisper, told Christy, "Honey, if old Mr. Simpkins comes through here again you're going to give him a heart attack. Your shirt has come unbuttoned, and I can see everything but."

Christy said, "Thanks, Cheryl," then winked at me and slowly buttoned her shirt all the way up to her throat.

Christy had been right about the food. It was great, and the wine was even better. Over my protests, she ordered a second bottle, and we lingered over dessert long enough for me to drink most of it while Christy watched and talked and laughed and drank just enough to keep me from feeling like I was drinking alone. Almost two hours after we sat down, we finally pushed away from the table. On the way out, I managed to pay Jimmy's wife for the meal while he was in back tending bar.

We were back at the cabin by a little after nine, and Christy invited me in for a nightcap. I knew I didn't need or want anything else to drink, but I didn't want to leave this beautiful woman who had lifted me out of my grief and go back home to deal with my parents or to make small talk with a bunch of geriatric relatives who would be sitting around "catching up on family."

Inside the cabin's great room, varnished cypress paneling contrasted with knobby gray carpeting; tapestry chairs and a linen sofa looked comfortable and expensive; and the walls held several good charcoals. A decent abstract oil hung over the fireplace. I had never thought of Hall as having much money or taste. It occurred to me that he must have been making real money moving drugs. It also occurred to me that, no matter how much money he made, Christy probably furnished the taste.

Christy touched a long match to wadded newspaper beneath the grate in the fireplace and went into the kitchen. The fire was built the way Zollie taught Hall and me when we were kids: wadded paper inside a tepee of pine kindling, placed beneath the grate holding good, seasoned firewood. One match would start the whole thing. All you have to do is turn a log every now and then. Christy came back in carrying two glasses. I said, "I can't handle anything else to drink."

"It's Coca-Cola."

"Oh. I was looking at your fire."

"Hall taught me to build one up that way. It's nice. You put everything out when you've got the time and a little energy, and when I feel like snuggling down all I have to do is strike a match. Help me move the coffee table, will you?" We moved the table to the side and sat on the rug with our backs against the sofa and our feet pointed at the fire.

"Christy, you've really helped me tonight. I feel better than I have in days. I really appreciate it. But there are some things I need to know about Hall."

She turned sideways, leaned her elbow on the sofa, and curled her legs under her so she could face me. "What do you want to know?"

"Tell me what you know about Toby Miller."

"Not that much. Everyone knows he takes bets on football and stuff. Hall used to bet with him a good bit."

"Did he win?"

"I really don't know. He always had plenty of money."

"What kind of person is Miller?"

"Like I said, I don't know him that well. I know he thought he was some kind of tough guy. I also know he was scared to death of Hall, though."

"How do you know that?"

"I've seen him out places, you know, bars and restaurants, sometimes over at Jimmy Carpenter's place having dinner. He'd be swaggering around, talking loud, standing too close to other men's wives, looking too long, things like that. When Hall would come in the room Toby's whole personality would change. He'd just kind of shut up and look at the floor, start minding his own business, you know?"

"Did Hall have that kind of effect on many people around here?"

Christy looked me in the eyes. "Hall was a good guy."

"I know Hall was a good guy. I wasn't trying to say anything bad about him."

"I know, I know. It's just that he really *was* a good guy, but he wasn't someone you wanted to push. Toby tried to push him. Hall never said anything about it, but Zollie told me that Toby tried to get tough with Hall about some bet on a Florida State game. Toby said Hall owed him money, and Hall said he didn't. Well, apparently Toby got Hall in front of a bunch of people one night down at Big Daddy's bar and started calling him a crook for not paying off the bet. Zollie said Hall beat up Toby right there in front of everybody, and he kept beating him until Toby actually started crying and begging Hall to stop. Zollie said it was pretty bad, but there aren't but maybe four or five men in town who could've stopped Hall if they wanted to, and nobody can stand Toby Miller to begin with, so everybody just stood there and watched. Hall made Toby apologize in front of everybody."

"I wouldn't be surprised if Toby decided to sit out in the dark one night and put a bullet in Hall for that. Especially since, in his line of business, you can't afford to have people thinking they can just not pay you whenever they feel like it."

"I know what you mean, but I doubt Toby did it. I doubt he'd have the guts. And I think Toby was lying about Hall owing him money to begin with. Hall wasn't a Boy Scout, but he paid his debts, especially his gambling debts. I've got an idea that Toby just wanted to see how far he could push Hall, and he found out."

I said, "Hall was always tough, but he never was really mean. It doesn't sound like Hall to degrade a man like that in front of other people, no matter what he's done. I could see Hall popping him a few times, but what he did sounds sadistic."

"Hall changed the last few months. He started doing too much cocaine. I never would let him do it here in the house, but I could tell when he'd been in it. I didn't say more because I thought I knew why he was doing it. Back around the first or second week in July—wait, I remember, it was right after the July Fourth weekend—Hall started having these nightmares. He'd wake up screaming. The stuff he slept in would be soaked with sweat. It was really frightening. I'd get him calmed down, and he'd go take a shower and sit up in the living room the rest of the night watching television or just staring out at the river."

"Did you ever think it might be that using the coke was causing the nightmares, instead of the other way around?"

"I guess it could have been that way. But the nightmares started at least a month before I noticed Hall was getting messed up more than usual."

"What happened July Fourth? Anything unusual?"

"Nothing I know about. Look, I've had two drinks, a bottle of wine, and a Coke. Nature's calling. I'll be right back." Christy trotted out of the room and down a hallway. When she came back, she had brushed her hair and freshened her makeup. She sat on the sofa behind me.

I said, "Are you okay?"

"I'm fine. The floor was just starting to get a little hard."

"I know what you mean. I'm starting to tense up again too, but I guess it has more to do with the conversation than the floor."

She reached down and squeezed my shoulder. "You are tense. Scoot forward."

"What?"

"Scoot up a little so I can sit behind you." She slid down between the sofa and my back and began to rub my neck and shoulders. She said, "I'm through answering questions for tonight. We're both getting tense, and the whole point was to cheer each other up a little."

"Christy, if you feel better, I'm glad, but that wasn't my whole point. I need your help finding out what happened to Hall."

"Hush. I'll answer anything you want me to tomorrow or the next day or the next day, but not tonight."

I said, "You win," and got up to poke at the logs in the fireplace. The bottom logs had burned almost in half. The ends were thick and black, but the middle sections had burned into thin red embers where the fire was hottest. I broke a couple of the logs in two and flipped the butt sections into the fire, then rolled over the top log to get the up-draft side to burn. The flames caught and filled the fireplace, and I walked over and sat back down in front of Christy. She started mas-saging my shoulders again.

She said, "You like that, don't you?"

"Who wouldn't?"

She reached around and unbuttoned my shirt, pulled it off my shoulders, and started to massage the muscles between my shoulder blades. I could feel the tension flowing away as she worked the thick cords of muscle that stretched from the base of my skull and along ei-ther side of my spine. After a few minutes, she pulled the soft hounds-tooth shirt back up over my shoulders, pulled me back against her, circled my shoulders with her arms, and patted me on the chest like a protective older sister. "I'm glad you invited me to dinner tonight. I don't know what I'd have done sitting around here by myself."

"Christy, you've helped me in more ways than you know. Just get-ting away from the house has helped."

"Yeah, Sam and Elizabeth are a fun couple, aren't they?"

As we talked, she started to absentmindedly draw designs on my chest with her fingernails, and I became aware that I could feel the warmth of her breasts pressed against my back. It was one of those sit-uations where women do offhand things that seem not to mean anything to them but are arousing to men, maybe because they are so offhand and natural and feminine. I tried not to think about the touch and smell of her and what I could almost see when she unbuttoned her blouse at dinner, but I couldn't seem to think of anything except the roundness of her breasts and the way her open shirt had fallen apart, clinging just inside her nipples, teasing with something yet to be seen.

The fantasy exploded when she said, "Looks like the floor isn't the only thing that's getting hard down here."

"God, Christy. Haven't you embarrassed me enough for one night?" I sat up and started to stand. She pulled me back, laughing.

"Relax. I'm sorry. Those lightweight cotton pants aren't real good for keeping secrets, are they?"

"Apparently not."

She hugged me and laughed again, a beautiful, full, feminine sound. She patted me on the chest again in that way that made me feel like her little brother, then, without warning, reached down and began running her fingernails along the khaki ridge produced by my unsummoned erection. I made a gentle effort to sit up away from her, and she just as gently but firmly held me against her.

"Christy, this isn't right."

"What? That you've got a hard-on, or that I'm touching it?"

"Christy . . ." She slid out from behind me and sat back on her heels. She looked into my face as she laid her hand back onto my lap and continued to gently stroke the source of my embarrassment.

"Tom, until you got here tonight, this was the worst day of my life. You're funny and nice and beautiful and I don't know why but I knew I wanted to make love with you the minute I saw you." I started to talk, and she gently placed her finger on my lips. "I don't know if I just don't want to be alone now or if I need to feel alive or what. Let's don't try to do the right thing. Let's just enjoy each other."

Christy slowly unbuttoned her blouse and let it drop from her shoulders. She leaned down and pushed my shirt aside and pressed her breasts against my bare chest. The one person who had been able to bring life into that horrible day looked into my face and began to brush her lips lightly along my lips, then slowly downward over my chest to my stomach where she began to unbuckle my belt.

I awoke Sunday morning next to my dead brother's girlfriend, feeling a little less satisfied with the world and myself than I had been the night before. A bottle of wine and a little skin and I'm ready to go. If I'd been a girl, I certainly would have been popular in high school. I eased out of bed and closed the door to the bathroom. I had a sudden queasy premonition that Hall's razor and toothbrush and personal things would be all over the bathroom, but there was nothing there to indicate a man had lived in the house, just powders and moisturizers and other girl stuff everywhere I looked. It occurred to me that I hadn't seen any of Hall's stuff in the house—no diving or fishing equipment, no guns, nothing. Maybe being surrounded by Hall's things after the murder had been too painful for Christy and she had cleared everything out.

I was in the shower with a head full of shampoo when I heard the door open.

Christy said, "Want me to wash your back?"

I said, "Tell you the truth, I'd rather have some coffee if you've got some."

"Thanks a lot."

"Sorry. I didn't mean it that way. My head has felt better, and I've got to get going anyway. Zollie is expecting me this morning," which wasn't exactly true, but close enough.

"I'll put some on. I put a fresh towel on the sink for you."

A few minutes later, I had dried off, used a Lady Schick to shave, and put my dirty clothes back on. I ventured out of the bathroom thinking . . . *gee, this should be awkward.* In the kitchen I found a fresh pot of coffee and a note:

Dear Tom,

> *I like you. Do you like me? If you want to get laid again tonight, check the box below.*

☐ *Yes*   ☐ *No*

> *Your friend,*
> *Christy*

P.S. I've gone for a run. Call me later.

Cute. I wrote the same note, without the getting laid part, to a little brown-eyed girl named Amy in the fifth grade. Hall found it, showed it to just about everybody he could find, and I beat the crap out of him. Apparently, Hall told the story to Christy, probably during the course of a night like the one I'd just had with her. It occurred to me that, after living three or four years with Hall, there probably wasn't much she didn't know about me.

I rummaged around in her kitchen cabinets and stole a mug with a blue sailfish on one side and "Redneck Riviera" printed on the other, filled it with black coffee, and drank it on the way to Zollie's house.

When he opened the door, Zollie said, "Where the hell have you been?"

"You don't want to know."

"I can guess. Your mother called here about midnight last night looking for you."

"Oh, hell."

Zollie said, "Yeah, she just put one child in the ground, and you go out catting around and it don't occur to you to maybe at least call and make something up?"

"I wasn't catting around, but you're right about the rest. I better go by the house and try to smooth things over. I'll see you back here at noon."

"You feel like a asshole?"

"Yes. I feel just like an asshole."

"Good. Come on in and have some breakfast. I told your mother last night you'd gone to see some old friends and that I asked you to stay over here. I had to tell her I'd call if you didn't show up, but I knew as sure as anything you wouldn't. Come on in the kitchen and sit down. I'll scramble some eggs."

"Thanks. I still need to go by the house and get some fresh clothes."

"You got plenty of time. We got three or four hours to kill."

"Before what?"

"We got an appointment with Toby Miller at two o'clock this afternoon." He smiled. "Only he don't know it yet."

chapter six

I T WASN'T THAT Zollie hadn't heard of fat grams, cholesterol, and triglycerides, it was just that he didn't care. Fifteen minutes after I came in the door, Zollie set the table with a mound of scrambled eggs, bacon, sausage, hot toast, honey with pieces of waxy comb floating in it, a pitcher of orange juice, a carton of milk, and a pot of coffee.

I said, "Do you eat like this every morning?"

"So far."

"I can feel my arteries clogging. It's great, but every morning? You keep it up, it's going to kill you."

Zollie bit off a piece of bacon, shoveled eggs and honey onto a wedge of toast, popped it in his mouth, happily munched awhile, and swallowed. As he crunched on the next strip of bacon and started to load up another piece of toast, he said, "Got to die of something." That was pretty much it for breakfast conversation.

We took our coffee out on the porch and plopped down in the same chairs we had used the night before. I felt sluggish and full and wonderful. I wanted to go stretch out on the lawn like a black Lab and take a nap with the sun on my face, but I had more important, and much more unpleasant, things to do. I said, "How do you want to handle it this afternoon?"

"Not much to handle. Toby was out at Big Daddy's until around one last night, doing some business, getting shitfaced. Picked up a little eighteen-year-old girl and took her home, or, at least, she followed him home in her car. I got me somebody watching his house. We'll give him to around two o'clock to get the girl out of there."

"What if she doesn't leave?"

"We go in anyway and suggest to her that she take herself somewhere else. She been up there screwing all night. She ain't going to go get her daddy, and I don't guess Sheriff Nixon cares if we beat on Toby a little." He paused and emptied his coffee cup. "It'll be better if we can wait for her to leave on her own, but it's okay either way."

I told him what Christy said about Hall humiliating Toby one night out at Big Daddy's bar. Zollie said that the way Christy told the story was pretty much the way it happened and that it wasn't Hall's finest hour as a human being. I also asked him about the Fourth of July and any changes he might have seen in Hall around that time.

He said, "I think Christy's wrong about that. She probably like to think something serious happened to Hall to change him overnight, but somebody don't change like that over a weekend. Years of messing with drugs and doing business with hard people is what changed Hall." Zollie got out of his chair and walked over to the banister. "Hall wasn't the man you remember. Hadn't been for a long time." Without meeting my eyes, he walked over and put his hand on the screen door handle. "Go on over to Mr. Sam's. Change clothes and be back here by one." He disappeared inside.

Five minutes later, I parked next to Sam's garage and went inside to make excuses. Mom was nowhere to be found. Sam was in his study.

I said, "Where's Mom?"

"Gone to church. You find out anything last night?"

"Yeah, as a matter of fact, I did. I'll know more after this afternoon. We can talk about it tonight."

Sam looked down at the Sunday newspaper on his desk and said, "Nice of you to call last night."

He always knew just what to say to piss me off. I took a deep breath and said, "Yeah, I thought so," as I turned and headed for the stairs. Two days in this place and I had reverted to high school comebacks.

Upstairs, I brushed my teeth and changed into a gray T-shirt, cut-off sweatpants, and running shoes. One o'clock was an hour and a half away; plenty of time to run off some of the filet mignon, hollandaise sauce, wine, scotch, eggs, bacon, sausage, and butter I had consumed during the past fourteen hours. I got a little sick just thinking about it.

On the way out, I passed Sam in the hallway. We each pretended the other wasn't there. I started jogging toward town, figuring I could loop out toward the Carpenter place if I had the energy. The first half mile, Zollie's breakfast shook and bubbled every time a running shoe jarred against pavement. A mile after that, sweat trickled between my shoulder blades, and stiff knees and ankles began to feel lubricated. I decided to try the south highway.

I had made it about two miles out toward Jimmy's place and was halfway back to town when an old Monte Carlo with blacked-out windows slowed to a crawl and cruised along next to me. A few seconds passed. I looked over and nodded at the black passenger window, figuring some brothers were trying to figure out why this crazy white man was out running in the middle of nowhere. Self-induced exercise is not real big in a place where most people perform physical labor for a living. It then crossed my mind that someone I knew was messing with me. It had just crossed my mind that someone I didn't know could be planning to seriously mess with me when the driver sped up, slammed on brakes, and turned the car sideways twenty feet in front of me.

Adrenaline is a wonderful thing. I had cleared the drainage ditch and was hurdling a barbed-wire fence by the time I heard a door open and someone say, "Shit." I ran perpendicular to the road and put about thirty yards of thick woods between me and the car before I stopped to listen. I couldn't hear anything, so I moved parallel to the road until I was ahead of the car and circled around to a thicket near the edge of the trees. A tall, skinny white guy in his twenties was staring off into the woods where I went in. He walked back and forth along the ditch a few times looking down into the trees. He had the appearance of someone who wanted to look serious and aggressive to impress whoever was in the car, but who didn't really want to play tag in the woods.

After he seemed sure I wasn't going to walk out of the woods and give up, he walked back and leaned down to talk to someone in the car.

"Did you see that? Looked like somebody shot him out of a cannon."

A male voice inside the car said something I couldn't make out.

The guy who didn't want to go in the woods said, "Yeah, well, he's either figured out he's in trouble, or he's scared of his own shadow. The guy moves like a fucking jackrabbit."

The man in the car raised his voice and said something very like, "Shut up and get in the car."

The Monte Carlo sat on the shoulder for a long minute or two while, I guessed, they were having a conversation about my favorite person, then the driver pulled back onto the road and started toward town. As the car passed, I could see Jefferson County plates. Someone had driven all the way from Birmingham to pay me a visit. I somehow didn't think they planned to go home and report that their mission was unsuccessful because I ran into the woods.

I sat still in my little thicket and waited. A few minutes later, the car came by headed south. I thought briefly about keeping to the woods along the road on the way home, but decided it would take at least an hour to cover the mile that separated me from town and relative safety, and I had an appointment to keep with Toby Miller. Instead, I crossed the barbed-wire fence, checked the road once more, and ran the first seven-minute mile I had run in a very long time. Back in town, I went by the sheriff's office. The deputy at the front desk said Nixon was out on patrol, which was pretty unlikely at lunchtime on Sunday. I left a message for Nixon to call me at my parents' house if he checked in during the next half hour.

I got back home at a quarter to one, went up to my room, sat on the bed, and stared at a spot on the rug. My brain was on sensory overload and apparently had decided to zone out for a few minutes. The room slowly came back into focus. I looked over at the other bed, with its old chenille covers and the cowboy-print comforter folded at the footboard, and heard myself say, "Hall, what have you gotten me into?"

There are very few problems in life that cannot be made better by a hot shower. As I stood there letting the spray beat down on the back of my neck, it occurred to me that I was preparing to go do to Toby Miller something very like what the men in the Monte Carlo wanted to do to me. It also occurred to me that it hadn't taken long for someone—probably the same person I was hunting—to start hunting me.

I dried off, combed wet hair out of my face, and pulled on jeans, white leather sneakers, a short-sleeved, red knit shirt, and a soft pigskin jacket. Then I went downstairs and asked Sam for the key to his gun cabinet.

He said, "You're just supposed to figure things out. Don't go do something stupid."

I said, "I just don't want to get killed while I'm doing something smart."

I followed Sam into his study. Next to a half bath was a big walk-in closet where Sam kept his hunting and fishing equipment. Inside, camouflaged clothing and waders hung from pegs, scarred decoys lined shelves beneath a dozen fly rods collected over a lifetime, and in one corner sat an ugly green gun safe. Sam worked the combination and opened the tall door on the front of the thing. It held a rich man's toys: an Orvis side-by-side, a matched pair of Beretta over-and-unders, a Belgian-made Browning twelve-gauge, and several Remington and Winchester rifles with Redfield and Nikon scopes. The long guns were stored vertically in the top of the safe. The bottom third of the cabinet held three drawers. Sam pulled open the top drawer, which contained a square, flat, walnut case, a Nikon F3, and several telephoto lenses in black cases that rolled around when the drawer moved.

Sam reached in, picked up the walnut case, and handed it to me.

"Sheriff Nixon gave me this for helping him in his first election. I've never even shot it, but I've kept it clean and oiled like I do all my guns." I opened the presentation case and found a Browning 9mm, with an extra clip and a little brass cleaning rod. Sam opened the second drawer, which was full of bird shot, thirty-aught-six cartridges, and other ammunition that went with his toys. He handed me a box of 9mm cartridges, closed the safe, and spun the combination lock.

He said, "We buried one son this week. Your mother couldn't stand to bury another one. Neither could I." He walked quickly out of the closet and the study, leaving me there with my special, presentation 9mm Browning.

Inside the Jeep, I loaded both clips, seated one in the gun, which I put in the back of my waistband, and put the other clip in the pocket of my jacket. I tossed the box of cartridges in the glove box, threw the walnut presentation case in back, and started out for Zollie's house. It was nearly two when I knocked on his door.

He said, "I hate to ask you this twice in one day, but where the hell have you been?" I told him about the Monte Carlo south of town and what I could hear of the men's conversation.

Zollie went in the other room to get his coat. When he came back into the living room, he said, "I got a call from the boy I got watching Toby. Said the girl left, and he was afraid Toby was going to head out too. I told him to stop him."

I said, "Can he do that by himself?"

"Most likely."

"Must be more of a man than a boy then."

"You might say this one more brain than brawn."

We took my Jeep. Zollie drove. We wound out through the country north of town, turned off on a gravel road, and took two forks off of that.

"Where does this guy live?"

Zollie said, "Toby got this little piece of land from his daddy, who used to make a little shine out here before people found out they could get just as drunk on Mad Dog and not go blind." As he finished talking, he pulled off into a little logging road, stopped the car, and beeped the horn one time. Twenty seconds later, a ten-year-old boy came running out of the woods.

"Is that the boy you told to stop Toby?"

"Yep. He's my grandnephew. Don't look like much, but he's smarter than God. Already skipped two grades in school."

Zollie's grandnephew came around to the driver's side, and Zollie rolled down the window. "Rudy, this Tom McInnes. Mr. Sam's son."

Rudy looked at me like I was some kind of specimen in formaldehyde, nodded almost imperceptibly, then looked back at his uncle. "That girl left at twelve-forty. I called you when Toby got in the shower. I was scared he'd go catch the afternoon games somewhere where he could take a few more bets."

I said, "Is he still there?"

Rudy looked over at me. He was not impressed. And he didn't answer me.

Zollie grinned. "What'd you do?"

"Pulled his coil wire. He came out at one-thirty and tried to start his truck. When it wouldn't turn over, he tried to ruin his starter, cussed some, slammed the door, and went back inside. I figured he was too lazy to look under the hood with a game about to start, and I figured he was too cheap to call a tow truck." Rudy switched his gaze and looked directly into my eyes before he said, "And I was right."

Zollie handed him twenty dollars and said, "Thanks, Rudy."

"Any time."

As we drove away, I said, "Sweet kid."

Zollie started chuckling. "Don't need to be sweet. Already smarter than any of his teachers. He'll calm down when he gets older. Hard being a ten-year-old man."

Sixty yards from the logging road where we had met the charming Rudy, we came up on a driveway that curved around a small pond and ran up to a red cottage trimmed in white. It would have been quaint if not for the three rusted-out cars in the front yard and the remains of a washing machine sitting off in the grass to the side. Zollie parked next to one of the old junkers.

"Tom, you go up front. I'll cut around back and make sure he don't slip out." As I started for the front door, Zollie put his hand on my shoulder. "Ain't nothing to Toby. He ain't you. You understand? He got nothing to lose. He ain't no high-powered lawyer with a rich daddy and friends. He figures you a problem, he'll put a bullet in you, drop you in a hole somewhere, and take a chance he'll get away with it. You understand?"

"I understand." I took Sam's 9mm out of my waistband and chambered a round.

Zollie looked down at the gun and back up into my eyes. He just said, "Good," and trotted off to work his way around the house. I gave him a little time and walked up and knocked on the front door. No one answered. I switched the gun to my left hand and laid it flat against the house just to the left of the door where it would be impossible to see from inside. Then I banged harder on the door.

"Who's there?"

"My Jeep ran out of gas. I need to use your phone."

"Who are you? Do I know you?"

"No. You don't know me. I just need to use the phone to call somebody to bring me some gas."

Toby opened the door about a foot and glared at me. He looked like every New Yorker's mental picture of Southern manhood—the kind of face you see on the evening news explaining how the tornado tore up his trailer and destroyed all his worldly goods. Toby Miller had a long, bone-thin face, mousy brown hair, a two-day beard, and teeth that would have benefited from braces and whitening, or maybe extraction.

I decided that talking my way in would be preferable to butting him out of the way. I began, "My Jeep ran out of gas. I was riding around looking for deer signs so I could maybe get one tomorrow morning, and I guess I wasn't paying attention 'cause . . ."

An expression of recognition swept over his face. We had never met, but it seemed my resemblance to Hall had started to filter through the fog of his reptilian mind. Some tiny thought of subterfuge flittered across his face before he thought better of it and jerked his head back inside with the idea of slamming the door in my face. I slammed my full weight into the door, and poor old Toby went flying across the room and landed in a pile of bones and joints and bad teeth. Unfortunately, I dropped Sam's prize gun in the process. When I bent down to pick it up, Toby scrambled to his feet and started running toward the back of the house. To my surprise, I picked up the gun, carefully pointed it at Toby's thigh, and pulled the trigger. I probably would have shot him if I had remembered to switch off the safety.

I was standing there feeling a little impotent when Zollie came into the room, pushing Toby ahead of him.

I said, "Sorry."

Zollie said, "Nothing to be sorry about. That's why I went around back. We figured he'd run. At least you didn't shoot him." I started to say something and thought better of it.

Toby stammered, "He tried to shoot me. Had his gun pointed right at me."

Zollie spun Toby around and threw him down on an old print sofa covered with tiny log cabins and spilling stuffing from several worn places. "Boy, if this man wanted to shoot you, you'd have been shot." I tried to look dangerous. "Do you know who this man is?" Toby just sat there trying to process what was happening. Zollie shouted, "I said, do you know who this man is?"

This time Toby was able to get out a barely audible "no."

Zollie said, "Come on, Toby. You picking the wrong time to be fucking around. You run, didn't you? So you know who this is."

Toby said, "He looks kind of like Hall McInnes. I reckon he's Hall's brother from Mobile."

Zollie walked over to a little dinette in the corner, dragged a chair over, and straddled it with his arms resting along the back. "You smarter than you look, Toby. That's right, this man here is Tom McInnes, and, if you don't listen real careful and tell us what we need to know, he's going to put a bullet in your sorry, white-trash head. See, Tom and me are going to find out who killed his brother, and right now it looks like it could've been you. Now, I'm going to ask you some questions. If you lie or don't answer the way we want, Tom there's going to shoot you in the knee. If we get another answer we don't like, he going to shoot you in the other knee. And, you know, Toby, I believe me and Tom can go on like that longer than you can."

I had been nervously pushing the safety on and off while Zollie tried to scare Toby. I finally had to say something. "Zollie, come over here a minute." Zollie and I walked across the room, and I whispered, "Don't you think you're laying it on a little thick? Do you really think he's going to believe we came here to murder him? You sound like you've been hanging around with Quentin Tarantino."

"I don't even know no Winston Valentino."

"Quentin Tarantino. He's a director."

"I don't know him either. Look, Tom, if it turns out Toby killed Hall and you won't shoot him, I swear to you I'll gut him myself right here on his living room floor." This situation was getting away from me fast. Zollie went on, "Before we came in here, I asked you if you understood the situation, and you said you did. That man over there probably killed your little brother, and he would kill you and me both this minute if he could."

I said, "Well, let's try to find out what he knows before we start gutting anybody."

"That's what I thought I was doing."

Zollie walked over and sat back down in the chair. He said, "Did you kill Hall?"

Toby said, "Hell no. Hall was a friend of mine. We did business together."

Zollie said, "Your friend whipped your ass in front of half the town out at Big Daddy's one night last summer."

"Friends get in fights. I remember hearing Hall and his own brother, Tom here, used to go at it pretty good."

"Toby, you ain't answering me right. You ain't nobody's brother, 'cept maybe some other redneck piece-of-shit that shot out of your Momma's ass."

That was more than Toby could stand. He shot off the sofa and grabbed Zollie around the neck before I could get between them. It was not a smart move. Zollie spun Toby around like a rag doll, pinned

Toby's arm behind him, and pulled a Buck folding knife out of his hip pocket. I thought that was the end of it until I looked into Zollie's eyes. He wasn't there. In all the years I'd known him I had never seen that look, and I knew he was going to kill Toby. I shouted, "Goddamnit, let him go."

Zollie said, "Tom, this little bastard killed Hall. I'm done talking."

I moved closer. "Zollie, let him go. Even if he did kill Hall, we don't know anything yet."

Zollie said, "Nothing else to know." I saw his bicep flex in anticipation of the cut, and I grabbed his wrist and yanked it as hard as I could to get him off Toby. Zollie lost his balance, and Toby shot through the front door like a rat let out of a trap. I ran after him and just caught sight of him as he hit the woods behind his house.

Zollie ran up beside me, and I said, "Think we can catch him?" He walked back to the Jeep and got in without answering. We drove back to Zollie's house in silence. I pulled up and let him out at his front door. When he turned to look at me, I said, "Well, I think that went well, don't you?"

He said, "Not everybody thinks you're funny."

"Actually, no one thinks I'm funny. And I don't think that shit you pulled back at that house was funny. What happened to you? You got better sense than that."

"I just couldn't stand that little shit sitting there alive while Hall is lying in his grave. You don't understand. He came after me 'cause we caught him."

"He came after you because he thinks he's a tough guy, and he wasn't going to let a nigger talk about his mother."

"I never heard you use that word."

"It's not my word, Zollie. You know that. I just mean it's the way Toby was thinking. And instead of just roughing him up a little and going on trying to find out what we could, you decided to cut his throat. Hell of an idea. What were you thinking? Hall was my brother, and you didn't see me turning into Jack the Ripper."

"I just couldn't stand it," he said again.

"Next time you invite me to a murder, I'd appreciate knowing about it ahead of time."

He said, "Sorry, Tom. Sorry about all of it." He turned and walked away. I scratched off like a high school kid, swerved onto the road, and headed back to my parents' house. This whole thing was going about as wrong as it possibly could. It seemed that Hall and everybody around him went crazy while I was away. It was time to slow down and bring this mess back into a world I could handle.

When I got to the house, no one was there. I sat down at Sam's desk in the study, put the Browning on the desk within easy reach in case my friends in the Monte Carlo decided to visit, and started making phone calls. It took about an hour to find the person who could set up a meeting with Toby Miller's boss.

I STARTED BY CALLING my secretary, Kelly, in Mobile. I needed phone numbers, and I needed a sounding board. I told Kelly about Hall's connection with a local bookie who worked for a gangster in Birmingham who apparently sent several unpleasant, if somewhat incompetent, people to find me. She said, "Don't call me. Call the police."

"Kelly, I wish it were that simple. I can't talk about it much on the phone, but the local sheriff also has a connection with the problem in Birmingham, if you follow me. And the state cops aren't going to be interested in investigating why someone pulled off the road in front of me while I was jogging."

"What are you going to do?"

"I'm doing it. I'm calling you, and when I'm through talking with you I'll call someone else and then someone else until I can bypass the local talent and get a meeting with the head man in Birmingham."

"What good is that going to do?"

"If someone is looking for me with the intention of doing me harm, it makes sense to find him before he finds me. I can't deal with someone if I don't know who he is. Hell, I guess I could always come home and hope the whole thing will just go away, but I don't really think that's a realistic option."

"What do you need me to do?"

"I need you to call Joey and get him working on this. We pay him to be an investigator. Let's see if he can investigate something more complicated than insurance fraud."

"I'll call him first thing in the morning."

"Call him now, and tell him I said to start investigating today, now. Tell him to find this guy fast. Okay?"

"You got it."

"Thanks. Now, I need some home phone numbers. Have you got your Rolodex at home?"

"I can access the one on my computer at the office from here. What happened to the one on your laptop?"

"Someone broke into my room during the funeral and bashed it to pieces."

"God, Tom."

"Yeah, I know. Tell me when you've got the address book on screen."

I swiveled Sam's leather chair around so I could look out the floor-to-ceiling windows behind his desk. Long afternoon shadows mottled the back lawn. Two white tree trunks with jagged limbs framed the window from outside. Against the limbs, bright red pigments burned the edges of maple leaves shaped like small hands. In a month, the leaves would be a startling, fiery yellow. A month later, they would be gone. I found myself scanning shadows along the edge of the property to see if one looked like it could have been cast by a tall, skinny guy who hadn't wanted to play chase in the woods.

When Kelly came back on, she had downloaded the whole address book onto her home machine and disconnected from the office. Ten minutes later, I had the home and office telephone numbers of maybe half of the leading criminal attorneys in the state.

Kelly said, "Anything else?"

"Yeah, one more thing. How about getting me another laptop in the morning. I need you to load it with our word processor, the database program, my address book, and the scanner software, then overnight it to me."

"Want me to drive up there and wash your car in my spare time to-morrow?"

"Cute. Can you get the computer?"

"Of course. I'm wonderful. Remember?"

"I remember."

I started calling attorneys in Mobile, since I knew them best. Specialists tend to know others in their specialty all over the state, sometimes all over the country. So, even if my Birmingham bookie wasn't known among the criminal attorneys in Mobile, I figured someone could at least introduce me to a criminal lawyer in Birmingham who could help. First, I called Harvey Stimler, an ancient trial lawyer who had made it his life's work to defend the rights of the worst drug dealers, smugglers, and other assorted scum to wash up on the Gulf Coast over the past forty years. Harvey knew every criminal lawyer in the Southeast. He listened for about twenty seconds, told me to call him at the office on Monday, and hung up. Professional courtesy.

The second number didn't answer. The third call went to Sullivan Walker, a young attorney about my age who was not as well connected in the legal community as some, but who was one of the young turks who would have his own firm one day if he didn't burn out first. Sully's family has been in the shipping business in Mobile for about two hundred years. He is the kind of polished, well-educated, and thoughtful man that old money is supposed to produce and so seldom does.

After he had soaked up all the facts I could give him, Sully said, "I don't personally know who this person would be, but he sounds like a major player. If he is and if he lives in Birmingham, his attorney, or one of his attorneys at least, is going to be Spencer Collins. I can call Spencer on your behalf tomorrow morning if you think it would be helpful."

I said, "I went to undergraduate school with Spence. I heard he went to night law school and was practicing criminal law in Birmingham, but I haven't really heard much about him. I figured he was pretty small-time."

"Spencer is about as big-time as you can get. He's in a firm with

a bunch of Ivy League types who handle the regular corporate matters for some, shall we say, colorful businessmen around the state.
Spencer's job is to take care of them and their employees in criminal
court."

"Thanks, Sully, I really appreciate your help. All right to call you
back if I need some help dealing with Spence?"

"Sure. You need to pay me something on retainer, anyhow. We've
talked pretty freely here. I'm sure both of us want the conversation to
be privileged. Have your secretary send me over a check for a hundred
dollars tomorrow, and we'll be in business."

"You're not going to get rich like that."

"Wanna bet? Who are you going to call the next time one of your
clients needs a criminal attorney?"

"Oh. You're right."

"I better be. Good luck and be careful."

I called Kelly about the retainer for Sully before it slipped my
mind, then dialed the home number of Spencer K. Collins, attorney-
at-law.

When the phone rang, a woman with a Caribbean accent said,
"Collins residence." It sounded like *Coleen's rese'daunce*. I asked for
Spence Collins. After I had stated my business and given my name to
his housemaid for clearance, Spence actually picked up the line.

"Tom, how the hell are you doing?"

"I'm fine, but I wish I had a nubile little upstairs maid to answer
my phone on the weekends. What's she wearing? One of those little
French-maid costumes with fishnet hose? Probably carrying a white
feather duster for show."

Spence laughed, just the right laugh to show me that he appreci-
ated what a witty fellow I was. He said, "Actually, she's not bad-looking, but she wears this austere gray uniform, with a white cotton apron
and sensible shoes. But if you know where I could get one of those
French-maid outfits, maybe when Sally's out of town . . . who knows?"

It was my turn to laugh. We had now exchanged good-old-boy
pleasantries and established that we were good enough friends to call

each other at home on Sunday and make bad jokes. All of which was bullshit, since we hadn't seen each other, except at a few state bar meetings, in about ten years, but it's the way the game is played, and we both knew it. Spence knew I had called for a favor, and I knew he knew it.

I began, "Look, Spence, I've got a serious personal problem, and I think maybe you can help. My little brother, Hall, was murdered last week."

"Oh, God, Tom. I'm sorry. What happened?"

"We don't really know. But it seems to be connected somehow with a local bookmaker in Coopers Bend, a fellow named Toby Miller. Let me make this clear up front, though, I am not accusing Miller of killing Hall. It just looks like he may have some information." I was trying to soft-pedal my interest in Toby. There was nothing to be gained by throwing around accusations of murder at this point.

Spence said, "Sorry, Tom, but I don't see what I can do. I'm a criminal lawyer, but I've never even heard of this Toby Miller. Sometimes I act as a go-between, set up meetings where everybody can feel safe to talk, stuff like that. Is that what you want?"

I decided to go ahead and dive in. "I need a meeting, but not with Miller."

"I'm listening."

"Miller works for a big-time bookmaker in Birmingham, who apparently also is pretty big in the drug trade."

"Are you on a cellular or a remote phone of any kind?"

"No."

"Hang on a minute." Spence did something with his phone, and I heard a number of clicks followed by a low-level buzzing sound. When he came back on, the buzzing continued.

I said, "What was all that about?"

"Don't worry about it. Just some kind of high-tech privacy thing I paid a fortune for. Probably doesn't do anything but buzz." He said, "You were saying?"

"I was saying that this Miller character has a boss in Birmingham, and, to hear the people around here tell it, he's some kind of major-league bad guy. This afternoon a couple of guys in an old Monte Carlo with tinted windows tried to waylay me in the middle of nowhere. The car had a Jefferson County tag."

"Are you okay?"

"I'm fine. I just want to handle this, whatever it is, before it gets out of hand. If bad guys in Superfly-looking cars keep trying to nab me, I'm afraid somebody's going to get hurt. And I'm afraid it's going to be me."

Spence sat quietly for a few seconds, then said, "Tom, most of my clients are businesspeople accused of tax fraud or EPA violations. I'm not sure what I can do to help you."

I said, "Uh huh," with as much incredulity as I could infuse into those two syllables. "Spence, we've known each other a long time, so let's cut through the bullshit and see if we can find a way to handle this, because whoever I'm looking for seems to want to find me, too. So, it looks like you could make two people happy at the same time. Now, let's say I'm not looking for one of your clients, and you're not volunteering any information about any past or present clients. I'm just asking you, as a well-connected attorney in this state, if you have ever heard of a person who has contacts and business interests of the kind I am describing."

Spence didn't say anything for maybe a full minute. The annoying, high-tech toy continued to buzz over his labored breathing. When he finally spoke, Spence said, "I don't know who your local man—what's his name, Miller—I don't know who he would work for here in town. But there is a man I could check with. He may or may not know some-thing. It would be, uh, unusual for anyone in this part of the state to be involved in those activities without this man's knowledge and, uh, his understanding."

That was it. Spence had come as close as he was ever going to come to discussing the activities of one of his clients. I asked, "Should I come to Birmingham?"

"Not yet. Let me check on some things first. I'll call tomorrow or

Tuesday. If I can do anything, I will need a letter from you requesting my representation and stating that you are enclosing a retainer check in the amount of ten thousand dollars. I'm telling you now so you can make arrangements. If I can help, and only if I can help, I'll need the letter and the check by the end of the week."

I was stunned. "What?"

"What part didn't you understand?"

"Spence, this is horseshit. I'm a sole practitioner now. I can't afford ten thousand dollars."

"You're breaking my heart. You live in a beach-front house on the most exclusive real estate this side of Palm Beach, and your father has his own frigging town. I like you, but I don't make a living giving my time away, not even to friends. You're a lawyer. You know how this works. Everyone who comes to us for help is in trouble. Now, maybe I'll do a little more for you—maybe go a little farther out on a limb—than I would for most clients, but I'm not going to act as a go-between for you and the most dangerous man in Alabama without some privilege attaching."

I said, "And you're not going to do it without some money going into your pocket."

He said, "You got it."

Spence's comment about the "most dangerous man in Alabama" suddenly hit me. I don't know if he let something slip or if he was trying to do me a favor and let me know what I was dealing with or if he was just trying to justify his retainer, but it was a disturbing comment. Spence sat silently and let me think.

I finally said, "Assuming you can help, you will send me a letter referencing a conversation during which I contacted you about representation. The letter will state, in no uncertain terms, that you have agreed to act as my attorney. It will set out the terms of your representation, and it will state that I have agreed to pay a two-thousand-dollar retainer against ten hours of your time at a rate of two hundred dollars an hour."

"Been nice talking to you. I don't walk across the street for two thousand dollars."

"You know, I've actually heard of lawyers giving other members of the bar a break on retainers. Maybe a hundred dollars."

"Some lawyers are trying to build up a client base. I've got one. With me, you pay a lot, and you get a lot. If one of your hundred-dollar lawyers could set up this meeting, that's who you'd be calling."

"Spence, you're a smart guy. Always were. And I'm getting something I need from you. That's why I'm willing to pay you two thousand dollars, even though you will get five times that from the guy who's looking for me. A very important person, who you either have a relationship with or you want one with, is trying to find me, and here I've fallen right into your lap. Hell, I've probably done you a favor."

Now it was his turn to sound incredulous. "How can I ever thank you?"

"You can set up the meeting, and you can send the retainer letter. I'll send out a check upon receipt of your letter."

"What difference does it make who writes the letter?" I breathed a sigh of relief. I had called his hand on the retainer, and he knew it. He had moved on to trying for a little advantage on the letter. If things later went south, he wanted the option of saying he had received a letter from an old college friend requesting representation, but that he had never agreed to do it. He would just put the check in a trust account until he could see how things were going to come out. If things worked out, he would be two thousand dollars richer. If not, he would return the retainer, together with a note apologizing for the delay and stating that he was unable to undertake the representation of Tom McInnes at that time. The whole thing was a game to him, the same nasty game he played every day of his life.

I said, "We both know it makes a difference who sends the representation letter. It's the way things are done, and anything else would look suspicious."

"Suspicious to whom?"

"Just do it, and don't mention my brother or the investigation in your letter."

"Thanks for the advice. I didn't start doing this yesterday."

"Yeah, I know. It takes years of practice to become the bastard you are today."

"You should know." He was laughing his good-old-boy laugh again.

I said, "Thanks. I have to go see if I can get two thousand dollars for my Jeep."

He said, "You're breaking my heart," and hung up.

I could hear Mom in the kitchen. Sam came into the study around five and I filled him in on my encounters with Toby Miller and Spence Collins.

By the time I finished my story, dinner was ready. We shared a brown and green casserole with yellow stuff on top. I helped Mom clear the dishes and went upstairs. It was early, not even eight-thirty, but the last two days had left me feeling like I had the flu. I stripped down to boxers, turned out the light, and tucked the Browning under my pillow, which, as it turned out, probably saved my life.

I
N THE EARLY morning hours, some old-house sound—a creak or thud or maybe a wind noise—pulled me out of sleep and back into the pitch-black bedroom. Red dots on the digital clock formed 3:22. I lay still and tried to amplify and shape small noises into the footsteps of faceless criminals, but the house just kept on sounding like an old house. I drifted back off to sleep.

I am not someone who wakes easily. I have to push sleep away, to transition slowly into reality. A blaring alarm clock cannot move me, but unaccustomed noises—a hotel's cleaning staff or the rhythm of an unfamiliar air-conditioning system—set off some kind of primeval, internal alarm that jars me out of sleep for no good reason. Now, some small noise pulled me once again into the dark bedroom. I lay still again, listening for nothing, thinking about Hall and Zollie and Christy and Toby Miller.

Someone moved inside the room. Floorboards creaked lightly as some person, invisible in the dark, shifted his or her weight a few feet to the left of the bed. My own breathing grew loud in the dark. Concentrating, trying to hear or see movement in the room, I felt for the square butt of the Browning under my pillow. Nothing moved. Ten seconds passed, then a full minute. I had begun to think I had dreamed or imagined the movement, that I had created the sound of weight shifting on floorboards from the innocuous sounds that fill every old house, when I heard the floorboards again and caught a vague, swift movement to my left. I rolled hard to the right, taking the covers with me, and hit the floor in a tangle of sheet and blanket just as a loud *thump* shook the bed.

This time I remembered the safety. Lying next to the bed, I quickly pumped three rounds under the bed, hoping to hit a foot or ankle on the other side. Something crashed into the wall behind me. I spun, put two rounds in the wall, and dove toward the foot of the bed in case he or she thought to shoot at my muzzle fire. While I was springing around athletically on the floor, my attacker ran out of the bedroom door. I was as mad, as insanely angry, as I have ever been in my life. I ran hard after the sound of footsteps. Downstairs, the front door stood open. I hit the porch in time to see a tall, skinny white guy open the passenger door on an old Monte Carlo and dive inside. I aimed and fired five rounds at the car. The window in the open door exploded, and the car screeched away with the passenger door waving in the night air.

A few seconds later, Sam stumbled stiffly out onto the porch holding a twelve-gauge pump. Gray hair fanned around his crown like a turkey tail; water and sleep filled lower lids beneath unfocused eyes. He looked like an old man.

Sam said, "What the hell was that?"

"My friend in the Monte Carlo paid a visit. I woke up with the guy in my bedroom. Better call Sheriff Nixon and get him over here. Tell him I've got the tag number."

As Sam walked back inside, he said, "You call him yourself. I've got to go take care of your mother."

Nixon was not on duty, but the night deputy promised to send a car around.

In the bedroom, something had gouged a large oval hole in the Sheetrock at about chest height. Beneath the hole, an aluminum baseball bat with a black foam grip lay next to the baseboard in a confetti of paint and Sheetrock. On the bed, the crumpled bottom sheet held a perfect imprint of the business end of the bat just where my chest would have been if I had moved a half second later.

My bedroom seemed suddenly unwelcoming. I could talk to Nixon in the morning. I jotted the car model and the tag number on a phone pad and gave it to Sam.

I found the musty guest room at the end of the hallway, felt ridiculous while I looked in the closets and under the bed, and climbed into the antique cherry four-poster. It seemed I had just closed my eyes when someone knocked on the door. Light streamed through double windows over the headboard.

Sam said, "It's seven o'clock. You've got an appointment with Nixon at eight."

I lay there trying to wake up.

Sam said, "You hear me?"

"I hear you."

"Good. Come down to the office when you're through with Nixon. I need to talk to you."

I was at Nixon's office by seven fifty-five. He wasn't. I sat on a hard deacon's bench in his secretary's office and waited. At exactly eight, Nixon marched into the office, produced a ring of keys, and fitted one into the dead bolt on his office door. When he had it open, he said, "Come in."

I followed him in and looked around for a soft chair. Pressed sheet paneling covered the office walls, which were checkered with awards and mementos collected over a twenty-year military career. Pieces of walnut and particleboard bearing knives, insignias, and engraved brass were interspersed with ribbons, patches, and certificates preserved inside thin black frames.

Nixon hung his park-ranger hat on an oak hat tree and sat down behind his desk. He said, "I hear you've managed to piss off someone."

"Looks like it," I said. "You know, if you had called me yesterday after I came by your office we might have been able to get these guys before one of them tried to bash my chest in."

"I didn't need to call you. You told my deputy what kind of car the suspects were driving."

"I didn't give him the tag number."

"We didn't need the tag number to look for him. There aren't that many ten-year-old Monte Carlos driving around the county with blacked-out windows. All the tag number would have done is give us a home address. And your perpetrator wasn't at home in Birmingham, because he was here. If you hadn't given us the license number by this morning, we would have been in touch."

"You seem to be taking this awfully well. Do you think you could work up some enthusiasm or indignation or maybe a little false concern over an attempted murder?"

"It's not my job to be enthusiastic or indignant. It's my job to stay calm and focused when terrible things happen to other people."

"Well, Sheriff, so far it looks like you're so calm and focused that you're practically comatose. Not only are you not providing information you promised Sam, but you don't even bother to return my phone calls. Do you think you could manage to shift into high gear and help me figure out this thing before I end up dead?"

"Faster isn't always better. Some stranger might not be trying to kill you if you learned how to move a little slower and work with people instead of banging around like a bull in a china shop. Try pretending to be friendly. It won't kill you."

"First of all, you're not my friend, and you weren't Hall's friend. You're helping me because Sam pays you to be his friend, and I guess we know what that makes you. So just cut the bullshit. You don't like me, and I don't care. But you promised Sam and you promised me that you'd help. I think it's time to start keeping your word."

Nixon subjected me to one of his interminable pauses, then said, "I have every intention of keeping my word. But you should know that I work with Sam because it benefits both of us. I'm not afraid of Sam and I'm sure as hell not scared of you."

I said, "I don't give a shit whether you're scared or not. Someone killed my brother, and now it looks like they're trying to kill me. You tell me, what do you think Sam is going to do if another son winds up dead because you were sitting around playing 'who's got the biggest balls?' If that happens, you better be as tough as you act, because Sam's going to take care of business."

"Is this a variation on my daddy can beat up your daddy?"

"This is just the way it is. I'm not trying to act tough. I'm just explaining real life to you. It's time for you to quit playing both ends against the middle, time to quit waiting to see who's going to come out on top so you can jump to the winning team. Goddamnit, somebody's trying to kill me. I take that very seriously." He just sat there looking at his desk. I said, "Well, do we work together?"

He reached inside a bottom desk drawer and pulled out a curled sheet of fax paper. He said, "The car you spotted at your house last night belongs to Rodney Shelton. He's a petty thief. Been getting arrested regularly since he was thirteen. The car was reported stolen by his sister at four-eighteen yesterday afternoon." Nixon stopped and looked into my face before going on. "The foam grip on the bat wouldn't hold prints, but I think we can safely assume that Shelton was the one in your room last night."

"How can you be sure?"

"I looked over Shelton's rap sheet. There was something interesting under 'known associates.' Toby Miller was listed. I checked around early this morning. Your intruder is Miller's first cousin."

He seemed to be trying to decide whether to tell me something else. I said, "And?"

"And I was able to find out that both Shelton and Miller work for the same, the same general organization in Birmingham."

I said, "Shit."

He said, "You better believe it."

I stood to leave, and Nixon said, "I must be getting old. Two years ago, if you came in my office and talked to me like that, somebody would be carrying you out on a stretcher no matter what might happen later." He paused and drew a breath. "Don't do it again."

I walked out of his office.

October was only two days away, and the wind held the promise of coming cold and the scent of dry leaves. The temperature had fallen off into the high sixties that morning, and, except for a few hot peaks in the days ahead, the temperature would continue to fall over the next month so that kids out going door-to-door on Halloween would need sweaters under their costumes. Cool wind swept into the Jeep through open windows as I scanned the highway and the side roads for Toby's cousin and his semi-stolen car. I pulled into Sam's parking lot and stopped next to his Blazer. Inside the office, the air conditioner continued to push filtered air into the building.

Sam's little secretary had pulled her frizzy permed hair up with a yellow ribbon and produced what has got to be the oddest of female hairdos: a sideways ponytail over her left ear. She looked like a surprised, one-eared dog. No flirtation today. She was all business.

She looked up from her keyboard and said, "Mr. Sam said you could come on in when you got here."

I said, "Thank you." She flashed a perfunctory smile and resumed her typing. She was frowning at a page full of Sam's scribbling as I went into his office.

Sam looked up from his desk and said, "Have a seat. Be with you in a minute." He ran a thick index finger down a column of numbers while his other hand danced over a ten-key calculator. After he was satisfied with whatever numbers he was checking, he turned and shifted his full attention to me.

He asked, "Did you learn anything from Nixon?"

"Yeah. The old car at the house last night is registered to Toby Miller's cousin from Birmingham, a guy named Rodney Shelton." Sam pulled out a yellow pad and made a note of the name. I went on, "It was the same car I ran into south of town yesterday. Turns out that a little over three hours after I saw them, Shelton's sister called the Birmingham police and reported the car stolen."

"Pretty bush league."

"Yeah, I thought so too. Anyway, Sheriff Nixon says this Shelton fellow works for the same, quote, 'general organization' that Toby works for in Birmingham."

"That doesn't surprise me. Nixon tell you anything else?"

"Nope."

"You make up with him?"

"We're not going to be hanging around the Dairy Queen together, but I think we have an understanding. I can't say you're getting a lot for your money there, though."

"Did he give you another copy of his file on the murder?"

"I don't need one." I watched Sam's face and realized I was hoping for some look of surprise or confusion or maybe even respect, but, as always, he remained nonplussed, refusing to rise to such obvious bait. I said, "I copied everything but the coroner's photographs onto computer disks the night before the funeral. Whoever broke in—probably Shelton or Toby Miller—left the disks lying in the desk drawer where I put them. My secretary is getting me a new computer today. It'll be here tomorrow, and I'll be able to get back into the file then."

"Where do you think you are? I don't run this place on stone tablets, you know. I've got twenty computers scattered all over the mill. Hell, the empty office I was going to put you in has one on the credenza. You do need somewhere to work, don't you?"

"Yeah, I do. Where's the office?"

He ignored my question. He asked, "Does Nixon know you have a copy of the file?"

"No. He hasn't felt right, if you know what I mean, from the start of this thing. I don't see any reason why he needs to know everything I'm up to. He's not paying us a thousand a month."

"Did you tell him about your and Zollie's meeting with Toby?"

"No."

"Good." He pressed a button on his phone and said, "Ginny, come in here a minute." His secretary came in carrying a steno pad and a pencil in the ready position, like a pre-Dictaphone secretary out of a Tracy / Hepburn movie. Sam said, "Tom's going to be working here in the office for a few days. Get him set up in Barney's old office. He's doing something for me, so get him any supplies, food, coffee, anything he needs."

Ginny said, "I'll take good care of him, Mr. Sam."

Sam began looking for something on his desk, and I gathered that I was dismissed. Ginny led me down the hallway. Her fuzzy blond ponytail bounced with each step. She pushed open a paneled pine door and stepped aside to let me enter a large, square office wrapped in cream-colored tongue-and-groove one-by-fours. Varnished pine planks covered the floor, and wide double-sash windows behind the desk looked over a hayfield that hit a barbed wire fence and then timberland a hundred yards back.

The "credenza" was a small gray-metal desk pushed up against the windows. A larger desk in a slightly darker shade of gray faced out into the room. An oak swivel chair with a green vinyl cushion separated the desks. The only decoration was a dusty eight-point rack someone had nailed up over the door that led back out into the hallway.

I said, "Are there any legal pads or pens or pencils in the desk?"

Ginny shook her head. "No one's been in here for over a year. Just tell me what you need and I'll get it."

"I need three or four pads, some black and red pens, and a box of floppy disks for the computer. Does the lamp work?"

She walked over to the desk and pushed a black button on the base of the goose-neck lamp. The metal dome glowed but threw no discernible light in the sunlit room. She said, "It works," and walked down the hall to round up my supplies.

The computer under the window was an old 286 model. I hit the power buttons on the computer and the monitor and watched green gibberish scroll across the screen as the poor thing crawled through its start-up routine. Finally, a c-prompt popped up in the top corner. It took some fiddling to figure out that the hard disk held an antique version of WordPerfect that had no idea of what to do with my disks. Ginny came back in balancing notepads, pens, a stapler, tape, and a tape dispenser on a month-at-a-glance desk pad with a John Deere tractor advertisement across the top.

She said, "How do you like your coffee?"

"I like to get it myself. I'm sure you've got your hands full with Sam."

She shrugged and started to leave. I was beginning to gather that I had hurt her feelings on Friday. She had picked a bad time then to be flirtatious, but sound judgment in social matters is not really to be expected from a young woman two years out of high school.

I said, "I hope I wasn't rude the other day. This is just a bad time for my family."

She smiled and said, "I didn't give it a second thought," but I could feel the tension melt out of the air. She lingered a second. "Do you need anything else?"

"Maybe. This version of WordPerfect is ten years old. My document disks won't even work with it. Do you have an updated version?"

She laughed. "Mr. Sam thinks a computer is a computer. He doesn't know that thing is a dinosaur. It's about lunchtime. Why don't you go get something to eat? I don't know if we've got a spare Pentium, but I'll at least get you a four eighty-six in here with Windows and a new version of the word processor."

"Don't you need to eat?"

"I bring a sandwich. Don't worry about it. Go eat. By the time you get back, I'll have you fixed up."

I dropped the disks back into my pocket for safekeeping and headed down the hall and out the front door. I was halfway down the walkway when I saw Rodney Shelton leaning against my Jeep. I thought briefly about going back inside. Instead, I walked up to him and said, "Get off my Jeep."

Rodney just folded his arms and smiled at me with the same dark-edged teeth that bad genes and worse hygiene had bestowed on his cousin Toby.

chapter nine

I LOOKED INTO RODNEY'S dull, cocky eyes and remembered what Zollie told me about Toby. *He ain't like you. You understand? He got nothing to lose.*

I took a deep breath and said, "I told you to get off my Jeep."

Rodney didn't move. He stopped smiling and furrowed his brow to squint into my eyes. He was about six feet and weighed maybe one-thirty-five with his shoes on. His most prominent feature was a bobbing Adam's apple that looked like a jawbreaker trying to dislodge from his windpipe when he talked. He had a hard narrow face, sunken cheeks, high, thin cheekbones, and a small, almost effeminate nose that clashed with, but softened, the rest of his features. Above arched eyebrows and a shallow, simian forehead, his black hair was slicked back from a widow's peak and collected into a slimy little ponytail at the base of his neck.

He had quite a little tough-guy costume put together: black T-shirt, black jeans, and two-tone lizard cowboy boots, all overpowered by a thigh-length deerskin coat with Daniel Boone fringe and bead-work on the chest and shoulders. Something about the squint and the ponytail and the clothes rang a bell, but I couldn't decide who he was supposed to be. It had been so long since I played dress-up.

Rodney said, "I don't like being shot at. Don't tell me you went out this morning without your little gun to protect you." He spoke in an affected baritone whisper, no doubt like the quietly dangerous man he imagined himself to be.

I said, "I've got it."

"You've got what?"

"Who you're supposed to be. You've got kind of a Steven Seagal meets *Deliverance* look going there."

Rodney's face reddened and he forgot to squint for a few seconds. He said, "You're not funny."

"I hear that a lot." This whole situation was just a little too strange. I had taken ten shots at this action-hero wannabe nine hours earlier for trying to kill me. It dawned on me that the Monte Carlo was nowhere to be seen. I asked, "Where's your boyfriend?"

"If Eddie hears you call him that it won't matter what we been told."

"Who's Eddie?" Rodney's squint faded again and his features took on the blank, uh-oh expression of the perpetual fuck-up that he no doubt was. I said, "We'll deal with Eddie later. Right now you're going to get your skinny butt off my vehicle, and we're going to go inside and have a little talk."

He finally pushed away from the Jeep and came up within a foot of my chest. He was squinting again, and he had thrown in the added intimidation of clenched teeth. I was getting the full treatment. Rodney said, "I been told to give you a message. My boss says to apologize about last night and to tell you you won't be having no more trouble till you two can meet. I'm supposed to tell you you'll be getting a call."

"Who's your boss?"

"That's all you get." He paused for effect and stared intently into my eyes. "But if you and your nigger friend mess with Toby again, family's gonna take care of family, no matter who don't like it."

I had had just about enough of being threatened by this delusional, anorexic high-school dropout. I said, "You tried to kill me last night, you little piece of shit. The only reason I'm not kicking your ass all over this parking lot is because it won't do any good and meeting with your boss in Birmingham might. Now why don't you get the hell out of here before I change my mind."

Rodney turned and walked out into the parking lot, and a light blue Taurus backed out of a parking space and pulled up beside him. The driver was a middle-aged man of medium build. He had thick, curly black hair turned white at the temples. His tanned head sat like a box on a muscular neck. I guessed I was looking at Eddie.

The office door opened, and Sam walked out onto the brick walkway. Rodney looked over at me and said, "You're a big guy all right, probably hell on a Nautilus machine, but this ain't the Sports Club in Mobile. Careful you don't let your mouth write a check your ass can't cash."

I had never seen anyone move so fast from frightening to preposterous to ridiculous. And I hadn't heard that particular threat since the seventh grade. The driver's-side window rolled down and, in a bored monotone, Eddie said, "Shut up and get in the car."

Rodney walked around the front of the Taurus and saw half a dozen mill hands walking across the yard in our direction. Apparently, Sam had noticed my encounter from inside the office and made a call for reinforcements. Rodney looked back at me and smiled. "You're a bad man with your daddy's men around, aren't you." He got into the car, Eddie pulled out of the lot, and the rental car disappeared down the highway.

Sam walked out across the yard and met his posse halfway. They talked a few minutes, and he came over. I wanted to get away by myself and try to piece things together. The day before, I had jumped in headfirst and nearly helped kill a man. Now I planned to do things differently. After quickly filling Sam in on my conversation with Rodney, I started up the Jeep and headed for town to get something to eat.

The sequence of events over the last twenty-four hours kept bothering me. Toby probably was drunk or stoned last night. It's hard enough for Sam to get all his employees to work sober at seven in the morning. Someone like Rodney would almost certainly be on something if he had stayed up until three in the morning, but that didn't explain everything. It had been clear just now in the parking lot that he was being controlled by Eddie or someone higher up. He also seemed to make it clear that he swung the baseball bat because of the confrontation Zollie and I had with Toby. *Zollie.* Damn. I picked up the car phone and punched in Zollie's number. A child answered.

I said, "Is Zollie there?"

"Who's calling?" I realized it was Rudy on the line.

"Tom McInnes. I need to talk to Zollie."

"He's not available."

God, this kid was irritating. I said, "Is he all right?"

"Of course he's all right. He just can't come to the phone."

"Look, Rudy, you need to warn him. Toby Miller's cousin came to my house last night—"

He said, "And beat up your bed with a metal bat. Yeah, we know."

I was really starting to hate this little bastard. I managed to say, "How the hell?"

Rudy said "small town" with exactly the same inflection Zollie had used when he said those same words on his front porch after Hall's funeral. Rudy apparently had been within earshot that morning without my knowing it. Zollie hadn't told me he was around.

"I guess I'm supposed to say, 'It's not that small.' I believe that's what I said to Zollie on Saturday."

Rudy let out a high-pitched, ten-year-old laugh before he caught himself. "You're not as dumb as you look," he said. "But I'm not sure that's possible."

Rudy was smart enough not to waste time amusing himself at my expense if Zollie were hurt or in trouble. I said, "Nice talking to you again, Rudy."

"No problem." He said, "But next time you think somebody's planning to take a bat to Zollie, you might not want to wait ten hours to tell him," and he hung up. Nothing like being made to feel like a schmuck by a ten-year-old.

I needed someone to talk all this over with, so I headed for

Christy's place on the river to see if she was interested in a lunch date. Ten minutes later, the carriage light she had lighted for me after the funeral came into view.

As the Jeep rolled to a stop next to her cabin, Christy walked around from the lawn overlooking the river. Her thick auburn hair was pulled back with some kind of wide, black, stretchy thing. She wore a green knit shirt, black jeans with dirty knees, and white gardening gloves caked with black potting soil. She beamed a wide smile and said, "Well, hello there."

I said, "Hello yourself," and swung the door shut on the Jeep. As I walked over to meet her on the lawn, I wondered how I was supposed to greet her. Did she expect me to treat her as a lover or as a friend or as some kind of extended family member, the live-in girlfriend of a deceased brother? I thought back on Saturday night and decided that treating her like a member of the family was definitely out. By the time I reached the lawn, I had decided that a short hug, with maybe a dry cheek kiss, was about right. But I stopped short before I got within striking distance when she laughed and said, "Don't look so confused. I'm glad you came. Just let me put these filthy gloves and my tools away, and I'll make us some iced tea." She turned and walked away. I wondered what she would have done if I had looked like I wasn't going to hug her.

I followed her around to a new flower bed full of purple and yellow blooms with black, clover-shaped faces and watched her collect three or four small gardening tools with wooden handles. She stowed them on a shelf in a little outbuilding, draped her gloves over a boxwood to dry, and led me inside. When she was at the kitchen sink washing her hands, I said, "I really came by to take you to lunch, if you want to go."

"I can make some sandwiches here."

"No. Don't do that. We can go out somewhere."

She said, "I'd really rather have a sandwich here than have to get all fixed up and go into town, if you don't mind."

"No. I don't mind at all. I was just trying to save you the trouble. I didn't come by here for a free lunch."

Christy winked and said, "What did you come by here for?"

"Cute. I came by for someone to talk with, to bounce a few ideas off."

"Fine. Do me a favor. There's all kinds of sandwich stuff in the refrigerator. How about getting everything out while I go take a quick shower. I've been working in the yard all morning."

I said, "Want me to wash your back?"

"To tell you the truth, I'd rather have some coffee."

"I was kidding."

She said, "So was I. Get busy," and walked down the hallway toward her bedroom and bath.

Barely ten minutes later, she reappeared in the kitchen wearing a blue knit shirt like the green one she had been wearing in the yard, khaki safari shorts, gray rag socks, and hiking boots. Her towel-dried hair was combed straight back, and she had scrubbed her face pink. I had just finished making a smoked turkey and roast beef sandwich with mayonnaise, mustard, slices of Vidalia onion, and two kinds of cheese.

Christy said, "When I said there was all kinds of sandwich stuff in the refrigerator, I didn't mean you had to put it all on one sandwich."

"Hey, I offered to buy lunch. It was your idea to feed me. Don't blame me for your foolish decisions." She laughed. I motioned at my sandwich and said, "Do you want me to make you one?"

"Thanks all the same. I think I'll just have turkey with a little honey mustard and low-fat cheese. Move over."

"No way. The least I can do after cleaning out your refrigerator is make your lunch. By the way, you're never going to get big and strong eating like that."

"Well, let's just say I won't get big."

Christy and I took our sandwiches and iced tea out onto the deck overlooking the water and stretched out on a pair of white deck chairs. Between bites of sandwich, I filled Christy in on everything that had happened since leaving her house Sunday morning, including the details of my confrontations with Toby and his Birmingham cousin with a Steven Seagal complex. I told her my theory that Rodney Shelton had temporarily escaped Eddie, or some other controlling influence, around three that morning, when family pride—in combination with a controlled substance or two—prompted him to attempt violence in my bedroom. She said the theory made perfect sense.

She said, "Let's assume for a minute that whoever killed Hall knows about you and your investigation. You really haven't had time to find out anything yet. The killer would probably at least wait until you were on to something before he tried to get to you or stop you somehow. Otherwise, he'd just be stirring up more interest in the murder by trying to kill the brother of the murder victim."

I said, "You're assuming Toby Miller wasn't the murderer. I went straight to his house, and Zollie accused him of the murder. Also, Toby's too stupid to understand that killing me would make things worse. He'd just call his cousin in Birmingham, and they'd do me in."

"Yeah, but that isn't what happened. Your theory is that Toby's cousin . . . What's his name?"

"Rodney Shelton, Esquire."

"Your theory is that this Rodney guy was actually just sent to talk to you, but then worked himself into a mad in the middle of the night and came calling with a bat in hand."

"Not exactly. My theory is that Eddie probably came down from Birmingham to talk to me and that Rodney was sent along because he knows this part of the state. I figure that after they botched the job on the highway yesterday afternoon, Eddie went to his hotel room, or wherever he was staying, and Rodney went out drinking, smoking, or snorting something with cousin Toby." I said, "Keep in mind that I'm pretty much making this up as I go, but it looks like the cousins got worked up sometime after midnight and decided to pay me a call while Eddie wasn't around to interfere."

Christy said, "Okay. That makes sense. Now do you think Toby Miller sent for this Eddie when he found out you were in town?"

"No. Eddie was clearly Rodney's boss, and I would hazard a guess that Toby thinks of Rodney as his big-time gangster cousin from the big city. So I don't think Toby would have the balls or the juice to *send* for Eddie."

"So, where does that leave us?" Christy leaned over to reach a pair of Wayfarer sunglasses on a small table and put them on.

"That leaves us with Eddie or his boss thinking I know something that he wants or needs to know. Which, by the way, I don't know." I couldn't see her eyes. She just smiled up at the sky. I said, "Bottom line. First, Spence Collins' big client in Birmingham thinks I know something valuable. Second, I better figure out what it is, or he may let our two genetically impaired, brown-toothed cousins gnaw me to death."

Christy said, "Gross."

"Sorry, I got carried away." We lay back in the deck chairs. Clouds floated across the bright sky. I don't know what she was thinking; I was thinking about what she might be thinking. I sat up and said, "Thanks for lunch and for helping me work through this mess. Got to go see if I can figure out what I'm supposed to know."

"Any time. Come on, I'll walk you to your car." We walked down the steps and around the house to my Jeep. Christy walked up and stood about the same distance from me that Rodney had earlier that morning. This time being crowded was considerably more pleasant. She said, "I'd kiss you goodbye if you hadn't been eating onions. Was that some kind of ploy?" I smiled or, rather, laughed a little feebly and uncomfortably. She said, "Thanks for coming by. The invitation on the note's still good. Anytime you want to check the yes box, just let me know."

"Christy, the other night was great, and I think you're great . . ."
She smiled. "I know."

"But this thing is just too complicated right now. I'm probably going to need to talk to you several more times about Hall as I find out more, and I want to be able to come by to see you without your thinking I have ulterior motives and without feeling guilty about it."

"It's okay, Tom. I understand. We'll let some time pass."

"Thank you."

"Then I'll stretch out naked in front of the fireplace and let you kiss my lips and my breasts and my stomach and . . ."

I shook my head and said, "You are evil." She stood there laughing as I drove away toward the unlit carriage light and the turn onto Cedar Lane.

Back at the sawmill office, Ginny had rounded up a brand-new Pentium machine with a color monitor and a version of WordPerfect newer than the one Kelly and I used in Mobile. I was beginning to understand why Sam had hired this flirty little girl to be his link with the world. I said, "Bless you. Whose computer did you steal?"

"Don't tell him, but it's your father's. It came in a couple weeks ago. I've been holding it back in case somebody needed one who actually knows how to use it. Everybody knows Mr. Sam's a smart old man, but for him this thing's just gonna be decoration."

"You are full of surprises, Ginny."

She said, "Ain't that the truth," and bounced off down the hall to her station outside Sam's sanctum.

I snuggled my backside into my green vinyl cushion, leaned back against the slats of the oak desk chair, turned on the goose-neck lamp that lighted without making any light, and loaded up my computer disks. In less than a minute, Sheriff Nixon's file began scrolling across the screen.

chapter ten

T HE FRIDAY NIGHT before Hall's funeral, I had pretty thoroughly reviewed the autopsy report, the investigative report on the murder scene, and Nixon's notes on his interviews with Zollie and Christy. That left the assorted reports on Hall's criminal activities over the past few years. I decided to put the various reports in chronological order, since they had to be put in some order and that approach seemed as good as any.

For an allegedly notorious drug dealer, there wasn't a hell of a lot there. Hall had been a guest at the county lockup on exactly three occasions: once for selling a few ounces of marijuana when he was nineteen, once for assault when he got mixed up in a bar fight, and once last August for striking an officer. God only knows how many digressions were ignored, covered up, or disappeared from the police blotter as a result of Sam's monthly contributions to past and present sheriffs. But other notes and memos made it clear that, despite Sam's generosity, the Sheriff's Department had been keeping a close eye on Hall's activities. There had been lots of supposition about his possible connections to drug seizures and to rumors of large sums of money moving through the county, but the department apparently had been unable or unwilling to directly link Hall to anything that was unavoidably illegal.

The only really interesting materials supplied by Nixon were in a partial report concerning the second murder he had mentioned when he first handed over the envelope containing his files on Hall. William "Bird" Fitzsimmons, a local artist, had been murdered by an intruder last summer. Nixon had given me only the initial report filed by the first officer on the scene, together with a later memo to file noting that "the fingerprints of Coopers Bend resident Hall McInnes, 10 Cedar Lane, were lifted from various surfaces in the victim's art studio as follows: the entry doorknob, the door frame adjacent to same, a small wooden chair splattered with various colors of paint (# F-33), and on a long Formica table that the victim reportedly utilized as a work desk (# F-4)." A photocopy of Hall's fingerprints was attached to the memo.

I turned to the investigating deputy's notes to see if, chronologically, the report should go into my master file before or after Hall's August arrest. When I pulled the first page up on screen, the shock felt like a physical blow to my chest. Bird Fitzsimmons was murdered just before midnight on Thursday, July 2—twenty-four hours before the start of the July Fourth weekend and, according to Christy, about the same time Hall had started to come unglued.

I picked up the phone and called Zollie. Once again Rudy answered.

I asked, "Is Zollie there?"

"Who's calling?"

"Rudy, you know who this is."

"He's busy. Can I tell him what this is about?"

"Rudy, put Zollie on the goddamn phone. Now."

A loud *clack* came through the earpiece as Rudy dropped the receiver and walked away. A few seconds later, Zollie said, "Hello, Tom."

"Zollie, tell that little prick to let me talk to you when I call."

"I'll talk to him. Got to remember, he's just ten. His judgment get away from him sometimes." He said, "You planning to ever come back out here to see me?"

"Sure I am, Zollie. We both just let things get away from us yesterday. I've been trying to figure out how to find out what happened to Hall without killing anybody or getting killed in the process."

"You making any headway?"

"Some. I'll tell you about it later."

"Rudy said you sounded upset. What can I do to help?"

"How well did you know William Fitzsimmons?" Zollie didn't say anything for a long time. Maybe Rudy had figured out a way to cut us off in retaliation for my snapping at him. I said, "Zollie, you there?"

"Yeah, I'm here. I was just thinking. I knew Bird. Hard not to know everybody in a town like this."

"Was he a good friend of Hall's?"

"I don't know if they were good friends, but they spent some time together. You know how Hall liked to dive in the river. Well, Bird just about lived out on the water. Most folks figured he was about half crazy. Spent all his time floating around out there with a camera. Even had a big yellow camera Hall said cost a fortune, that he'd take pictures underwater with whenever enough mud dropped out of the water. Him and Hall got to diving together, and Hall used to go by and hang around Bird's old barn some. Said Bird had a bunch of maps of the river that he made hisself. Hall said Bird's maps were better than the ones put out by the Corps of Engineers. You know, Bird was the one they used to call when someone drowned. They say he could hook a body faster than anybody. Hall said Bird knew every sandbar and stump hole on the river for twenty miles north and south of here."

"What did they do together? Did you ever go out to Fitzsimmons' studio with Hall?"

"Nope. I went by the house to pick Hall up once or twice, but I never been to that old barn where Bird painted his pictures."

"Why not?"

"Never had a reason. He wasn't no friend of mine, and I sure as hell wasn't going to pay a thousand dollars for a picture of a alligator eating a crane, or some such foolish thing that's supposed to be art."

"Okay. Thanks, Zollie."

"I don't guess I was much help, but you're welcome."

"Is there anyone else, other than Christy, who might know more about any connection between Bird Fitzsimmons and Hall?"

"Yeah, Bird's wife still lives out at their place. I guess she'd know as much as anybody. Her name's Susan."

I said goodbye and promised to drive out as soon as I could and fill him in on what was happening, but he and Rudy seemed to have a pretty good pipeline without any help from me.

After I hung up, I walked down the hall and asked Ginny if Sam was in. She told me to go on in. Sam was sitting at his desk looking out the window at his mill. I said, "Sam, I've come across something that may or may not mean anything. I need an introduction to Susan Fitzsimmons."

"You think the murders are connected?"

"I don't know."

He flipped through a Rolodex on his credenza and reached for the phone. "Want to see her as soon as possible?" I nodded as he punched in the number. Sam started talking, and I could tell from his tone that he was talking to a person and not an answering machine. Sam is part of a generation that considers speaker phones to be bad manners, right up there with wearing a hat in the house, so I was left out. I just stood there uncomfortably, examining every word spoken by Sam in an effort to ascertain what was being said on the other end, while simultaneously suffering the vague feeling that I was somehow behaving inappropriately or intrusively because Susan didn't know I was standing in Sam's office.

Sam said, "Susan . . . Sam McInnes . . . Good to talk to you too. I want to say again how sorry Elizabeth and I are about Bird . . . Yeah, it's a hell of a thing to have in common . . . Thank you. Everyone's been very kind. Elizabeth would like that. Listen, my oldest son, Tom, is in town . . . Yeah, that was him. He's trying to help me make some sense out of what happened to Hall, and I'd like you to talk with him if it's not an imposition . . . I don't know. He's come up with something he wants to run by you. He won't be in town that long, and he was hoping you were free this afternoon or tonight." I waited through the last and longest silence while Sam continued to stare out the window and I continued to wonder what Susan Fitzsimmons was saying. Finally,

Sam said, "Thanks, Susan. I'll tell Elizabeth you asked about her. Goodbye."

When the receiver was back in its cradle, I said, "I gather that Mrs. Fitzsimmons is willing to see me."

"She said she'll be home all day. Come by whenever it's convenient."

"Thanks."

He said, "Sure," and turned his chair around to look back out at the mill. I caught on faster this time. I was getting pretty good at being dismissed.

I grabbed a few things from my borrowed office and, armed with directions from Ginny, headed out for my meeting at the Fitzsimmons place.

chapter eleven

I T WAS MID-AFTERNOON, and the temperature had reached a high of seventy-one degrees. The wind pulled at my hair and clothes as I followed Ginny's directions out of town. Susan Fitzsimmons' home was out Whiskey Run Road, ten or twelve miles past the first turn onto Cedar Lane. My highway map showed that the river lay to my left, and that, for some reason, the road's twists and turns reflected the shoreline that ran along some distance away across the hardwood forest that covered the old floodplain. Cedar Lane, where Christy lived, splits off Whiskey Run and divides the larger road from the river, running parallel to both, before slanting back into the highway a little over eight miles later.

I saw Cedar rejoin the highway and, as directed by Ginny, began looking for an old general store. Coming up on the right in a tangle of weeds and kudzu stood a simple, formerly white building with a rusted tin roof and a wide, drooping porch across its front. The store sign was long gone, but a broken and overgrown cement island marked where gas pumps had stood, and *Colonial Bread* was painted in faded blue script diagonally across the heavy double doors. I wasn't sure, but I seemed to remember stopping here for gas with Sam a few times when I was around five or six years old. The face of an Indian, a wrinkled face fringed with gray wisps and centered around a dark, toothless mouth, was connected in my memory with that store.

On the far side of the building lay a dirt road with a strip of clover down the middle. I turned my tires into twin ruts and, four or five hundred yards later, found a mailbox with WM. FITZSIMMONS painted on each side in architectural lettering. Just to the right of the lettering was a line painting of a comical-looking, long-legged bird. The road into the property ran along the top of an earthen dam that separated two old fishing ponds. On the right, the feeder pond rippled just two feet below the roadbed. On the other side, the water level dropped ten feet. White pipes ran under the road and protruded from the left side of the dam to funnel water from the higher pond to the lower.

At the end of the dam-top road was a Victorian farmhouse that looked like every farmhouse should—not a trendy restoration, but a perfectly preserved home place with white sideboards, gray porches, and hinged shutters painted a green so dark they were almost black. The yard was beautiful without looking overly planned or self-consciously *landscaped*. Around the edges of a wandering yard, thick grass faded into brush and forest and, in front, into the gravel drive. Rosebushes clustered against the front walk, and a controlled jumble of flowering and evergreen bushes swirled around the house.

I pulled across the front and nosed the Jeep in behind an ancient Ford pickup whose back bumper hung outside a small barn that shaded the cab and truck bed. I walked between the mass of rosebushes and mounted the porch. On the screen door was a note written in a flowing hand. It simply said: *I'm in back.* The porch turned around the left side of the house and I followed. Steps led off the porch into the side yard, and fieldstones dotted a worn pathway that hugged the swirls of greenery next to the house. I found Susan Fitzsimmons in the backyard, sitting on a porch swing hung from a thick limb that reached out parallel to the ground from an old oak with splattered, deformed branches. Over to the right was a huge red barn. Susan Fitzsimmons looked like a younger Martha Stewart with a few more curves, and she was smoking a long cigar.

She watched me approach without saying a word. She looked to be somewhere in her early forties. Her short blond hair was streaked by sunshine, and her blue eyes looked younger than the small crow's-feet and laugh lines on her lightly sunburned face would indicate. I stopped five feet in front of the swing, and she continued to un-abashedly look me over like a piece of livestock.

I said, "Are you Susan Fitzsimmons?"

She said, "You look like your father." Her voice was calm, and it had a Midwestern sound about it.

"You know who I am then."

"Anybody who has ever seen your father or your brother would know who you are."

A bull bellowed somewhere in the distance. She put the cigar in her mouth and took a couple of preliminary puffs to heat the ash before taking in a long draw and blowing it out in a long, thick stream.

I said, "Can I ask you a few questions?"

"Sure."

"Well, could we go somewhere where I could take some notes, maybe inside or up on the porch."

"I just lit this, and I don't want to get the smell in the furniture inside. We can talk here." She took another long pull on her cigar. "Do you want one?"

"What is that? An Avo?"

"Very good. Yes, it's a double corona."

"Sure. I'll take one."

She said "Here, hold this," and handed me her cigar. It seemed to me that holding someone else's cigar, with smoke curling from one end and teeth marks on the other, is a pretty personal gesture, but she apparently didn't share that view. She disappeared inside the back door and came back out with another cigar. She had clipped the head and lighted the foot. She said, "I don't smoke them inside, but you pretty much have to light them in there. It's nearly impossible to get one going out here in the breeze."

I thanked her. She sat on one end of the swing and motioned for me to sit on the other. I sat down.

She puffed on her Avo double corona to get it going again, then said, "So, you're the smart one."

I said, "The smart one of what?"

"Hall used to talk about you. That's what he called you: 'The smart one.'"

I didn't really know what to say to that, so I smoked on my cigar. I don't smoke at home, but I've played enough poker to know when I am smoking a very expensive cigar, and this one had cost more than Sam pays for an hour's work hauling lumber in July. People can have strange and incongruous habits, but Susan did not seem the kind to smoke expensive, hand-rolled cigars. Susan seemed exactly right living on a farm in a Victorian farmhouse with flowers and horses and an old pickup truck. She did not seem exactly right smoking. It also seemed odd that someone who lived alone and smoked cigars wouldn't want the smell inside.

I said, "How long you been smoking these?"

Susan rolled her cigar between her thumb and forefinger and smiled up at the limbs overhead. She said, "Just two or three months."

I said, "You wouldn't let Bird smoke in the house." It was a statement, and she didn't respond. I tried again, "Is this swing where your husband smoked these things?"

She looked over at Bird's old barn and smiled. "You are the smart one."

I said, "They say the sense of smell is more closely tied to emotion and memory than any other sense."

She turned sideways on the swing to face me. "What did you want to ask me?"

"I wanted to ask you about your husband's relationship with Hall, and, if it's okay, I'd like to talk with you a little about Bird's murder." I asked, "It is okay for me to call him Bird, isn't it?"

"It's fine. It's what everyone called him."

"Can I ask why?"

"Bird grew up on the Tennessee River. He got a degree in fine arts from Vanderbilt, and, like all serious young art majors, he was about to starve painting abstracts, which is what you paint if you want to make A's in university art classes. Just a few months out of school, he came down here on a boat trip from the Tennessee and fell in love with the place. He said the humidity here softens and gives color to the light. Anyway, he started painting the river. Particularly the water birds that live there. His style was more or less in the vein of Audubon, but with a modern, hyper-realism look. Pretty soon, he developed a market through a gallery in New Orleans. But the gallery owner kept complaining that Bird's signature was indecipherable, and he begged Bird to make it clearer so his work would be more easily recognizable. Bird pretty pointedly informed the gallery that his work was plenty recognizable because of its quality. But the gallery kept after him, and he eventually compromised. He refused to change his signature, but he started painting a quick little sketch of a crane next to his name. So all someone had to do was see the little crane, and they knew it was one of his. The gallery turned it into a marketing tool. Somewhere in the middle of all this, I met Bird at one of his showings in New Orleans. The first thing I ever said to him was: 'So you're the Bird Man.' After I moved to Coopers Bend to be with him, I kept calling him Bird Man, which eventually got shortened to Bird. The name caught on with his friends, I think, because he was always too Bohemian to be a William to begin with."

I smiled. "You tell that well."

"I've told it a hundred times. Everyone wants to know."

I asked, "Were he and Hall friends?"

"Nice transition. What are you asking? Were they buddies, drinking pals, soulmates? No. Did they hang around together sometimes and go diving in the river together? Yes, they did."

An edge had crept into her voice. I knew I was imposing, but I had other concerns. And if I figured out what happened to Hall, along the way I just might stumble onto an answer to who killed her husband. I said, "What did you think about your husband hanging around with a known drug dealer?"

She smiled at me. "You know how to use that soft Southern thing, but you just cut right through the bullshit when you need to, don't you?"

"Yes."

"I didn't like it. I didn't like anything about Bird's relationship with Hall. I don't mean to offend you, but I don't think I would have cared much more for Hall if he had been a college professor."

"And he wasn't any college professor."

Susan smiled. "That's true, and in light of his chosen profession, I was particularly unhappy about his hanging around the studio."

"Did you tell Bird that?"

"Yes."

"Why didn't he listen?"

"Bird was not really good at taking instruction. He was a great husband and a wonderful person. I don't expect to ever meet someone again with his confidence and intelligence and humor, but artists are, almost by definition, supremely confident. Most have spent a lifetime ignoring the advice of parents, teachers, and counselors to get a real job. They are who they are, in no small measure, because they didn't listen to anyone." She stopped to draw on her cigar, then went on. "And you have to understand that Bird was spoiled. He never spent a day of his life working in an office where he had to do what other people wanted."

"He was lucky."

"Yes. He was." She paused. "So was I."

Susan and I talked for another hour, sitting under her oak tree, drifting in small circles with the swing and the wind. She told me that Bird and Hall were fellow river rats, but that they seemed to have little else in common. Their only time together was either passed on the water or spent in Bird's studio poring over Bird's collection of river maps and charts. She never said so in so many words, but woven throughout her conversation were hints that she believed Bird's murder was somehow tied to his relationship with Hall. Because of her suspicions, she was not inclined to speak charitably of Hall or to apologize for not doing so.

Everything about Hall's relationship with these people seemed to center around the river, so I asked if I could see Bird's studio and maybe look over some of his maps. Susan said, "Come on," and led the way. The big, standard-issue, sliding barn door was bolted shut. Susan went to a human-sized door on the side. She fished a ring of keys out of her jeans and unlocked two dead bolts. She said, "Just a second," and stepped inside to work an alarm pad to the right of the entrance. I was beginning to suspect that Bird had been more than a little paranoid when Susan flipped on a light and told me to come inside. Warm light flooded the barn. Two or three hundred completed canvases lined wooden shelves built at waist height along the two longer walls. Everywhere, the Alabama river flowed and swirled in sunshine, rain, fog, night, day, winter, summer, fall, and spring. Wildlife peered out from every canvas—in one, just a silhouetted kingfisher, small against a moonlit river; in another, a close-up study of two bull alligators in amorous battle. Bird had found the colors in fog and night and winter. His paintings made the river look the way it feels.

And Bird had not been paranoid. This stuff had been worth a small fortune when he was alive. Now, Susan Fitzsimmons was fixed for life.

Almost as striking as the canvases, and considerably more important to the task at hand, was a scroll of the river running across one entire wall from end to end. I walked over for a closer look. The scroll was one continuous piece of heavy cotton artists' paper about four feet high and thirty feet long. The river was drawn in flowing strokes of ink, like a Japanese ink brush painting, and nearly every turn and dip in the channel was decorated with drawings of riverboats or old coins or grizzly, misshapen bodies. In a few places, Bird had drawn mythological figures. Everywhere, there were blocks of notes in the same neat, architectural lettering I had seen on the mailbox. Altogether, the map looked like nothing more than a beautiful, fanciful, artistic impression of the river's wanderings, until I looked closer and saw a light grid with survey markings done in pencil.

I said, "This looks too artistic to be accurate."

"That's what everyone says. A friend of Bird's with the Corps of Engineers came out here once with a leather case full of little silver map-maker's instruments to try to prove it couldn't be as accurate as their boring little gray maps. When he was through, he said it had some small variations from his maps in places because of the width of brush strokes and that sort of thing. But he said that overall, if he were asked in a court of law, he'd have to say it was as accurate as anything produced by the Corps' own mapmakers. Bird wasn't satisfied with that. He maintained that his handmade map was more accurate than any other map he'd seen, especially when it came to geologic formations. The engineer finally admitted that Bird's map was more complete, if not more accurate, than anything else he'd seen, but I don't know if that was because it was true or because Bird had just worn the poor guy down."

"Why did he do it?"

"Do what?"

"Oh, I'm sorry. Why did Bird spend all that time making this map? I mean, it's beautiful, but why make over a map you can buy at the courthouse for twenty dollars? Looks like he would've just done a rough job on the technical part and spent his time and talent making it a work of art."

"Art was Bird's profession, his business. This, the river, was his hobby—although he would not have liked hearing it described in such pedestrian terms. I think it appealed to his need for precision." Susan walked over to stand next to me and looked up at the map. She said, "I asked him one time why he spent so much time trying to be more exact than the professional mapmakers. He said it was like the medieval monks who illustrated manuscripts. Bird said if you're decorating a hand-calligraphed history of the Crusades, then you're creating a work with overlapping layers of technical, scholarly, and artistic merit. But if you're decorating a shopping list, then you're just doodling."

I said, "And if he did this, taking measurements, recording observations, making notes on feeder streams and cave formations, then he wasn't just floating around on the water taking pictures. He was doing something serious."

She said, "Men need that, don't they? They need to feel like what they're doing is serious."

I said, "Not just men."

Susan reset the alarm and locked up. As we walked around to my Jeep, I thanked her and asked if I could come back. She said I could. I left her sitting on the front steps of her farmhouse, watching me over the tops of rosebushes as I drove back across the earthen dam a little after five o'clock.

I was back at the sawmill office before the six o'clock mill whistle sounded. Ginny was still at her desk. When I came in, she said, "Mr. Sam wants to know if you found out anything new."

"Tell him no. Do I have any messages?"

"You sure do. Your secretary, Kelly, called. We had a little talk. She seems like a great girl. And you got a call from a man named Spencer Collins in Birmingham."

"Have you got his number?"

"Didn't leave one. Just left a message." She leafed through a short stack of pink message slips. "Here it is. He just said for you to, quote, 'get your butt up to his office by noon tomorrow.' He said you have a meeting at two."

"I don't have his address." She held out a typed sheet of bond containing the name of Spence's firm, the address and phone number of his office, and directions on how to get there, beginning at Sam's driveway. I said, "Thank you."

Ginny just said, "Uh huh," and looked down to busy herself with the next project, but she was grinning. Ginny was teaching me a little lesson about judging people. As I turned to leave, Ginny said, "One more thing. Mr. Sam had your stuff moved out to the lake house. He said he thought you would be more comfortable with your own place to work at night."

"That's what he said, huh?"

"Actually, he just said to tell you you'll be staying out there from now on."

"One little attempted murder and I'm kicked out."

Ginny laughed.

Back in my borrowed office, with my vinyl cushion and my anemic desk lamp, I made some notes on the computer about Susan Fitzsimmons and the map in Bird's studio, then placed a call to Kelly. When she heard my voice, she said, "So you're still alive, and I'm still gainfully employed."

"So far. It's been another interesting day, though. Why did you call?"

"Because Joey called me. He started working on your problem in Birmingham right after we hung up yesterday. I've got a preliminary report."

"Good. I'm meeting with the guy in Birmingham tomorrow at two. Maybe Joey got something that will help."

"From what Joey tells me, you're going to need all the help you can get. You ever heard of Mike Gerrard?"

"No."

"Sit back and listen. We've got problems. You know that favorite line of yours from *The Verdict?*"

I said, "You mean when Paul Newman tells his mentor, that red-headed character actor, I can never remember his name. Anyway Newman tells his mentor that his opposing counsel is a 'good man,' and the mentor says, 'Good man? He's the prince of fucking darkness.'"

"Yeah, well, you get to meet the prince at two tomorrow afternoon."

chapter twelve

THE LAKE HOUSE smelled, not surprisingly, like a musty, seldom-used, waterfront house—lots of dust, stale air, and mildew odor. I opened the doors and a couple of windows to get a cross draft going, turned on the ceiling fans downstairs, and waited for nightfall. A little after eight, I closed the doors and switched on the television. The cast of a sitcom that had been on a year too long was busy doing a caricature of the show they used to do. I changed the channel to *Monday Night Football*. After gathering up three bottles of Foster's lager and a sack of sandwiches I had picked up in town, I turned on the cold water in the shower, walked out the side door, and got comfortable behind a row of dogwoods.

Watching an empty house is not as entertaining as you might imagine. By ten o'clock, I had eaten three sandwiches and was finishing off my last beer. By ten-thirty, the part of me in contact with the ground had fallen asleep and refused to wake up even though I shifted position every three minutes. Eleven o'clock came and went. I was beginning to feel ridiculous—a little like one of the Hardy Boys, and I was about to call it a night when the hum of a motor and then the sound of tires on gravel interrupted the quiet. A few seconds later, a pickup truck rolled slowly into view with its headlights off. The truck stopped a hundred feet from the house and idled there for exactly six minutes, then backed onto the shoulder, turned around, and drove away into the night. I walked over and looked at tire tracks on the soft shoulder, peered intently down the road for a few seconds, walked back to my hiding place, and sat down. A man of action.

At one in the morning, I stumbled into the house and turned off the shower. In keeping with the Hardy Boys theme, I rigged up makeshift alarms by stacking pots and pans inside each door and across the hallway to the bedrooms, then went to bed.

Seven A.M. came fast. I spent most of the next hour hitting the snooze button every ten minutes before finally rolling out of bed. I used every drop of hot water in the tank to shower and shave, then went to the closet to try to figure out what one wears to meet the most dangerous man in the state. I decided I had better look like someone who would be missed. I pulled on a starched white shirt, a charcoal-gray, tropical-weight wool suit with a muted pinstripe, and a dark red tie with small gold dots. I slipped on black tassel loafers and a black alligator belt and looked in the mirror. I looked just like one of the hundreds of standard-issue, overpriced lawyers who overpopulate every large city in America.

Four days earlier, the trip from Point Clear to Coopers Bend had been one of moving from sandy coastal plains to rolling timberland. Now, as I followed the blacktop north toward coal mines and dormant steel mills, rolling hills grew into mountains, and the pumped-up, steroidal trees of the Black Belt shrunk to scruffy, undersized pines. At Calera, a rumpled little railroad town south of Birmingham, I cut across to the east to finish the last twenty miles on the interstate.

Spence's office was on the corner of Twentieth and Fifth Avenue North. According to Ginny's notes, he was on the thirtieth floor of an office building covered with pink granite. I turned right onto Fifth, turned left into the attached parking garage, and went looking for Spence. The building lobby was modern and sort of narrow and stingy with the usual blue-green and purple accents that designers seem to be getting a deal on these days. I pushed the button with a 30 on it and watched lights dance back and forth on the stainless steel panel as I passed twenty-eight floors of lawyers and bankers, stockbrokers and accountants.

The doors opened onto a different world. The firm's interior designer had decorated the passageway outside the elevators to look like the entry hall in an expensive home. Dark blue, plush carpeting stretched underfoot; carved oak paneling—not the stained veneer found in most lawyers' offices—covered the walls; and wing-backed chairs flanked an antique library table that held an oversized arrangement of blue and white silk flowers. Overhead, someone had actually painted a mural on the frigging ceiling. Clouds and cherubs swirled around a scene of Alabama industry from cotton and soybean fields to mining, steel mills, and timber. To the left, a wide, arched doorway opened into a waiting area that looked like the smoking room in a men's club: leather chairs, antique oriental rugs scattered across edge-grained hardwood floors, Waterford and Stiffel lamps, and what looked to be hand-tinted English hunting lithographs on the walls. In one corner behind a mahogany desk with leather inlays sat an absolutely beautiful young woman with long brunette hair and deep blue eyes. As I entered the room, she turned a brilliant, practiced smile on me and said, "May I help you?"

"I'm here to see Spence Collins."

She said, "Yes, sir," and looked down to examine an appointment book on her desk. "You must be Mr. McInnes." I admitted that I was, and she asked me to have a seat. I sat on a sofa beneath an old tapestry of a lot of skinny white women dressed in medieval costumes and lounging with a unicorn on the banks of a small stream.

I was ruminating on the possible relationships between unicorns and medieval women and trying to get interested in a *Fortune* article on NAFTA when I heard my name. A rigid woman in an olive-green tailored suit was standing in the doorway to the right of the receptionist. She said, "I'm Mr. Collins' secretary. Please follow me." As we started down the hall, she said, "You can get comfortable in the conference room while Mr. Collins is finishing his telephone conference." She seemed to like using the word *conference*.

When we were inside the conference room, I asked, "What's your name?"

She said, "Debbie." I smiled. She looked about as much like a Debbie as the receptionist looked like an Ethel. Debbie peered at me from beneath a short semi-beehive of indeterminate, artificial color. She was wearing black half-glasses suspended from a silver leash that circled behind her neck. Over the years, I have become convinced that you cannot rise to the level of senior legal secretary unless you agree to wear those glasses. Debbie said, "Would you like some coffee?"

"Sure. Thank you. Black with two sugars."

She said, "Yes, sir," and walked away with her head, neck, and spine in perfect, almost arthritic alignment.

I was sipping my coffee and staring out the window across a church roof at the fountain in Linn Park when Spence came in. "Tom, how are you? Glad you could make it."

I said, "I appreciate your moving so quickly on this, Spence."

"No problem." He reached inside his coat and produced a white envelope. "Here's the letter you asked for." I opened the envelope, scanned the letter, and put it in my inside coat pocket, then handed him my envelope with a two-thousand-dollar check inside. Spence put the envelope away without opening it. He sat in one of the leather conference chairs and motioned for me to do the same.

Since I had last seen him, Spence had gained about fifteen pounds, which he carried around his waist and beneath his chin. His thinning, reddish-blond hair was trimmed in a short Ivy League cut, and his round face was ruddy from weekends of golf at the country club. He wore a dark blue three-piece suit, cut to de-emphasize his girth, a blue and white striped shirt, and a yellow bow tie with tiny black dots. A pair of hexagonal wire-rimmed glasses peeked out from inside the front pocket of his suit coat.

Spence opened a tan leather folder, laid a fountain pen on the blank legal pad inside, and said, "Before I tell you who you're meeting with today, we need to get some ground rules straight."

I said, "Unless I'm meeting with Mike Gerrard, the ground rules won't matter."

Spence smiled. "You are."

"Good."

"How much do you know about Mr. Gerrard?"

"As much as my investigator could find out in a day and a half."

"Well, don't believe everything you hear. Mr. Gerrard is one of the most successful businessmen in the state. His family was in steel mills here in Birmingham seventy years ago. He's one of the few who was able to hold onto the family fortune after the mills closed."

"And he is, as you said, the most dangerous man in the state."

"Tom, I'd appreciate it if you didn't repeat that. I was trying to do you a favor by telling you what you were messing with."

"No problem, Spence. I just didn't want you to get too carried away with what a fine, upstanding citizen Gerrard is."

"That's the thing, Tom. In many ways, Gerrard is just that. He's on the boards of half the charities in town. He's a member of the most exclusive country club in town, has been since his daddy got him in as a junior member in his twenties, and he's pretty well respected. Everyone, or at least everyone in the top levels of the business community, knows Gerrard has unconventional business interests, but he's so well connected and he does so much for the community that folks don't really hold it against him."

"So long as he's not selling dope to their kids in Mountain Brook, nobody really cares. Is that it?" Spence frowned. Mountain Brook is an incorporated town contiguous to Birmingham, and it was where Spence and most of his friends lived. It has one of the highest per capita incomes in the nation. It is sometimes referred to by those who work but cannot afford to live there as "The Tiny Kingdom."

"No one here has said that Gerrard sells drugs to anyone and, as his attorney, I feel that I should deny that on his behalf. But the answer to your question is no. I don't think anyone's that shallow or perverse. Gerrard's image among his peers is that he's kind of a romantic scallywag. Someone who does things they wouldn't do, but who is basically a good guy."

"My investigator tells me that Gerrard's reputation is somewhat different among certain socioeconomic groups outside Mountain Brook."

"What else does your investigator tell you?"

"That Gerrard's in drug smuggling and gambling. That he's responsible for at least half the marijuana and cocaine that flows into Alabama through the Gulf Coast. My investigator also heard that if an independent bookie starts making any real money anywhere in the state, one of Gerrard's men pays a visit and the bookie either ends up working for Gerrard or he's out of business. And there are rumors that a couple of people who refused to do business with him had fatal accidents shortly thereafter." I stopped and waited for Spence to jump down my throat about the last comment, but he just looked at me and then let his eyes drop down to his yellow pad. I went on, "I hear he's smooth and well connected."

Spence said, "It's no secret that Mr. Gerrard is one of the largest contributors to political campaigns in the state."

"So you're telling me to be careful."

"I'm telling you to be very, very careful."

I said, "I understand that Gerrard is supposed to get here at two."

"He's not coming here. You're going to his office for the meeting."

"Don't you mean *we?* You're my attorney."

"I wasn't invited. He wants to see you alone."

"Why?"

"No idea. You'll find out when you get there."

"Am I in danger?"

Spence looked down at a doodle he had been working on while we talked. He said, "I have not been told and I do not know the answer to your question, and guessing is not my job. Just be careful. I can tell you from personal experience that Gerrard will not respect anyone who is afraid of him, but he won't abide an open challenge either."

"Thanks. I'm glad you cleared that up."

"Just remember, the guy is smart. And I don't mean smart like a lawyer, like you and me. Gerrard is as smart as lawyers like you and me *think* we are on our best days."

I smiled and said, "Come on. Nobody's that smart."

Spence didn't smile. He said, "Mike Gerrard is."

As Spence and I were leaving for lunch, the receptionist with the deep blue eyes called my name. "Mr. McInnes. Your two o'clock called. Mr. Gerrard would like you to dine at his home with him at one-thirty instead of meeting at two."

"I don't know where he lives."

She said, "They've arranged for a car and driver to meet you on the Fifth Avenue side of the building." The phone on her desk rang, and she turned her attention to charming the client on the other end of the line.

I looked at Spence and asked, "What does that mean?"

He said, "Beats the hell out of me."

Spence rode down on the elevator with me either out of courtesy or because he was going to lunch and it was on his way. He didn't look like a man who missed a lot of lunches. As we walked around to Fifth Avenue, I half expected to see a Sicilian chauffeur in full livery standing next to a stretch limousine. What I saw was a pimply high-school kid leaning against a two-seater Mercedes. Spence said, "That's one of Gerrard's cars. Good luck. Come up to the office and see me when you get back. I'd like to know what happens."

I introduced myself to the driver. He offered a small, damp hand for me to shake and told me his name was Freddie. Once the Mercedes was up to speed on the expressway, he said, "All right if I listen to the radio?"

I said, "Fine with me." Such was the full extent of our conversation. My new friend Freddie and I reveled in the more or less musical sounds of Nashville until he pulled into a circular, brick driveway that curved in front of one mansion and between two others. He didn't say anything, but I gathered that I was supposed to get out. I thanked him for the ride, and he bobbed his head once in response. The Mercedes disappeared around a service drive. I was left standing there alone, looking at one of the most pretentious houses I have ever seen.

In Mobile, most people with money have generally had it for a century or two. Probably for that reason, they don't seem to feel much need to impress the peasants with their liquidity. Mobile is also still Southern enough to consider obvious displays of wealth to be tacky. Birmingham, by contrast, is a relatively modern city, and the people who came in this century to build steel mills were from the rough society of old Pittsburgh, where displaying wealth was considered one of the main reasons for acquiring it. As a consequence, Birmingham in general, and Mountain Brook in particular, has more than its share of mini-castles, and I was standing in front of one of the most impressive or pretentious, depending on your point of view.

All ten or twelve thousand square feet of the house was encased in manufactured stone. The place actually had a small turret that rose up next to the entrance and ended forty feet in the air, poking up ten feet above the rest of the stonework. A visually irreconcilable roof strained under the weight of overlapping orange Mediterranean tiles. Clouds passing overhead reflected off leaded glass in the windows.

I approached the front door and rang the bell. At least I think I did. This was not a house where one could hear door chimes ringing from outside. A few seconds passed before the door opened and Eddie—Rodney Shelton's friend with the expensive tan—asked me to come in. He led me down a central corridor, through a paneled library, and out into a glass room that appeared to be a solarium; although it seems odd to call a room a solarium if it doesn't have any plants in it. In the center of the room, a small dining table had been set for four. Eddie said, "Make yourself comfortable. We'll be in in a minute." He left the way we had come in. I walked over to look out the windows. The house had been built on a mountain ridge, and the informal dining room looked out over the city. Gerrard's view didn't look like much in daylight, just a lot of scruffy apartment buildings, railroad tracks, and, in the distance, the downtown business district; but I guessed it would have been beautiful at night when darkness obliterated railroads and smokestacks, and scruffy apartments transformed into thousands of tiny lights in the distance.

Voices floated in from the library. Eddie and a vague-looking, well-tended man strode into the room immersed in conversation. Rodney Shelton followed a couple of steps behind, looking as out of place in Gerrard's mansion as a rat on a silver tray. The well-tended man, who had to be Gerrard, walked over and offered his hand. I shook hands with the most dangerous man in Alabama, who, it seemed to me, looked like one hell of a nice guy. Gerrard appeared to be in his late forties, but could have been older. Thick blond hair, parted on the side and salted with gray, swept back from a tanned forehead in a sharp widow's peak. A long, straight nose dominated the rest of his features, and, when he smiled, he showed expensive teeth and his blue eyes narrowed to slits. Gerrard wore a tailored gray flannel suit over a starched white shirt. A gray fleck in his perfectly knotted oxblood tie precisely matched the flannel, which, in turn, matched the ribbed socks that disappeared into narrow tasseled loafers that had been polished to a hard shine.

Gerrard said, "It was good of you to come. I hope I haven't inconvenienced you by moving up our meeting at the last moment. Something unavoidable came up that I have to take care of later this afternoon, and I wanted us to have enough time together. We're going to have some lunch while we talk." He turned to Eddie and Rodney and said, "I believe you've already met Mr. Shelton." Neither Rodney nor I made any move to shake hands. He motioned to Eddie and said, "Mr. McInnes, this is Eddie Pappas. Eddie is the president of our little mining company. Eddie and Rodney are going to join us for lunch."

I said, "Mr. Gerrard, I requested this meeting, and I honestly appreciate your taking time to meet with me. But Mr. Shelton here tried to kill me in my sleep with a baseball bat."

Gerrard interrupted, "Unless I'm mistaken, Rodney has delivered a personal apology for whatever errors in judgment he may have made. If you want this meeting to go forward, you're going to have to put that incident behind you."

I said, "I'm not going to sit across the table from him."

Gerrard suddenly didn't look like a guy you would want to hang out with. Eddie stepped in quickly and said, "Mr. McInnes, Rodney knows your part of the state. He has contacts there. He can help you with your problem. We all need to show some restraint here."

"The fact that Rodney got back to Birmingham in one piece is evidence of my restraint." I was looking at Rodney now. His face was growing progressively flushed as I talked. "But I'm not going to have lunch with someone who broke into my parents' house in the middle of the night and tried to kill me. In fact, it's insulting for you to bring your trained dog to this meeting."

The room got very quiet. My sentiments were genuine, but I was also playing a hand. Everyone in the room—well, everyone but Rodney—knew there was no legitimate reason for his being at the meeting. Executives as smart as Gerrard was supposed to be do not bring entry-level thugs to meetings if anything important is going to be discussed. So, if anything substantive was going to happen over lunch, Rodney had to go. Otherwise, the meeting would be a waste of time, and I would be better off leaving with my dignity intact.

It also looked like Gerrard was trying to find out just how much shit I was willing to eat. Spence told me Gerrard doesn't respect anyone who is afraid of him. If I had been willing to break bread with a lowlife who tried to murder me, then Gerrard would have assumed, rightly, that I was terrified of what I had stumbled into and that I would be willing to do anything to feel safe again. They needed to know that selling my soul or my dignity was not going to be part of the equation.

After my "trained dog" comment, bluish veins popped out on either side of the little fist formed by Rodney's Adam's apple, and his face slowly turned purple until it looked like it might explode like a blood blister. Eddie looked bored. Gerrard had begun to look a little amused.

Gerrard said, "Eddie, ask Rodney to excuse us." Eddie looked at

Rodney and nodded at the door. Rodney shot one last look of hatred my way and left quickly with Eddie close behind. My attempted murderer had been humiliated in front of men whose opinions he cared about. Sooner or later he would have to do something about it.

I smiled at Gerrard and said, "Thank you." It was time to get the meeting back on a professional level.

Gerrard returned my smile and said, "Eddie should be back in a minute. Let's go ahead and sit down." No sooner were we seated than a brittle old man in a white coat and black trousers entered the room with, I noticed, three, not four, salad plates bearing chunks of fresh fruit sprinkled with coconut shavings and poppy-seed dressing. Gerrard picked up his fork and I followed suit. I soon realized that I was just picking at my food, which is a sure sign of fear or nerves in a guy my size, so I started to concentrate on eating in a comfortable, unhurried way. Gerrard was working his way through the fruit, chewing each bite thoroughly as he delicately balanced his fork on long, tanned fingers. He was looking out the window now and then and not saying a word. If the silence made him uncomfortable, he didn't show it. He looked like a man enjoying eating alone, which, it seemed to me, was pretty much what he was doing.

When we had finished our salads, Gerrard said, "You asked for the meeting," as if he had been waiting for me to break the silence.

"Has Spence Collins discussed my problem with you?"

"He told me a little, but I would like to hear from you why you're here."

"My younger brother, Hall McInnes, was murdered on the river down in Coopers Bend last week. I asked around and found out he was betting pretty heavily with a redneck named Toby Miller, who is Rodney Shelton's cousin." I paused to see if my story was having any effect on Gerrard.

He said, "You were going to tell me why you're here."

"Rodney and, I think, Eddie tried to stop me when I was out running Sunday afternoon. I didn't know who either of them was at the time. Later that day a friend of mine and I went by and had a pretty serious talk with Toby Miller. He ran. That night Miller's cousin, your employee, came by and tried to kill me with a baseball bat." As I finished the story, Eddie came back into the room, sat down, and started eating.

Gerrard said, "You had Spence Collins ask for a meeting. I heard about Rodney and made him apologize. What else do you want me to do? From what I hear, you did threaten his cousin's life. Rodney acted irrationally, but I can understand why he took the action he did. He was trying to help out a family member. It seems to me, if you leave Rodney's family alone, he will leave you alone. And your problem will be solved."

"Bullshit."

Gerrard truly looked surprised. "What?"

"Bullshit."

Gerrard said, "Young man, do you know who you're talking to?"

"Yes. I know exactly who I'm talking to, and I mean *exactly*. This is not a family dispute that got out of hand. Rodney works for you, and Eddie works for you. And both of them were after me before my friend laid a hand on Toby Miller. After your employees ran me off the roadside Sunday afternoon, I heard Rodney tell Eddie that I must have figured out I was in trouble. I even heard Eddie here tell him to shut up when he said it."

Eddie said, "You don't know half of what you're saying."

Gerrard looked at me. "Do you really think you're that important to me?"

I said, "It doesn't make much sense, does it?" Gerrard didn't answer. In fact, while I was clearly the focus of his attention, he didn't seem particularly interested in what I was saying. Eddie had stopped eating and was watching me the way a cat watches a cornered mouse. I kept talking to Gerrard. "Spence tells me you're smarter than God. Tell me. Why in the hell did you send down people who could be traced to you? Hall whipped Toby Miller's ass in front of half the town last summer. I might have just figured it was personal. You could have given me Toby, and I might have just gone away. But no. For some reason, you couldn't stay out of it."

Gerrard said, "Mr. McInnes, you can get up and leave here right now, and I guarantee that I will gladly leave you alone to work through this mess by yourself. If I need to remind you again, I will: You asked for this meeting, not me."

I said, "That's not exactly right. I asked Spence to set up a meeting with someone who's well connected in the kind of businesses that employ people like Toby and Rodney. Spence came up with your name, but he didn't do it until after he checked with you. So you told him you would meet with me."

Gerrard said, "Yes, and I didn't have to do that. I would think you'd take a more appreciative tone."

I said, "Oh, I appreciate it all right. And I'm sure you appreciate Spence dropping me in your lap. I keep hearing how smart you are, but you've got the same failing that most gifted people have. You think so little of the rest of us mortals that you think no one is able to even grasp your most obvious plans, much less meet you on equal terms."

Gerrard said, "Are you going to dazzle us with your superior intelligence, Mr. McInnes?"

"Let's find out," I said. "It seems to me that Hall knew something that you need to know, something he took to his grave. That's why I don't think you killed him, or had him killed, I should say."

Gerrard said, "That's very generous of you."

"I put my little brother in the ground last Saturday. I'm not in a generous mood. I'm just telling you what makes sense, or at least what makes sense until I learn something that changes my mind. Anyway, based on your connections to Coopers Bend through Toby and Rodney, and based on the business interests that you and my brother shared in common, it would not surprise me to learn that Hall also had some kind of business relationship with you."

As Eddie watched me talk to Gerrard, deep frown lines crept into the space between his eyebrows, and he began to rhythmically clench his jaw. He finally spoke up. "What kind of business interests do you think a man like Mr. Gerrard would have with a redneck hustler like your brother?"

Gerrard said, "Eddie, Mr. McInnes is understandably upset about his brother's death. I'm sure he would appreciate your refraining from any further disrespectful comments." Eddie accepted his boss's reprimand in stride. Not only did he not get red in the face as Rodney had, but he actually seemed to grow calm and relaxed again. Gerrard had this one well trained. He turned back toward me and said, "Eddie asks a good question, though. What business interests do you think I had in common with your brother?"

"You have gambling interests. Hall gambled. You import controlled substances into the state. Hall was also in that business." Again, Gerrard just looked at me without responding, so I went on. "Getting back to why I think you and Hall may have done some business together. First, as I just explained, Hall was in your line of business. Second, a week after Hall's murder, you send two thugs—no offense, Eddie— to talk with me. Not to kill me or, it seems, to do me harm, but just to talk with me."

Gerrard interrupted, "You just said Rodney did, in fact, try to kill you."

I said, "Yeah, but you didn't send him to do it."

Gerrard said, "Thank you for that."

"You just picked the wrong man for the job. You sent a lowlife who got stoned in the middle of the night and got to feeling macho. Or at least that's how it seems with what I know now." I said, "Getting back to my line of reasoning. Where was I? Okay, three, Rodney—who is your employee—announces on the highway Sunday afternoon that I'm in trouble. But, and now we're up to reason number four, when you hear from Spence, you call off Rodney, make him apologize, and invite me to your home for lunch. All of which means that you had some connection with Hall and that now you want something from me. Otherwise, I wouldn't be sitting here."

Gerrard said, "That's what you think?"

"That's what I think."

He said, "Just out of curiosity, what exactly is this invaluable information that you claim I've gone to all this trouble to discover?"

I said, "That, Mr. Gerrard, is the problem. I've got no earthly idea."

"Then why did you want this meeting? Just to tell me your patchwork theory about your recent bad luck and to insult me in my own home?"

"No. I came here to find out what you need to know. I don't really care what your business is, so long as you had nothing to do with Hall's death. If there's something in Hall's papers or his safety deposit box that you need to know about, I'll be more than happy to pass it along."

Gerrard said, "And you want me to ensure that you have no further problems with Rodney."

I said, "The hell with Rodney. I don't know what you know about me, but I am not afraid of some skinny, amateur hardass who thinks he looks like Steven Seagal. If Rodney comes after me again, whether it's his idea or yours, I will take care of him."

Eddie smiled and said, "Looks like we got a tough guy on our hands."

Gerrard held up his hand at Eddie and shook his head, then he said to me, "If you're so sure of your ability to deal with Rodney and his cousin, what is it you want from us?"

I said, "I want to know who killed my brother."

Gerrard pushed back from the table and held his palms in the air in feigned exasperation. "Mr. McInnes, I'm quite sure you do want to know what happened to your brother. I would too in your circumstances. But you're asking the wrong person. Regardless of what romantic stories you may have heard about my business dealings, I can assure you that the closest I ever come to murder is watching *Mystery* on PBS."

I said, "I'm not accusing you of anything. It just seems to me that you need some kind of information from me, and I'm telling you what you have to do to get it."

Gerrard said, "Even assuming your suppositions are true, you've already said that you don't have any information that I would be interested in."

"Maybe I just don't know what to look for. All I can say is, if you point me at Hall's killer, I will make every effort—that does not expose me to criminal prosecution—to provide you with whatever it is from Hall's estate that you want."

Gerrard said, "You've made a number of unusual and, I must say, ridiculous accusations. However, I understand that you have suffered a great loss, and I will chalk your attitude up to grief and to the understandable need to fight one last battle for your younger brother. Let's leave it there for now. You've made your position clear. Eddie and I will discuss our impressions of your ideas and, if we decide to talk further, we will contact you through our mutual counsel, Spencer Collins. Is that satisfactory?"

I said, "Not completely."

He said, "I have no doubt that that's true, but for now, let's turn our attention to lunch." As if on cue, the old houseman appeared bearing dinner plates. After removing the remains of our salads and arranging the table for the main course, he returned with what was, as it turned out, a very good meal. As we began to eat, Gerrard said, "Tell us about your practice in Mobile. What kind of attorney are you?" And that was about the most substantive sentence uttered for the rest of the meeting.

B Y THREE O'CLOCK, I was back in Spence's self-consciously impressive offices, wondering what, if anything, I should tell him about the meeting with Gerrard. Fortunately, Debbie came out into the waiting room to tell me Spence was in another "conference" and to ask me to, once again, have a seat beneath the medieval women with the pet unicorn. I thanked her for her hospitality and got out of there before she had time to warn Spence that I wasn't willing to wait. What I was willing to do was get the hell out of Birmingham. The meeting with Gerrard had been frustrating and surprisingly unsettling.

After working through the sheriff's file and an autopsy report on my little brother's murder, after stopping Zollie from killing Toby and Rodney from killing me, after using every professional connection I had to find and meet with the most dangerous man in the state, I had been able to do nothing more than ask a favor of someone with a demonstrated lack of concern for his fellow man. In exchange, all I was able to offer was the promise that I would provide something—I didn't even know what—that I wasn't even sure existed. I was feeling foolish and impotent and like I should have handled things differently. For nearly three hours, every word, expression, and implication of the meeting swirled over my mind as the Jeep carried me through farm towns, college towns, pastureland, and decimated, clear-cut timberland on the way from Birmingham to Coopers Bend.

I wanted to talk the day over with someone, to work through the conversation bit by bit and hear that I had done all I could do, that I was making more progress than I knew. On the outskirts of Coopers Bend, I pulled over at a bait-and-tackle shop, filled my gas tank, and placed a call to Christy from an outside pay phone. She wasn't home. I said "shit" to no one in particular, got back in my Jeep, and headed for the lake house.

When I drove up to the house, I was surprised to see a pickup and a Japanese convertible parked under the same stand of young oaks where I had spotted Sheriff Nixon's Caprice four days earlier. I was trying to decide whether to take my Browning out of the glove box or turn tail and find Nixon, when Zollie came walking out onto the long porch overlooking the driveway. He motioned for me to come inside. I parked the Jeep and walked up on the porch. Zollie said, "I came over to see what you found out in Birmingham."

I said, "Whose Miata?"

"Christy's." He looked disgusted.

I ignored him. We both went inside. Christy was standing next to the round dining table at the far end of the living room. Her hair hung down around tanned shoulders, which were accentuated by the straps of a white sundress.

Christy said, "I came by to make you some dinner. I thought you'd be tired after spending the whole day on the road."

Zollie said, "That why you came by?"

Christy said, "Actually, I thought I might also screw his brains out after dinner if we can get you out of here."

Zollie said, "That's how you usually get what you want, ain't it?"

This was not developing into a pleasant evening. "Shut up. Both of you." I said, "Y'all must've been having a wonderful time before I got here." Nobody said anything. I said, "Look, we're all interested in finding out what happened to Hall, and everybody's on edge. But it looks like you could control yourselves a little. We've got enough problems without starting in on each other."

Zollie said, "I should've kept Hall away from this little piece of ass. I don't want you to end up with the same troubles he had."

Christy raised her voice. "I was the only one who tried to help Hall. Everyone else let him down, and you were the worst one. For some stupid reason, Hall looked up to you, and you just let him ruin his life."

Zollie started moving toward Christy. I stepped in front of him and said, "Time to go home, Zollie."

"Get out of my way, Tom. I'm just gonna talk to her."

"I said it's time to go home."

Zollie said, "Nobody else gets in front of me. You know that, don't you? Just you. Just 'cause of who you are to me."

"I know." I said, "Let's call it a night. We'll talk later."

Zollie walked over and picked up a worn canvas hunting coat off the sofa, looked sideways and held Christy's gaze for a second, and walked out the door. I looked at Christy and said, "Well, that certainly was pleasant."

She said, "I don't know what his problem is."

"I wasn't just talking about him."

"I didn't do anything. He's just never liked me for some reason. I came by here to do something nice for you, to make sure you got a good meal after being on the road all day."

"I appreciate your thinking about me, Christy. I really do. But I'm tired. I just want to go to bed and not have to deal with any of this until morning."

Christy smiled. "I thought you'd never ask."

"Like I said, Christy, I appreciate the thought, but I'm completely exhausted. Right now I need for you to go home. We'll talk later. I promise."

"You don't really want me to leave."

"Yes, as a matter of fact, I do."

She walked over, put her arms around my neck, and gave me a long kiss. The woman knew how to kiss. She said, "I'm not wearing anything under this dress."

I took her by the hand, led her over and opened the outside door, and said, "I'll call you soon. Thanks for coming by." Christy froze. Her eyes glazed over, and color burned her cheeks. For a count of three, she didn't move a muscle, then she snatched her hand away, spun, and slammed the door in my face. A few seconds later, I heard angry tires tearing down the gravel road and away into the dark.

All in all, it had been one hell of a day.

The place was dark; it smelled old and tired. I went to bed.

Somewhere in the dark someone screamed, over and over and over. I wanted it to stop. I wasn't alarmed, I just wanted it to stop. Around the sixteenth scream, the voice turned into a telephone ringing. I was carefully weighing whether the energy expenditure necessary to roll over and reach the receiver would be worthwhile when it stopped. I smiled and closed my eyes. Just enough time passed for someone to redial my number, and the ringing started anew. I gathered up all my resources and reached for the phone. "Hello?"

"Mr. McInnes, this is Mr. Collins' secretary in Birmingham."

"Debbie, how the hell are you?"

"Uh, well, I'm fine. If you can hold for a minute, Mr. Collins would like to speak with you."

"He's not in conference again, is he?"

"Mr. McInnes, perhaps it would be better if we called you back in, say, fifteen minutes. I apparently have called at a bad time." Debbie thought I was goofy with sleep, which was pretty much true.

I said, "Yeah, do that. Make it twenty. I'm going to go get some coffee." Debbie apologized for disturbing me, although I think it may have been the other way around, and said she'd call back. I managed to get more or less vertical and stumble into the bathroom, where I found myself gazing at a pitiful sight in the mirror. Eggbeater hair, pasty complexion, and eyes swollen almost shut—Christy didn't know what she was missing. I splashed cold water on my face and brushed my teeth. No coffee in the house. By the time Debbie called back, I was sipping a cold can of Coke. Caffeine is caffeine.

"Mr. McInnes?"

"Yes, Debbie. Good to hear from you."

She didn't sound amused. "Hold for Mr. Collins." I heard a click and found myself humming along with "Ride of the Valkyries." Another click, and Spence was on the line.

He said, "Tom."

"Yeah, Spence. I'm here."

"Sorry to interrupt your beauty sleep. It's damn near ten o'clock."

"One of the pleasures of being self-employed."

He said, "That and poverty."

I said, "Yeah, that too. What can I do for you?"

"What happened to you yesterday? I thought you were going to come up here and fill me in on your meeting with Gerrard."

"Debbie said you were *in conference.*"

"Debbie says I'm in conference if I'm taking a shit. I need to talk to her about that."

"Well, that's why I didn't wait. There wasn't much to report anyway. I tried to be straightforward with Gerrard, and he pretended to be a choirboy. I didn't think it accomplished much."

"I got a call this morning from Eddie Pappas. From what he said, you managed to accomplish quite a bit. I hear you refused to meet unless they threw an employee out of the meeting, that you called Mr. Pappas a, quote, 'thug,' and that you pretty much called Mr. Gerrard a gangster to his face."

"Winning friends and influencing people."

"Mr. Pappas was not amused. I don't know what Mr. Gerrard thought."

"He actually did look kind of amused."

"May have been. You never can tell with him. Like I said, he likes guts, so long as you don't get too carried away."

I asked, "Is that why you called? To find out about yesterday?"

Spence said, "Partly. I've also been asked to deliver a message. Eddie Pappas said Mr. Gerrard has decided to help you. You're supposed to go home to Point Clear and wait at your house. He said you'll get a call tomorrow or Friday at the latest."

"Spence, I can't go home. Everything I'm checking on is here. Why can't you just tell Gerrard to call me here?"

"Tom, I didn't get the impression that this was negotiable. You've pushed your luck with Mr. Gerrard about as far as you can and remain in the world. I strongly suggest that you get your ass down to Point Clear and sit by the phone."

"I didn't think that Gerrard controlling where I sleep was going to be part of the deal."

I could hear Spence's heavy breathing on the line. He said, "You started this, Tom. You asked Gerrard for help. I thought you understood what you were getting into. Gerrard doesn't do anything where he's not in control. Maybe he's got a good reason for sending you home, or maybe he's just showing you that he's pulling the strings. Whatever the reason, you better decide right now whether you want to play in his jungle. If you do, you better know that he's the king." Spence paused. I didn't know what he expected me to say, so I didn't say anything. When I didn't speak, he went on, "Tom, I knew you at Auburn, and I've done some checking on you since you called me about this mess with your brother. I know you're smart, and I know you grew up in a South Alabama sawmill town around some tough people. But Gerrard isn't going to come straight at you. He's not going to challenge you to an IQ test, and he's not going to ask you to arm-wrestle. He's just going to slowly bring you into his world, just far enough so you can't get back out. Whatever happened to your brother, it looks like he saw it before he stepped in it. Your brother chose his life. There's no reason for you to let this mess screw up your life too. Look, Tom, you can probably still walk away, and if you take my advice, that's what you'll do."

I said, "Tell Gerrard I'll be in Point Clear by dinnertime tonight."

Spence hung up, and I headed for the shower.

chapter fourteen

A LINE OF LOG trucks flew by throwing clouds of grit and sawdust in gusts that gently lifted the near side of the Jeep as each truck blew past. Inside the sawmill office, Ginny's fuzzy blond ponytail had migrated from the side of her head to the top, halting just a couple of inches behind a shelf of sprayed bangs. The impression was one of a small fountain spouting sand into the air over her head. She was busy filling in blanks on a long yellow form, while chattering into a receiver cradled in the crook between her neck and shoulder. She waived me into Sam's office without breaking stride on either the form or the telephone conversation.

Inside, Sam's guest chair was overflowing with an impossibly large black man, whom I recognized as one of the longtime supervisors in the main mill. Sam reintroduced me to his guest, who offered a calloused hand the size of a catcher's mitt. Shaking hands with this giant felt the way it had felt to shake my father's hand when I was a boy, just learning the manly art of combining the right hand position, grip pressure, and eye contact to produce a proper, businesslike handshake. After the supervisor had left the office, stooping his head to miss the top of the door frame and closing the door behind him, I took his seat and filled Sam in on the status of my investigation. Sam made copious notes and very few comments. Our meeting lasted less than ten minutes.

I placed a call to Kelly in Mobile, asked Ginny to keep my temporary office ready for me, and pointed my Jeep at the Gulf of Mexico. Two hours later, I pulled into the familiar concrete severity of the office parking deck, crossed into the lobby of the forty-year-old Oswyn Israel Building, and rode the elevator up to the ninth floor, which I shared with two other lawyers, a collection agency, and a chiropractor. The walls above the wainscoting were real plaster, original squares of white marble paved the hallway, and the woodwork was varnished Alabama curly pine. The rectangle of frosted glass in my outside office door read: THOMAS McINNES, ATTORNEY AT LAW. As I turned the brass knob and pushed open the door, I thought about Spence's offices with silk flowers, expensive art, hurried workers, and murals on the ceiling. I felt lucky not to be Spence Collins.

I didn't have a receptionist. Kelly could see the door and most of the waiting room on a small video screen in her office. She could also turn on the alarm system, turn the office lights on and off, and even lock any door in the office from an electronic pad hidden inside her credenza. Burglar alarms are not optional equipment in a seaport city like Mobile, and the addition of a closed-circuit system to cover the front door and reception area had cost less than two months' salary for a receptionist. The whole thing had worked out pretty well. All I really needed was some clients.

Kelly walked into the waiting room. Apparently, she either heard me come in, or she saw me on her little video screen.

She said, "So, the weary traveler returns."

I said, "God, it's good to be home. Is everything okay here?"

"Everything's fine. Joey will be here at three-thirty for your meeting, and I've taken care of the other items we discussed this morning."

"What about the phone lines?"

"That's where Joey is. He swept the ones here in the office this morning. He's been out at your house since then."

"Did you get hold of the phone company?"

"Yep. They promised to install call forwarding at the beach house between eight and ten tomorrow morning." We walked back to my office as we talked. When my coat was on the back of the door and my backside had found its imprint in the cracked leather seat of my desk chair, Kelly said, "What are you grinning about?"

I realized I felt almost giddy. "I can't believe how happy I am to be back."

She said, "I can believe it. It's like coming home after a lousy business trip. You can put your feet on the furniture, and the refrigerator is full of everything you like."

"Huh?"

"I was speaking metaphorically."

"Oh."

Kelly smiled. "Maybe I should make some coffee before Joey gets here."

I said, "I make my own coffee, remember."

"Then maybe you should make some coffee."

"I'm okay. It's just been a lousy week."

"About as bad as they get." She said, "Lots of people have called to ask about you."

"Any of them want to sue me for malpractice?"

"Nope. When I talked to Sully about his retainer, I asked him to take over your caseload for a while. He's a good guy. I knew he'd do a good job, and I knew he wouldn't use the opportunity to steal your clients. I hope that's okay."

"Sure. It's fine. I should have taken care of it myself. You probably saved me from a lawsuit."

"Don't worry. I wasn't going to let a filing date or a court appearance get by. It just seems this thing with Hall is going to take up your time for a while. Sully can stay on top of the cases, and he'll turn them back over whenever you say. By the way, I forged your name on a letter to Sully giving him the right to sign your name to pleadings."

I started laughing. "Damn, Kelly, do you need me for anything around here?"

"Not much. I can run the office just fine and keep you out of trouble most of the time. But your clients do need you. You're the one who keeps *them* out of trouble." I didn't say anything. Kelly said, "I guess for now your only client is Hall, huh?"

"Huh."

We both heard the little ding-dong the front door makes when it's opened. A few seconds later, Joey walked into my office.

Most people are surprised when they first meet Joey. The name doesn't really go with the package. I'm six feet, and I have to crane my neck backward to keep from staring into his neck when we stand face-to-face. He claims to be six-five. I suspect he's at least an inch taller. Joey looks a little strange, probably because he's the only man that height I've ever seen who is proportioned like a smaller man. From a distance, you think he's a normal-sized guy—maybe five-ten or so— but as he approaches he seems to grow larger than life, like a 3-D movie at Disney World. His strength is also proportionate to his size. Joey has probably never touched a barbell in his life, but I've seen him pick a grown man up off the ground with one hand. I always think of a line from *Three Days of the Condor* when describing Joey: Robert Redford describes the European hit man as being "strong like a farmer."

Joey has blond, almost white hair, eyes the color of old aluminum, and perpetually sunburned skin, crinkled with lines and character from ten years in the Navy. Over fifteen years in law enforcement, he has served on Shore Patrol, as a Naval Intelligence officer for a short time, for the Alabama Bureau of Investigation, and now, as a private investigator. He's good at his job. Like me, I think, he just keeps looking for some place to make a living where sucking up isn't part of the job description.

As he entered the room, Joey said, "Tom, I was sorry to hear about your brother. I lost my brother in a car wreck in high school. Hard thing to get over."

I said, "Yeah, it is. Thank you. And thanks for your fast work checking on Mike Gerrard while I was out of town."

"No problem. I just got back from checking out your phones at the beach house. No taps there or here at the office so far." I thanked him. He said, "Now that I've done what you wanted, how about telling me what kind of a mess you've gotten yourself into. You're yanking the dick—sorry, Kelly—of a guy who'd just as soon kill you as look at you, and it sounds like you want me to help you yank."

Kelly smiled and said, "Don't tell me you're afraid of some Ivy League business type from Birmingham."

Joey said, "Hell yes, I'm afraid of him. These aren't a bunch of drunk sailors or even run-of-the-mill street criminals. From everything I hear—and I mean everything—if you tick off this Gerrard character, you just drown the next time you go swimming, or you get mugged and shot on the way home one night, or the next time you drive along a lonely road you just happen to have a wreck."

Kelly teased, "You sound like a bad movie of the week."

Joey ignored her.

I said, "Look, Joey, Hall was my brother. I've got to do something. You didn't even know him. If you don't want to get in this, there won't be any hard feelings. As a matter of fact, I would probably think more of you for having the good judgment not to risk your life for seventy-five dollars an hour."

"I have no intention of putting my balls on the chopping block—sorry, Kelly—for seventy-five dollars an hour."

I said, "Don't blame you. Thanks for the help you've given so far."

"Glad to do it. You helped me get started down here after I left the ABI." Joey paused, then said, "You and me aren't exactly the Rotary Club type, so, even if we don't hang around each other's houses on the weekend watching ball games, I figure we're about as good of friends as either of us has got. I don't charge for helping friends in trouble. Somebody killed your little brother. I say we find who did it and fuck 'em up. Sorry, Kelly."

Kelly said, "Couldn't have said it better myself."

The next morning, Joey came out and rigged up a machine to record any calls I might get from Gerrard or his minions, and BellSouth

called at midmorning to let me know call forwarding had been acti-
vated. The idea behind getting call forwarding was to free me from my
beach house. It would allow me to forward calls to my car phone and
be pretty much anywhere I wanted when Gerrard called. And it provided me with at least the illusion of a small victory against Gerrard's
effort to control my movements. It really only provided minimal free-
dom, but I didn't like Gerrard trying to pin me down in one place while
he went about the business of trying to end-run me and get to whatever information he needed from Hall's estate. The strange thing was
that, despite Gerrard's effort to hold me at home, I found that I wanted
to stay there at the beach.

For the rest of the day, I puttered around the house, read over my
notes for the umpteenth time, walked on the beach with a mobile
phone in my pocket, and talked with Joey. We talked about Hall and
about Joey's brother who died in high school, about women and scotch
and fishing and boats, but mostly we talked about Gerrard and how to
deal with him.

On Friday just before lunch, the phone rang. I switched on the
recorder and picked up the receiver. Spence was on the line. After saying our hellos, Spence said, "Tom, I've finally got a message from Gerrard. He wants you to fly over to New Orleans."

"What for? Is the killer over there?"

"Tom, I don't want to know any more than I do now, which ain't a
hell of a lot. Don't ask me any questions. I'm working here as a go-between for two clients. I don't know any details, and I don't want to know
any details. And I sure as hell don't want to talk about some goddamn
killer. Okay?"

"Fine. I'd just like to know what I'm walking into."

"I told you two days ago what you were walking into, and, against
my advice, you insisted on going forward. Now, this is what you get.
You get to walk down blind alleys and fly around at Gerrard's command
without even knowing why he wants you to do it. In other words, you
asked for it."

"When am I supposed to be in New Orleans?"

"Monday. Go to the Mobile airport. There'll be a ticket in your name waiting for you at the Delta ticket counter. You're booked on a noon flight. You got that?"

"Yeah, I got it. What do I do when I get to New Orleans?"

"You take a cab to the Quarter. There's a little bar there on an alley off Bourbon Street called Yabeaus."

I said, "You mean like 'look at the yabos on her'?"

Spence said, "That's probably the general idea, but it's spelled with b-e-a-u on the end. Kind of a half-assed attempt at giving the place a Creole flavor, I guess. Anyway, just ask the cabdriver where it is and he'll take you to it. Just make sure you tell him you know it's right off Bourbon, so you don't get an eighty-dollar tour of Southern Louisiana."

I repeated the name as I wrote it down. "Yabeaus. Okay. Anything else?"

"Somebody'll meet you there around three Monday afternoon."

"Who?"

"Didn't say. Just said they'll find you at the bar."

"Wonderful." I imagined some faceless hoodlum walking through a strip club with my picture and a small handgun. The term *sitting duck* came to mind. I asked, "Why a noon flight? I'll be at the bar by one-thirty or two. I don't want to sit around some sleazy bar named after mammary glands for over an hour."

"Like I said, Tom, I'm just delivering a message. But I was told that you are to do exactly what I've told you or the contact won't show up. Anyway, I've been to Yabeaus. It's not that sleazy, and you can get some lunch. Just don't eat at the bar unless you want some twenty-year-old stripper shaking her ass over your club sandwich."

"Thanks for the advice. You're right, Spence, this place doesn't sound sleazy at all. Maybe I could take a date."

Spence laughed. "Good luck, and—"

"Yeah, I know. Be careful."

"You got it. Goodbye."

. . .

I located Yabeaus a few minutes before two o'clock Monday afternoon. Diagonally across the street from the bar sat one of those overpriced New Orleans antique shops where desperately artistic clerks sell architectural details that have outlived the antebellum houses they once decorated. I was able to watch the door of the bar through the front window of the antique shop while pretending to examine a matched pair of gargoyle finials. Across the street, a dozen flush-faced sales and middle-management types carefully exited the bar, casting furtive glances up and down the alley before venturing out into full view. The noon lunch crowd.

The shop manager ignored me. He had a couple of blue-haired ladies from Greenville, Mississippi, on the line, and he was reeling them in with a swishy Southern drawl and a raised pinky. I slipped out the front before he so much as looked at me. Back on Bourbon Street, I bought a street hot dog from the busiest vendor I could find—a harried Cajun kid who slopped steamed franks, relish, onions, chili, ketchup, and mustard onto open buns and swapped them for cash without ever looking up at his customers' faces. Unless the guy was a hand identification expert, he was unlikely to remember my patronage.

After polishing off my chili dog with onions, I bought a black cap with the words *They Don't Call It Bourbon Street For Nothin'* stenciled across the front. I put on a pair of cheap sunglasses from home and stopped to examine my new look in the window of a T-shirt shop. The guy reflected in plate glass looked very much like someone trying not to be recognized, which was going to make me fit in like one of the regulars at Yabeaus.

Slinking New Orleans style in a doorway across the street, I watched the bar until three o'clock, hoping to recognize someone going in, coming out, or just hanging around like me. Nothing. Five more minutes. Still nothing. I began to worry that I had missed my contact and my chance to find out something about Hall's business or his murder. I sucked it up and headed for the black vinyl, brass-studded front door of Yabeaus.

Just inside the door, a fat man in a tank top sat on a stool behind a maître d's lectern. He mumbled, "Five-dollar cover." I handed him a five and went in, determined to find a very dark corner. That proved an easy task. Nearly every table was situated in as much darkness as possible without the waitresses falling all over themselves. Only the show bar was lighted for the strippers and the few brave souls who were more interested in the girls' gynecological gyrations than in maintaining anonymity. Seated in a back corner, I ordered a pitcher of draft and paid cash with a stingy tip so the waitress would stay away for a while. After the mostly naked waitress had collected my money and walked away saying something that sounded like, "Nice tip, asshole," I finally removed my sunglasses and let my eyes adjust to the room.

We were between shows, which was fine with me. I studied every dark figure in the room for something familiar or unusual or I didn't really know what. It just seemed like I should be on the lookout, so I was. The draft was ice-cold Abita, and there are worse ways to kill time than sipping good beer in a dark bar. I restricted myself to taking small, well-spaced sips. After ten minutes, I had grown bored enough or calm enough to notice the unmistakable bar smells of spilled beer, fried food, sweat, and disinfectant that permeated the room. I was about to sneak outside for some fresh air when tiny Christmas tree lights began twinkling around the edge of the horseshoe-shaped show bar, and a red spotlight hit a red-sequined curtain at the far end of the bar. Oh boy, a floor show.

A scratchy recording of "Eye of the Tiger"—possibly the worst movie theme of all time—came over the sound system, and a tall, buxom redhead threw the curtains aside with a theatrical sweep and stepped out onto the bar. Holding her hands over her head in the classic ta-da position, she froze for a count of five so we could marvel at her gifts, which were not inconsequential. Either she was a freak, or strippers have changed since my undergraduate days when we occasionally drove from Auburn to Columbus, Georgia, where aging hookers strutted on runways in semi-darkness, which was as necessary to their charms as it was to our bravado. Now, this Yabeaus redhead—a Miss Pussy Flambé, as it turned out—looked like a bodybuilder who had undergone breast augmentation at the hands of a very serious surgeon. Miss Flambé started out in a tiger-skin leotard—which kind of explained the song—and ended up wearing nothing but a thong and a pair of black sequined high heels. In the interim between leotard and thong, she did back bends, splits, and twirls, and finished with that time-honored New Orleans tradition of bar dancers—she humped the top of the bar for a good two minutes.

The proper thing to do these days would be to condemn the bar for exploiting the stripper, condemn the stripper for perpetuating female stereotypes, and condemn my own interest as a base, filthy, Neanderthal reaction rooted in unhealthy, media-imposed appetites. But it was something to see. I think I actually said "golly" out loud at one point.

As Miss Flambé wiggled off stage and the lights died down, a tall, skinny silhouette entered the room and approached the bar. As he neared the lights, the dark form turned into Rodney Shelton. I slipped my glasses back on and moved around Rodney's back and toward the door. When I was sure I had a clear path, I stopped and listened. The bar was quiet after the performance, as each customer struggled with the flush and confusion of unsatisfied titillation. In the midst of that silence, Rodney asked the bartender in a too loud voice, "You seen a guy here named Tom McInnes? He's supposed to be here."

The bartender said, "No," without looking up.

Rodney persisted. "Well, he's supposed to be here. Can you page Tom McInnes?" Again he said the name unnecessarily loudly.

The bartender looked tired. "Look, buddy, these guys come in here for a good time. They ain't hurting anybody, and I ain't gonna call some poor guy's name all over the bar who might not want everyone to know he's here."

Rodney said, "I told you he's a friend of mine."

"Don't make no difference."

Rodney slid something across the bar, and the bartender shook his head from side to side. The conversation was over. I headed for the door. As I did, the wall disappeared into a dark passage. RESTROOMS was painted vertically in white paint on the wall beside the hallway. I slipped inside. The L-shaped hall was painted black and lighted by a single, tired bulb hanging from the ceiling. The men's room was empty. No one answered my knock on the women's-room door. Miss Flambé had temporarily emptied out the restrooms. After unscrewing the light bulb in the hallway, I removed my sunglasses and walked back out to the main room. Rodney was sitting at a table, staring into a drink. I walked a few feet out into the room and coughed—not very subtle, but then neither was Rodney. He looked my way, squinted to focus in the dark, and smiled.

He started talking loudly, "Well, there's my friend—"

That's as far as he got. As he began speaking, I spun and headed quickly into the restroom hallway, trying my best to look like I was making a run for it. Just around the elbow in the dark hallway, I stopped and waited. When Rodney's silhouette turned the corner, I swung hard, aiming an uppercut for his middle and hoping to catch him in the solar plexus and knock the air out of him. The punch hit him full in the stomach, which is just as effective, but messier. Rodney lifted off the ground and fell facedown on the carpet, vomiting on the way down. Working blindly in the dark, I dropped a knee into his back to pin him and lifted an automatic pistol out of a shoulder holster beneath his fringed leather jacket. Rodney was easy to read. I knew he'd come hard, and I was all but certain he'd have a shoulder holster, just like all the tough guys in the movies.

By the time I got the barrel pressed to the back of Rodney's head, he had begun to cuss between spits as he expelled the rest of his disturbed lunch from his mouth. I held the gun in my right hand and rifled his pockets and patted him down for more weapons, finding a snub-nosed automatic in his waistband and a hunting knife hidden in his boots—shades of Daniel Boone. As I lifted the knife and stood up, Rodney had gotten far enough past the pain and nausea to figure out what was happening to him. He said, "I'm gonna fucking kill you."

I grabbed him by the collar, snatched him to his feet, and shoved him through the door into the men's room. In the light now, the guy was a mess. Vomit covered his face, his neck, and the top of his signature black T-shirt. I said, "Get cleaned up."

Rodney was so mad he could barely talk. He kind of sputtered. "You motherfucker. Gerrard's going to kill your fucking ass for this. I'm going to kill you. I'm going to kill your whole fucking family. I'm gonna go to Coopers Bend one night—"

I moved the gun to my left hand and slapped him hard with my right palm, catching him in mid-threat and spinning him into the wall behind him. I said, "Shut up." He looked back and started to talk. I said, "Goddamnit, shut up and listen, or I'll break every fucking bone in your body." He shut up. I went on, "Get over to the sink and get cleaned up before somebody comes in."

He started up again, "I hope they do, you motherfucker. I'll tell them you tried to queer me in the men's room. That'll go over pretty good back home, won't it."

I said, "Get your ass over to the sink and wash up." He finally walked over and did what I said, but he was probably just getting tired of wearing a face full of vomit. I said, "If someone comes in, I'll tell them you tried to roll me. You're a sleazeball with an arrest record a yard long, and I'm an attorney with friends all over the state. Who do you think they'll believe?" He didn't answer.

When he was presentable, or as presentable as Rodney Shelton ever got, I told him to keep his mouth shut and pushed him out ahead of me. Just outside the bathroom door, we met a chubby guy who had to turn sideways to pass. I tilted my head down to hide behind the visor of my Bourbon Street cap. Rodney noticed and took a quick step forward and said, "That's right, Tom . . ."

I had to give Rodney credit. He was thinking, but thinking too late. The fat man had already passed and was more interested in draining his bladder than he was in us. I stepped quickly forward and hit Rodney with my fist right above his little ponytail. I connected with him just as he got to the turn in the hallway. He pitched forward and hit the wall.

I leaned down and said, "See you outside."

Dropping the larger automatic into my hip pocket, I walked out to the showroom and slipped out the front door into blinding sunshine. I turned right and headed away from Bourbon Street. There was an off chance that Rodney would try his luck reporting me to the police. He seemed desperate to establish my presence in New Orleans that afternoon, and having me arrested, or even interviewed by the police, would accomplish that nicely. Considering Rodney's history and his occupation, the cops were probably the last thing he wanted to see, but I didn't want to risk being arrested carrying unlicensed, probably stolen firearms around a strange city in a state whose indecipherable laws are still based on the Napoleonic Code.

Three or four storefronts down, a narrow service drive cut between two old buildings and dead-ended into a dumpster. With the clips removed, both guns hit the dumpster. The loaded clips and Rodney's knife went up onto the roof of a one-story warehouse. Back out on the side street fronting Yabeaus, Rodney was nowhere in sight. He was probably inside, spreading my name around—which wouldn't make much difference if no one saw me. Maybe he was trying to buy a gun or a knife off of the bartender.

Six minutes later, Rodney came squinting out into the alley looking blankly around for his lost game. I let a couple of tourists pass before I approached him with my hands in my coat pockets. My right index finger was pointed to look, I hoped, like the barrel of a gun. I said, "This way. And I'm tired of your bullshit. Keep your mouth shut." I thought I was sounding pretty Steven Seagalesque myself.

Rodney walked ahead of me into the service drive. I shoved him face forward into a brick wall and held my finger on him while I patted him down for the second time in ten minutes. In his back pocket, I found a butter knife he had lifted from Yabeaus. I said, "Kind of gives a whole new meaning to 'spread 'em,' doesn't it?" He didn't laugh.

"Okay, what are you doing here, and what was that bullshit with my name in the bar?"

"I was just looking for you."

"Right. And why were you looking for me?"

"I'm supposed to take you to a meeting."

"Let's go."

Rodney led me to a rental car parked three blocks over. We climbed in, and he began to weave through traffic. New Orleans suffers one of the worst street systems in the country. After forty-five minutes of side streets, four lanes, and bumper-to-bumper traffic, I figured out that we were headed for the industrial docks.

Make-believe guns stayed buried deep in my pockets.

chapter fifteen

IN EARLY OCTOBER, endless sunshine had faded into brisk days and early evenings despite the best efforts of daylight saving time. As Rodney pulled into a warehouse complex near the docks, the sun hung just above the horizon, and long afternoon shadows had begun to merge into dusk. We drove through an open, double-hinged gate that briefly interrupted a line of hurricane fence that stretched beyond view on either side of the road.

Rows of cavernous warehouses hunkered inside chain-link fencing topped with swirls of razor wire. Inside the complex, Rodney followed the entry road to a dead end, turned left, and drove parallel to the shore, which was hidden by rows of cinder-block buildings that I knew would be stacked full with wooden pallets bearing crates and boxes and mechanical equipment deposited from, or destined for, the cargo holds of merchant ships. A couple of hundred yards down, Rodney hung a right, nosed the rental car in between two identical warehouses, and honked his horn three times. A sliding metal door rolled open on the side of the warehouse to our left. Rodney pulled the car inside and shut off the engine. Although someone had obviously operated the overhead door, the place looked deserted. I said, "What now?" Rodney didn't answer. I tried harder. "Rodney, you want to get hit in the head again?"

He spit on the floor of the car—very impressive—and said, "Just wait."

I was about to ask *wait for what* when the overhead door closed. I could feel the adrenaline kick in. Every ancient warning device my brain and glands could muster screamed at me to bolt out of the car and find a rock, or a big black guy, to hide behind. I was struggling to stay calm and concentrate on the available, realistic options, when Eddie Pappas seemed to just appear in front of the car. Rodney stepped out. I got out and left the passenger door open between me and Eddie. I reminded myself that these people had gone to a lot of trouble to bring me to New Orleans and to establish my presence in the city that afternoon. It seemed that if you planned to kill someone, you wouldn't draw a map to the place where you intended to do him in. As I said, it seemed that way, but I still felt better with a metal car door separating me from Eddie.

Eddie looked at Rodney and said, "Leave your gun in the car."

Rodney turned red. He looked uncomfortable, so I thought I'd help him out. "He doesn't have any guns. I took them away from him at the bar, along with a hunting knife he had stuck in his boot."

Eddie looked at Rodney, who didn't say anything. Eddie said, "Shit," then looked back at me. "Give me the guns."

I said, "I don't have them either."

Rodney now had something to say. "Bullshit, Eddie. He's got them stuck down in his coat pockets. He held a gun on me the whole way here."

Eddie crooked two fingers at me and said, "Come over here." I walked over and let him search for the guns. When he was done, he said, "He's clean. Rodney, you say he pointed a gun at you in the car."

Rodney said, "Yeah, well, I didn't see the gun. He had it in his pocket."

I patted my pockets to show they were empty, slid my hand inside the right side pocket, pointed my finger at Rodney through the coat, and said, "Bang."

Rodney was not amused. He started cussing and came at me fast.

Eddie called his name. When he didn't stop, Eddie stepped quickly to the side and kicked Rodney's feet out from under him as he lunged for me. Rodney landed facedown on the concrete floor. I said, "Rodney, is there anyone who can't kick your ass?"

Eddie said, "Shut up, McInnes. Next time I'll let him come on at you."

I said, "He's already come at me once today with two guns and a knife, and he ended up pretty much in the same position he's in now."

Eddie said, "Well, now that we know what a tough guy we're dealing with, why don't we try to go get this meeting over with. Mr. Gerrard has gone to a lot of trouble to help you with your problem." He turned to Rodney, who was still prostrate on the concrete floor, and said, "Get up." Eddie motioned with his hand. "We're going to meet in a little tool room back over that way." Rodney led the way, I followed, and Eddie brought up the rear.

As we neared the far side of the building, a thick-necked man stepped out next to a cube structure that stuck out into the warehouse. A closed door was centered in the end of the cube. When we got to the door, Eddie pulled Thick Neck over and said something to him, then pointed back at Rodney's rental car. Thick Neck headed for the car. Eddie opened the door and told Rodney and me to go inside.

A wall of chicken wire stretched from floor to ceiling and from one side wall to the other, dividing the room's interior into a front tool-storage section and a larger back office. Crowbars, hammers, saws, and huge metal hooks with crossbar handles hung from nails driven into the three wooden walls in the front storage section. Boxes, stacked two and three high, lined the bottom of the wire screen from the right wall over to a doorway that had been framed into the chicken wire. A bare bulb shone through from the other side, where two men stood next to a desk and chair. In the chair sat Toby Miller, slumped over and half dead.

Toby looked like he'd tried to kiss a moving train. His shirt was ripped and stained. Blood caked his nose, dribbled from his mouth, and crusted over his left eye, which protruded beneath his brow like a purple tennis ball glued into the socket where his eye should have been. Blood and tears oozed from an ugly slit where his eyelids used to open.

Rodney went in through the outside door first, but it seemed to take him four or five seconds to comprehend what was going on. When he did, he bolted through the door in the wire screen and caught the man closest to the door with a roundhouse kick that landed the heel of one expensive cowboy boot next to the guy's left ear and put him down. Still moving fast, Rodney dove across the chair that held what was left of Toby, apparently with the intention of throttling the second man who had been beating up on his cousin. That was his mistake. Rodney's body was too slight to make much of a missile. The second man just stepped back and brought his fist down on the base of Rodney's neck as Rodney hurdled forward. For the third time in as many hours, Rodney crashed facedown into the floor. The man who dropped him fell on him and pinned his arms, the guy who got a boot in the ear stumbled over, and both of them tied his hands with grass rope. The guy with the earache told his cohort to hold Rodney and stepped back with the intention of busting him up a little.

Eddie interrupted them. "Let him go."

Earache said, "Bullshit. He's getting popped for that kick."

Eddie calmly said, "Hit him, and I'll shoot you."

Earache said, "What? That's bullshit, Mr. Pappas. I ain't gonna kill him. He just ain't gonna get away with that shit."

Eddie raised his hand, which now held a nickel-plated automatic. "Go ahead."

Earache put his hands down and backed away from Rodney. "Shit, Mr. Pappas, that ain't right."

"Shut up." Eddie motioned at the door with his free hand. "Go outside and tell Nate to come in."

Earache said, "Yeah, okay."

Eddie said, "Stay out there and watch the door while Nate's in here."

Earache nodded and went outside. Rodney looked like he might cry or scream or maybe explode into bones and muscle and guts and mess all over the room. Eddie said, "Rodney, don't say anything." Rodney opened his mouth and nothing came out. Eddie repeated, "Don't say anything. You're going to get through this if you do what I say." Rodney looked dazed. "You got that? I said, you *got* that?" Rodney closed his mouth and looked at the floor.

Thick Neck, whom I now knew as Nate, had come into the room and closed the door behind him while Eddie talked to Rodney. When Rodney surrendered to the reality of what was happening and dropped his eyes, Eddie walked over to talk with Nate. The nickel-plated automatic had somehow vanished from Eddie's hand. Eddie spoke in a normal, conversational tone. He didn't seem to care if Rodney and I and the guy who dumped Rodney on the floor heard every word.

Eddie said, "Where'd you get that guy?"

Nate said, "He's worked for me before. He's got some mouth on him, but he knows the business, and he keeps quiet."

"He damn well better. It's your responsibility. If he messes up again, you messed up."

"Yes, sir."

"You understand?"

"Yes, sir."

"Good. Get him out of here. I don't want him around this."

"Yes, sir. He's gone."

Eddie said, "What about the car?"

Nate said, "No guns. Nothing. Just some change in the driver's seat."

Eddie nodded, and Nate left the room to deal with Earache. At Eddie's instruction, Rodney walked back out into the storage section and sat on a box of rags in the corner. He still had his hands tied. Eddie extended his hand, palm up, at the door to the office and said, "Inside." I walked in. Eddie followed and approached the one remaining nameless thug in the room. "That guy a friend of yours?"

"Billy? No. Never seen him till today."

Eddie nodded at Toby's slumped figure. "Wake him up."

Toby mumbled, "I am awake." It sounded like *Eh bum a bake*.

Eddie's thug produced an ammonia capsule from his shirt pocket and snapped it under Toby's bloody nose. Toby's head snatched backward, and he said, "I told you, I am awake." *Eh tole ooh, eh bum a bake*.

Eddie said, "Tell this man. Who killed Hall McInnes?" Toby dropped his chin to his chest and shook his head back and forth. Eddie said, "Toby, I thought we were through this. You're going to tell who killed McInnes, and you're going to tell the truth, or"—nodding at the thug—"your friend here is going to have to hurt you some more. And, Toby, I don't think you can take much more."

"Gonna die anyhow." *Bonna die aennehow*.

Eddie said, "That's true, Toby. You're going to die anyhow. So, wouldn't you like to tell the guy who came into your house with a nigger to beat on you—the man who is responsible for your being here and responsible for you probably dying out here tonight in the middle of nowhere—wouldn't you like to tell that man you killed his brother?"

Toby raised his head and tried to smile through swollen, cracked lips and broken teeth. "You're right. You're right." *Ooh rye. Ooh rye*. "I killed Hall. Did it with a thirty aught six." *Eh keel Haw. Deh ih whe' a thurry augh seh*. "Followed 'em on the river till they looked like they was lost. Him and that nigger stopped in a slew to look at a map. Stupid pricks. Worked around and shot the bastard from the bank."

His slurred words took a few seconds to sink in. I said, "What? Who was with Hall?"

"That nigger. That nigger you and Hall think is your daddy." Toby tried to smile again. "Probably is your daddy. Probably been slipping it to your mother for years while Big Sam out strutting around the mill."

Eddie turned to me. "You hear that?"

I said, "Yeah, I heard him."

Eddie pressed the muzzle of a small, black revolver behind Toby's ear. I thought Eddie was going to threaten him again—to push him for more information—until I heard a loud *crack* and saw a spray of blood, bone, and tissue explode from Toby's head and spatter the metal office desk. I think I cussed and grabbed for Eddie. I remember being held by the thug while Eddie talked in hushed tones to Rodney in the other room. The room swam. I don't think I tried to get loose from the grip that held my arms. It felt almost reassuring to be held up, to be in contact with someone.

Minutes passed as Eddie whispered to Rodney. Finally, Eddie stood, walked to the door, and knocked. Nate came in. Eddie said, "Can your man get Rodney out of here and somewhere safe for the night? Keep him quiet?"

Nate said, "Yes, sir. He can do that." Nate looked over at the still nameless thug who held me in his grip and said, "Let go of him and come over here." My captor shoved me away and walked out. He and Nate half guided, half lifted Rodney off the box and to the door. Nate, I think, asked Eddie if he'd be all right, and then left Eddie and me alone with Toby's battered corpse.

Eddie walked into the office and stood looking at Toby. A full minute passed before he said, "You're his brother." It took a few seconds to understand he wasn't talking about Toby. "Mr. Gerrard wants to know where he put our merchandise."

"What?"

"Since he got killed, we found out your little brother was ripping off Mr. Gerrard. We've checked around. Can't find where he sold anything. So, he must have stashed it somewhere. Mr. Gerrard intends to have it back."

"I don't know what you're talking about. I haven't lived around Coopers Bend since I was eighteen years old, and I haven't talked to Hall more than twice a year since then. If you want to find your 'merchandise,' you've got the wrong man."

Eddie motioned at Toby's body. "Mr. Gerrard thinks enough of your lawyer friend in Birmingham to find this scum and make him talk. But liking someone doesn't buy a killing. Now you owe Mr. Gerrard a favor, and he wants you to find out where the drugs are. If you can't, that's fine. We are businesspeople. We do not expect you to give us something you don't have."

"I don't have what you want, and I don't have any idea how to find it. And I did not ask Gerrard or you to kill this man. I didn't want you to kill him. I wanted him turned over to the police. Then maybe they could've learned a lot more about what was going on, and found out why Toby killed Hall or maybe even who paid him to do it."

Eddie said, "We did not kill your brother or ask anyone else to do it," then he just stood there looking at me, waiting for it to sink in.

A light began to shine through the emotion clouding my mind. I said, "You don't want him alive and telling the police anything, do you? You want me thinking I owe you. You want me to think I owe you so I'll cooperate if I come across your stuff. But you killed him because he was a liability to your business, not as any favor to me. And you brought me here to involve me in this so I would keep quiet." Eddie didn't say anything. He just let me talk, let me work through it on my own. I said, "Now you're rid of your problem and you think I'm mixed up in it enough to keep quiet. You people are idiots. You want to claim you killed this poor bastard for me. You want me to feel like I owe you some favor. Well, I don't owe you shit. Tell Gerrard he's watched *The Godfather* too many times. In fact, you can just tell him to kiss my ass. I'm done with this."

I didn't see the fist coming. Eddie caught me in the solar plexus with a right uppercut and opened my eyebrow with a left hook. No more cool. Eddie was screaming, "Who the fuck do you think you're talking to? You think we didn't do you a favor. If Mr. Gerrard didn't like Spencer Collins, we would work you over the same way we did this piece of shit," he said, gesturing to what was left of Toby Miller, "find out what you know, and dump your dead ass in the Mississippi."

I struggled to get some breath back into my lungs. I was making that embarrassing honking sound everyone makes when they've had all the air slammed out of them. Between first breaths and before I could stop the words, I said, "You try to do to me . . . what your men did to Toby . . . and you damn well better kill me."

Eddie said, "Shut the fuck up." He was breathing deeply and seemed to be struggling to regain control. It dawned on me that he couldn't kill me without checking with Gerrard first. When he spoke again, Eddie's voice was back to a normal level. "Look, you're a lawyer. You know how the real world works. A man doesn't do another man a favor unless it benefits both of them. We found Hall's killer for you, we let you hear him confess, and we paid him back for murdering your only brother." Eddie walked over to the outside door, opened it a crack, looked out, and came back into the office. He went on as if there had been no interruption, almost as if he had his little speech memorized. "And I don't give a damn whether you asked us to kill him or not. If you kill the man who murdered your friend's brother, you've done your friend a favor, even if it turns out that maybe you wanted the same guy dead for some other reason." He paused. When I didn't respond, he said, "Do you follow me?"

I had my wind back now and, for the first time, noticed blood trickling down my right cheek from the eyebrow where Eddie's left had landed. I said, "Yeah, I follow you. Gerrard does Spence a favor, which he will no doubt collect, he gets rid of an employee who's murdering people in his spare time, and he not only can claim he did me a favor but he manages to expose me to murder and obstruction of justice charges while he's at it, all of which means that he thinks he owns another lawyer in Mobile."

"You *are* a smart lawyer," Eddie said. "But Mr. Gerrard doesn't think he owns your ass. He knows it. And if you call him Gerrard again without putting a Mr. in front of it, I'll close the other eye for you."

I said, "You try to hit me again, and you'll have to kill me. I promise you, I will kick your fucking ass."

I could sense Eddie stiffen, and it occurred to me that maybe he could kill me without his boss's permission. It was not a comforting thought. All he said was, "Whatever. Let's go."

Outside the tool room, the warehouse was deserted. No Nate, no Billy with an earache, no thug, no Rodney. Even Rodney's rental car was gone. Eddie reached in his coat pocket and pulled out the black revolver he had used to kill Toby. After wiping down the snub-nosed .38 with a white handkerchief, he swung it in an arc from his hip to over his head and tossed it up on top of the tool room with kind of an uncoordinated-looking hook shot, then he cut around the left outside corner of the tool room and headed for the end of the warehouse farthest from where Rodney and I had entered. Just inside an open overhead door and beneath a yellow bug light sat a black, 700-series BMW with Alabama tags. It looked like Eddie had driven his own car to avoid airline or car rental records of his trip to New Orleans. I made a mental note of the tag number as I walked to the passenger door.

Eddie cranked the engine, drove slowly out of the complex, and left the razor wire, the warehouse, the tool room, and Toby's remains behind. When he had put four or five miles between us and the murder site, Eddie shifted in his seat and looked over at me as he continued to navigate through dark city streets. His tanned face was turned a sickly green from the lighted instrument panel. He looked like a camp demon in an episode of *Tales from the Crypt*. He said, "The fact that you think you have us figured out does not change the fact that you owe Mr. Gerrard a favor. We want to know where our property is."

"Don't you mean Gerrard's property?"

Eddie said, "Son, you have a death wish, and if you keep fucking with me it's going to come true." This seemed like a good time to quit talking. He went on. "You find Mr. Gerrard's property and we're even. If you won't or can't find it, well, we'll find some other ways for you to help us out in Mobile."

I asked, "Why am I supposed to believe you'll leave me alone if I find your dope?"

Eddie said, "I don't really give a shit what you believe. I'm just telling you the terms." He pulled over and said, "Get out."

I got out of the car and found myself standing on a dark street paved with old brick that had been laid out in a herringbone pattern a hundred years ago. Dawn-to-dusk streetlights illuminated lines of clapboard shanties interspersed with overgrown industrial junkyards. Tiny dirt yards ran up against chain-link fences topped with razor wire. There seemed to be a theme here. As I stood there thinking about just how unwelcome a white man would be in that particular New Orleans neighborhood, I heard the electric whine of the passenger window rolling down. I leaned down and looked into the car. Eddie said, "By the way, the gun that killed Toby was registered to your old man."

"What?"

"Remember the Smith & Wesson thirty-eight you claimed was stolen during the funeral?" I didn't answer. Eddie was smiling. "Well, believe it or not, you just used that same gun to kill poor old Toby Miller." I could almost see Eddie grinning in the rearview mirror as he drove away.

As Eddie's taillights disappeared into the night, a pair of headlights flashed on in the opposite direction. A few seconds later, Joey pulled up in the 4x4 pickup he had borrowed for the night. I yanked open the passenger door and said, "Get back to the warehouse, fast."

I jumped in and Joey floored the accelerator. He said, "I don't think you want to do this."

I said, "I'll explain as we go. Just get me there. We've only got a few minutes before that prick in the BMW calls the police."

chapter sixteen

B IG-CITY POLICE officers are overworked, underpaid, and in-
fused with cynicism and hostility from days and nights of scraping society's underbelly. In New Orleans, just like everywhere else, the
cops do not expend a lot of time and energy guarding the safety of
streets like the one Eddie left me on, where, sadly, a good percentage
of the residents are the ones committing crimes in other, wealthier
neighborhoods. It's not a politically correct statement. It's just true.

In our red 4x4 pickup with its row of spotlights across the top of
the cab and its oversized tires, we met only five or six other cars on the
way back to the warehouse complex, and those were low-riding Chevys
and overly accessorized foreign models—the kind favored by gangs
these days. I was shocked at how fast we got there. It became clear
that Eddie had driven in a circuitous, zigzag pattern for four or five
miles and then dumped me within walking distance of the docks—
putting one last finishing touch on his orchestrated effort to establish
my presence in the area that night. It seemed that Gerrard and company were going to extraordinary lengths to frame someone whom they
allegedly wanted out on the street and helping them find their "merchandise." Apparently, Gerrard had more faith than I did that I would
be able to sufficiently extricate myself from the night's adventure to
stay away from a grand jury.

Joey, who seemed to know New Orleans as well as he did Mobile—

and his knowledge of that city's streets, neighborhoods, bars, and docks always amazed me—zoomed through the gate to the complex no more than two minutes after I jumped into the truck. He followed the entry road to its dead end, killed the headlights, and turned left. For the first time, we were moving at less than the maximum speed allowed by the road conditions. About sixty yards from the warehouse where Toby's body and Sam's handgun waited for us, he pulled into a drive between two dark, cinder-block warehouses and shut off the engine.

Joey said, "I've already pulled the wires to the interior lights, so we won't light up when we get out."

"That's smart."

"Basic shit every PI in the world does. Don't talk. Just listen. We gotta move fast. Leave your door open when you get out. Don't even think about closing it quietly. I'll lead. You come up behind. There's probably nobody there. Probably cleared out so this Pappas guy could make an anonymous call to the cops." He handed me Sam's Browning 9mm. "If you see someone, freeze. I'll hear you stop and look around. You just point out the trouble, and I'll take care of it. Okay?"

"Yeah, okay."

Joey pulled a box of disposable surgeon's gloves out of the glove box, tossed me a pair, and pulled a pair on his oversized hands. We both eased open our doors and headed for the warehouse. Joey moved quickly, picking the darkest routes as if by instinct. Within thirty seconds, we were outside the open door where Eddie's BMW had been parked. Joey whispered, "Wait here," and ducked inside the building. A minute passed, then two. Now still, the fear and sickness of the night worked on me. When Joey popped back out of the door, I almost wet myself. He whispered, "Let's go," and took off at a run directly for the tool room. I followed, awkwardly gripping the Browning in my right hand as I ran. When we got to the side of the cube, Joey put his huge hand on my chest and pushed me back against the wall, like a father holding his child out of oncoming traffic. His face was within a foot of mine. Joey said, "Nobody's here yet. There's boards nailed to the other side. Kind of like a ladder. Probably store stuff up there sometimes." He held a penlight up in front of my face, and I took it. He said, "Go around, get up there, and find the gun. Move fast, but careful. Don't trip up and get hurt up there, and don't let anything come out of your pockets. Go. I'll be inside." Joey disappeared around the front of the cube. It took me a couple of beats to get moving. The ladder was where Joey said—just two vertical two-by-fours with one-by-four crosspieces at two-foot intervals. I dropped the Browning in my coat pocket, put the dark penlight between my front teeth, and started up.

Climbing a completely vertical ladder messes with your center of gravity. You have to really grip the rungs to keep from going over backward. At the top, I had to press up on the tops of the two-by-fours, like a vertical shoulder press between parallel bars, and swing my knees onto the roof in the dark. As I did, a nail gouged my left thumb. I yanked it away and nearly lost balance. Flicking on the penlight, I examined the puncture wound—a purple hole that wasn't spilling any blood yet. I pressed it shut with my index finger, found a wadded sheet of brown paper on the roof, and wrapped it up. I could hear myself chanting under my breath, "Shit, shit, shit, shit, shit . . ."

First things first, the gun was easy to find. It lay among trash and rusted nuts and bolts and broken tools. Lots of metal, but the Smith was the only piece without layers of rust; it was the only piece that reflected the light beam. Back over at the ladder, the nail that got me was a crooked half-inch point inside the left two-by-four where a top crosspiece used to be. No sign of blood around or beneath the nail. I wiped at it with the brown paper and headed down.

Joey was nowhere to be seen. I found him inside the tool room. He was soaking Toby's corpse with kerosene. I almost screamed, "What the hell are you doing?"

Joey's voice was low and calm. "Gotta burn him. Too much blood. Some of it's gotta be yours. Also, you were in here a long time. We'd have to wipe down everything in the place to be certain about getting all the fingerprints."

"Shit, Joey. I didn't touch anything."

He said, "Gotta be safe. You find the gun?" I said I did. Joey asked, "Any problems?"

"I managed to stick a nail in my thumb up there in the dark. I checked. No blood, but I wiped down the nail anyhow with some paper."

"You keep the paper?"

"Yeah, it's in my pocket."

"Good." He walked out to the tool storage area and pulled a rag out of the box Rodney had squatted on while Eddie killed his cousin. Joey poured kerosene on the rag and handed it to me. "Go back up and rub this over the nail and the places around and under it. Soak it as much as you can. It'll screw up the blood analysis, if anybody is interested enough in a dead redneck bookie to do one."

"If you're going to set the place on fire, what difference does it make?"

Joey had finished spreading the last of the kerosene around the office. He took out a serrated Spyderco pocketknife and started cutting open a can of motor oil he had fished out of a case of the stuff he'd managed to find on his tour of the building. Pouring the thick yellow fluid around the tool storage area, he said, "Fire may not get up there. I'm not a goddamn maniac. The warehouse is full of industrial water sprinklers. Just none in here. Looks like they added this little shack on later. But soon as this place gets hot enough to flame up on the outside, the sprinklers are gonna flood the place, and the fire department's gonna come tearing in. I'm not trying to burn down the frigging docks. We just need to burn up your buddy over there and gut this tool shack." He looked up at me from his work. "Now will you please get the hell out of here and take care of that nail. We're in kind of a hurry here. And bring that rag down when you're through with it."

I was up and down in ten seconds and found Joey standing outside the open door to the tool room. He snatched the rag out of my hand and threw it inside, then ripped the cover off a book of matches from Yabeaus, lit the whole book at once, tossed the burning matches into a pile of rags just inside the door, and put the matchbook cover in his hip pocket. He pulled the door shut softly, which seemed kind of polite for an arsonist, until I realized Joey had accomplished his whole job without making a sound that could even have been heard on the other side of the warehouse. I was the one who didn't know what the hell I was doing.

As soon as the door clicked shut, Joey took off running without a word. I had to pump to keep up. The man covered a lot of ground with each stride. Back in the truck, Joey said, "Ease the door shut." He backed out and negotiated the roads between rows of warehouses as quickly as he could with no headlights. As we turned onto the road that led through the gate and out of danger, Joey cussed. "Too damn easy."

"What?"

"There's a car coming. See that glow outside the gate. Looks like they're gonna just about meet us going out."

Up ahead, a vague ground glow moved to the right as someone took the last curve before heading into the complex. Joey said, "Put your seat belt on."

"What are you going to do?"

"Win."

I started to ask more and decided I might not want to know. Joey jammed the accelerator to the floor and headed directly for the gate and the oncoming car, whose headlights were now plainly visible and growing larger. It looked like we might just beat them to the gate, when, a hundred feet from a head-on collision, Joey reached down with his left hand and flipped a switch under the dash, then pulled on the head-light control. When he did, all five spotlights across the top of the cab, the high beams, and a pair of halogen fog lamps flooded the ground between the truck and the gate and lit the place up like a football sta-dium. The headlights ahead wiggled back and forth and then dove to the left as the driver slammed on brakes before taking to the ditch. The poor bastard must have thought he was headed into the grill of an eighteen-wheeler. Joey was laughing uncontrollably. Next time he said he wasn't a maniac, I might have something to argue about.

As we passed the car, Eddie's man, Nate, was crouched down in the ditch on the left side of the road. He was halfway hiding behind Eddie's black BMW, whose front end looked to be pretty well wedged into a narrow gully. From his angle in the ditch, all Nate saw was Joey, a laughing, red-faced giant having an absolutely wonderful time.

Joey kept going until Louisiana was behind us and the sands of the Mississippi Gulf Coast whirred by in the night like a white ribbon separating the highway from a perfect black ocean decorated with scattered lines of whitecaps. Across the ocean highway from the beach, fruit stands, hamburger and pizza joints, package stores, cheap motels, and dingy quick marts with self-serve pumps out front punctuated scruffy timberland.

Joey found an aqua-blue, cinder-block motel with a pay phone outside, pulled our conspicuous vehicle into a dark spot around the side, and went to use the phone. When he came back, Joey was smiling. I asked, "Did you get him?"

"Yeah, I got him. I had to hire a guy I didn't know. But Loutie Blue said he'd do, and he was where he was supposed to be. I was about half afraid he'd screw the whole plan by being laid up drunk somewhere after having to kill most of a day in New Orleans."

"What's his name?"

"Parveez Mullona."

"What?"

"You heard me." Joey pulled out of the motel parking lot and pointed the pickup east toward Mobile." He said, "We needed someone to take your flight who didn't look anything like you; the only person I know who looks less Mediterranean than you is me."

"Did you tell him to do something to be noticed on the plane?"

Joey started laughing. "I been waiting to tell you this. That's the beauty of the whole plan. You know how we wanted somebody to take your place on the flight from Mobile who didn't look like you?"

"Yeah."

He was laughing again. "Well, we hit the goddamn jackpot. Loutie

Blue found me a guy that looks pretty much like your buddy Eddie Pappas. I mean, he ain't no twin, but he's about the same size and has curly black hair. Of course, our man's Libyan and Pappas is Greek, but, all in all, it ain't a bad match."

"Does that make sense? Eddie Pappas flying in from Mobile instead of Birmingham? And now, unless he works fast, it looks like the cops are going to find his BMW jammed in a ditch next to a murder and arson site."

Joey said, "You're probably right. But, we needed someone who doesn't look like you and this guy fits the bill. I think it gives us another option in the future, though, if the guy who used the flight reservation that Gerrard's people set up just happens to look like Gerrard's right-hand man."

I said, "Yeah, that makes sense, so long as he didn't go around telling people on the flight that he was Pappas."

"Hell no. But that brings me to the best part. We wanted him to be remembered, right? So, I found out from a contact in Birmingham that Pappas drives everywhere he goes. Flying makes him sick."

"He didn't."

"Hell yeah, he did. I told him to eat a big meal before takeoff and stick his finger down his throat after he was in the air and nobody was looking. Mr. Parveez Mullona just told me on the phone that he threw up a spaghetti lunch all over this poor bastard in the seat next to him." Joey was laughing again. "I think we can be pretty sure the flight crew will remember his ass."

"What'd you tell him to do now?"

"Told him to cancel the return flight to Mobile, fly to Birmingham using the name Eddie Pappas, and then get a rental car in his own name and drive back to Mobile. He bitched a little, but I told him you'd put another five hundred on him for the trouble."

"Thanks."

"Any time."

I smiled. "Is he going to throw up again?"

Eddie said, "Nah. A second time would be overdoing it. Got to use some subtlety in these things."

"And subtlety is your middle name."

"Goddamn right."

At a bustling self-serve station in Biloxi, I went in with my *They Don't Call It Bourbon Street For Nothin'* cap pulled down low and paid for a tank of gas. Joey, being somewhere in the neighborhood of six-foot-eight, is poorly equipped for not being remembered. I brought candy bars, chips, honey buns, and canned Cokes back to the truck. Small-town traffic crowded the highway. We moved along at a crawl until traffic thinned and we were back in the night.

We drove in silence for a while, savoring full bellies and the after-glow of a major sugar buzz. The highway angled away from the coast and moved through thick pinewoods that rose up on either side like the walls of a fort. Joey said, "I guess you better tell me what went on inside the tool shack."

I went through the whole thing twice, trying to remember every word, gesture, and impression. When I was through, Joey said, "Go back over what Toby said one more time. That fits in with the murder, doesn't it? Your brother was killed from the riverbank with a thirty aught six."

I said, "Yeah, but that was in the papers."

"You think he was lying?"

"No. I guess you'd be ready to say about anything if you'd been worked over the way Toby was. But, no, I believe he shot Hall. I just don't know why. I think there's more to it."

"Well, you got the killer. Unless you just wanna decide Gerrard told Toby to do it and kill Gerrard in his sleep, there ain't a hell of a lot more you can do." Joey slowed to look at a white-tail doe on the shoulder of the road, then went on, "What about the guy Toby said was with Hall. Is that the black man you always talk about who raised you?"

"Yeah. Zollie Willingham."

"You believe Toby about that?"

"I'd like to say no. But Zollie's changed a lot since I saw him last. I told you about him trying to cut Toby's throat in Coopers Bend."

"What are you gonna do?"

"I'm going to go on with our plan to make it look like I was never in New Orleans, and I've got to find a way to get Gerrard off my ass. But I don't plan to get mixed up in stolen drugs to do it, and I sure as hell don't plan to spend the next thirty years doing nasty little favors for him."

Joey said, "Sounds like a pretty good trick. How are you gonna do it?"

I said, "Damn if I know."

Joey's borrowed 4x4 rolled onto the white gravel drive at my beach house a few minutes after eleven. That morning before leaving for New Orleans with Joey, I had hooked up timers to the lights and the television, and programmed everything to go off after the ten o'clock news. Now, the house was dark. As I stepped down out of the truck, Joey got out of the other side and said, "Give me your clothes."

"I beg your pardon?"

"You've probably got specks of Toby's blood all over you, and you'll be covered with dirt and fibers from the warehouse. Strip."

I emptied my pockets onto the hood of the truck and started handing my clothes to Joey. He turned my coat inside out, spread it out on the ground, and piled my shirt, pants, belt, socks, shoes, and cap on top. I reached over, picked up my brown paper bandage, and tossed it on the pile, then started to gather up my keys, money, and wallet from the hood. Joey said, "Need the boxers, too."

"What are you going to do with this stuff?"

"Burn it. I'll burn my clothes too before I get in my car. Now, go inside and shower, and I mean scrub yourself top to bottom, then clean your shower with Clorox bleach, or whatever the strongest thing you've got is."

"Aren't you getting a little carried away? Like you said, Toby was a redneck bookie with an arrest record. I can't exactly envision an expensive, O.J. Simpson–type trial with fiber evidence and DNA testing."

Joey said, "Do it anyhow. Probably isn't necessary. But, in case you forgot, we just did a very bad thing. There's a hundred ways to mess up and get caught. I'm just trying to cover twenty of 'em."

Joey made a quick search of the house and the beach before leaving to return the truck. I did as instructed, scrubbing every inch of me from toenails to crown, gagging on fumes while scrubbing out the shower with Clorox and, the whole time, keeping the Browning within easy reach. A little after midnight, I tucked the gun under my pillow, fell on top of the covers, and slept like a dead man.

Someone hammering on the front door woke me. It was about eight-forty-five, according to my Rolex, which was good for swimming and diving but basically kept pretty lousy time. The hammering started up again. I got up, climbed into a pair of Timberland shorts and a green T-shirt that my cleaning lady had stashed neatly in the chest of drawers, and walked into the front bedroom to peek out the window. A patrol car, with CITY OF MOBILE painted above a shield on the door and the words POLICE DEPARTMENT below, sat in pretty much the same spot where the 4x4 had been the night before. I took about ten deep breaths to get my heart out of my throat and headed downstairs to answer the door.

chapter seventeen

I PADDED DOWN THE hallway on bare feet, shuffled quickly downstairs into the living room, and hung a right through the entry hall. Stopping just inside the front door, I paused to pull in more air, trying to clear the sand and mush out of my skull. I wanted to call Joey to see if the police had talked to him first. I wanted my head to clear and my stomach to quit churning. Basically, I wanted the police not to be on my front porch. The banging started again. I opened the door.

On the other side stood a young cop in a blue polyester uniform with sharp, vertical creases sewn into the petroleum-product fabric. He said, "Mr. Thomas McInnes?" I said I was. He said, "Where have you been all night?"

My brain still felt slow and mushy from yesterday's sensory overload and from being jarred out of a deep sleep. I asked, "What's this about?"

"Mr. McInnes, we are investigating a crime, a kidnapping. Now could you tell me where you were last night?"

"Officer, I don't mean to be a problem, but I'm a lawyer. You can ask all the questions you want, but I'm not going to answer any of them until I know what this is about."

"Like I said, there's been an apparent kidnapping. We were told to contact you last night about this matter. We called your house four times and got no answer."

I was ready, at least, for this question. It was one I knew would be asked if someone tried to reach me while I was away visiting Miss Pussy Flambé and Eddie Pappas in New Orleans. I said, "I turned my answering machine on and cut off the sound."

"Why would you do that, Mr. McInnes?"

"I just got home a few days ago from my brother's funeral. I wasn't much in the mood to talk to anyone." It takes a real jerk not to empathize with the death of a brother. Officer Bobby Treeton, whose name I now knew from the gold rectangle above his right pocket, was not a jerk. He visibly relaxed his intimidation technique. I said, "Who was kidnapped? Is this about one of my clients?"

Officer Treeton said, "Mr. McInnes, I'm sorry to inform you that your secretary—"

My voice sounded like it belonged to someone else. "Somebody took Kelly?"

"Yes, sir. She was at a restaurant with a Mr. Sullivan Walker, a local criminal attorney, last night from seven until approximately nine-fifteen P.M. As they left the restaurant and went to Mr. Walker's car, two attackers grabbed her. Mr. Walker attempted to defend her. He received a pretty good beating."

"Is Sully okay?"

"You know Mr. Walker, then?"

"Sure I do. We've worked on some cases together."

"Have you worked on any criminal matters with Mr. Walker?"

"I asked you if Sully's all right. How bad was he hurt?"

The officer looked down, then back up into my eyes. "Mr. Walker was treated at Mercy Hospital and released last night. Our concern now is with the kidnap victim."

"Sure. Of course. What do you need from me?"

"We need to know if you've heard from her or her abductors. We understand that you come from a wealthy family. We may be dealing with a ransom situation."

"What makes you think it wasn't, God forbid, a couple of rapists or something like that?"

"Mr. Walker said the men were middle-aged and wearing business suits. And the kidnapping was pulled off pretty professionally. Can we come in and review your messages to see whether someone besides us has tried to contact you?"

I said, "Who is we?"

He said, "Me and my partner."

"And he would be where?"

Officer Treeton looked uncomfortable. "He went around to the other side of the house when you didn't answer the door."

I said, "And I guess he's still lost back there, huh?" He didn't answer. "I'll do anything I can to find Kelly, but please tell your partner to get his butt back around here and off my property unless he's got a search warrant."

The good officer no longer looked sympathetic. He picked a small square transmitter off a polyester epaulet and pushed a button. "Buddy, come back around to the front. Mr. McInnes is out here and concerned about protecting his constitutional rights." A few seconds later, a paunchy, baby-faced officer walked around the corner and leaned against the banister at the bottom of the steps.

Officer Treeton said, "Now can we come inside and check your machine for any messages?"

"No."

"Mr. McInnes, we're trying to find a person who is very close to you before any harm comes to her. I would think—"

"Officer, believe me, I want her to be okay a lot more than you do, but I'm an attorney with clients who sometimes leave messages on that machine in there. I cannot, in good conscience, allow you to listen to messages that I haven't reviewed." Officer Treeton's face flushed a bit. His round-faced partner just stared blankly at the ground, while absentmindedly poking a stubby thumbnail into his right nostril to scratch at some offending presence. Apparently, the case had failed to fully engage Officer Buddy's imagination. I said, "Let me review the messages. If there is anything that is in any way related to Kelly, I'll bring the tape to the police station myself."

Officer Treeton pressed. "Could you listen to those messages while we wait here?"

I tried to look beaten. "Sure." As I turned to go inside, I said, "And you and your partner will wait here on the porch, right?"

"We'll wait here."

The mini-blinds were closed in the little library off the living room. I sat at the desk and tried to calm my thoughts enough to consider what to do about Kelly. After placing a call to Joey, I walked back out to the porch and said, "Nothing on the tape."

Officer Treeton said, "Sir, we know that's not right. We called you four times last night."

"Nothing on the tape from Kelly or any kidnapper is what I mean. I've got a number of messages. Just none of them is what you're looking for."

Officer Bobby Treeton didn't look like he believed me. He gave me the universal law-enforcement "yes, sir" that sounds condescending and a little threatening when spoken, but which would sound polite and professional if repeated in court or in front of a superior.

I said, "Please keep me informed of what's happening."

I got another "yes, sir," with a disgusted lilt to it.

The officers climbed into their blue-and-white patrol car. As Treeton backed around to head out, I could see his partner, Officer Buddy, sitting in the passenger seat. He was closely examining the end of his thumb.

A shower cleared the mess in my brain. I placed a call to Sully from the library phone. Our conversation was brief. Sully said he had asked Kelly out the morning he came by to pick up my case files. They had been seeing each other for lunch or dinner every couple of days since. He repeated the information I had gotten from the police about the professional appearance and performance of the attackers but had nothing new to add. I promised to keep him informed of any developments, then hung up. The poor guy sounded like he wanted to cry.

Joey had yet to appear. I waited five more minutes, while I opened all the blinds, walked out onto the deck overlooking the Gulf, drank a Coke, and finally walked out and stood in the driveway staring down the road. I told myself that I didn't know why I was waiting for a private investigator to make a phone call to Gerrard. I could keep Joey out of it.

Ready to unload on someone, I flipped on the tape recorder hooked to the phone and called Spence. His anal secretary, Debbie, answered. I said, "This is Tom McInnes. I need to talk to Spence."

"I'm sorry, Mr. Collins is in a conf— He can't come to the phone right now."

It looked like Debbie and Spence had had that discussion about her affinity for dressing up phone calls and bathroom trips as "conferences." I said, "Debbie, unless he's dead you better put him on the phone. I'm getting ready to send one of his clients to jail, and I mean I'm going to do it this morning unless something happens fast."

An indignant silence lingered a few seconds before Debbie said, "Hold on. I'll just have to interrupt him."

I said, "You do that, Debbie," and Paganini filled the earpiece.

A half minute of a violin concerto floated through the earpiece. A loud click, then Spence's booming voice. "Goddamnit, Tom, who the hell do you think you are. Pulled me out of a goddamn meeting with a client who pays real money with some bullshit threat. What the—"

I interrupted. "Shut up, Spence."

"What?"

"If you want to keep Gerrard and Pappas out of jail, you're going to shut up and listen." I could hear him breathing hard, but he did shut up. I said, "Somebody messed up. Messed up bad. I know it was Eddie Pappas. I just don't know if he had Gerrard's blessing."

"What are you talking about, Tom?"

"I'm telling you. They got pissed at me over something—you don't need to know what—and they had a couple of goons grab my secretary out of a restaurant parking lot."

"Now, Tom, I'm sorry about your secretary, but I don't think you can assume—"

I cut him off again. "I don't want to hear it, Spence. You're talking your clients into jail."

"What do you expect me to do?"

"Get Gerrard on the phone. Now. If I don't get a call from Gerrard in the next twenty minutes, I'm calling the police. And tell him I don't give a shit if we share the same cell. He went too far. He messed up, and he's got to fix it fast."

Spence asked where I was and hung up.

Seven minutes later the phone rang. Eddie Pappas said, "Spencer Collins called and said you have a problem."

"If Spence said that, he got the message wrong. You're the one with the problem. You and Gerrard. And I didn't ask to speak to a flunky. Put Gerrard on."

After the confrontation in the warehouse, I could tell when Eddie was losing it, and he was losing it. "You think you're a tough little fucker, don't you? You think you got away with something last night, and you're gonna just keep pushing it. You're really one smart lawyer. I gave you a way out last night, a way to get even and out of this and you had to start striking matches."

"I don't know what you're talking about, Eddie. By the way, how's that pretty black BMW of yours?"

"Keep laughing, asshole. 'Cause of that shit you pulled last night, we had to torch my car. You think you cut us off from keeping you under control, so we just found another way to do the same thing. You may not care about yourself, but we're gonna find out if you care about that little piece of ass we picked up at the restaurant. Whatever happens, though, you and me are gonna deal with each other when this is over. In the meantime, that sweet little girl of yours is gonna be a guest until you turn over the stuff your junkie brother stole from Mr. Gerrard."

"Like I said, Eddie. I didn't call to talk to the hired help. I want to talk to Gerrard in the next fifteen minutes, or I'm going to the cops with everything. You messed up. You kept pushing until you raised the stakes too high. If it means Kelly getting hurt, I just ain't gonna play anymore."

Eddie said, "Bullshit."

"No, Eddie, that's real shit, and it's going to land right on top of you if Gerrard doesn't call in, let's see, now it's fourteen minutes."

Eddie said, "Fuck off," and slammed down the receiver.

The doorbell chimed. Locking the library door, I jogged upstairs to get the 9mm and look out over the driveway. Joey was standing on the white gravel. He waved at me when I parted the blinds to look out. Very funny. I brought him into the living room, then went to the kitchen, pulled a couple of bagels out of the refrigerator, and put cream cheese, orange juice, glasses, and plates out on the counter. I zapped the bagels in the microwave, smeared some cream cheese on them, and took everything into the living room, where a two-story wall of windows looked out onto perfect white sand beaches and the dark, choppy waters of Mobile Bay.

While we gnawed on the bagels and drank orange juice, I filled Joey in on my conversations with the police, Sully Walker, and Eddie Pappas. Joey said, "You really going to the cops?"

"I will if I have to, and it's starting to look like I have to. I don't know what else to do. I'm not going to let Kelly get hurt to save myself."

"What about me getting hurt?"

"Don't worry. I'm still a pretty good lawyer. I'll keep you out of it."

"Damn right you will. I don't mind flaming up a couple of corpses for you, but I draw the line at volunteering to be somebody's fuck buddy in prison."

I said, "Joey, you're damn near seven feet tall. You got sixty pounds on me, and I'm a pretty good-sized man. Not that I expect you to go to prison for me, but who on God's green earth do you think is going to be able to fuck you if you don't want to be fucked."

Joey smiled. "I was illustrating my point with obvious dramatic license to make a stronger impression. You're kind of a dumbass for a hotshot lawyer."

It felt good to laugh. I said, "Well, what do I do?"

Joey said, "Call Gerrard and make your point. Doesn't sound like Eddie believes in selfless acts."

"I already called for Gerrard and got Eddie. I wouldn't even know how to get him."

"Remind me to reevaluate my relationship with you when this is over. Damn, Tom. Think. You know people like Gerrard never get more than twenty feet away from a phone. Too much in his kind of business can go wrong. You call your attorney friend in Birmingham back. You give him enough incentive, and I guaran-fucking-tee you he'll find Gerrard."

I headed into the library, and Joey followed.

Spencer Collins said, "This shit's getting old, Tom."

"Just think how I feel. I'm about to turn myself in to the cops just to bury one of your clients."

"What happened? I set up the call. You don't like the way these people play? Well, guess what, I did everything I could to warn you off this. You want to bury yourself, your career, and your family just to get even with somebody, there's nothing I can do to stop it."

"That's the problem, Spence. I'm not the one acting irrationally, trying to get even for personal reasons. Eddie is pissed, and he's doing things that I don't think Gerrard even knows about." I paused a few beats for effect and said, "Eddie kidnapped my secretary, Spence. He's going to hold her unless I do everything he says. And he just doesn't get it that I would rather go to jail than sacrifice Kelly to this mess. He wouldn't do it, so he thinks nobody else will. But I got no choice. If you can't put me in contact with Gerrard where Eddie can't get between us, then I have to go to the police and make the best deal I can, which will involve serving up your clients on a platter."

Spence's labored, out-of-shape breathing rasped over the line while he moved the conversation around in his mind, poking and prodding to find a loose end to tie me down. Finally, he said, "I'll see what I can do."

"Thanks, Spence, but it's got to be fast. I'm not going to sit around here for an hour while Eddie calls a couple of locals to come out and bust me up, or worse."

Spence said, "I understand. Sit by the phone." I heard the line go dead.

I filled Joey in on the conversation and said, "Looks like you were right."

Joey said, "What else is new. I'll bet you twenty he calls in the next ten minutes."

"Nope. Gerrard's going to call Eddie first. I say—if he calls—it won't be for twenty minutes."

"You're right. Forget the bet. Look, I'm going outside and put my car in your carport. You stay here and wait for Gerrard to call. I'm gonna find somewhere where I can keep an eye on traffic."

"You think he's going to send someone out here?"

"Probably not, but it's possible. Better to be safe."

"Better keep an eye on the beach too."

"Yeah. Good idea. Don't forget to record the call, and, by the way, remind me to get your used tapes before I leave. You got stuff on there that'll send us both to jail. I'll put 'em somewhere safe."

Joey left. Twenty-three minutes later, the phone rang. I punched the record button on the black box attached to my phone and said, "Hello."

"Tom. This is Mike Gerrard."

"Do you know what's going on?"

"Yes. I just spoke with Mr. Pappas. You had a busy night last night. You're a much more creative fellow than we gave you credit for."

"It's how creative Eddie's gotten that I'm worried about. He doesn't get it. He went too far. I told him I'm going to the police with everything if Kelly isn't back here safe and sound this morning."

"Do you really think that's smart, Tom?"

"No. It's probably stupid as hell. But I'm not going to gamble with Kelly's life over this."

"Has it occurred to you that, if you go to the police, that will be exactly what you will be doing?"

"This is not up for debate, Gerrard. Either Kelly is delivered to my house this morning, or I'm going straight to the cops. Eddie thinks I'm bluffing because there's nobody he cares about more than himself. You may not either, but I'm guessing you're smart enough to understand there are still a few stupid souls in the world who believe in something besides self-preservation. Whether you *understand* me or not, though, you'd better *believe* me. Eddie played a stupid hand, and I'm calling him on it. At least I thought it looked like something Eddie would come up with on his own. Or is this cluster fuck your idea?"

"Don't worry about whose idea it was. It is now a reality that must be dealt with. Hold on for a moment." The phone stayed dead for nearly three minutes. "Excuse me, Tom. I had to speak with someone else for a couple of minutes."

"What did Eddie have to say?"

Gerrard ignored the question. He said, "Now what do we do here? I need some level of cooperation from you, and you've gone to what I must admit are extraordinary lengths to distance yourself from last night's events. Although, we still have evidence that you flew into New Orleans yesterday. We made sure you were on the flight before Rodney made contact."

"Bad news, Gerrard. All you know is that someone used the ticket. If you had checked a little further, you might have found out that person looked very much like Eddie Pappas."

Gerrard actually laughed. "Tom, I really did underestimate you. Are you sure you aren't interested in working with us in the future?"

"I'm sure."

"Well then, what can we do about this little impasse we've reached? I must have my property."

"I told you at your house in Birmingham that I would turn over anything that belonged to you out of Hall's estate if you'd just find out who killed Hall. You just couldn't leave well enough alone. You had to try to pull me further in. You weren't happy to just have a chance to get your stuff. You had to have me by the balls, and that's when the whole thing went south."

"Yes, Tom, but you've put your finger on my problem. You see, the *chance* that I would recover my property simply was not good enough. I believed you needed some additional incentive, and I still believe that." He paused for a few seconds, then went on. "Let me tell you how we will handle this. Your secretary is still in Mobile. She will be returned to you within one hour. I understand your concern for her, and I believe your threat about going to the police. You should know, however, that you are not the only one who can obliterate the evidence of last night. In fact, I'm not sure you'd have much to tell the police that either you or they could prove."

"That's probably why you're sending Kelly back then, huh?"

Gerrard laughed again. He had a casual, comfortable laugh. "No, Tom. Your secretary will be returned because it was a bad decision to take her. It created more loose ends than it tied up. I'll tell you what we're going to do. We're going to just handle this the old-fashioned way. No more fancy plans. You have ten days to find my property and return it to me."

"That's not enough time."

"It's enough for you to use your contacts around Coopers Bend and your knowledge of Hall. It's enough time for you to do anything we couldn't do. If you're just going to start looking from scratch—you know, just asking questions and maybe leaning on people—well, we can do that better than you can. No, Tom, if you can't find what we're looking for fast, then I would have to agree with Eddie that you're more trouble than you're worth."

"I've already said I would do that if I could without exposing myself to prosecution." Gerrard didn't say anything. I started to think about the next ten days. I asked, "What happens if I can't find it? What happens if Hall sold it and spent the money or stashed it in an offshore bank account? I can't be responsible for delivering something that isn't there."

"But, Tom, you are responsible. We offered you an alternative last night. You had the opportunity to help us out in Mobile, do a few favors for us, if you honestly could not find our property. Now, I'm afraid we must, as I said, handle this without elaborate plans or counter-offers. If you do not return my property within ten days, the same men who abducted your secretary, or other men very much like them, will take you and your secretary. What's her name? Kelly? They will take you and Kelly to a quiet place and put a bullet in your head. Then they'll put a bullet in Kelly's head. Or, better yet, the other way around. You know, ladies first and all that. But I should tell you that the sort of men who do this kind of work are not raised to be gentlemen, as you and I were. I expect Kelly would suffer some rather rough sexual experiences before she eventually felt a gun pressed to her temple."

I was too shocked to think or speak intelligently. All I could get out was, "You son of a bitch."

"Yes, Tom. I thought you knew that." Gerrard said, "Kelly will be safely delivered to your home within the hour. Her companions should have already left for Point Clear."

A little more than thirty minutes later, a faded blue Cadillac turned into my driveway.

chapter eighteen

I WAITED IN THE entry hall, peering out at the entrance road through a column of small panes next to the door. When the car started into my driveway, I walked out onto the porch and waited in plain view. Sunlight bounced off white gravel and sand, making the day look hotter than it was, and a harsh glare flashed from the windshield as the car rolled forward. It was not until the driver cut the wheels and stopped at an angle to the house that I could see who was—and who was not—inside. Two middle-aged men in dark business suits sat in the front seat. Kelly was nowhere to be seen. Neither of them moved. They sat there like a pair of homely mannequins. I headed down the porch steps and across the gravel to have a closer look and maybe get someone inside the car to actually move a minor appendage.

Standing next to the passenger window, I saw sunlight reflect off a blued revolver in the driver's right hand. He still didn't move. I did. Ducking quickly toward the back of the car so that any shots would have to be fired awkwardly over his shoulder, I managed to get to the other side of my Jeep and put it between the armed occupants of the Cadillac and my body parts.

As if on some silent cue, both doors of the Cadillac opened at once. The driver, who was on the far side, stood erect with his revolver grasped in both hands but pointed at the clouds. The guy riding shotgun stepped out but kept the car door between us. The driver, a short, swarthy man in his thirties, did the talking.

"Step out from behind the Jeep."

I said, "I don't think so."

He looked at me for a few seconds. "Then put your hands on the top of the vehicle where I can see them." I was thinking about how that position would put nothing but glass in front of my chest and abdomen, when he said, "If you want the girl, put your hands on top of the vehicle."

Figuring I could drop to the ground faster than he could level his gun, aim, and fire, I did as instructed. When I was in position, he said, "My partner's going to move around and open the trunk. If you move, I will shoot you."

The man in the passenger seat slowly moved out from behind the door. He was about ten years older and forty pounds fatter than his partner, and he had a gauze bandage on his right hand. He headed back to the trunk. I kept watching the guy with the gun. The trunk popped open. Something was making scuffling noises inside. The fat guy yanked Kelly out and propped her against the back bumper. Her hands, her feet, and her mouth were bound with gray duct tape, and she looked reassuringly angry. I quickly turned my eyes back toward the driver to make sure small pieces of lead weren't about to come whizzing at my head.

He wasn't there. I cussed before I thought. The fat guy struggling with Kelly, apparently believing I was mad about her condition, said, "Don't worry about it. She's fine. Just had to do this to get her here." As he spoke, I saw Joey's huge hand appear over the hood, looking for all the world like the disembodied hand called Thing on *The Addams Family*. Joey's hand floated above the hood for a second, waved at me, gave me a thumbs-up, and vanished. The fat guy in back wrestled around with Kelly, trying to cut the tape off her ankles with a small pocketknife. He mumbled, "The hell with this," as he pushed her down on the gravel and turned back toward the passenger door of the Caddy.

When he had taken two steps away from Kelly, I pulled the Browning out of my back waistband and yelled, "Freeze." Surprisingly, Fat Guy did freeze, for about two seconds, before he tried to dive behind the open door, lost his footing on loose gravel, and landed with an "oomph" on his round gut next to the Caddy's back tire. I put a bullet in the rear car door over his head and said, "I told you to freeze. Get your hands out where I can see them." He did.

I said, "Joey," and my Viking friend rose up on the other side of the Caddy's hood and came walking around to the near side holding a .45 automatic in one hand and dragging the unconscious driver with the other.

Joey said, "Not much traffic out here, but better to have both of 'em on this side of the car, away from the road." He nodded at the driver and said, "Keep an eye on this one for a minute," then unceremoniously let go of the driver's collar and dropped the man's limp face into the gravel. I switched my sights to the driver, which seemed kind of silly considering his condition. Joey walked over and frisked Fat Guy, finding a small, nickel-plated automatic and the little pocketknife he had used to try to cut the tape off Kelly. When Joey was satisfied, he looked up, shook his head, and said, "Hey, Einstein. I was kind of kidding about holding a gun on Sleeping Beauty there. Go over and take care of Kelly."

I shoved the Browning back into my waistband, ran over to Kelly, and hugged her until I realized she was grunting at me through the duct tape over her mouth. I carefully lifted one corner and said, "Fast?" She shook her head. So I very, very slowly peeled the thick tape away from her face. When it was half off, I could see why she said no to having the tape yanked off in one quick pull. The right side of her mouth was swollen, and her bottom lip puffed out in purple eruptions on either side of a deep split. When the tape was peeled away from both lips, I asked, "Are you all right?"

Kelly said, "I will be," and for the first time, tears began to fill her eyes. She asked, "What happened? They wouldn't tell me what this was about."

Joey tossed me Fat Guy's pocketknife. As I dropped to one knee to reach down and slice the tape from her wrists and ankles, I said, "We'll talk about all that inside, Kelly." Motioning at the men on the ground, I said, "We'll talk all you want after we've figured out what to do with these two." Kelly nodded. When her hands and feet were free, I helped her over to my Jeep, opened the door, and lifted her into the driver's seat. Joey busied himself with tying up Eddie's men with their own belts and stuffing both of them in the Caddy's trunk.

Joey walked over and looked from Kelly to me. "Is she all right?"

Kelly said, "She's fine." Joey smiled. I asked what happened to her mouth. Kelly said, "Those two beat up Sully and stuffed me in the backseat of that car last night."

I said, "We know what happened at the restaurant. I talked with Sully this morning."

Kelly sat up a little straighter and turned her head to look out the windshield as she blinked away tears that had begun to collect along her lower lids. "Is he okay?"

"He's fine. Just worried about you. We'll call him in a few minutes. But right now, I want to know how you got hurt."

Kelly said, "That fat pig in the trunk held me down in the backseat while his partner drove away. He had one hand over my mouth, and he had his other arm wrapped around my body to pin me down." She stopped.

I took her hand and said, "What happened, Kelly?"

"We got on some old dirt road about thirty minutes after the mess outside the restaurant. Everything got real dark. That greasy-looking guy in the front turned on the radio to some kind of hillbilly station, and the fat one decided to try something." She stopped and took a few breaths the way people do to try to hold back tears. "Anyway, he started working his hand inside my shirt." She stopped again. Her face got hard. "The whole time he had his right hand over my mouth, I guess so his partner wouldn't know what he was up to. So I started kicking the door. When I did, he took his hand off my breast. I thought maybe he had quit because his partner could hear. Then . . . then he reached up my skirt and started pulling off my panties."

Joey said, "That sonofabitch is dead, Kelly. I swear to God, he just died."

Kelly reached out and took Joey's huge thumb with her free hand. She squeezed so hard her knuckles turned white. She said, "He didn't do what you think, Joey. When he started pulling at my underwear, I figured it was rape, and I had nothing to lose. I screamed bloody murder. The guy in front slammed on brakes, and that pig clamped down on my mouth so hard that two of his fingers went inside. I bit down as hard as I could until I felt my teeth hit bone."

Joey said, "I think I'm in love."

Kelly smiled and continued to squeeze his thumb. She said, "It was the only thing I could think to do. He started screaming like an animal and slapping at my head like a little kid. Finally, he managed to hit me in the mouth with a fist and give me this lip. That's what made me let go."

I said, "Was that the end of it?"

Kelly said, "Well, he wasn't much in the mood for sex anymore. But he started yelling about how he was going to kill me, calling me a bitch. Stuff like that. I was scared to death until the guy in front pulled him out of the car. They stood out on the side of the road for about five minutes and shouted at each other. By the time they came back, I had locked all the doors. The windows were already rolled up. Anyway, when they came back, they got really mad about the doors. They both pointed guns at me through the windows and talked about how they were going to shoot me right there if I didn't open up. But, you know, I thought, you know, good God, they're probably going to kill me anyhow if I let them in and maybe even rape me for a few hours first. So I just held on and waited for them to . . . you know." She stopped to take a deep breath that trembled her body like a forced vibrato. "So, the driver finally pulled some kind of metal thing out of the trunk and bashed out a back window and unlocked the door. I thought that was it, but they just pulled me out and threw me in the trunk. Maybe ten or fifteen minutes after that the trunk opened, and they took me in some old cabin in the woods. I've been there until this morning."

Joey said, "You sure that's it, Kelly?"

She said, "I'm sure. What time is it?"

I said, "A little after ten."

Kelly said, "I haven't even had a sip of water since nine last night. Can I please go in and get cleaned up?"

Joey asked, "Can you get inside by yourself? Me and Tom need to stay out here for a few minutes."

Kelly looked me in the eyes. "Tom, I'm not even going to try to talk sense to this guy"—motioning at Joey—"but I want you to use your head. It's not going to help anything, it's just going to make things worse if you two do something stupid."

I said, "You expect us to just let them go?"

Kelly said, "Hell no. I would be forever grateful if you would kick that fat one in the balls a few times, but just don't get too carried away. I'm alive. I'm not raped, and I'll be okay in a few days. All I'm saying is, nobody needs to do anything permanent here, okay?"

"Okay."

"You promise?"

"I promise, Kelly. Go inside and take care of yourself. There are clean towels in the guest bath upstairs and some girl clothes in the bottom of the dresser."

Joey lifted her out of the Jeep like he was lifting a child and walked her to the steps. When he got back, he said, "Girl clothes in the dresser, huh?"

"Yeah, I like to play dress-up sometimes."

Joey smiled. "Thought it must've been something like that. What do you wanna do about that trunkload of shit over there?"

"I want the fat one. I'm going to take him out and untie his hands and then beat the shit out of him. You can do whatever you want with the other one."

"That probably isn't too smart, Tom. He may look out of shape, but he does this kind of shit for a living. Leave him tied up. Make him feel as helpless as Kelly did last night."

"Can't do it. Wouldn't feel like I'd done anything. I need to do this for Kelly."

"Well, just for argument's sake, what do you expect me to do if Fat Boy whips your ass?"

I pushed off from the Jeep and started toward the Caddy. "I expect you to break his spine."

Joey said, "Can do."

Joey walked to the Caddy's passenger door, reached in, and clicked open the glove box. He motioned at me again to stay back and pressed the remote trunk release. The trunk lid popped up, and four feet shot out, kicking like a couple of groggy frogs on a dissecting tray. When Gerrard's thugs figured out we weren't around to be kicked, they started scuffling around, trying to sit up with bound hands and jump out of the trunk. Joey stayed back, watching through the crack on the hinged side of the open lid. When they had their knees hooked over the edge of the trunk, and as they sat up and tried to dive out head-first, Joey stepped forward and slammed the lid down.

A second later, a torrent of filth, insults, and threats spewed from the trunk. Joey walked to the back of the car, pulled out Fat Guy by his shirtfront, and dropped him on the ground. Then he grabbed the driver and tossed him backward over his right shoulder like a child tossing a rag doll out of a toy chest. The driver's nose poured blood, and Fat Guy's forehead began turning purple. Joey looked over at me. "We better take this around to the beach, away from the road." Fat Guy had already gotten to his feet. Joey kicked the driver in the ribs and told him to get up.

We herded them around to the beach and into a protected corner where the end of the lower-level deck joins the house. Joey pushed the driver down against one of the deck pilings and told him not to move, then he walked around behind Fat Guy and untied his hands. He said, "What's this?"

Joey nodded at me. "Tom here is gonna have a little talk with you about how you treated his secretary."

Fat Guy smiled. His partner snorted and said, "Shit."

Joey looked at the driver. "What's your problem?"

"Old pussle gut here don't look like much, but he was welterweight champ of some kind of fleet or something in the Navy."

Joey said, "Must've been twenty years and about a hundred pounds ago. Tom, you ever fight an old, out-of-shape, piece-of-shit, ex-bush-league welterweight before?"

It was a rhetorical question. I handed my gun to Joey, leaned over to stretch out my back, and picked up a handful of sand. As I walked up to Fat Guy, he dropped into a classic boxer's crouch, which is designed to protect the body and face since you can't hit someone below the waist in the ring. This wasn't the ring. When he crouched, bringing his right up to guard his jaw and cocking his left to jab, I kicked him in the left knee. Fat Guy howled and brought up both fists and forearms to protect his face while the pain faded. When he did, I caught him in the stomach with a straight left. He saw me drop my fist for a body shot and let go a right hook that glanced off my forehead and felt more like a rug burn than a solid hit. Whatever it was, he was getting over the knee. I circled around to the right to throw off his jab and faked another punch to his gut. When he flinched and dropped his left elbow to protect his midsection, I swung a wild right cross six inches short of his nose and let a handful of sand fly into his face. He ground both fists into his eyes to rub out the grit. Once upon a time, he had been well trained. He kept his forearms in front of his chest and jaw for protection while he rubbed at his eyes. But his jaw wasn't the target. As his fists went into his eyes, I swung a right uppercut into his solar plexus and hit him the way I had meant to hit Rodney Shelton in New Orleans. My ex-welterweight champ bent double and, unfortunately for him, dropped his hands to grab at the pain in his stomach. I caught him on the way down, put both hands on the back of his head, and brought my knee up into his face.

He lay on his side squirming like a gut-shot animal, spitting red blood and broken teeth into the sand. Joey looked at the driver leaning against the piling and said, "If he's the fighter, you must be pitiful."

I looked down at Fat Guy. "Get up."

Fat Guy said, "Fuck you," and stayed down. I kicked him hard in the lower back, just below the rib cage.

The driver said, "You're gonna bust his fucking kidneys."

Joey said, "I believe that's the general idea, if Tom can do it through all that lard."

Fat Guy had been quietly catching his breath for one last lunge. Now he jumped to his feet and came at me as fast as he could, which wasn't very fast. I spun to the right and hit him just below the left ear and behind the corner of his jaw. He went back into the sand. I was tired of talking. Just mad. Mad about Kelly and Hall. Mad about Eddie and Gerrard screwing up my life. I pulled the bloody mess to his feet, pushed him against the house, and pinned him there with a forearm against his neck. I said, "You ever come near Kelly or me again and I'm going to kill you. You hear me."

He looked up and sputtered, "Fuck you."

Everything turned bright white, and I started pushing my forearm into his trachea. I was trying to push his filthy, bloody, bloated head through the wall, when something that felt like my father's hand grabbed my bicep and spun me easily into the sand. Joey was standing over me. "You're the smart one, remember? I thought we weren't going to kill anybody." I couldn't say anything. He smiled, the way you smile at a funeral to give comfort. "Go inside. I'll take care of this and be in in a minute."

I walked up on the lower deck, went inside to the kitchen, and washed my hands and face in the stainless steel sink. There was a cold Coke in the refrigerator. I killed half of it, then ran to the bathroom and vomited.

Kelly heard the retching. She came in and found me sitting on the floor. She looked clean and fresh again in white shorts, a red top, and bare feet. Kelly bathed my face with a cold washcloth and walked back upstairs to my room with me, then left to finish getting ready. By the time I had changed shirts and brushed my teeth, Kelly was back and standing in the bathroom doorway. She said, "I thought you did something awful." I didn't say anything. She said, "I saw Joey putting them in the car. What is that all about?"

"What are you talking about?"

"They were both naked as jaybirds."

I suddenly felt much better. We both stood there in the bathroom and laughed like idiots. In a few seconds, we heard the front door and went downstairs. Joey was on the phone.

". . . trying to get Sergeant Rick Otter . . . Thank you . . . Rick? . . . Joey. How are you? . . . Look, you're not going to believe what I just saw. Two middle-aged guys, buck naked on the coast highway . . . Hell no, I'm not kidding. Looked like one of 'em had beat the crap out of the other one and was butt-fucking him right there on the side of the road. Had the guy bent over his hood. I swear . . . No shit . . . Yeah, a light blue, seventies Cadillac. Alabama tags. 3BUC6436 . . . Yeah, I was headed out here to Point Clear to see a client. If you got some-body out this way, you should be able to pick 'em up . . . Yeah, I guess you're right, it could've been rape. Good luck. Keep me out of it . . . Good deal. Thanks. Goodbye."

Kelly was laughing uncontrollably. When she could get her breath, she said, "See. I told you he was crazy."

Joey said, "Lots of that going around," then nodded at me. "Damn, Tom, where'd that come from outside? I had no idea." I didn't say any-thing.

Kelly said, "What are you talking about, Joey?"

I shook my head at Joey and said, "Nothing."

Joey said, "Tom, we've known each other a long time, been through a lot of business, lots of problems together. We always got along pretty good, right?" I nodded my head. "Well, after what I just saw on the beach, I want you to promise you'll never forget what I'm going to say." He paused for effect and said, "I'm on your side."

The three of us talked through the afternoon and into the night, ordering in pizza, arguing between ice cold swallows of Foster's lager, and slowly working out a plan for trying to stay alive. By nine, we knew I would head back to Coopers Bend to find Gerrard's drugs and whatever; Joey would go to Birmingham to dig up everything he could on Gerrard and Eddie Pappas; and Kelly would—until something changed—live night and day with a female friend of Joey's, known as Loutie Blue, who had agreed to shoot anyone who came near Kelly.

A little after eleven, the phone rang. Kelly was in bed. Joey and I were polishing off a case of Foster's and telling each other lies about how we would own Gerrard by the time we were through. I walked into the library, flipped on the recorder, and lifted the receiver. A familiar voice said, "Tom?"

"Yeah, Gerrard. It's me."

"I thought we had an agreement?"

"We do. Kelly's back, and I'm headed to Coopers Bend tomorrow morning to look for your stuff."

"You nearly beat one of my men to death this morning. That was not part of our agreement. I said the girl would be safely returned, and she was. Your actions seem to violate the spirit of our contract, if not the letter."

"Our agreement was that I find your drugs in ten days, or you kill me and Kelly. I don't think you can really say that kind of agreement has much in the way of a spirit."

"Maybe so, but Eddie is, ah, concerned about whether we can trust you to live up to the bargain. If it were up to him, we would call off our deal right now and cut our losses with you."

"Eddie Pappas is the class bully who wants to slap the other kids in the head when nobody's looking. He can't believe it when someone slaps him back. He's making this thing personal, and—worse than that—he's screwing up the works every time he tries to use his limited intelligence to solve problems that aren't even there. I don't have the time to untangle any more of Eddie's brainstorms. If you want your stuff, you've got to keep him out of my way and let me work."

"Oh, I want it, Tom."

"What about Eddie?"

"Don't worry about Eddie. If you deliver my merchandise, you'll have no problems from Eddie or his people. If you don't, you're developing a long list of enemies who would love the job of putting a bullet in you." Gerrard said, "That brings me back to this morning. Our Mobile attorneys just bailed out a couple of our men charged with public indecency." I started laughing. He said, "Very creative, Tom. But like I said, I wasn't laughing when I found out you nearly killed one of my men."

"One of *your* men—that fat jerk who thinks he's Mike Tyson—held down Kelly in the car and felt her up, then tried to rape her. If he had done it, he'd be dead. It's that simple. As it was, I untied his hands and gave him the chance to defend himself. He couldn't. The guy who left Kelly alone, we left him alone."

"Yes, Tom. Our other man who was there tells pretty much the same story. It just seemed to be an overreaction—one that could have gotten you and Kelly dead."

"I'm funny that way. I tend to overreact when someone tries to rape a friend of mine. Look, we have an agreement. I expect to be left alone, and I expect my friends and family to be left alone while I'm trying to do what you asked. Right now, we both have some incentive to get through this. But if Eddie keeps raising the stakes, he's going to blow everything."

"We've already discussed Eddie. By the way, who's your new partner? I hear you've got some kind of white-haired giant backing you up."

"Doesn't everybody have one?"

I must have been slurring a little. Gerrard said, "Are you drunk, Tom?"

I said, "Pretty much."

"Well, I suggest you sober up and get busy." He paused, then said, "Ten days," and hung up.

The man loved a dramatic exit.

chapter nineteen

J OEY MADE BREAKFAST. Kelly looked pale and didn't seem to be able to eat; she just sipped coffee and nibbled at the edges of some toast. She told us she had tossed and turned with nightmares for most of the night. I admitted I woke up from a violent dream a little after five and never got back to sleep. Joey said he slept like a baby.

Around nine, Joey and Kelly left to meet Loutie Blue at her place. Twenty minutes later, I finished loading the Jeep and headed north once again across cow pastures, bridges, timberland, and harvested fields—all of them made possible by streams and creeks filled with rain and groundwater flowing south to the Gulf, moving from where I was going to where I had been.

An Alabama state trooper wrote me up for going seventy-eight in a fifty-five zone just below Monroeville. I realized I had been driving faster and growing more panicked as each mile passed. *Ten days.* Even if I failed and couldn't work out some kind of deal with Gerrard, we could probably get Kelly out of the country before he could get to her. But then what? I couldn't take care of her forever. I would get by for a while, but sooner or later the brakes on my Jeep would go out on a curve, or maybe walking on the beach one day I would feel the punch of a bullet or hear a gunshot and just stop feeling anything at all.

. . .

I had planned to go to the sawmill and bring Sam up to speed as soon as I hit Coopers Bend. Instead, I found myself headed out Whiskey Run Road toward Christy's cabin and Susan Fitzsimmons' farm. Cedar Lane—the road to Christy's place—passed. I was pushing to find the dilapidated general store that marked the turn onto the dirt road—the one with a strip of green clover down the middle. I found the road and the clover and the mailbox with a crane on it and, finally, the dam-top access road to the farm. As I started across, Susan's old step-side pickup came toward me from the other side. I braked and backed up to let her pass. She stopped alongside, and I rolled down the window.

Susan's windows were already down. She ran unpainted fingernails through blond hair to push it out of her face, and she smiled. "Hello."

"Susan. It's nice to see you again." She didn't say anything. "I need to bother you for a little more information, if you don't mind."

She looked at me with those intelligent blue eyes for a few seconds, thinking, it seemed, about why I might have shown up unannounced. She said, "You don't bother me."

"Can we talk?"

"I've got to go into town for a few minutes." She fiddled with the keys in the ignition and then reached her hand out the window. "Here. Let yourself in the house." I reached out, and she pressed a brass key with an octagonal head into my palm. "Make yourself comfortable. The alarm pad is behind the front door. Just punch in fourteen ninety-two and push enter to turn it off. I'll be back in less than an hour." She said, "I'll bring lunch," and put the pickup in gear.

I called her name. "Susan. I guess this is going to sound strange, but I don't really want anyone to know I'm back in town yet."

She nodded and drove away.

Inside the farmhouse, I found a phone in a paneled office off the living room and placed a credit card call to Kelly in Mobile. She was safe, and Joey had already boarded a plane for Birmingham. She gave me the number of the hotel where Joey would be staying and got off the phone. Kelly had been brave and then some while Eddie's men had her. Now the whole thing seemed to be killing her.

Inside Susan's eat-in kitchen, onions and garlic and charcoal-gray Calphalon cookware hung from the ceiling, mostly red wines were stacked in a wooden rack on a countertop, and the refrigerator held eggs and whole milk and butter and fresh herbs. No Cokes. The back door opened off the pantry onto the backyard. I walked outside and was trying to find a way to look into Bird's studio when the sound of tires moving across the dam floated into the yard. As I walked around to help Susan unload whatever she might have to unload, a fist rapped sharply on the front door. Since I didn't much think Susan would knock on her own door, I moved quietly to the corner of the house and peered around at the porch. Sheriff Nixon had his right hand on the doorknob.

As he pushed open the door and stepped inside, I said, "That's breaking and entering." Nixon stepped back out onto the porch and turned to face me. "Actually, in your line of work, I guess it's more of a Fourth Amendment thing. You know, illegal search and seizure. All that stuff you swore to uphold."

Nixon said, "You sure are not your father."

"Thank you."

"It wasn't a compliment. Sam's got as little use as I have for men who crowd the air with bullshit. Talking until they can think of something intelligent to say."

"Not that I don't appreciate your stopping off to explain my father to me, Nixon, but was there some other reason you dropped by to break into Mrs. Fitzsimmons' home?"

"I came here to find you."

"How'd you know I was in town? Nobody knew I was coming."

Nixon looked down at the gray porch and shook his head. "If you want to go somewhere without anyone knowing you're there, it's a good idea not to get ticketed for speeding on the way in, or to drive through the center of town once you get there. This isn't Birmingham or Mobile, and it certainly isn't New Orleans. It's a little harder to go unnoticed here."

Nixon caught me off guard, and he knew it. I said, "What are you talking about?"

He smiled, but there was nothing friendly in it. "Right, son. You don't have any idea what I'm talking about, do you?" I didn't answer. He said, "We need to talk."

"Is that what you came out here to tell me?"

"I came out here to tell you that you've been lucky so far. Luckier than you should have been. I know you've probably got some kind of new information now and that you came back here to do something about it." He stopped as if he expected me to fill him in. I didn't. He went on. "You started out in a bad place on this, and unless I miss my guess, you're in serious trouble up to your neck now." Nixon subjected me to another ten-second pause. "I owe it to Sam to tell you that working for these people is the wrong way to go."

"What makes you think—"

"Tom. Don't talk. Just listen. I'm not accusing you of anything. Just consider it free advice for now. All I'm saying is that if you made some kind of deal in Birmingham, they won't keep it. You need to understand that. These people do not care about keeping their word or about ruining other men's lives."

I nodded.

Nixon said, "And it's my job to tell you that—if you did learn something about who killed Hall—you cannot come back here and start taking your own revenge. Listen to me, Tom. I don't care who your father is. You are not going to come into my county and swap anyone else's life for Hall's or swap someone for a way out of your trouble in Birmingham."

I said, "I'm not a murderer."

Nixon spoke quickly. "Didn't say you were, Tom. I'm just trying to get the rules straight up front."

mike stewart

189

"They're straight."

"Good." Both of us looked up as Susan's pickup appeared across the dam. Nixon said, "You should have called me first if you wanted to come in unnoticed. I could have helped you. As it is, I've already been to Zollie's and Christy's trying to find you."

"Thanks."

"Can't expect someone to keep a secret unless he knows it's secret. By the way." Nixon looked past me, focusing on something in the distance that seemed to give him a bad taste in his mouth. "I believe I got, uh, too aggressive about what happened to the files I gave you. You and your family had just gotten back from Hall's funeral." He paused to take in a deep breath. "I should have handled it better. Come by the office. I'll make you another copy of Hall's file if you still need it." Nixon turned his back and walked away through Susan's rosebushes.

By the time Susan pulled her pickup under the barn and carried a couple of grocery sacks up to the porch, Nixon had disappeared across the access road, driving too fast and leaving parallel dust clouds hovering over the dam.

Susan said, "He always drive like that?"

"I think I irritate him."

She handed me one of the brown sacks and said, "Imagine that."

We unloaded the sacks in the kitchen. Susan had brought barbecued pork, potato salad, coleslaw, and two six-packs of Sol. She said, "If you squeeze a lime into that beer, you have to leave."

"I may have to leave then. I'm a pretty stylish guy. By the way, have you seen this month's *GQ*?"

She smiled as she arranged the food on stoneware plates. "No. And unless *GQ* has a new L.L. Bean edition, I don't think you have either." She put the plates on an antique butcher's table surrounded by four green, wrought-iron chairs. I took the chair facing her. Susan said, "What additional information do you want?"

"I wanted to find out more about what Hall and Bird did on the river. Where they went. If they ever went out on the water at night. Things like that."

Susan's features hardened. "I hope you're not trying to say Bird was mixed up in Hall's drug business."

"Hell no. I'm just trying to figure something out. You see, I found out that Zollie Willingham was with Hall on the river when he got shot."

"That doesn't surprise me. He and Hall were in business together. I always assumed Hall was up to no good when it happened." My face must have registered discomfort because Susan changed her tone. "I'm sorry. As much as you two look alike, I have trouble really seeing you as brothers."

"Don't worry about it. Everyone keeps telling me Hall had changed. Even his girlfriend says he turned mean the last few months." I stopped for a beat as something Susan had said earlier about Zollie hit me. I said, "Back up a minute. You said Hall and Zollie were in business together. And you more or less said that if Hall was up to no good, then Zollie was probably with him."

Susan said, "Sure. Bird told me, I guess it was last spring sometime, that Hall and Zollie were bringing drugs into the county. Bird said Florida cops have gotten so sophisticated at spotting drug couriers, you know, speedboats and private planes outside normal fly zones, things like that, that a lot of these little towns on the Alabama and Tombigbee rivers are used for drop sites for marijuana and cocaine flown in from the Caribbean."

"You sure Zollie was mixed up in it?"

"Well, Bird seemed sure about it. No offense, Tom, but Hall was no rocket scientist. Bird said Hall would've been caught the first month without someone to help him. He said Hall probably took the chances and supplied the muscle or whatever, and Zollie ran the business. Everybody knows Zollie's always been smarter than most of the people he's worked for. Apparently, there just wasn't a lot of opportunity for a black man around here twenty or thirty years ago when he was young, particularly for someone with a prison record."

"I'd forgotten about that. Sam told us one time when we were kids that Zollie had been to prison. Something about a fight. How'd you know about it?"

"Gossip. A lot of people knew Zollie spent a few years in prison. I guess until he and Hall got into the drug business, most people had pretty much put it out of their minds, though." Susan paused and took a sip of Mexican beer before she went on. "I guess you've probably gathered that I think Bird's murder had something to do with Hall and his business."

"Yeah, but why? That's the second time . . . Well, when I was out here before, I picked up on that without your saying it in so many words."

"I know Bird. He would not have gotten involved with drug runners. But he did seem to know a lot about what Hall was up to. I thought maybe Hall got drunk one night and told Bird more than he should have. I know it sounds cliché, but maybe Bird just knew too much. Also, one thing I know for sure is that they found Hall's fingerprints all over the studio."

"Yeah, but you've already said Hall was hanging around out there with Bird all the time."

"That's true, but the deputy who took the prints said they looked really fresh based on the way dust and some kind of film from artist's turpentine had settled over most of the others. And there's something else. They found Zollie's prints in there too. And as far as I know, Zollie Willingham had never been in Bird's studio in his life."

I seemed to remember Zollie telling me pretty much the same thing. "Did you tell Sheriff Nixon that?"

"Yes. He didn't seem interested. I think he said they found fingerprints for something like thirty people in there. He said I couldn't possibly know every person who visited Bird when I wasn't home."

I said, "Wait here for a minute," and ran out to the Jeep for my laptop computer. I grabbed the computer and my briefcase and went back to the kitchen table.

Susan asked, "What are you doing?"

"Hang on. I'm trying to find something." It took a few seconds to get the laptop booted up and to access my WordPerfect files on the investigation. When the program was on screen, I typed in a directory-wide search for the word "Bird" and found thirty-four references, which were way too many to be helpful. I tried to think back. Zollie said something that day about not liking Bird's paintings. He used an example. I asked Susan, "Did Bird ever paint a picture of an alligator?"

"Sure. He painted pretty much everything that lived on the river."

I typed the word "alligator" into the search screen. Ten seconds later, just one file popped up. I opened the file I had named ZolliePhone.wpb, and my notes of a telephone conversation with Zollie, dated the Monday after Hall's funeral, scrolled across the screen. The search word was highlighted.

> *Asked Zollie if he'd been to studio.*
> *Ans.: "Nope." Said he went by Bird's house to pick up*
> *Hall 1 or 2 times, but never been in barn where Bird*
> *painted.*
> *Question: Why?*
> *Ans.: "Never had a reason. He wasn't no friend of mine."*
> *Said he wasn't going to "pay a thousand dollars for a*
> *picture of an **alligator** eating a crane, or some such*
> *foolish thing that's supposed to be art."*

Susan was looking over my shoulder. She said, "Zollie was in the studio, Tom. I can't say Zollie killed him, but he had to be in the studio pretty close to when Bird was murdered."

"How do you know?"

"The night Bird died he had been working on a large canvas of an alligator pushing up through floating plants and holding a crane by the legs as it tried to fly away. It was something he actually saw on the river. It's still not finished."

"Where's the painting?"

"Still in his studio. You didn't see it because it's covered with a drop cloth."

"Has that painting, or a photograph of it, ever been outside the studio?"

"No. Un-uh. Bird photographed works in progress, but the pictures were for his use. He didn't show them to anybody. I'm sure about that. And I'm even more sure that that canvas never left the studio. Zollie was there, all right. And he was there during the last four or five days before the murder. That's when Bird started the painting."

I asked, "Can I use your phone?"

"Sure. There's one over on the desk there." As I walked away, Susan took my chair and started rereading Zollie's words on the screen.

The phone was on the side of a cabinet above a small, built-in desk. I dialed the sheriff's office. After explaining to the operator, the desk deputy, and the sheriff's secretary who I was and that I needed to speak with Nixon personally, I finally heard the sheriff's voice on the line.

"Sheriff."

"Yes?"

"This is Tom McInnes."

"I know."

"I need a favor." Nixon didn't say anything. "I need to know why Zollie Willingham went to prison about thirty years ago. Can you pull his file for me?"

"Not necessary. Zollie went up for manslaughter. We pulled his records in the course of investigating Hall's murder."

"What about in connection with Bird Fitzsimmons' murder?"

"Tom, what's Susan Fitzsimmons been telling you? Don't let her problems get to be yours. Not right now. You've got enough on your plate."

"I need some of that help you promised Sam. Can I get a look at Zollie's old arrest records and look at the file on Bird Fitzsimmons' murder?"

The line stayed silent while Nixon thought or sent out intimidating brain waves or scratched his balls or whatever he did during all those long pauses he loved so much. Finally, he said, "I can't spare anyone to do the research right now. I'll have to pull the files myself. Come by the office between six and six-thirty. I should have what you want by then."

"Thank you."

Nixon said, "No problem," and hung up.

I stood there trying to reason through my new, paper-thin theory. I knew that something—frustration or maybe greed—had pushed Zollie into the drug business; I knew that Zollie tried to cut Toby Miller's throat using pretty much the same technique that someone used to kill Bird Fitzsimmons; and, while Zollie claimed he had never been in Bird's studio, I knew that he had not only been there, but that he had been there close to, if not on, the night of the murder. Maybe Zollie was going around slicing up people who got in his way, and maybe I was full of shit. But I finally had a loose thread to pull. I wasn't just reacting to pressures from Gerrard or Eddie or Rodney. I actually had an idea. Hell, I had a clue. The only problem was that it seemed to lead to one of the best friends I'd ever had.

Susan had moved back around to the other side of the table and was staring out a window at her yard. I sat down and started eating. Susan turned to face me. "What did the sheriff say?"

"He's going to let me see the files around six tonight."

"Why didn't you tell him about Zollie?"

Susan still didn't understand. She thought the cops were going to arrest Zollie and end her pain. The truth was that nobody would be arrested—much less convicted—based on a few notes of a conversation that Zollie would deny having. And putting Zollie in jail, even if that were possible, was not going to keep Susan from missing her husband, just as the bullet that Eddie pumped into Toby Miller's battered head had only worsened my feelings of guilt and anger and loss about the way Hall died. I said, "Nixon wasn't interested in talking about Zollie. Just like he didn't listen when you talked to him about it, remember. I've got to come up with something else."

"I guess." She said, "What are you going to do until six?" I looked up. She must have been lonely living alone on that farm for the past three months.

I said, "I'm going to visit an old friend."

chapter twenty

A COOL WIND BLEW in from the west, rippling the uneven ponds on either side of the dam and giving jagged edges to gray clouds reflected on the water's surface. Like Sheriff Nixon, I drove too fast across the narrow crest of earth separating the ponds. Susan had wanted to talk more about Bird and why I hadn't argued with Nixon about Zollie's guilt. All I could tell her was to trust me, which felt like a lie. Seeing the pain in her face had hurt, but Nixon had been right about priorities. I could not afford to make her problems mine. Anger and depression were eating away at Susan, but she was alive, and I thought then that she was safe. Another woman close to me had been kidnapped, nearly raped, and threatened with death. That had to take precedence over everything and everyone else. I eased back on the accelerator and tried to concentrate on where I was going and what I would do when I got there.

On the other side of town, I veered off the highway onto red gravel and sped between lines of same-age pines laid out like row crops by some paper company. Two miles in from the highway, natural growth rose up in a jumbled line perpendicular to the road, marking the end of the plantation and the beginning of Zollie's land. His mailbox was a quarter mile ahead. I turned right into the plantation and drove between rows of young loblolly pines. About ninety feet in, I turned left toward Zollie's house and nosed the Jeep into a narrow clearing that looked like the end of an old logging trail. Tall pines and bulging oaks rose up on either side as the Jeep rolled over swirls of dormant honeysuckle and blackberry vines.

Vines gave way to saplings and delicate silk trees that bent double, scraping the undercarriage, then snapped up behind the rear bumper. Finally, the last remnants of the logging trail disappeared into thick bottomland. I cut the engine and stepped out less than eighty yards from Zollie's back door.

I covered the remaining ground on foot, moving as quietly as possible over dry leaves and underbrush. Within sight of the house, I circled the edge of the yard, staying well inside the surrounding cover.

Zollie's truck was gone.

I sat on the ground and leaned against a smooth poplar trunk to think. Not much time passed before I began to feel ridiculous squatting in the woods, *lying in wait,* for God's sake. Zollie might do a lot of things—steal from Gerrard, head for Argentina, maybe even kill Bird or Toby Miller—but he would never shoot me, and he would never leave me to be shot by Eddie Pappas if he knew the situation. But, of course, he didn't know the situation, and it was entirely possible that, if he wasn't gone already, he would soon head for parts unknown with Gerrard's "merchandise" in tow.

I walked through the yard, up onto the porch, and knocked on the front door. No one answered. I sat on the porch and waited; at least, I waited about three minutes before it occurred to me that maybe he *was* gone for good. I tried seven or eight locked or painted-shut windows before giving up and kicking in the back door. Everything looked normal: dishes in the cabinets, food in the refrigerator, clothes in the closets. But if you were, say, a drug runner who was about to be arrested for murder, you might not pack the good china and vacation clothes before heading for Mexico.

I looked for something that might tell me where he had gone and whether he planned to come back. I'm not sure what I expected to find. There were no airline tickets, no hoards of cash in the mattresses, no travel brochures for South America. Two hours later, after rifling closets, drawers, cabinets, and every other hidey-hole that looked suspicious, my only accomplishment had been to trash Zollie's house. I was on my third tour of the downstairs rooms, looking behind pictures and under rugs for wall safes and secret passages. Really. I just thought I felt ridiculous squatting in the woods; now I was reaching a whole new level.

As I started up the front stairs to ransack the bedrooms one more time, I caught a glimpse of a doorknob sticking out behind a chifforobe next to the staircase. I walked around to the side of the stairs and leaned close in to the wall to peer behind the antique wardrobe. My doorknob protruded from an old door put there to allow access to storage space under the stairwell—one of those little doors with a slanted top that follows the incline of the staircase above. It looked promising. A brass padlock hung a foot above the knob.

Bracing my shoulder against the wall for leverage, I got a grip on the left side of the chifforobe and swung it out and away from the wall, then borrowed a crowbar from the garage out back and popped the lock off, along with a chunk of Zollie's door frame. It was a little late to start worrying about screwing up the house. But it occurred to me that if I was wrong, if he did not kill Bird, if he was just out, for example, fishing for crappie or buying sweet potatoes, Zollie was going to kick my ass.

I opened the door.

Nothing. Just an unlighted closet with a couple of worn hunting coats hanging from hooks. I had closed the door and was lugging the chifforobe back into place when some ancient memory started squirming around the back of my brain. I let go of the chifforobe and pulled the door back open. The coats were the same style Zollie had worn as long as I could remember: tan canvas, with large game pockets and brown corduroy collars. I remembered something too full, too detailed to represent just one childhood experience. I had stood in that same spot, in front of that door, many times. Scattered fragments clicked into place and my mind poured full of the feel, the look, even the smell of standing in front of that odd little door looking up at Zollie's face on some distant winter morning twenty years before. I could see him coming out of the closet, hunched over and carrying his scarred Winchester pump in one hand and a box of shells in the other. I could see him stepping down into the closet. *Stepping down.*

I found a flashlight in the kitchen and went back to the closet. Dark brown paint covered all four walls. But, while three walls were paneled in four-inch planks, the wall on the right—the one toward the bottom of the steps that angled overhead—that wall was made of plywood.

After ten minutes of pushing, pulling, tapping, and kicking, I dropped to my knees and peeled back the square of green carpet that covered the closet floor. There, in the floor at the foot of the plywood wall, was a pine one-by-ten with a one-inch hole drilled a few inches from one end. I shined the flashlight down through the hole. Nothing was visible except more boards a few inches down. I carefully pushed my right index finger down into the hole as far as it would go. Nothing. But when I tried to pull it out, the board lifted easily out of its space, leaving a ten-inch gap running the length of the wall. A brass cabinet handle curved out from the bottom edge of the plywood about three inches below where the floorboard had been. I tossed the one-by-ten out of the way, took hold of the handle, and pulled like a madman. Nothing happened. I pushed with everything I had and got the same result. So much for brute force.

I stood up and ran the flashlight over the wall hoping for some scratch or nick that might indicate that the wall had moved one way or another in the past. The side edges were clean and the joints tight. Finally, the flashlight beam picked up faint vertical scratches beginning in a straight line six inches from the top of the wall and disappearing into the ceiling.

I placed the flashlight inside the well and pointed the beam at the brass pull. Leaning over and gripping the metal handle with both hands, I bent my knees, set both feet, and pulled up hard with arms, back, and quadriceps. The wall flew up six inches and swung away from me so fast that I lost balance and yanked back on the handle to keep from falling. When I did, the wall slammed shut and fell back into place like a guillotine blade, snatching the handle out of my hands and shooting me backward. My tailbone hit the wall behind me, then nose-dived into the floor. I sat crumpled in the far corner of the closet cussing the door and rubbing my butt. It was not impressive.

A couple of minutes of behind rubbing and vector analysis and I was ready to give it another try. This time, I held the handle with one hand, lifted straight up, and then carefully swung the wall up and out of the way. Aged wooden steps led down into the dark. Overhead, a bent coat hanger hung down so that it could be hooked around the brass handle to keep the door suspended against the inclined ceiling. I picked up the flashlight and started down. This, I thought, is not the fun part.

Wooden steps followed the angle of the main staircase overhead, whose structural supports and subflooring acted as a miserably low ceiling that descended at the same angle as the rough steps underfoot. The feeling was one of descending into the earth's bowels through a narrow and unstable orifice.

Ten or twelve steps down, the angled ceiling leveled out to follow the line of hardwood flooring that stretched out from the base of the stairs above. But, while I no longer had to hunch over to keep from banging my head, the end of the low passage was also the end of fresh air. Odors of earth and mildew, mixed with something that smelled like old sweat, wafted up and filled the cellar.

I thought about the graveside service when Hall was lowered into something like this, something immeasurably worse than this, where he would lie and rot and crumble until he became part of the earth and smells that crushed in on his casket. My little brother was dead. I had no more sympathy, no more feeling for anyone mixed up in this nasty, inhuman business. Zollie had better pray to God that he had left in time. The hell with Zollie. He was with Hall when he was killed. Zollie could have helped, but kept quiet just to protect himself—just for money.

I stood and trembled in that filthy, dark place. Some time passed before I could refocus on the job at hand.

Near the bottom of the steps, I swept the flashlight's beam across mounds of fresh dirt, tools, worktables, and an antique coal-burning furnace. I understood now that I was entering an old coal storage basement. Somewhere, high up on the black walls, there would be a rusted iron gate and a chute for dumping coal in winter. Close to the center of the cellar, a bare bulb hung down. I switched it on and looked around. The furnace was ancient and unused for decades. Worktables, roughed together out of two-by-fours and plywood, looked only a few years old. Piles of fresh black dirt lay next to three identical two-foot cubes that had been dug into the earthen floor. Someone clearly had emptied the holes of dirt and whatever else was in them during the last day or two.

For a little-used cellar, the place was unusually neat and free of the junk and trash that naturally live and multiply in every other basement. There wasn't an old newspaper or a broken chair in the place. Everything except the rusted-out furnace seemed to have a purpose. A shovel and pick lay against the wall next to the holes. On one table, Zollie had laid out plastic shipping tape, scissors, and a spool of grass rope next to gallon cans of tar and nautical-grade polyurethane. Two fresh trays of rat poison were tossed in opposite corners. I tried to make sense of the odd assortment of items. All I could figure was that Zollie dug up three boxes, tied them with rope, taped them shut, and, hell, maybe patched a boat later in the day. It didn't make much sense. It was an interesting puzzle, but it did not explain where Zollie was or what had been in those perfectly square holes.

I reached up and clicked off the light bulb, then quickly switched it back on. An off-the-wall thought came flying in from the logic-free region of the brain where foolish ideas form and wait to be thrown into action by desperation. Everything in the basement—everything but the furnace—had a use. Most people don't remove coal furnaces from old houses because it costs a few thousand dollars to have one cut up and taken out. It's usually easier to put up with a little lost storage space. But, I had come this far. It was worth a look.

The latch on the cast-iron door would not budge. A few vicious swipes with the shovel accomplished nothing more than a scratch or two on the cast iron. The pick snapped off the latch with one blow. I expected to contend with rusted hinges, but the door swung open easily. Inside, something was jammed into the back corner of a space the size of a doghouse. Squatting to get a better look with the flashlight, I could see the end of a large corrugated box that looked to be about eighteen inches square. On top of the larger box sat two white shoe boxes.

The boxes looked too new to have been put in before the latch rusted shut. I shined Zollie's flashlight on the spot where the latch had hooked to the body of the furnace. A small hole had been drilled into the center of the space where the latch came to rest when the door was shut. The broken latch lay on the floor next to my foot. A quick examination showed it had been drilled to line up with the hole in the furnace. I knew what I was looking for now, and it was under my foot— a headless three-inch nail. Zollie had rigged up the door the way cops tell you to secure windows from burglars. He had drilled through the latch and into the furnace, then pushed a headless nail deep into the hole. He probably used a magnet or a small wire to remove the nail when he put the boxes inside. It wasn't exactly Fort Knox, but it was just difficult enough to dissuade most people from poking their heads into the furnace out of curiosity.

As I squatted there on the dirt floor congratulating myself on my tenacity, it occurred to me that I hadn't found anything yet except some old boxes. I only assumed that I had found Zollie's drug stash, and not the hiding place for his grandmother's silver.

A grown man could not fit through the furnace opening; and the boxes were, of course, just beyond reach. I ran upstairs for the crowbar and stopped to listen for someone in the house. Nothing. A quick trip to the window verified that Zollie's truck had not returned. Back in the basement, I reached out with the crowbar and tried to hook the large box, which showed no discernible interest in cooperating. Finally, I drew the crowbar back against the side of the coal bin, swung hard, and jammed the hooked end of the bar into the side of the box.

It was more difficult than I expected to pull the boxes across the grate on the floor of the bin; but the crowbar was solidly hooked into the cardboard and into whatever was inside. When the large box finally slid through the feeder door and plopped out on the floor, both shoe boxes fell open inside the furnace, spilling out twelve neat bricks of cocaine wrapped in plastic and sealed with shipping tape from the worktable. Bingo. The larger box had a picture of the Green Giant on the side and was taped closed, but its heft indicated that it had the same stuff inside. I could find out for sure back in the woods, locked securely inside the Jeep.

I stacked white bricks back inside the shoe boxes, placed them on top of the larger box, and lugged it all upstairs. Still, the house seemed empty. I dropped the boxes at the foot of the main staircase. Back down in the basement, I threw the broken latch inside the furnace, closed the door, ran up the narrow steps at full speed, and lowered Zollie's false wall into its slot. When the floorboard and carpet were in place, I closed the closet door and stepped back to put my shoulder against the chifforobe. As I shoved to swing the monstrous antique into place, something slammed into the left side of my head. An explosion of pain clouded the room. I saw the floor coming but was gone before I could feel it hit.

chapter twenty-one

SOMEONE MOVED IN the next room. My arms and legs felt paralyzed. A fuzzy lamp, floating among other, darker shapes, hurt my eyes; I closed them and tried to call out. Some time later, a warm wet cloth bathed my face. Someone was talking. The world faded away.

It was dark now. The lamp had grown brighter and clearer. I tried to be quiet and bring the room into focus. Life flowed back inside, like blood into a sleep-dead limb. I was tied to a chair in the living room. Zollie walked in and smiled.

"You been gone a long time. Afraid I killed you."

I managed to say, "Tried to."

"No, Tom. You be all right. I didn't hit you hard enough to mess you up for good. Just had to stop you. You had a gun under your belt, and you were stealing my property. I did what I had to do. I'm too old to stand toe-to-toe with a young man your size." I was still too fuzzy to argue, but everything looked clear and normal again. I just stared at him. Zollie said, "You got in it too far, Tom. Should've left well enough alone. Toby's dead. That ought to be enough." He walked over and wrung out a washcloth in a plastic bowl of water on the floor next to my chair. I tried to jerk my head back as he reached to wipe my face. Everything went black again for a few seconds, then eased into focus. New rule: no quick movements for a while. Zollie said, "Calm down. You going to have a pretty good headache. Probably going to need a few stitches too." He walked out of the room and came back with four tablets and a glass of water. "Take these." I did. "You going to be fine. Take a few minutes, let the pills work and try to come to. I put some butterfly bandages over the cut. Somebody'll be by to get you tomorrow."

I could finally think a little. My first sentence was, "What if I have to take a leak?"

Zollie laughed. "Wet your pants. I'll be in the bedroom taking care of some things. Check back with you in a few minutes." There was no one to hear a yell for help. I tried the ropes and was ineffectually picking at a knot next to my left wrist when Zollie came back in. "Looks like you getting well enough to try to get away."

"What the hell are you doing?"

Zollie said, "I could ask you the same thing. I wasn't the one who came looking for you with a gun."

"I know you killed Bird Fitzsimmons."

Zollie stopped and looked at me. "I figured you did. You always were about the smartest boy I ever saw. At least, until Rudy came along."

"How did you know Toby Miller was dead?"

"Found out from the same folks who took you to New Orleans to kill him."

"I didn't kill him."

"That's not what I hear. But, to be honest, Tom, I don't much care if you did. You can bet your ass I'd've killed him when I got hold of him."

"I didn't kill him, but your buddies in Birmingham are trying to make it look like I did."

"Yeah, they good at that."

"I need you to help me."

"You noticed by any chance that I had to hit you upside the head this afternoon to keep you from stealing my property and maybe shooting me if you got the chance? It don't look like we're helping each other much these days." Zollie walked out again and came back with my

Browning in his hand. "You figured out what happened with Bird. If you worked it out, well, that means, sooner or later, somebody else is going to do the same thing. I been to the river to get what I need. I'm gone from here tonight."

"Gerrard and Eddie Pappas say they're going to kill me and my secretary."

"Well, if they want you dead, you going to be dead. All I can tell you is to get some cash and head out of the country yourself." Zollie turned and looked out a window at the night. "I'm sorry you got in this, Tom. You should've left it alone."

"That's bullshit. You wanted to kill Toby yourself. And whatever Hall may have meant to you, he was my brother."

"I know, but you in something now that nobody, at least nobody I know, can get you out of."

He started to go upstairs again. I called his name. "Zollie. What happened to Hall? Toby said before he died that you were in the boat with Hall when he got shot."

"Yeah. I was in the boat. Somebody on the bank—well, I guess we know now it was Toby—anyway, Toby saw us and yelled out. Hall stood up to answer him, and Toby shot him in the neck." Zollie walked over and sat in a wooden chair next to a small oak table. "I guess there's more to it than that, but I can't prove nothing. I moved the body the next night 'cause it was in a place I couldn't afford to have people poking around in."

"You couldn't put him on the bank somewhere? I saw the autopsy report. Do you know what the turtles did to him?"

Zollie pulled out a cigarette and lit it with a kitchen match. "Sorry, Tom. There ain't nothing in this whole situation but bad. You got to remember, though. Hall was dead. Wasn't nothing going to hurt him any more then." He paused to think and draw on his cigarette, then went on. "One thing I never understood, though, was why Toby didn't come back for the money. It looked like he must've known where the stuff was if he was waiting out there on the bank to take a shot at us."

"He didn't know what he'd found. In the warehouse in New Or-

206

leans, Toby said he followed you and Hall that night on the river. He thought you were lost out there in the dark. Said it looked like you stopped to look at a map."

"Isn't that some shit? Boy was in the wrong kind of business to be that stupid. Hell, somebody like that was just waiting to be dead. Anyway, he killed Hall, and now he's where he ought to be." Zollie balanced his cigarette on the lip of a glass ashtray, rested his elbows on the tops of his knees, and looked down at the floor for a few seconds before he started. "I want you to know, I didn't bring Hall into the business. Hall was betting everything he had, then turning around and selling dope to get more money to bet, before he was out of high school. After screwing up for three or four years, he asked me to come in with him three summers ago. At first, I didn't want no part of it. Hall didn't have enough sense to know that he'd of been locked up twenty times if Mr. Sam wasn't his daddy. And I guess you know I been to prison. I wasn't real interested in going back."

"Then it should have been pretty easy to say no, Zollie."

"Yeah, but it wasn't. Even messing up the way he did, Hall was making a shitload of money."

"Sorry. You're right. Money makes it okay to fuck up people's lives."

Zollie looked up from the floor and met my eyes. "Tom, you asked to hear this. You want to shut up and let me tell it, or do you want to sit there acting like a rich white boy and preach at me?" I shut up. Zollie went on. "I told myself I could help Hall run it right and keep him out of jail. But I know it was mostly the money. Tom, you got no idea how much money you can make running a little dope. So, we got to growing marijuana back up in the woods, then we found some cocaine suppliers in Pensacola and Houston. Before long we was making maybe ten or twenty thousand a week."

I said, "You don't exactly live like someone making six figures."

"You're right, and we didn't plan to for a couple more years. We been putting most everything away. Put a good bit of coke away in storage for a rainy day too. We figured to head down to Belize or somewhere like that after we was set."

"How did you get mixed up with Gerrard?"

"Same thing usually happens in this kind of business. Couple years back, we got to making too much money. Gerrard found out about it because Hall could live without spending money, but he didn't seem to be able to get by without betting some of it on ball games. Gerrard sent Eddie Pappas down, and he made us one of those offers you can't refuse. Pappas said we could make three times the money working for them. Working kind of like a warehouse operation. Their planes would bring stuff up from Texas, Florida, sometimes all the way from the Bahamas. We'd keep it somewhere safe and get it to a commercial barge operation that Gerrard owns. And they said we could keep the four counties where we was already doing business."

"Pretty good deal if you don't care who you work for."

"Yeah, well, Pappas said if we wasn't interested in that, Gerrard would be glad to take over our operation. And he said he'd be taking all our money we'd made so far."

"So you just started working for a gangster?"

"By that time, me and Hall wasn't much better."

"Zollie, you used to be the best man I knew. What happened to you?"

"Got tired of working for white men half as smart as me. Wouldn't you if you was me?"

"Probably, but there are other things you could have done."

"Name one. A fifty-two-year-old black man with an eighth-grade education? Shit. Besides, it looked like nobody was really getting hurt. Folks been doing coke since before my daddy was born. Nat King Cole sang about it forty years ago. Hell, Tom, somebody was going to make the money. We didn't see a reason it shouldn't of been us."

"And now Hall's dead."

"Yeah. I'm sorrier about that than you'll ever know, but, Tom, it wasn't my fault. Hall was in this mess up to his ass before I ever made a dime. I like to think he stayed alive a little longer, or at least stayed out of prison, 'cause I got him to stop taking stupid chances and run it like a business. Anyway, there's nothing we can do about it now. Hall's dead, rest his soul, and I got to get out of here before either Nixon figures out what you did about Bird, or before Gerrard decides killing Hall ain't going to get him his drugs back."

"Zollie. Now I've got to get Gerrard's drugs back or he's going to kill me and my secretary in Mobile. They already kidnapped her. I was just lucky I could make them bring her back. I know you aren't going to leave me here to get killed over some dope money."

"Maybe you don't know me as good as you think. I'm getting ready to go to another country. You can do the same thing. I don't see why I'm supposed to go back to being your father's poor nigger so you can go home and live on the beach and be a fancy lawyer in Mobile. For the first time, I got as much, maybe even more, money than you got. As far as I'm concerned, me and you and your secretary can all go to Belize and play in the water."

"That's it? You're just going to take me and a woman you never met down with you?"

"You ain't going down. I'm just coming up where you are."

"Zollie. I've always thought I had a way to go as a man to get to where you were. I guess your murdering Bird Fitzsimmons kind of killed off that illusion."

"Guess so, Tom. I don't know. I don't know if I was ever what you thought I was. I'm not now. Just tired. I'm ready for my time. And I couldn't give you most of the drugs anyway. It's long gone. Sold it to hurry up the Belize deal. Things were getting scary. We figured if we could skim a little from Gerrard's shipments, we could be in Belize by now."

"Hall didn't quite make it."

"No."

"Neither did Bird. Why would you do that to someone? I hear he was a pretty good man."

"Bird was okay. About half crazy I guess, but okay. The fact that you been out there screwing his old lady don't make him a saint, though."

"Zollie, you know me. You just about raised me. There are some things nobody's going to say to me."

Zollie said, "You ain't in a real good position to be threatening anybody." I kept looking at him. He said, "You right. Sorry. I know she's a fine lady, she just had a dumbass husband."

"And I'm not screwing her."

"Okay. I said I was wrong."

"Susan thinks Bird found out what you and Hall were up to. She's guessing Hall got drunk and ran his mouth in front of Bird."

"Naw, that wasn't it. You see, me and Hall had a hiding place in the river."

"*In* the river?"

"Listen. You know how Hall loved to scuba dive in the river." I said I did. Zollie said, "Well, Bird spent all his time on the river too. He'd take pictures and go home and paint up what he saw and sell it to whoever was interested. Almost two years ago now, him and Hall got to diving together. You probably heard about that Civil War paddle wheeler that sunk out near the old ferry run. Bird got his gear and dove on that thing and brought up all kinds of stuff. Some gold and silver coins, but mostly just old junk. Hall helped him."

"Hall told me about it."

"Yeah, well, one day Hall was with Bird in that barn where he paints, and Bird tells Hall about a cold water cave he found on the river. Hall said Bird called it the 'River's Womb' 'cause of the narrow tunnel leading into a round cavern that, I guess, seemed like a womb to him. Bird said he never went up in the thing. He used some kind of sonar or something a teacher friend of his loaned him."

"A teacher?"

"Yeah. Some kind of geology teacher up at the college in Auburn."

"Oh."

"Yeah. Anyway, Hall acts like he's not interested, then, the first chance he gets, he goes looking for the cave. I don't know if he had something in mind, or he just thought it was something fun to do. But it took him about a week to find it. You know, you can't see shit in that muddy water. Finally, Hall gets a big underwater flashlight-like-thing and finds the opening. You ought to see that damn thing, Tom. It ain't but maybe three feet across, and you can't see where the hell it comes out, even with the light. It would take someone as crazy as Hall to try to swim up inside the thing."

"Hall wasn't afraid of much."

"Neither one of you boys was ever scared of much, but Hall was always about half crazy on top of it. So, he swims up this little old cave for about thirty feet, and he says it comes out into this big round-top cavern that curves way up above the water level. And this is the part I couldn't believe till I saw it. The cave had these big iron screws in the walls with rings on them. All we could figure was the rebels kept valuables in there during the war."

"I know they kept munitions in river caves up around Selma, but I never heard of anything like that around here."

"Me neither, but when Hall told me about it, I figured we had the perfect place to keep our stuff. The only other person who seemed to know about it was Bird, and I figured even he wouldn't be crazy enough to swim up in there by hisself. So, little by little at night, we strung up nylon ski ropes and bought a bunch of those backyard hammocks made out of nylon rope. We'd roll up the hammocks to get them in the little tunnel and then hang them up from the ski ropes inside the cave. Tom, it's really a big damn place. First we started storing Gerrard's shipments in there until we could unload them on one of his barges. Then, later on, we decided it was a good place to keep the money we were saving up for Belize. Whenever we got up enough money to worry about, we'd put it in plastic freezer bags, then inside garbage bags, and then we'd put it all in old paint cans with half a brick to weigh it down. About every few weeks, we'd go out there at night and put the cans on one of those hammocks."

"So when I got here today, you were out collecting your cans of money."

"No. Not exactly. I been out getting *half* the money. At least, it's about half. I kept a record of every can, how much was in it, and the date when we put it in the cave. But you nosing around has hurried me up a little, so I just took half the cans. The rest was Hall's. Now it's yours. I also left a pretty good load of cocaine in the cave."

"I don't want Hall's drug money, but I need the cocaine to stay alive. Is it enough coke to get Gerrard off my back?"

"Not if he got any idea how much me and Hall really took."

"You think he knows?"

"Once he got on to us, yeah, he could figure it pretty close. But there's enough money for you and your secretary to live large, as Rudy says, down in Central America."

"That's not my idea of a solution, Zollie."

"Well, you might feel that way right now. But from what you say, Gerrard's got you by the short and curlies, and you may be needing to find a new home whether you want to or not. Use it, or don't use it. It's yours. I've told you enough to find it. Go to your girlfriend's house. Bird's maps are still there. But I'm leaving. I hope you have some luck."

Zollie stood up to leave. I said, "You still haven't told me what happened to Bird Fitzsimmons."

Zollie looked uncomfortable. "I thought you would've figured it out by now." He paced the room now while he talked. "I was wrong about Bird. One day he was piddling around the old ferry landing and decided to find out where the cold water cave went, and he brought up a couple of our cans. I guess he probably just about shit hisself. Somebody was looking out after me and Hall, though, 'cause Bird decided to come to his old diving buddy to help him get the rest of the money up fast. He knew Hall wasn't above breaking the law, and he wanted help getting the stuff up without getting caught by the folks who put it there. He said he figured he needed a lookout, and I guess it made him feel safer to have a man like Hall next to him. Anyway, he promised to give Hall twenty percent of the money for helping."

"That was nice of him."

"Yeah, we thought so. And I thought later that maybe Bird was kind of feeling Hall out to see if the money was his, but Hall just kept quiet and listened. Anyway, Bird thought he hit the jackpot. Turns out he didn't exactly report all the gold and jewelry he found on the paddle wheeler either. Can't really blame him. The folks it belonged to was dead, and he'd of just ended up giving most of it to the government. So now he figured he was lucky a second time. Bird figured it was drug money, so, to him, it was fair game. Hall listened to Bird and agreed to help him that night. Around midnight, me and Hall drove over to Bird's place to have a talk with him. He was back in his barn, and goddamn, when I came in he went crazy, yelling at Hall for messing up the deal and screaming about us being low-life drug dealers. I listened to his mouth for a few minutes before I had enough."

"So you just killed him?"

"I hadn't planned to. I started out to just scare him, but Bird was a strong man. He spent his whole life outside, swimming, diving, going places nobody else wanted to go. He came back at me and we tied up pretty good. I figured it was him or me, so I got his arm pinned behind him and did what I had to do."

"Good to know the man who raised me turned into a drug runner and a murderer."

"I know what I am. Hall knew what he was too and couldn't take it. Before he died, he started having nightmares about Bird, waking up screaming next to that white-trash girl he lived with."

"At least Christy was there to help him. She's not headed for Belize with Hall lying dead in the ground."

"Like I said, Tom, I know what I am. Your trouble is, you don't know what Hall was, and you sure don't want to be finding virtue in Christy."

Zollie walked out and came back in with two large duffel bags.

I said, "You got that cardboard box full of cocaine stuffed in one of those?"

Zollie asked, "The big, heavy box in the furnace?"

"Yeah."

"That wasn't coke, Tom. It was full of cash."

"Shit."

"Yeah. I know. You starting to see what I been talking about." As he headed out the door, Zollie said, "I'll call someone to come get you tomorrow. Turning me in won't bring back Bird or Hall, it'll just screw things up worse. By the way, I'm taking your Jeep. I'll leave your stuff in the woods back there—that was pretty pitiful, by the way—and I'll let you know where you can find the Jeep."

Zollie stopped with his hand on the doorknob and said, "Use the money in the cave. Hall died for it." Then he was gone.

An hour later, I was contending with the pins and needles of a dead backside and trying to get comfortable for the night, when a car drove up out front. It was around eight-thirty. Maybe Zollie sent someone early, or maybe Susan had gotten worried and come looking for me. I yelled for help until footsteps echoed on the porch. Zollie would probably send Rudy, who was not one of my favorite people. But at that particular moment, Rudy might get his first wet kiss from a white man if he came through the door and untied me.

I yelled, "Who is it? Rudy?" No answer. "Susan?"

The front door swung open. Rodney Shelton stood in the doorway wrapped in his trademark buckskin coat. And he was smiling.

chapter twenty-two

D URING OUR SHORT acquaintance, I had never seen Rodney look this happy. "Well, well, well, what have we got here?"

"That's original."

"Huh?"

"Nothing. What we have here is a tied-up white guy in his early thirties, who did not kill your cousin." Rodney stopped smiling. Maybe bringing up the murder of his cousin at the warehouse was a bad idea.

Rodney said, "Save your breath. Eddie told me they had to make Toby talk and then kill him to keep you from going to the police. He said you claimed you found something in Hall's stuff that'll send us all to jail. I think you're full of shit."

"And you believe Eddie?"

"I been working with Eddie since high school. Started out driving him around. Worked my way up." All I could think was *up to what?* Over ten or more years Rodney had moved all the way from gofer and driver to gofer and wannabe hired muscle, which didn't exactly seem like the career path of the next Godfather. I kept these thoughts to myself. Rodney went on while I won my internal, one-sided argument. He said, "Eddie's never been anything but good to me. But you. I've known you a week, and you tried to kill me two times so far."

"Rodney, if you'll think back, you might remember that it was *you* who tried to murder me twice, and I had to defend myself." It was pretty clear that he had not come to rescue me. The next best thing was to keep him talking as long as possible. Maybe someone would stop by. If not, well, better to die in twenty minutes than two.

Rodney self-consciously furrowed his eyebrows and lowered his voice to a dangerous whisper. "I made the mistake of coming after you drunk the first time. The second time in New Orleans, I wasn't trying to kill you. If I had been"—he paused for dramatic effect—"you'd be dead now."

Staying alive was one thing, but if I was going to die anyhow, there was no reason to listen to any more of this shit. I said, "Rodney. In New Orleans? Were you holding yourself back before or after you puked and fell in it?"

Rodney used some very unbecoming language and, as he walked forward, pulled a huge revolver out of his shoulder holster. He backhanded me across the cheekbone with his free hand and pressed the muzzle of his revolver to my forehead. It looked like it was time to go. No need to make friends now. I said, "You hit like a faggot."

Rodney smiled. "Goodbye, asshole."

I waited for the explosion. Time moved deliberately. I had always heard that, if you survive, the fear comes later. Now, I thought only of whether I would hear or feel the bullet before it ripped apart my frontal lobes. A gun fired—not as loudly as I expected—and Rodney staggered and fell back onto his rump. He sat upright for a full second or two, staring past me with the flat dull eyes of a cadaver. I saw the ugly hole through the bridge of his nose before he rolled backward in a lifeless free-fall that ended with a sickening thud as his punctured skull hit the hardwood floor.

Something like shock blotted out everything except Rodney's corpse and my own unfocused fear. Floods of adrenaline flowed and quivered through my hands and stomach, while on the floor at my feet, blood flowed out of the jagged hole in Rodney's nose, soaking his hair and building an expanding circle around his head like a dark red halo.

Sheriff Nixon walked in the front door and stood over the body. I couldn't tell how much time had passed since the shot. I hadn't even thought about who fired it. I just felt sick and numb. Nixon said, "You okay?" I couldn't answer. "Tom! Are you all right? Do you need a doctor or an ambulance?"

"No, no I don't think so. Just feel kind of numb."

"You're in shock. Here." Nixon walked over and untied me from the chair. Pulling my arm behind his neck, he helped me out onto the porch and told me to lie down. He walked inside, then came out with a glass of water and a cushion from the sofa. He slid the pillow under my head, sat the water next to my hand, and pulled a porch chair around and put my feet up. He said, "Stay like that. Sip some of that water if you can. I've got to call this in and get some people out here." A few minutes later, Nixon came back out and spread one of Zollie's quilts over me and sat down to wait for his deputies and the coroner to arrive. He asked, "You feeling better?"

"Yeah. I don't know what happened to me. I didn't even think I was that scared. As dumb as that sounds."

"Doesn't sound dumb. I saw it in 'Nam. Once a man accepts that he's going to die, he gets almost peaceful. What's really happening is your body's putting you in shock." A patrol car turned into the driveway. Its revolving emergency lights swept over the surrounding woods, intermittently staining tree trunks, shrubbery, and the house with a blue wash. Nixon stood up and gazed out at the patrol car. He continued to look away from me as he spoke. "You showed a lot in there. Don't worry about it hitting you hard now. If it didn't, you'd be a fool." Nixon walked down the steps and across the yard to talk with the deputy.

In addition to the crime-scene people, Nixon also had called Dr. Pearson to come out. While the sheriff and his deputies worked inside, the doctor hovered over me, prodding, poking, and checking temperature and blood pressure. He gave me a shot of something in my shoulder and said, "You're going to be fine. I'll ask Sheriff Nixon to go easy on you tonight. You need rest. Stay in bed as much as you can over the next couple of days." As he stood to leave, Dr. Pearson said, "By the way, somebody did a good job on your head. Keep those butterfly bandages on tonight, and come by the office tomorrow. Doesn't look like you'll need stitches, unless you're worried about having a scar under your hair."

Nixon came out around ten and asked me where my Jeep was. I said, "Zollie's got it."

"Did Zollie tie you up like that?"

I had thought about how to handle my run-in with Zollie. Being tied to a chair gives one time to think, since there's not much else one can do. My first instinct had been to bury Zollie, telling Nixon everything I knew about Bird's murder. I even fantasized about testifying against Zollie in court—sending him away to spend the rest of his life on a work gang. As it always does, though, the anger passed, and, having cleansed the emotional trash from my thoughts, I endeavored to apply a little logic and perspective.

If Zollie were captured, he would likely trade the cocaine and the money in the cave for whatever leniency he could get. In which case, any possible leverage I had for dealing with Gerrard would be gone.

I also recognized that Zollie was harboring more resentment than I ever imagined. Zollie had loved Hall and me on some level, but, as I sat immobilized in his living room chair, I had had time to think back on all the mornings when Zollie left his own children at home while he took Hall or me hunting, spending the time with us that a man usually spends with his own kids. I remembered all the Friday and Saturday nights when he drove us to movies and ball games and parties, all the weekends he spent teaching us to shoot and fish and drive a straight shift and everything else Sam wanted us to learn while he put in eighty-hour weeks at the mill. I thought of all the time Zollie was paid to be with us instead of home with his own children and his wife, who left him when I was fourteen. We weren't responsible for his wife leaving, but a man blames a lot and carries a lot of baggage when his home life falls apart. For the first time in my life, I understood that while Zollie had been a friend to me—maybe the best friend I would ever have—to Sam and at times to Zollie, he was just hired help.

Now, Zollie refused to lose everything to save my career. Instead, he gave me half the money he and Hall made together. He gave me enough money to take care of Kelly and to move to another country and live out *his* dream. Just like when I was a kid, Zollie had looked out for me. Only this time, he had done it his way. I owed him for all those years. No matter if he was paid to spend his life with us instead of his own family, he had done it with kindness and patience and intelligence, and most of the things I could do well in life were because of him, because he took the time to teach me. Most of the bad stuff came from somewhere else.

Zollie thought he had sacrificed enough of himself to the McInnes clan. I would not turn him in to Sheriff Nixon. I just didn't know what to tell Susan Fitzsimmons.

Nixon said, "I asked you if Zollie was the one who tied you up."

"Sorry. I'm still a little foggy," I said. "No, or, I guess I should say, I don't know. Zollie borrowed my Jeep this afternoon to run up to Montgomery for some shopping. I was waiting around here, doing some thinking about how to handle things, about what you said this afternoon, things like that. Somewhere around mid-afternoon, I walked through the hallway on the way to the kitchen to get something to eat, and somebody popped me with a nightstick or something and"—I motioned at my head wound—"gave me this."

"You didn't see who it was?"

"Nope. Just woke up after dark and sat there until I heard someone drive up. I started yelling for help, and Rodney came in."

"Yeah. I saw that much."

I asked, "What were you doing here, hanging around outside the window?"

Nixon said, "I told you. Sam asked me to keep an eye on you."

"And you just happened to pop up just in time to shoot Rodney Shelton?"

"I thought you'd be glad I did." I thanked him. He looked at me for a few seconds and said, "When you didn't show up for our meeting, I tried to call you at the Fitzsimmons place. Mrs. Fitzsimmons said you had gone to see an old friend. Something about the whole thing bothered me. So, I started going through the two files I pulled for you—Zollie's file and the file on Fitzsimmons' murder." Nixon stopped talking. He was looking into my eyes, trying to find something. He went on. "Kind of looked from the files like Zollie may have killed Bird. That fellow Zollie killed thirty years ago had his throat cut almost exactly the same way Bird did." Nixon paused again. "You knew about that, didn't you, Tom?"

There was no use denying my suspicions. Susan Fitzsimmons already knew that much and more about evidence pointing to Zollie. I said, "Yeah, I knew. That's one of the things I came out here to talk to Zollie about."

"And after you told him your suspicions, he just happened to borrow your Jeep for a long drive. And you just happened to end up whacked on the head and tied up in Zollie's living room. I'd say that's an interesting coincidence, wouldn't you?"

"When you put it that way, I guess it is. It just seemed more likely to me that Rodney hit me and tied me up. He said he'd get even about my shooting at him when he broke into Sam's house that night. I thought he probably wanted me to wake up so he could enjoy slapping me around before I got dead. Of course, like I said, I couldn't see who hit me."

"And I guess Zollie denied everything about Bird?"

"Yep. I told him about the cut throat, you know, the way it looked like someone had stood behind Bird and cut his throat like a wounded deer. Zollie pointed out that half the men in the county cut at least one deer's throat that way every hunting season. He said I would probably be hard-pressed to find a grown man in South Alabama who didn't know how to use a knife that way."

Nixon said, "He had a point."

I said, "Yeah, that's what I thought."

Nixon looked up as a couple of EMTs crossed the porch and started down the steps. Between them, they carried a white stretcher bearing a black body bag filled with Rodney Shelton's lumpy remains.

Nixon called one of his deputies over and, looking at me instead of the person he was addressing, said, "Zollie Willingham is on the road in Mr. McInnes' vehicle. Wilbur, I want you to stay out here until midnight. If Willingham is not back by then, I want an APB out all over the state. And I want you to call me by twelve-fifteen to tell me you've done it."

The deputy said, "Yes, sir," and went to help the EMTs load the corpse into a waiting ambulance. The emergency vehicle pulled slowly out of the dirt driveway and headed for the hospital where Dr. Pearson would stay up late that night performing an autopsy.

Nixon dropped me by my parents' house. I assured Mom that everything was over and that Hall's killer was dead, and I let her believe I was talking about Rodney. She seemed relieved. Sam and I went down to his study to talk.

Sam said, "Now, tell me everything," and I did—everything except the parts about the stowed drugs, the cans of money, the River's Womb, and Zollie killing Bird. It doesn't sound like there was much left to tell, but the story took most of an hour. Sam listened until I was done, never uttering a word or exhibiting any emotion. When I was through, he asked, "Are you going to be able to get out of this?"

"I don't have much choice. So, yeah, I'll get out. I've got good people helping me, and Gerrard's got a bunch of morons working for him." I tried to sound convincing.

Sam said, "What do you need from me?"

"I need two sets of scuba equipment, masks, fins, wet suits, weight belts, tanks, everything. And I need some explosives."

"Why?"

"If I'm still around, I'll tell you when it's all over."

"What kind of explosives?"

"Nothing fancy. Just enough to . . . I'll tell you what, figure how much dynamite it would take to blow a stubborn old stump out of the ground and multiply it by about four."

"You got somebody who knows how to use it?"

If Joey hadn't picked up that particular skill in the Navy, he'd know someone who had. No matter what strange knowledge or ability might be needed, Joey always seemed to know someone who could do the job and keep quiet about it. I said, "I've got somebody. I just need for you to get the diving equipment and the explosives as quietly as possible and then forget you ever saw them. And one set of the diving gear needs to fit a man who wears about a fifty regular."

Sam said, "Damn. Is he as big as Zero?"

Sam was referring to the mill supervisor who had been in his office last week. Zero had ducked his head to keep from banging it on the door frame when he left. I said, "Just as big, but not round like Zero. This guy's built like me, only he's half a foot taller."

"Glad he's on our side."

"Me too."

Sam said, "Go get some sleep. I've got to get some friends out of bed."

"I can't go to sleep yet. I need the keys to your Blazer." Sam started to say something, then pulled open a desk drawer and tossed me a spare set of keys.

He said, "You'll have what you need by noon tomorrow. Call after then." As I left, Sam was thumbing through a leather address book on his desk.

Just as he had promised, Zollie had deposited everything on the ground next to the spot where the Jeep had been parked. I loaded my duffel bag, laptop computer, portable printer, briefcase, and other odds and ends into the Blazer and started for Susan's farm. The River's Womb waited to be found on Bird's maps. I could get some sleep if I could just find the location on the map; then I would at least have a concrete objective in the morning. On the way out Whiskey Run, I turned down Cedar and stopped at Christy's cabin to tell her as much as I thought I safely could. At least, she deserved to know that Hall's killer was dead, and I needed to smooth things over after the confrontation between her and Zollie at the lake house. After all, if I couldn't get out of trouble within the next nine days, I might not be around to tell her anything.

Christy answered the door wearing a white lace nightgown that would have looked right on only one woman in a hundred. It was straight out of Victoria's Secret, and it was the kind of nightgown that I would have guessed Christy would choose.

I asked, "Are you alone?"

Christy said, "You look like hell."

"Been a tough night. Can I come in?" She said sure, and I walked into the great room. The fireplace was cold, the room was well lighted, and David Letterman was rambling through his top-ten list on the television screen. Christy seemed more reserved than usual, which was understandable since I more or less threw her out of the lake house the last time I saw her. I said, "I wanted to bring you up to speed on what's happening with the investigation." Christy just nodded at me, then walked over and flicked off the television. Her nightgown was shaped like a one-piece bathing suit with a short gown over it. All of it was lace. She looked like every thirteen-year-old boy's late-night pubescent fantasy. "I also wanted to apologize if I was abrupt the other night at the lake house. It had been a lousy day, and refereeing a fight between you and Zollie wasn't what I needed right then. I hope we're still friends."

Christy walked over and stood facing me. She smelled like soap. "I'd say we are, at the very least, friends. Now come back to the bathroom and wash up. You look like you've been in a car wreck."

"Thanks. But I don't have time."

"You said you were going to bring me up to speed on the investigation."

"I am, but—"

"Then you can sit still and let me clean those cuts while you're doing it." Christy took me by the hand and led me down the hall and through her bedroom into the master bath. She motioned at a small bench in front of a built-in vanity next to the sink. "Sit there."

I sat down and looked in the mirror. No wonder she wanted me to get cleaned up. She probably couldn't stand to look at me. Blood had caked the hair above my left ear and dribbled thick stains down onto my shoulder and chest. Rodney's backhand had raised a mouse under my eye, and I already had a bruise on my forehead from the glancing blow delivered by Eddie's overweight welterweight in our fight at the beach. I said, "Would you buy a used car from this man?"

Christy smiled and opened a louvered door in the wall behind me. She pulled out cotton balls, alcohol, gauze, and antibiotic cream and stacked them all on the vanity. I wasn't crazy about her fooling around with the cut over my ear, but she seemed to know what she was doing, and she had the soft, gentle touch that God gives only to women. She said, "What have you found out?"

"Oh. I'm sorry. I was staring at myself in the mirror. I didn't know until right now that I looked like this."

"I told you you were a mess."

"You were right," I said. "Okay. I've been in contact with some of the men Hall worked with around the state. Through them, I was able to find out who killed Hall."

Christy stopped working on my cuts and met my eyes in the mirror. The blood drained out of her face. All she said was, "Who?"

I almost told her and thought better of it. I thought she could probably keep her mouth shut, but knowing that kind of information about Gerrard's operation or his people was not a particularly healthy situation. I said, "I know this isn't fair, but I can't tell you. At least, I can't tell you now." Christy started to say something, and I cut her off. "I *can* tell you, though, that the man who killed Hall is dead."

"Did you . . . ?"

"No. I didn't kill him. But I know he's dead. No question about that." Christy looked over at the wall, then turned back and started cleaning my cuts again. Tough lady. I said, "Did you know Zollie was in business with Hall?"

She looked startled. "Sure. That's not who's dead, is it? There's not much love lost between Zollie and me, but I know he didn't kill Hall."

"No. It wasn't Zollie. He's fine, but why didn't you tell me about their being in business together?"

"I honestly thought you already knew it, Tom. I mean, it wasn't common knowledge, but the people close to Hall all knew it. I just figured—"

"I wasn't exactly close to Hall the last few years."

"Sorry. I guess I knew that. I wasn't trying to bring up something, uh, uncomfortable. Look, you started out to find out what happened. Sounds like you did it, and it sounds like the killer got what he had coming. You've done more than anyone else would."

I looked at her reflection in the mirror, then glanced at my own. She had done a good job cleaning my wounds. I said, "Well, at least I don't look like something you'd find lying by the side of the road anymore."

Christy laughed and squeezed my shoulders. "Unfortunately, you still smell like it."

"That's not very polite."

"Neither is the way you smell." Christy walked over and turned on the hot water in the shower. "Get undressed."

"Christy, I've stayed too long already. I can't."

"What you can't do is go anywhere or take care of anything smelling like that."

"Christy . . ."

She dropped her short gown and peeled the lace bodysuit down over her hips and kicked it away with her toes. "You're not going to leave me standing here naked all by myself, are you?"

This was not going the way I had planned. I said, "I'm afraid I am. Like I said, Christy, I've got to go. People are depending on me." I knew that leaving her standing there in her birthday suit wasn't exactly a kind thing to do. As I stood to leave, I said, "Look, Christy, the man who killed Hall is dead, but this isn't over yet. I've got about two weeks to find something, or there's going to be hell to pay. Until then, I can't think about anything else."

Christy picked up her gown and pulled it on. She walked with me to the door without speaking. I said goodnight and stepped out onto the porch. She looked upset, but I had other things to worry about. I walked away, climbed into Sam's Blazer, and pointed the headlights in the direction of Susan Fitzsimmons' farm, where, I hoped, the map of the River's Womb waited to be discovered.

chapter twenty-three

TEN MINUTES LATER, Susan Fitzsimmons' farmhouse floated into view across the dam. Susan was sitting on the front steps, backlit by yellow light pouring into the night through her open front door. It was after midnight and black in the shadow of the little carport-barn where I parked the Blazer. Susan watched me approach through dark clusters of rosebushes. When I stepped into the light at the foot of the steps, she gasped. "You're hurt."

"I'm okay."

She was genuinely distressed. "What happened, Tom?"

"A lot's happened. I'll tell you as much as I can later." My throat felt dry. "Right now, you need to know that I ran into Bird's killer at Zollie's house this afternoon." Susan stood slowly. She descended the steps until she stopped in front of me on the brick walkway and I was looking down into her sunburned face. I went on. "Nixon showed up as I was getting in real trouble and killed a man named Rodney Shelton. The coroner's got him." It wasn't exactly a lie. I never said Rodney killed Bird, just that I ran into Bird's killer and that Nixon shot Rodney. This, I thought, is why people hate lawyers.

Tears filled her eyes and began rolling down her cheeks. Susan reached out and hugged me hard around my chest. She managed to say "Thank you" before burying her face in my shirt. Her crying came in spasms as she finally let go of three months of hurt and anger. As each sob racked her small body, I felt more and more despicable, and I knew that I would never want to see or speak with Zollie again. I put my arms around Susan and tried hard to believe that it was for the best, that she could get on with her life now. Then, forcing myself to look beyond emotion and stay focused, I began repeating another sentence over and over in my mind like a mantra: *Kelly could still die.*

Before Susan could regain enough control to ask, I said, "I'm sorry, Susan, but I can't tell you any more than I have. Maybe I can some-day, but not now. Right now, I need your help." She had stopped sob-bing. She pulled back to look into my face. "Susan, I need to get into Bird's studio. I need his maps to stay alive and to keep a friend alive."

"Why?"

"I can't explain now. I just need your help."

Susan said, "Anything. Anything you need. You don't know how it feels for all this to finally be over."

I felt like I was being stabbed in the chest. It hurt to breathe. "Come on," I said. "We've got work to do." I took Susan's hand and led her around the side of the house toward Bird's studio. I had already purchased my ticket to hell. No need stopping now.

Susan unlocked the barn, punched her code into the control pad, and switched on fluorescent lights. The stacks of Bird's lush paintings lining the walls were overwhelming, just as they had been the first time I entered this old barn with Susan. It wasn't the unexpected number of finished works that shocked me before; it was the paintings them-selves. Zollie had murdered a lot with his knife that night.

The studio proper occupied about two-thirds of the barn. Tucked under the old hayloft at one end was Bird's makeshift office, which he had cordoned off with furniture and equipment creating a distinct work space apart from the studio. The floor of the loft made up the ceiling of the office and helped set it apart from the rest of the barn. Susan took me to a back corner of the office and pulled open a wide, flat drawer full of maps. The drawer was one of many stacked verti-cally into a map cabinet four feet wide and about as tall. She showed me an index to the maps that Bird had organized into a three-ring notebook. Each page of the index was protected by clear plastic sheeting. I was surprised. Bird had been anal retentive enough to be a lawyer.

Susan excused herself and went to the house, where I expected she would cry or drink or scream or whatever she did to make it through life's bad stuff. I couldn't think about that now. I started with the index. Twenty minutes later, I had scanned most of the sheets in the binder. There was no mention of the River's Womb, just technical map coordinates occasionally supplemented with Bird's physical descriptions of the areas. I was running a finger down the last couple of pages when Susan came in with a plate full of sandwiches and a couple of beers. I said, "Bless you."

Susan said, "You don't look much like you had time for a leisurely dinner."

"So much has happened since I left here this afternoon. I hadn't even thought about it. Thank you."

"Sure. Come on over and eat. We can look through that stuff for the rest of the night if you want."

The lunch with Susan seemed like it had happened days before. We each had polished off two sandwiches, and I was politely refraining from grabbing the last remaining sandwich off the plate between us. Susan noticed and smiled. "Go ahead. Two's my limit. That one's for you. You kind of look like someone who would eat three or four sandwiches at a sitting."

I said, "Thanks a lot," but I reached for the sandwich anyhow.

"Don't be silly. Anybody can see you're not fat. You're just, ah, big." I looked up, and she added, "In a good way."

"I feel so much better now." I asked, "You ever heard Bird mention a place called the River's Womb?"

"Sure." I put down the sandwich. She said, "It's some kind of cave with ice-cold water. Bird said it flows out of a cavern and empties out into the river."

"Where is it?"

"No idea. Is it important?"

I broke off a corner of the sandwich and popped it into my mouth.

Knowing how much to tell different people was getting complicated. But it seemed right to tell Susan most of what Sam knew; plus she needed to know about the cave and how important it could be. She needed to know, or at least I needed her to know, that my life depended on finding the River's Womb.

I said, "Hall and Zollie weren't just in business for themselves. They worked as a link in a cocaine distribution network for a well-educated sociopath in Birmingham, who, by the way, has offered to let me live if I can find some drugs that Hall and Zollie stole from him. I found out from Zollie that the stuff's hidden in this cave that Bird called the River's Womb." Susan opened her mouth to say something, and I cut her off. "Zollie can't tell us anything. He's gone. He left the state this afternoon. In a few days he'll be somewhere in Central or South America."

Susan nodded and asked, "You let him go?"

"It wasn't up to me to let him. He gave me this," I said, pointing to the cut over my ear, "and took off. I tried to stop him at the time. Now, for a lot of reasons, I'd just as soon let him go. We got Hall's killer, and earlier tonight his cousin, Rodney Shelton, caught a bullet in the nose from Sheriff Nixon, who, by the way, doesn't know that Zollie's the one who hit me." I broke off another piece of sandwich. "It's all connected. Like I said, I can't tell you everything yet. You just need to know that you were right about Bird. He was not tied up in the drug business. He just stumbled into something and got in the way of some dangerous men. The same kind of men, by the way, who are going to kill me and my secretary in exactly nine days if I can't find their merchandise."

"Go to the police. Maybe not Sheriff Nixon, but the state police could do something. You can't get mixed up in supplying drugs to gangsters. Not even once."

"Susan, it's not that simple. This Gerrard character lives in a mansion in Mountain Brook and contributes more money to politicians every four years than most people make in a lifetime. Calling the cops won't do anything but get the guy's lawyers busy and get me dead." Susan looked doubtful. I said, "Hey, I'm the smart one. Remember?"

She smiled. "For now, I've got to find the drugs. After that—after I know I'm going to live and my secretary's going to live—I can figure out how to keep from getting in any deeper."

"What's your secretary got to do with it?"

"These guys already kidnapped and almost raped her." Now Susan cussed. I said, "I was able to call their hand and get her back. I said I'd go to the cops no matter what might happen if they didn't let her go. They decided from that that Kelly meant something to me. So they threw her murder in as a little added incentive to get me moving."

"Tom, Hall's killing you from his grave. He's already been responsible for three deaths. Don't be the next one."

"Hall's not killing me. The men who killed Hall are doing it, or at least trying to do it. And believe me, I don't plan to be next. Now, I've told you more than just about anyone else, including my father. If you go to the police with this, *you* will be the one killing me."

Susan got up and walked over to gaze at Bird's thirty-foot scroll map. She said, "Then I guess we better get busy and find this scum's drugs."

Susan went back to the map drawers while I started at one end of Bird's handmade map and began reading every block-printed notation and abbreviation on the thing, searching for anything that even came close to looking like "the River's Womb." When I was about half through, Susan joined me. By 4 A.M., we were finished, and we were no closer to finding the River's Womb, if it existed, than we had been when we started.

Under the map, about a third of the way from one end, Bird had pushed a double bed against the wall. It was covered with a tie-dyed spread—probably from his undergraduate art-major days at Vandy— and either he or Susan had tossed a half dozen pillows on top to make it look something like an oversized daybed. Bird probably had crashed there after long nights in the studio.

Susan stretched out on Bird's anachronistic, psychedelic bedspread to rest. I placed a call to Joey in Birmingham. Joey sounded wide awake when he answered the phone, but Joey always sounded wide awake.

"Joey?"

"Tom. What's going on?"

"I need you to come to Coopers Bend, if you can. I've got a lead on where Gerrard's drugs are, and I need some help getting them."

"Fine, but I haven't found out that much here yet. Just been one day—hell, less than one day."

"Got anything?"

"Sure. Ran a credit check, went by the courthouse and checked out Gerrard's car, his property, lawsuits, shit like that. And I had a look at his house, but that's about it. I just got back from digging in Eddie Pappas' trash, and that went pretty well. Got his checking account number off a canceled check, and got one of his credit card numbers off a receipt."

"Sounds like a pretty good day to me."

"Yeah. But that's all shit anybody could find out. I need a few more days to get into Gerrard's operations, find out who's close to him, maybe find out if there's something or somebody he cares about more than the drugs."

"I know we need to do that, Joey. But I don't see how I'm going to get the stuff up without some help. I'd appreciate it if you could come down in the morning."

"I'll do it. But what's this shit about getting the stuff *up*? Is it in a frigging hole in the ground or under the water or what?"

"Yes."

"Shit. You're getting to be a pain in the ass, Tom. I'll see you around noon tomorrow."

"One more thing, Joey."

"What? You gonna ask me for my left nut now?"

"I need someone who can handle dynamite. You know anything about it?"

"About enough to be dangerous."

"Do you know someone who can show up on short notice and keep his mouth shut?"

"Do you need him tomorrow?"

"No."

"Then I'll think about it, and we can talk over lunch tomorrow. I know somebody. I just don't know if he's available. Probably be able to find out between now and tomorrow, though."

"Thanks, Joey. Get some sleep."

Joey must have picked up on something in my voice. He paused a couple of seconds and said, "You okay, Tom?"

"I'm fine, but Rodney Shelton is real dead."

"Good for you. Did the world a favor."

"I didn't kill him. The local sheriff managed to put a bullet through Rodney's nose as Rodney was just about to kill me."

"You're a strange man, Tom. You never actually kill anyone, but everyone who pisses you off seems to wind up dead. You've got an interesting talent there."

"Don't worry. You're on my side, remember?"

Joey said, "Damn straight," and hung up.

Susan snored quietly on the tie-dyed bed. Her shirt had twisted and ridden up to her chest, baring her tanned stomach. The shirt fell apart at the center of her bra where a small pink rose decorated the V where the lace cups came together. I walked over to Bird's paint-stained sink and splashed water on my face. I sucked a mouthful of water from the faucet and went to have one last look at the map—this time looking for a line drawing that might represent a thin cave leading to an underground cavern. Five minutes later, I gave up, stretched out next to Susan, and fell asleep.

A little after ten, the sun was far enough above the trees to angle through Bird's huge skylight and hit the psychedelic bed. Bright sunlight stung my eyes and Susan's head felt warm and heavy on my shoulder. Her right arm was thrown across my chest. I had no illusions. It wasn't me. In her sleep, Susan had moved into the same comforting position she had snuggled into when she shared her bed with Bird. I lay still looking around, trying not to disturb her, and hoping she wouldn't be embarrassed when she awoke.

Sunlight brought the studio to life, bouncing off rows of river paintings, vibrant blobs of splattered paint, rolls of white canvas, sable brushes with slender wooden handles, and, above it all, swirls of dust that danced in the light and spiraled up toward dark timbers and the bright skylight.

I rubbed my eyes with my free hand and looked up at Bird's hand-made map on the wall above the bed. The thing might never do me any good, but it really was beautiful with its pen-and-ink sketches of shells and paddle wheelers and skiffs and ghosts and mythological figures. *Damn.* I gently rolled Susan off my shoulder and sat up on my knees to get a closer look. There on the map, over the bed I had slept in for the past five hours, was a sketch of *Venus de Milo*. On the area between her navel and her pubis, Bird had drawn a north-wind face—the kind you see on antique American headboards and servers. The ghoulish face with rounded cheeks, squinting eyes, and a mouth pouring forth a gust of cold air sat precisely over the marble womb of Venus.

Susan had stirred when I rolled her away. Now, she said, "What is it?"

"I think it's a way to stay alive."

chapter twenty-four

I GRABBED A QUICK SHOWER in Susan's guest bath and headed back out to the studio to study Bird's map. Deciding I would be taking my life in my hands if I cut out the relevant section—not to mention defacing a work of art—I first tried to reproduce the map freehand on one of Bird's old sketch pads. The result vaguely resembled the scroll map, if you didn't look too closely and if you had the scroll in front of you to compare. It did not seem likely to lead anyone anywhere, however.

Taking a more logical approach, I located a Corps of Engineers map in the office cabinet and sketched the cave and the cavern on the printed map, using the engineers' grid to produce an accurate, albeit artistically unappealing, drawing of the cave. I finished as the sun neared its apex over the skylight and warmed the studio enough to stick the fresh shirt to my back. After rolling up my new map, I was walking across the back lawn when car tires crunched on the gravel drive in front. Joey pulled up in a generic American rental car as I rounded the corner and stepped onto the front porch. I said, "Thanks for coming."

Joey said, "I'm hungry."

So much for greetings. We went inside, got Susan and Joey introduced to each other, and built some sandwiches at the counter. Susan joined us on the front porch to eat lunch and to help bring Joey up to speed on the location of the River's Womb. And Susan tried not to look at Joey. She wasn't successful. I'm so used to him that I sometimes forget the effect he has on people. Not only is he somewhere between six-six and six-eight, but Kelly also has mentioned on more than one occasion that he's not a bad-looking man. And, since Susan is not a bad-looking woman, Joey's face had that immobile look of feigned intelligence that men adopt when someone of the fairer sex is checking them out. I tried to ignore all the body language going on and just get the story straight.

When I finished, Joey said, "Let's go."

I said, "Soon as I call Sam," and went inside to make the call. Sam, as always, had been as good as his word. Diving equipment and explosives were waiting in the attic of the lake house.

I had pulled on shorts, running shoes, and a New Orleans Jazz Festival T-shirt that morning in preparation for the dive. Joey was wearing a suit and tie. Back on the porch, I said "Ready to go whenever you are."

Joey walked out to his rental, popped the trunk, and pulled out a faded green duffel. "Where can I change?" Susan showed him upstairs; then she came back out and sat on the steps.

Susan said, "Tom, I used to do some diving with Bird. I could help you."

"The best way for you to help is to stay here and think about where we can hide the stuff we fish out of the river."

"No need to think about it. There's an old fifties-style bomb shelter out in back of the barn. Bird said the realtor who sold him the place didn't mention it, and no one else around here ever seemed to know it was there. He found it one day when he was bush-hogging the kudzu back there. He got the hatch open and working, then let the kudzu grow back. I think he liked having a secret hiding place. You know, one of those little-boy things that men do."

"I guess." I said, "Sounds like a good place, anyhow. I need something else from you too, if you don't mind."

"Like I said last night, anything you need."

Her misplaced gratitude brought back the now familiar stabbing pain in my chest. I said, "I understand Bird had a boat. Sam's got one at the lake house, but I'd rather not be seen around the cave in it. It's one of those big fishing rigs."

"Well, Bird's isn't that small, either. It's an open Boston Whaler, maybe fifteen feet. But it sits pretty low in the water. Whatever. You're welcome to use it if you want. Better take a can of gas though."

"Where is it?"

"It's docked at a friend's house on the river. I can draw you a map and call Mr. Simpkins to let him know you're coming so he won't call the police."

Christy had spoken to someone named Simpkins at Jimmy Carpenter's restaurant. I asked, "Is he a bent-over little man who walks with a cane?"

"Yeah, that's him." She said, "Bird's tools and some of his diving stuff are in a locked chest on the boat. I don't have a key. Feel free to break it open. It should have two or three diving lights inside. I don't know how much diving you've done in the river."

"Some, a long time ago."

"Then you know you're going to need the lights. You won't be able to find your elbow down there without them."

"Thanks, Susan. Can you stay by the phone in case something goes wrong?"

"Glad to."

Joey came out dressed in the same kind of clothes I had picked for the day. I filled him in on my conversation with Susan while she drew a map to Mr. Simpkins' house. Joey transferred a handgun and a long diving knife to the Blazer, and we headed for the lake house. We were halfway to town on Whiskey Run when Joey said, "You know we're being followed?"

"No. As a matter of fact, I didn't."

"One car about a hundred yards back. A five- or six-year-old Camaro."

"How can you tell?"

"He's tracking your speed. Staying the same distance away. Make a couple of turns, you'll see."

We took the bypass around town and turned down the road that passed by the sawmill. Our Camaro did the same. At the mill entrance, I turned in and the Camaro went past. The driver did look familiar, but if you grow up in a town this size almost everyone does. I stopped in front of the office building and ran in to see Sam. He wasn't in. Ginny loaned me the keys to a company pickup.

Joey and I took a few minutes to decide how to handle our new friend in the Camaro. I drove out in the pickup, followed by Joey in the Blazer. At the exit onto the main road, I could see the Camaro a couple hundred yards up, parked next to a vegetable stand. I turned in the direction of fresh produce and passed the Camaro while the driver pretended to be interested in a basket of yellow squash. Joey turned in the opposite direction. Two minutes later, the Camaro appeared in my rearview mirror. I circled around and led him back toward town. He kept coming. North of town, I turned into the gravel road to Zollie's house and, when I knew the Camaro driver could see me, jammed the accelerator to the floor. Just past Zollie's driveway, the road made a hard right and crossed an old creosote bridge. I slammed on brakes and stopped diagonally across the road, blocking the bridge. Five seconds later, the driver of the Camaro took the curve sideways, slammed on brakes when he saw the blocked bridge, and spun in a complete circle before stopping thirty feet from Sam's truck. It seemed to take a couple of seconds for him to regain his equilibrium after the spinout. When he did, the back tires spun hard against red gravel, throwing orange clouds of dust into the trees, and he tried to do a one-eighty and get away. It was a nice move. If the Blazer hadn't been blocking the road behind him, he would have made it.

The driver slammed on brakes, grabbed a cellular phone inside the car, and started punching buttons. Joey and I hit the gravel at the same time. I got to the Camaro first and yanked on the locked door. Joey ran up, swept me out of the way with one giant paw, and bashed out the side window with his handgun. The guy looked horrified. Joey reached in, grabbed the phone, and put it to his ear while he held the gun on our new prisoner.

After listening for a few seconds, Joey hit the off button and said, "He called the Sheriff's Department. It was just some operator answering the phone. I don't think he had time to get through, but we better get him out of here fast in case I had a good actress on the other end."

The driver looked scared to death. But, as Joey finished speaking, indignation finally overcame fear and the driver said, "I'm a deputy sheriff. You know what you're doing? I'm a goddamn deputy sheriff."

Joey reached in, unlocked the door, and said, "Get out." The deputy didn't move. Joey grabbed him by the shirtfront and tossed him into the road, then held the handgun out toward me. "Here, take this." I did. Joey brushed glass off the seat and climbed into the Camaro. It was still idling. He carefully turned the car around and pointed the front bumper diagonally across the road at the creek bottom below the wooden bridge. Just then, the deputy figured out what was happening.

He started screaming, "That's my personal car. I didn't do nothing to y'all. You can't wreck my car." Joey cut the wheels toward a stand of young pines next to the creek and got out. Our deputy was frantic. "Goddamnit, I didn't do nothing. Please, don't . . ." Joey gave the car a shove, and its overly tuned engine took it down the hill where it disappeared into the pines and brush lining the creek. The deputy was speechless.

Joey took the gun and motioned for me to get back in the pickup. He shoved the deputy into the Blazer and made room for me to pass. I drove into Zollie's driveway and parked under a pecan tree behind the house. Joey and I took our guest inside and tied him to my favorite chair. He started up again, "You can't do this. I didn't do nothing. Sheriff just asked me to keep an eye on you. I wasn't trying to do you no harm."

I said, "I don't know who you are. Some bad people are after me, and as far as I know, you could be one of them."

"My badge is in my pocket. Come on, at least look in my goddamn pocket."

"Wouldn't mean anything. Could be a fake badge, or you could be a crooked cop. Either way I'm screwed. We're just going to leave you here for a while until we know it's safe. If you are a deputy, you got nothing to worry about. The only way you're going to get hurt is if you try something stupid."

Joey came up with a pair of socks he'd found to use as a gag. The deputy was screaming. Veins stood out on his temples. "Goddamnit, you can't do this. If I don't call the desk every hour on the hour, Sheriff's gonna come looking for me. You're messing up."

Joey stuffed one white sock into the deputy's mouth and tied the gag in place with the other one. The deputy started squealing through the gag. Joey said, "Those socks came out of a chest of drawers upstairs. You keep fussing, and I'm gonna go get a pair out of the dirty clothes." The deputy got very quiet, and we walked out to the back porch. Joey asked, "You think he's telling the truth about checking in?"

I said, "Probably. From what I've seen, Nixon keeps his people on a pretty short leash."

"Shit. It's about one-twenty now. That gives us forty minutes before he's supposed to call. Ten minutes after that, somebody'll get worried and try to call him on this cellular phone I've got in my pocket. So, we've got maybe fifty or fifty-five minutes before the good sheriff comes looking for us."

"They won't know we did anything. They've got to find that deputy in there first."

"No they don't. Use your head, Tom. The sheriff sent his boy to follow you. His boy disappears. Unless this sheriff's stupid, he's gonna send his people out looking for you and the deputy at the same time."

"He's not stupid. We better get going. We can leave Sam's Blazer at the lake house and take the pickup. That ought to help a little. But it's kind of hard to get lost in a small town where everybody knows me and every member of my family."

Our prisoner started squawking again. Joey pushed open the back door and said, "I saw a pair of dirty rag socks sticking out of some hunting boots upstairs. They ought to be pretty ripe by now." The deputy got quiet again.

I said, "Nobody can hear him out here."

Joey winked at me and said, "I know."

We took both the pickup and the Blazer to the lake house. Five minutes after we drove up, we had the diving gear and explosives, a can of gas pilfered from Sam's fishing boat, and a two-hundred-foot roll of nylon ski rope loaded in the pickup and hidden beneath a tarp stretched across the truck bed. We left Sam's Blazer parked next to the lake house, loaded into the pickup, and followed Susan's map to the dock where Bird's boat was supposed to be waiting.

Mr. Simpkins lived in an unpainted house at the end of an old dirt road that angled off Whiskey Run across from Susan's farm. He did not live on Cedar Lane. His was a wholly different and a much older world, a place where country folks lived in cabins built along the river-bank by fathers and grandfathers. The dirt drive led past Simpkins' house and down the steep riverbank before butting into a concrete ramp that angled down and disappeared into muddy water. Next to the ramp, an old dock constructed of creosote timbers floated on oil drums full of Styrofoam. Bird's Boston Whaler bumped against tread-bare whitewall tires lining the far side of the dock.

We seemed to be alone. Joey got out and casually walked around the truck to my side, then leaned against the door and whispered, "We're being watched."

"What?"

He was smiling. "Look up at the house when you get a chance. Don't be obvious." I stepped down out of the truck and began untying the tarp. Joey was right. Every window was covered with drawn curtains, but at one double-sash window near the left corner, the curtains were parted into a dark oval just big enough for one eyeball to peer out.

"Don't worry about it. Probably just Mr. Simpkins." As I spoke, I turned toward the window and waved. The curtains snapped shut.

Joey said, "That must be that small-town friendliness I'm always hearing about. You ever get the feeling you're not exactly beloved around here?"

I said, "Beloved?" Joey just smiled and started unloading the truck and stacking our equipment on the dock.

Bird's Boston Whaler was filthy from months of disuse, but after a little priming, the motor sputtered and popped and kept running. The corner of a rusted gray toolbox protruded from underneath the raised midsection, and the locked chest Susan had mentioned was in the bow. Joey found a screwdriver in the toolbox and popped the lock off the chest. Mildewing fins, scuba masks, snorkels, and other assorted odds and ends that would have been useful to Bird on the water were jumbled inside. Three diving lights encased in yellow rubber and caked with scum and mildew lay beneath the black diving equipment. One worked. After trying five different combinations of batteries rolling around loose in the chest, we got another one to light up.

Joey untied us from the dock, and I backed around and started up-river. It was a workday for most people, and we saw only two other boats. Both were anchored in small slews and floated beneath gray-haired retirees getting in an afternoon's fishing. I had copied a couple of Bird's landmarks onto the Corps of Engineers map, and the Venus spot was easy to find. It lay inside a crooked slew filled with rotting tree trunks that pierced the surface and poked into the sky like giant burned matches. I steered the boat into a little cup of water that curved into the bank under the branches of a weeping willow. The slender leaves were gone, but the cascading streaks of branches were enough to provide cover from anyone on the main river.

Clouds covered the sun, and the world appeared in shades of gray. Joey said, "Shit, Tom. This is taking too long. It's already past two."

"Well, the phone hasn't rung. Maybe the deputy was full of shit."

Joey looked doubtful. "Maybe. Let's just get moving. Andy of May-berry ain't gonna find us in fifteen minutes, but it probably ain't gonna take all day either."

We both stripped to shorts and squeezed into wet suits. Joey checked out the tanks and regulators while I gathered the rest of the equipment. Based on the theory that I had dived in the river before and could, therefore, find my way around in the murky water, Joey stayed on board while I went looking for the cave entrance. When I came up to have another look at the map, Joey said the phone had rung.

I asked, "What'd you do?"

"Answered the frigging thing. Didn't know what else to do."

"What?"

"Sure. Told them everything was okay. Said I forgot to call in. I don't think they bought it. The guy on the other end asked me to hold for the sheriff."

"What'd you do then?"

"Hung up."

I said, "Smooth."

Joey laughed. "Worth a try. You think maybe you could find that cave now?"

I resurfaced twice more to look at the map before finding the entrance to the cave. Zollie was right. I did not want to go in there. The opening was about three feet across and only a little over two feet from top to bottom, and the water at the mouth of the cave felt twenty degrees colder than the rest of the slew.

I went up to get Joey. "You're not going to like this."

"I already don't like this." He put the regulator in his mouth and plunged backward over the side of the boat. We each had lights. I led him to the mouth of the narrow cave. Even through his mask, Joey was able to look at me like I had lost my mind. I turned and kicked into the opening. Brown water turned pitch black and grew even colder as the undiluted stream of frigid groundwater rushed across my face and shoulders. I had swum only a few feet when I felt someone grab my ankle. Joey pulled me back out of the tunnel and pointed at the surface. We headed up.

On top of the water, Joey pulled his mouthpiece out and spat into the water. "Shit, Tom. There ain't any way in hell that I'm gonna fit up in that thing."

"I'm sorry. You're right. I should have known that. Look, you just stay here, keep your eyes open. I'll check it out."

Joey said, "Hang on," and swam over to the boat. He came back with the roll of nylon rope. "Here, tie this to your weight belt. Get it on there good. I'll hook the other end on my belt and wait outside the tunnel. If you get turned around, just follow the rope."

"Yeah. I learned about cave diving and safety lines when I got certified. I just didn't think I'd ever be stupid enough to actually do this shit."

Joey said, "Just don't untie that line. It ain't gonna do you or me or Kelly any good for you to be floating around dead in some fucking hole in the ground." I nodded and pulled my mask down. Joey said, "Hey, wait a minute. You said that inside that thing there's some big-ass cave that's above water level, right?"

I pulled out my mouthpiece. "Yeah, that's right."

"You know not to breathe that air, don't you? Shit could have some kind of fucking prehistoric bacteria in it that's been dead everywhere else for a thousand years, or it could look okay but not have any oxygen. You need to keep your regulator in."

I had never seen Joey this nervous. I said, "Thanks, Mom."

Joey looked a little embarrassed. He said, "Eat shit," and popped his mouthpiece in. We headed back down.

Ancient seashells and smooth rock fragments covered the river floor just beneath the mouth of the cave, where the feeder stream had deposited them over the last few centuries. Joey pointed at the gravel and disgorged enough air from his flotation vest to settle on the bottom. I nodded and turned once again into the dark tunnel. I couldn't tell whether my light just wouldn't penetrate the black or there just wasn't anything there. The place was lifeless, not even a bubble to reflect the light.

Alone in the black freezing water, the pounding of my heartbeat echoed in my ears. I began to concentrate on the rhythmic thuds, listening for something. Zollie had claimed the cavern was thirty feet from the entrance. After it seemed that I had swum thirty feet three times over, the sides of the tunnel spread. I kept moving, but it seemed too far. A panicked thought jarred my concentration, and I grabbed at my weight belt. The line was still there. I was okay for another ten seconds of counting heartbeats until a worse thought wormed into my mind—maybe the other end had come loose from Joey's belt.

Shit. Breathe deep. Breathe deep. Slow.

Cold water continued to stream past. Up ahead, something caught the light beam. The walls were moving in again. The whole world contracted and focused into a black orifice tinier than the small opening where Joey waited on a mound of clean gravel. I had pushed into the tiny hole up to my waist before a logical thought finally pierced through fear and panic and my newfound fascination with my own heartbeat. I pulled back into the open space and found the inflation button on my vest. Letting in air from the tank little by little, I rose up until the water fell away from my head and I stared into total blackness—a void without sound or light or even the tactile rush of water.

I let more air flow into the vest to raise my shoulders above the surface, then raised the diving light out of the water and pointed it straight up. Scum-covered ropes and hammocks crisscrossed in the light beam, throwing sharp, cobweb patterns on a filthy stone dome that rose thirty or forty feet above my head. I realized I must have moved down as much as forward, and I thought I understood something else.

Picking the safety line out of the black water, I aimed Bird's diving light down the dripping yellow cord and saw it stretch out toward the opposite side of the cavern. My stomach muscles tensed. Wrapped in dark and cold and fear, I had kicked out of the tunnel and across the cavern floor and started into a thin artery of the underground stream.

I pulled my concentration back to the job and ran the light over the interior of the cavern. The round dome came down and bent into a more or less triangular shape twenty feet above the water. Beneath the ropes and hammocks, an uneven stone ledge formation ran around two of the three walls, providing a dry place to work about three to four feet above the water in most places. After a few false starts, I was able to pull up onto the ledge and stand there. My light beam found the iron rings Zollie had described. Nylon ski ropes, like the one tied to my belt, had been lashed to the rings. And a couple of feet out from the wall, Hall had tied battery-operated Coleman lanterns in four places. Only one worked.

Greenish- and brown-and-black-stained hammocks held more than a hundred paint cans dipped in black tar, and three sealed boxes strained the webbing of a large hammock that hung higher than the rest. It was time to see how much Zollie had lied about. Joey had the knife. I pulled the wire handle off one can and used it to scrape through the tar around the lip, then, between bouts of gouging myself in the palm, managed to pry the lid off. Too dark to see, I pulled over the diving light and shined its beam into the can. A brick stood on end in the center of a thick ring of crumpled black plastic. I ripped open what looked like a trash bag and found swirls of cash pressed into the can in layers. Mostly fifties and hundreds. Nothing smaller than a twenty. Unbelievable.

I got the wire handle back on the can and pressed the lid closed with my foot. Tiny fluorescent lines on my stainless steel Rolex pointed to two-thirty.

The slack line came easily. If the rope was two hundred feet long, the tunnel was only fifty, which was about half as far as I thought I had come. I was careful not to pull in all the slack, fearing that if Joey felt a sudden snatch on the line he might panic and haul me out butt first. When a hundred feet of line was stacked in loops at my feet, I put the can I had opened, along with three of its brothers, on the small ledge and tied the safety line to the handles, leaving enough slack so that, when I jerked the rope for Joey to reel in the slack, he would see the cans come out before he could snatch me back into the tunnel.

When the knots were secure, I hauled in every inch of slack line. Joey felt the line go taut and gave two quick yanks. I yanked back two times. Nothing happened. I yanked three times. Nothing. I grabbed the rope in both hands and yanked it as hard as I could three times. Joey nearly snatched me off the ledge. Yellow ski rope started shooting into the tunnel like a winch was hooked to the other end. My paint cans flew off the ledge and hit water. Now the rope slowed as the cans created a drag that made Joey work to move them through the narrow cave. Soon the line stopped moving. I guessed Joey had seen the cans. The line tightened again, and I got ready to untie the thing from my belt to avoid being yanked off the ledge. Then, as quickly as the line had pulled tight, it went slack and then tight again. I felt Joey give three quick pulls. The line went slack, and I hauled it in.

Forty minutes later, all but one hammock was empty, and I was coated from head to toe with brown and black slime. And it was about to get worse. I climbed up on the empty hammocks to reach the top webbing, where three boxes of cocaine waited to be unloaded. On the second hammock up, I slipped on the gunk covering the nylon ropes and hung there by one hand, twisting around and trying to get my other hand into the netting and scramble back up. That wasn't happening. I let go and hit the black water with a loud *bloosh* that was still echoing in the cavern when I came up.

Back on the ledge, I gave serious consideration to leaving the drugs where they were, but headed back up and managed to reach the boxes and line them up on the stone ledge. The smaller boxes went first and moved easily, if slowly, through the narrow cave. The last and largest box was almost as big as the tunnel, but Hall and Zollie had gotten it in, so I figured it would go back out. I wrapped rope around all four sides like a Christmas present and made a loop for my wrist about three feet on my side of the package. Then I put my fins back on, switched off the Coleman lantern, and gave the line the usual three yanks. Joey hauled in line, and I jumped into the water with the box to get a free ride out at Joey's expense. I put my left wrist into the loop and held the diving light in my right. The tunnel came up fast and swallowed the box and me. This time I was with the current, and someone else was furnishing the propulsion.

At least, it was a free ride until the tunnel narrowed just enough so that the box had to slide against the top and bottom to move forward, and I had to push to move it along. Then it stopped. I pulled back on the box and tried fitting it through at a different angle. Just as I had it cocked up to work it around a rock outcropping, Joey gave a yank that should have pulled a heifer through the tunnel. Instead, he wedged the tar-covered blob into the narrow cave like a wine cork.

Time to stay calm, just wait. Thudding heartbeats surged back into my ears. Seconds passed. *Don't just float here in this tube. Do something.* I put both hands against the box and pushed, then pulled, twisted, and finally clawed at it. Water pressed against my chest, suddenly making it hard to breathe. There was no way to turn around. I tried swimming backward. Maybe Joey was wrong, maybe I could breathe the air in the cavern until he could come back with someone to help.

And who would that be? I'm down here committing a felony. I tried to push at the water with my hands, to push backward into the cavern that lay twenty feet behind me now. The clumsy movement wasn't strong enough to move the tanks, a flotation vest, flippers, and a hundred and eighty pounds of me against the cold current. The diving light twisted and bumped awkwardly, finally falling and sinking into silt beneath my hips. I had to find a way to back up—at least enough to get the light. The light was the only reason I hadn't already lost it completely in this place. No stones or roots or hard earth to grab, I dug my fingers into the soft sides of the tunnel and felt them sink into silt and algae and ooze the consistency of mucus. I was starting to lose it. Flailing at the sides with both hands, I reached the light and plucked it out of the silt.

Something moved in front of me. I froze, then focused the light beam on the box. It didn't so much wiggle as jolt a little in the tunnel's grip. Suddenly, the tar-covered package seemed to explode, and white clouds of cocaine billowed out toward me in slow motion, clouding the dark water and looking like the pictures of Mount Saint Helens blowing clouds of smoke and ash into the sky. I thought Joey had pulled hard enough to rip the box apart. I didn't give a damn about the cocaine. I started swimming forward, kicking hard, undulating my body like a porpoise, trying to move through the sickly white cloud of drugs. As I entered the thick of dissolving cocaine, a pair of hands appeared out of the white soup and grabbed at the water a foot in front of my mask. One of the hands held a long knife. I swung the diving light and knocked the knife free before realizing the hands were Joey's.

He was frantically beckoning for me to grab his hands. I got hold of one huge palm with my free hand, and Joey clamped down hard, sending a shock of pain up my forearm. I tried to pull away. He wouldn't let go. I couldn't see his face, just his hands grabbing at me through white liquid. *Oh, my God.* The crazy sonofabitch had squeezed into the tunnel the only way he could fit—with his hands and arms pointed straight out over his head in a diving position. He was close to being wedged in. Joey yanked on my hand and made more grasping motions. *Shit.* I dropped the light and grabbed his other hand. Joey yanked three times—the signal we had used to mean pull, but he had to mean push. I flattened my palms against his and kicked.

Nothing happened for five or six extraordinarily long seconds; then Joey began to move. I tried to calculate the remaining distance to occupy my mind and push everything else away. But the distance didn't matter. I wasn't saving my strength for a sprint. This was everything I had. The flashlight faded away, and we inched through darkness. There was nothing but my heartbeat and exhaustion and burning and cramping in my legs. I wanted it to stop, but if it stopped we were dead.

Minutes passed, then Joey seemed to fall away. When he did, he snatched back on my hands and nearly pulled my elbow joints apart. We were out. Joey was a barely visible blob of black rubber in the brown water. I rose to the surface, and he followed. At the top we both pulled our regulators out and gasped in the cool autumn air. It tasted like copper and smelled of leaves and water and earth. Neither of us spoke. We didn't have wind enough to speak.

I swam to the boat and was inside sliding off my tanks by the time Joey started over. A jumble of tar-coated paint cans covered the floor of the Boston Whaler. Joey had lifted the two waterproofed boxes of cocaine into the bow and placed them next to Bird's old diving chest.

When Joey reached the boat, he just hung on the side, too exhausted to climb in. I said, "Thanks. Thanks, Joey." He just nodded. I asked, "You okay?" Joey still didn't answer. He just stared at the side of the boat. I could see his pale, shriveled fingers trembling where he had them hooked over the side. I gave him a few minutes while I peeled off the wet suit and put on a dry shirt. I reached out. Joey took my hand, threw one leg over the side, and climbed in. He got out of his gear, but then he just sat on the floor of the boat in wet shorts and no shirt.

I opened a can of money and held it out. "What do you think of this?"

Joey looked out at the water. "I dropped my knife down there."

I said, "Screw the knife. You almost killed yourself. You had more than a million dollars up here in the boat, and you came back down to squirm up in that hole and save me."

"Damn."

"What?"

Joey just shook his head and looked out over the water.

We loaded the money into one of the diving bags our gear had come in, sunk the empty paint cans in the slew, and placed a call to Susan on the deputy's cellular phone. She agreed to meet us on the bank and get the money and drugs hidden fast.

It was almost four-thirty when Mr. Simpkins' dock came into sight. Sheriff Nixon stood at the top of the concrete ramp flanked by two deputies. One was out of uniform and had been tied to a chair the last time I saw him. I slowed and pulled the boat in next to the dock. Joey secured the lines.

Nixon said, "Get out of the boat."

Joey said, "You caught the sonofabitch, Sheriff. That guy tried to run Tom here off the road this afternoon and ended up putting his car in a ditch. Lucky I came by. Lord knows what a man like that might have done if Tom was alone."

Nixon said, "Be quiet."

Joey went on, "Had to tie him up just so we could get away safe. You know, we think he's one of those big-time hired guns from up North. Maybe New York or Cleveland."

Nixon said, "I told you to be quiet."

Joey said, "Yessiree, that's a dangerous man you got there. Man just looks like a natural-born killer."

I smiled. Joey was back from wherever his mind had gone after the cave.

Nixon looked at Joey. "If you say another word, one more word, I'm going to shoot you in the leg." Joey did his best to look surprised, then held his palms up in the air in feigned surrender. Nixon said, "Now, get out of the boat." We climbed up on the dock. He asked, "Where have you been?" He was looking at me. I just looked back. He turned toward Joey. "What about you?"

Joey said, "Hey, you told me not to talk. I'm just trying not to get shot in the leg."

Nixon was not amused. He looked back at me. "I'm not going to ask again."

I said, "Good."

Nixon looked taken aback. "What?"

I said, "It's none of your damn business where we've been."

Nixon glared for a few seconds, started to say something, and changed his mind. Instead, he turned to his deputies and told them to search the boat. The uniformed deputy jumped down and went through our gear. The out-of-uniform Camaro-driving deputy frowned at us. Joey gave him his friendliest smile.

After tossing everything in the boat, the uniformed deputy said, "Nothing here, Sheriff. Just some fishing tackle, ski ropes, stuff like that."

Nixon looked hard at me, then turned to his deputies and said, "Let's go."

The plainclothes deputy said, "But, Sheriff, that big one there—"

Nixon said, "Get in the car. Now." And both deputies loaded into Nixon's patrol car. Nixon opened the driver's door, stopped to glare at us one more time, and stepped inside.

As the sheriff turned over his engine, the plainclothes deputy rolled down a back window and said, "I need my phone back."

Joey smiled a very becoming smile and said, "What phone?" The deputy cussed and rolled up the window. Nixon put the car in reverse and backed around before spinning his tires on the steep riverbank as he drove away much too fast. When the local law enforcement was gone, I pulled the deputy's phone out of my back pocket and punched in Susan's number. It rang a dozen times. Joey said, "She's probably out back hiding the stuff in that bomb shelter."

I said, "Probably," then turned and tossed the deputy's little black phone in the river.

Up at Mr. Simpkins' house, the curtains parted, and one eyeball watched us walk to the truck and drive away.

chapter twenty-five

AFTER MEETING JOEY and me to pick up the money and drugs, Susan stowed everything in Bird's bomb shelter, then pulled a batch of crawfish étouffée out of the freezer to thaw. By six, the red elixir was bubbling on the stove. By six-thirty, Joey was cleaning his plate with a chunk of sourdough bread to soak up the last of the sauce.

Susan asked me to open more long-necks while she went into the paneled office off the living room and came back with three cigars. She led us out onto the porch, where she told Joey to grab two wrought-iron chairs and bring them in back. Susan flipped a switch next to the outside door, and hidden bulbs lighted the swirls of greenery around the house. In back, stars speckled the sky around the dark mass of Susan's splattered oak. Someone, probably Bird, had placed the outside lights in a way that managed to retain the cozy, isolated feeling of nighttime, while providing enough indirect illumination to bring faces and gestures into focus. Susan asked Joey to position the chairs facing the backyard swing. She and Joey took the chairs. I had the swing to myself.

The breeze was cool and light, and we got our cigars burning with a minimum of fuss. I said, "I hate to ruin the mood, but I've got eight days after tonight to figure out how to handle this thing with my friend in Birmingham. By the way, Joey, I think it's better if we keep names to ourselves."

Susan said, "Thanks a lot."

I said, "I'm not trying to exclude you, Susan. I'm trying to keep you alive."

Joey said, "He's right, Susan." Then he turned to me. "What are the options? I assume you've probably given some thought to this, seeing how you're gonna be dead soon if it doesn't work out."

"Thanks for the sensitive reminder. I haven't thought about much else." I said, "The way I see it, we have three basic options. One, we could give the money and drugs to, uh, the Godfather, and hope it's enough to get him to leave us alone."

Joey interrupted. "That won't work."

I said, "Yeah, I don't think so either. But it is an option. Let me just get the possibilities out on the table before we start shooting them down."

Joey said, "Excuse me."

I said, "You're excused. Okay. Two, we could go to the police, tell everything, or mostly everything, and hope for the best." Joey started to say something and stopped. I said, "Yeah, I know. You don't like that one either. Third, we can use the drugs and money as leverage to set up some kind of Mexican standoff. Okay, Joey. Now you can tell me why the first two options won't work."

Joey said, "Nice of you to let me talk. I'm glad you know that giving our friend the money and drugs won't work, because it won't. Number one, you said that Zollie Willingham said there ain't enough money or coke to make—what'd you call him? The Godfather? There ain't enough to make what's-his-name happy. He's still gonna expect something else, and he's gonna put you to work in Mobile. And he's gonna make you do stuff that will even make a lawyer's stomach turn."

I said, "Thank you."

Joey said, "You're welcome. Anyway, it also won't work for another reason. The Godfather's right-hand man—I'll call him the Lieutenant—is not exactly your biggest fan. If you don't produce, he's gonna convince his boss to let him spread your guts over Mobile Bay.

Sorry, Susan. And Ed . . . , uh, the Lieutenant, seems to me like the kind of man who'd take Kelly out too, just so he could tell you he was doing it before he killed you."

Susan looked at me. "Is he exaggerating?"

I said, "Unfortunately, no."

Susan said, "I'm going inside for a while," and got up and walked back to the house.

I said, "Damn. I should have known she wasn't ready for this."

Joey said, "She'll get over it. People always do. She just ain't gonna have a whole lot of fun until she does. Anyway, we can stop using those stupid code names. Hell, even I was getting confused." I was still looking at the house. Joey said, "Tom. I like the lady too. But you can be her big brother later. Right now, we gotta figure out how to keep you alive long enough to do it. You hear me? Kelly's depending on us."

"I know."

"Good. It's a good thing for you to know. Now, to recap. You give the stuff to Gerrard, and he's gonna fuck up your life anyhow. And Eddie's gonna kill you the first chance he gets. What was the second option? Going to the police?" I nodded my head. Joey said, "Well, that's the real stupid move. All you're gonna do is embarrass Gerrard at the country club. I guarantee you he's insulated from all this crap. But when you embarrass him, he's gonna have to make an example out of you. You and Kelly are gonna end up dead in a very public and painful way, so everyone else will know that you don't screw around with Mike Gerrard. But let's consider what might happen if you lived. Gerrard can set you up for the murder of Toby Miller in New Orleans, and he can probably put me there if he works at it. He could also point out that earlier today you kidnapped a deputy sheriff, stole his cellular phone, vandalized his car, and you capped off the day by lying to the sheriff about finding a couple million dollars in drug money and two boxes of cocaine." Joey paused. "Bottom line. If you live, you're going to jail, where you'll be some buck's girlfriend until either you kill yourself or Gerrard decides to pay another inmate to do it for you."

"You certainly do paint a rosy picture." I said, "Please tell me this is the place where you tell me how much you like my third option. So far I'm screwed and screwed, according to you."

"You disagree with what I've said so far?"

"No. I'm just not happy about it."

"Tom, I ain't trying to make you happy. I'm trying to figure out how to dig you out of this pile of dog shit you've got yourself buried in. All right? Now, option three. Use the money and coke to 'leverage a Mexican standoff.' That right?" I said it was. Joey said, "Now that makes some kinda sense. Let's look at that. We've got maybe two million dollars in a hole behind the barn. And we've got a shitload of cocaine. The money's enough to buy off most people twenty times over, but these folks deal in that much money every day, so we need to think about how to use the money to manipulate Gerrard, 'cause it ain't enough for a straight payoff. We need to think about a way to make Gerrard leave you alone now and ten years from now. And we damn sure need to come up with some way to control Eddie Pappas."

I said, "And it'd be nice to bury some of these assholes in the process."

Joey said, "That would be nice. Look, from everything you know, what makes Gerrard mad? What makes him stop being careful?"

"Someone stealing from him."

Joey smiled. We had the same thought.

I asked, "You still got that stuff you found in Eddie's trash? Canceled checks and a credit card receipt, wasn't it?" Joey nodded. "We still need something to trade." We sat in silence, staring into each other's faces, trying to think. "Let's go inside. I need to make a phone call."

"Rudy?"

"Yeah."

"It's Tom McInnes."

"I know who it is." Pleasant as always.

"I need to get a message to Zollie." Rudy didn't speak. "Can you get in contact with him?"

Rudy said, "Maybe."

I took a deep breath. "Tell Zollie I need some information to stay alive. Tell him I didn't turn him in to the sheriff, and I need him to help me now. I need a list. I need a list of as many names, dates, routes, and contacts as possible from his days working with Gerrard. Also, get the name of the commercial barge company Gerrard uses to move drugs upriver."

"Heck, I know that."

"What is it?" Rudy didn't answer. I said, "I need to know, Rudy. I need to know bad enough to come over there and twist your skinny little arm until you tell me."

"Golly gee, Mr. Whitey. You're scaring me to death."

"I don't much care whether you're scared or not. Without that information, I'm going to wind up dead. I've protected Zollie as much as possible so far. But if you don't quit being cute, I'm going to do whatever it takes, including kicking your smart little ass and bringing Zollie back into this. The name of the barge company is no skin off your nose, but it could save me. And it could save your uncle Zollie a world of trouble."

Rudy was quiet for a while. I let him think. Finally, he said, "IBC. Industrial Barge Company, Inc. Zollie said it was part of a company called Alturo Shipping. Gerrard owns it."

"Thank you, Rudy."

"Uh huh."

"Can you get my message to Zollie?"

"I might get it to him. He might not answer it."

I said, "Just get it to him. I need the information within twenty-four hours."

Rudy said, "Uh huh," and hung up. I felt *so* much better.

Joey and Susan sat at the kitchen table, listening to my conversation with Rudy. Susan said, "Well, I know the Godfather's name now."

I said, "Better forget it." I sat down and looked at Joey. "What kind of credit card number have you got on Eddie?"

"American Express."

"Bless you. I need you to call your Eddie Pappas look-alike in Mobile. What's his name?"

"Mr. Parveez Mullona."

"Call Mr. Mullona. Tell him we need him to visit half a dozen banks in New Orleans and, I don't know, say Dothan, tomorrow afternoon. Tell him there's ten thousand dollars in it for him."

Joey looked puzzled. "What?"

I said, "Susan, you don't mind if I place a couple of calls to the Caribbean, do you?"

chapter twenty-six

J OEY AND I stayed up late into the night counting money, while Susan stayed in the house and watched the entrance road for surprise visitors. Zollie had left me exactly one million, six hundred seventy-two thousand, two hundred and forty dollars. Neither Joey nor I knew how to value our two boxes of cocaine.

The next morning, Joey left for Birmingham at daybreak. Susan left for Mobile, and I headed for a hastily scheduled meeting with a law school friend in Montgomery. By 7:45 A.M., I was sitting in a small conference room inside the offices of a Montgomery firm that occasionally used my old firm's Mobile offices when one of their lawyers was in town for a meeting or deposition.

At exactly eight-thirty, I called Joey's pager number. Three minutes later, the button-covered phone in the conference room began beeping at me. The receptionist informed me that a Mr. Bat Masterson was calling on line four.

I punched the blinking button. "Bat, how's Wyatt Earp?"

Joey laughed. "Thought you'd like that."

"How's it going?"

"Almost too good. Eddie's out of the state. In Georgia somewhere. I called his secretary this morning and said I had a lunch appointment with him. She said he was out for the day. I got indignant, and so did she. Hell, she got so indignant that she told me that the only thing on his calendar today was a trip to Georgia. She suggested I get my dates straight."

"Nice lady."

"Yeah. Just about who you'd think Eddie would have for a secretary. Anyway, we don't have to worry about Eddie showing up at the bank this afternoon. The secretary even said he was traveling by car and could not be reached by phone. She said his other car was 'in an accident,' and he didn't have a new car phone installed yet."

"What about Gerrard?"

"Called him after I hung up with Eddie's office. Said I was a computer salesman, and asked if I could fax him a proposal. His secretary told me to send the proposal to the purchasing agent. I pressed, and she admitted Gerrard was going to be in later in the morning, but she made it pretty clear that he doesn't have time for salesmen."

"Somebody's looking after us."

"So far, buddy. Don't get cocky."

"I need to get off the phone. I'm supposed to call Susan at Loutie Blue's house at eight-forty-five. Where are you going next?"

Joey said, "I'm headed over to the Jefferson County Courthouse to get a map of Gerrard's lot in Mountain Brook. Then I'll take care of the self-storage unit."

I said, "Thanks. Good luck."

Joey hung up. I ran the plan over and over in my head, trying to think of what we might have forgotten, thinking of what might go wrong. I decided that pretty much everything could go wrong. 8:44. I placed a long-distance call to Susan. Loutie Blue answered. I knew her voice, even though I'd never met her. Joey said she had been a stripper and a hooker ten years ago when she was in her twenties. He never said what she looked like or why she was so loyal. Joey just said I could trust her.

I asked Loutie, "Is she there?"

Loutie said, "Yeah. Both shes are here. Which one do you want to talk to?"

"You first. I wanted to thank you for your help on this."

"I owe Joey. Anything he asks me to do, I'm going to do."

"Can you control Mullona in New Orleans? He can't do us any good if he's shot. You've got to keep him straight with plain, old-fashioned fear. He's going to have eight hundred thousand dollars of my money in his briefcase."

Loutie said, "Don't worry about our little Lebanese friend. I'll explain things to him. Hang on. Susan wants to talk to you."

I heard voices in the background, then Susan said, "Tom?"

"Yeah, Susan. It's me. Joey's in place, and everything looks good in Birmingham. Are you set down there?"

"Well, Loutie seems to know what she's doing. I gave her the money. This guy who looks like one of your gangsters is supposed to be here in about five minutes."

"Make sure he looks right."

"I did what you said. I bought a gold Rolex in Fairhope on the way in this morning, and I picked up a pair of two-hundred-dollar sunglasses. Not much I can do about his suit, but if he needs them, we'll stop and get him new shoes, a tie, shirt, whatever he needs."

"Listen, Susan. *We* don't need to do anything. You just turn the money and the job over to Loutie Blue and get back to Coopers Bend as fast as you can. Let Loutie do what she's good at." I paused. Susan didn't argue. "Tell Loutie to give Mullona the ten thousand when he's through, and tell her *not* to let him keep the Rolex or anything else we've bought for him. We don't need any loose ends leading back our way." I said, "By the way, what does Loutie look like?"

Susan said, "She's beautiful. Why do you want to know?"

"Just wondered. Tell Kelly I need those numbers from the safe."

Kelly picked up the line and gave me the information I had called about the night before. She sounded tired. I gave her the telephone number in Montgomery and said goodbye. After I hung up, I placed a call to the National Bank of the Bahamas and asked for Mr. Michelle DuBois.

Like many attorneys along the Gulf, I had set up a dozen offshore accounts over the past few years for nervous clients who were worried about divorce or bankruptcy or whatever. I wouldn't help them secret funds, but setting up the accounts seemed enough like normal legal services to let me sleep at night and look in the mirror in the morning. By the time the fourth client requested that service, I had developed a relationship with one of the officers at National Bank of the Bahamas—a man named Michelle DuBois—and he had suggested that I set up a firm account for my clients' benefit, noting that, when offshore accounts are needed, they are generally needed quickly. So, I had established a professional trust account—somewhere to put client funds until I could arrange for an individual account. The trust account was numbered, and I could have stolen the clients blind if I wanted. But they seemed to trust me more than their wives and husbands and business partners, and it had worked out pretty well.

Now I needed to talk with my friend Michelle in Nassau. I asked him to use the information on file to set up a separate numbered account in another country. Michelle acted as though my request were routine, and he suggested Jamaica. I faxed him a waiver so he could send my new account information to Montgomery by telecopier. At 11:03 the phone rang. I had a new numbered account at Trinity Bank of Jamaica.

Everything was in motion. Time to go to lunch and be noticed.

At eleven-fifteen, the staff at the Capital City Club scurried from kitchen to dining room with stainless steel platters of trout almondine, roast beef, asparagus, new potatoes, salads, and desserts. In an hour, the place would be filled with politicians, bureaucrats, lawyers, brokers, and other assorted respectable hustlers. I was early and got a table overlooking Dexter Avenue and the distant Alabama River. At the top of Dexter, the State Capitol hovered over Goat Hill looking down on the historic capital. At the other end, a bronze statue in an antique fountain pointed away from the Capitol complex and toward the river.

I pestered the waiter for three refills of iced tea and tried to sound pain-in-the-ass pompous when I told him, "I'm Thomas McInnes. Tell the front desk I'm expecting Steve Mallory from the Attorney General's office. And tell whoever needs to know it that I left this number with my office." At 11:50, Steve strutted into the dining room five minutes late, looking like someone who clearly was too busy to ever be on time.

"Tom. Sorry I'm late. How are you? You look great. Getting rich down there in Mobile, I hear. Just let me make one phone call, and I'll be right with you." Steve didn't seem to require, or even want, responses to his monologue. He said, "Go ahead and hit the buffet. Be right back." Steve headed out to the large entrance hall to use the telephones.

Steve had spent his first year at Duke law school with me. The second year, he decided he needed to go to school in Alabama if he wanted to be governor one day, and he transferred from one of the top-ranked private schools in the nation to the University of Alabama, which is a good school but hardly the Harvard of the South.

Now, I sat and watched the traffic on Dexter and waited. Fifteen minutes later, Steve was back, apologizing for the delay and wondering why I hadn't been to the buffet. I smiled. Steve ushered me through the short line, talking constantly, pointing out the best dishes, and saying "no, no, no," whenever I took something he hadn't recommended. Back at the table, Steve rattled on for twenty minutes about the "AG's Office" and its investigation into the previous administration. Finally, as if it were an afterthought, he asked why I had asked for the meeting.

I looked deeply into Steve's eyes and told him I had grown disillusioned with private practice, that I wanted to explore opportunities in the Attorney General's office. The sudden transformation from strutting politico to hamstrung bureaucrat was something to behold. I heard about budget restraints, manpower problems, and the current Attorney General's campaign promise to cut staff. After Steve finished rattling off excuses why he couldn't hire me, he finished lunch in four minutes flat, apologized for his busy schedule, and headed for the exit. I was pretty sure he'd remember the meeting.

It was 12:55, and Mr. Parveez Mullona should have been preparing to leave New Orleans after visiting the four largest banks in the city. I signed the receipt for the meal and headed back to the law firm. No messages were waiting.

At 1:30, Bat Masterson called. Joey said, "Heard anything?"

"They left Mobile at nine. I haven't heard anything since, but Mullona should have deposited all the money by now. What's happening on your end?"

"Either Eddie's still out of town or his secretary's a good liar. Probably both. I've got the map, and I rented the storage unit over the phone with Eddie's American Express number. I'll give some kid a twenty to pick up the key later this afternoon."

"You been to his house yet?"

"No, but I checked it out the night I waded through his garbage. The guy's a fucking peasant, by the way. Drinks generic beer from Piggly Wiggly. Eats a bunch of those diet frozen dinners."

"Joey."

"Yeah, well, Eddie's house is wired for an alarm. But his garage is separate from the house, and it ain't wired. Hell, he leaves it unlocked."

"What if it's locked this time?"

"I'll unlock it. What do you think I do for a living?"

"Loutie's supposed to call at three-thirty. Call back at four. I'll tell you whether to go for it."

For the next hour and a half, I paced, drank Cokes, and tried my best to digest the lining of my stomach. At 3:15, the phone rang. Loutie was on the line.

"Tom?"

"Yeah, Loutie." My head was pounding. I asked, "Well, how'd it go?"

"It's done. We had a little problem at the bank in Dothan, though. I'll get to that in a minute."

"Shit. Don't do that to me. What kind of problem?"

"Just hang on. I thought lawyers had nerves of steel." She was laughing, and she was not laughing *with* me. "We got to New Orleans around eleven. Mullona worked out fine. He seemed to be happy with the ten grand, and he seemed to understand that Joey was going to turn him inside out if he got any bright ideas about the rest. Anyway, we hit the four banks you told us about. Each time Mullona deposited two hundred thou in a new account, and each time the bankers told him they'd have to report a deposit that size to the feds."

"What'd he say?"

"He told them that didn't matter."

"Good. When do we get to the problem?"

"Hold on. We're still in Dothan right now. Got here by about two-thirty and went straight to the main AlaBank branch down here. Mullona went in and asked to transfer some money from several banks in New Orleans to an offshore account in the Bahamas. He told them he'd been in Georgia and New Orleans today working on a financing package, and that he had to have the money in the Bahamas by morning to set up a deal in the islands." Loutie paused. "And now we get to the problem." She said, "Mullona used the same retouched driver's license he used in New Orleans to open the accounts, but the officer said he needed another piece of identification. Mullona made some excuse that must have sounded like bullshit, because the officer went and got some senior VP, who took Mullona up to his office. I thought we were screwed."

"What happened?"

"They clearly thought something was wrong, so the senior officer called his main office in Birmingham."

"Shit."

"Yeah, that's what Mullona thought. But somebody in Birmingham apparently told the Dothan guy what a valuable customer Eddie Pappas is, and must have told him something about Eddie Pappas' *unusual* business dealings."

"Did that do it?"

"The Dothan VP asked for a description, which fit Mullona to a T. Then he hangs up the phone and starts kissing Mullona's ass, feeding him coffee, 'expediting' the transaction. You know, generally showing what a shallow asshole he is."

"So, the eight hundred thousand is in the Bahamas, right?"

"It's in the Bahamas."

"Thank you, Loutie. Please get the fake ID and burn it in the rest-room of the first gas station you come to, then flush the ashes. Also get the watch and whatever else Susan bought for Mullona and toss them."

"Tom, that watch is worth nearly ten grand."

"Okay. You can hock it, but no ads and no records. Is twenty thou-sand okay for looking after Kelly and for your work today?"

"No. It's not okay. It's way too much."

"Don't worry about it. If we don't pull this off over the next couple of days, you won't get anything. If we do, well, I figure I'm giving away money that Gerrard thinks is his, and I'm kind of enjoying it."

Loutie said, "I argued about it once. That's enough to salve my con-science. Goodbye. I hope you live long enough to give me all that money."

It was still a few minutes before four, when Joey was scheduled to call. I placed a call to Susan in Coopers Bend to make sure she had gotten home okay. When she answered the phone, she sounded out of breath.

"Somebody's been watching us, Tom."

"What do you mean? Did Nixon have someone follow you?"

"No. It's worse than that. When I got home, something didn't feel right. I checked the house and the studio before going back to the bomb shelter. Tom, it was wide open."

"You took the money this morning, didn't you?"

"Yeah. Everything I didn't give to Loutie or spend on stuff for Mul-lona got put into your office safe."

"Then it's okay. I mean, I know it's spooky to have someone mess-ing around your house when you're not there. But nothing's missing, right?"

Susan said, "No. But while I was in back looking at the open bomb shelter, someone ran a wire from my starter to my gas tank. I saw it in a movie one time. It's supposed to blow up the truck when you crank it."

"You okay? How did you find it?"

"I'm fine. I just kept looking for something wrong after I found the open hatch on the bomb shelter. But, Tom. Somebody was here when I got home. Somebody who wants to kill me was here."

"Get out of there, Susan."

"No."

"Susan—"

"I'm not getting run off my own property. I've got a gun and an alarm. I'll be fine. Just get this over with."

chapter **twenty-seven**

THE CONFERENCE ROOM smelled of perspiration and worry; eight hours of strain does not help one's aura. And now, after the conversation with Susan, I was more frightened than I had been all day. Joey said that people I didn't like tended to end up dead. It was starting to look like I was having the same effect on the people I did like. The receptionist buzzed me and said Mr. Masterson was on the line again. I said, "Tell him to call back in ten minutes," then hit another line and called Sam. I told Sam that Susan was helping me, and I told him that someone had turned Susan's truck into a bomb about thirty minutes earlier while she was working in her own backyard. Sam agreed to send three men with shotguns over to the Fitzsimmons farm. I suggested that he call Susan first, unless he wanted Susan to shoot three of his men. Sam said, "Fine," and hung up. The man loved for me to give him advice.

Seven minutes later, Joey called back. He said, "This is a precision operation, hoss. What's this 'call back in ten minutes' shit? You sitting there playing with yourself?"

"Somebody's been in the bomb shelter." Joey cussed. I said, "It's okay. Susan got all the money to Mobile that you didn't take, and you've got the cocaine, right?"

"Yeah. We can talk about that in a minute. Is Susan okay?"

"She's fine for now. Somebody tried to rig her truck to blow while she was in back of the barn. I called Sam. He's sending over three men with shotguns. She should be okay. What's happening on your end?"

"The cocaine is packed in new boxes and waiting in a little storage building rented in the name of John Smith. Of course, that name may not hold up in court, though, since I rented it with Eddie Pappas' American Express number." Joey was enjoying himself. He said, "The kid who picked up the key gave me a receipt for the credit card charge. I'll put that in the garage with the money in case the cops need a little help."

"Good. Everything else is ready. The accounts are set up. As soon as I hear from you about Eddie's house, I'll make the last two calls. Now I'm headed back to Coopers Bend. You can reach me at the lake house in a couple of hours."

"It'll be more like the middle of the night before I have anything to report."

"Thanks, Joey."

"No problem. Shit, this is fun. Just keep my ass out of that river, and we'll be fine."

I said, "Call me when it's done."

After thanking the office manager for the use of her conference room, I climbed into the Blazer and headed south. Everything was going too well. I kept waiting for the problem that was going to get us all killed, tensing every time some high school kid in a sports car zoomed past, watching for the gun that was never there.

Darkness had enveloped the river by the time I hit the gravel road to the lake house. All the kitchen had to offer was sardines, crackers, and beer—Sam's idea of poker food. A bottle of Louisiana Hot Sauce spiced up a meal of sardines on saltines. The beer almost made it bearable.

It's miserable to be in the midst of battle with nothing to do. Kelly was hiding out in Mobile with an ex-stripper-slash-hooker. Susan was holed up in her farmhouse with a big gun inside and three armed mill hands outside, and Joey was getting ready to engage in a little breaking and entering, transportation of stolen property, and planting false evidence. I, on the other hand, was eating small oily fish and watching *Hard Copy.*

I tried to read, did some push-ups, and listened for assassins. By eleven, I was unable to find ways to further entertain myself, and I was sleepy. I went to bed. At 4 A.M., the phone rang. For the first time in memory, I had no trouble waking up. Joey was on the line, and he sounded giddy.

He said, "Everything's set. I put the hundred thousand in a toolbox and hid it under some boxes in a corner of the garage. Then I put the dynamite in the trunk of Eddie's new car, next to the map of Gerrard's lot in Mountain Brook."

"His car was there?"

"Yep. Bastard came home around ten. I figured that was better for us. It'd be hard for the cops to arrest him if he wasn't home."

"You got your friend in Mobile standing by?"

"Yeah. Rick knows I'm gonna call. I'll call at seven to tip him off. He'll get the Birmingham police moving."

"Tell me again that you're sure he'll do it."

"He'll do it. I'm a reliable source to him, and the Birmingham cops will think he's one. He's told me before that the Mobile and Birmingham police work together all the time on drugs coming in through the Gulf and headed for Birmingham."

"Let me know when you've gotten him."

"Sure. Just sit and wait."

"Joey. When you're sure everything is on track, get the hell out of there. You need to be somewhere besides Birmingham today. Come back here. Meet me at the lake house."

Joey said, "See you before noon."

I set the alarm for seven and fell back asleep. At 7:27, the phone rang. Joey said, "Go."

I said, "What?"

Joey said, "We're set. Go."

At 7:55 A.M., I started calling Michelle DuBois at the National Bank of the Bahamas. No one answered the first call or the second. I just kept hitting the redial button after every ten rings. At exactly eight o'clock, the bank operator answered the line.

I said, "May I please speak to Michelle DuBois."

She asked me to hold and, after a few seconds came back on the line. "I am sorry, sir. Mr. DuBois is not in today. Can someone else help you?"

Wild thoughts of Eddie Pappas holding Michelle at gunpoint cluttered my head. I said, "Is he ill?"

"Are you a friend?"

I was a friend, but not in the sense she meant. I said, "Yes, I am. I just wanted to be sure he's okay."

"Mr. DuBois' youngest daughter is getting married tomorrow. He has taken time off to prepare for the ceremony."

"Thank you."

She said, "Sir?" And I realized she had been holding while I tried to think about what to do next.

"Huh?"

"Can someone else help you, please?"

I was really on top of this situation. "Oh. Yes. Who's handling Mr. DuBois' accounts today?"

"Ms. Grieber should be able to help. Hold on. I'll transfer you."

"Thank you."

"Yes, sir."

Ms. Grieber's voice was as harsh as her name. After initial greetings and a short discussion of Michelle's absence, I said, "Ms. Grieber, I need to wire funds out of my account to another account in Jamaica. My account number is one-one-one dash two-three-seven-six-one. My access code is three-one-nine."

"Hold one minute. Yes, sir. I have your account on screen."

"Do you have completed and verified transfers dated yesterday in the aggregate amount of eight hundred thousand dollars?"

"Yes, sir."

I said, "Please transfer all but fifty thousand of that amount to Trinity Bank of Jamaica," then gave her the account number in Jamaica. "The privacy of this account and its activities are protected by law, correct?"

"Yes, sir."

"Please do me one more favor." I pulled over a handwritten list of addresses and phone numbers. "Send verification of the transfer of funds to Mr. Eddie Pappas, four-five-six Stoneledge Drive in Mountain Brook, Alabama. But do not include the account number."

"No, sir. We would never do that."

"Good. And do not mention my name. My associate simply requires proof that the funds have been transferred. Please have the note say the following: As requested, seven hundred fifty thousand dollars was transferred to an overseas account on this date. The account information is excluded from this letter as per bank policy and as per instructions." I said, "Did you get that?" She read it back to me word for word. I asked, "Does that language pose any problem for you or the bank?"

"No, sir. It will go out today by first-class mail."

I thanked her again and hung up. The toll-free number for Delta Airlines reservations was also on my list. I placed the call.

"Yes. My name is Eddie Pappas. I need a reservation on a flight leaving Birmingham, Alabama, this morning and flying into Nassau, Bahamas."

"Yes, sir. Please hold." Twenty seconds passed. "All we have left today is first class."

"Wouldn't have it any other way."

"Yes, sir. I can put you on flight three-five-one-four leaving Birmingham at ten-fifty. You will transfer in Orlando with a forty-minute layover, for an arrival time in Nassau of three-fifty-five this afternoon."

I said, "Great. Again, my name is Eddie Pappas. Please put that on my American Express card . . ."

Joey rolled in around one that afternoon. We drove out and checked on Susan, then took Sam's boat out on the river, where we quizzed each other for oversights and mistakes while throwing a hook in the water every now and then. Since talking with Sergeant Rick Otter at seven that morning, Joey hadn't been able to get hold of his friend to find out whether Pappas had been arrested. Pretending to fish was a way to kill an afternoon. We docked around four, picked up fried chicken in town, and got back to the lake house in time for the local news.

It wasn't the top story, but it was one of the top three.

"Birmingham businessman Edward 'Eddie' Pappas, president of Alturo Mining Company, was arrested this morning at his Mountain Brook home on charges of possessing cocaine with intent to distribute."

Joey said, "You know he's in deep shit when they use his nickname like an alias in quotes."

I shushed him as the female reporter went on. "Police reportedly found explosives and a hundred thousand dollars in Pappas' garage, along with a map of his employer's home. Police speculate that Pappas may have intended to blow up his employer's home, perhaps with his employer in it. Birmingham Police spokesperson Talia Blackmon stated that the garage also contained a receipt for the rental of a local storage locker that is said to contain boxes of pure cocaine with an estimated street value of over one million dollars."

As the reporter spoke, jerky video flashed across the screen showing a handcuffed Eddie Pappas being guided into the backseat of a patrol car by a blue uniform. The station tried to squeeze the story for a couple more minutes, but only repeated the same information they had already given.

Joey said, "I'll be damned. We did it."

I said, "Yeah, we did it all right, but what is it? We're either out of this now or we're going to be dead very soon."

"You're a cheerful sonofabitch."

"Joey, I've tried Rudy four times today and couldn't get him. Without Zollie's information, I don't know if we have enough to stalemate Gerrard."

"You're a sleazy lawyer," Joey said. "Lie to him."

I said, "That's the plan."

chapter twenty-eight

THE ALARM BUZZED me out of a deep sleep at seven A.M. Gerrard hadn't called. Joey was still sacked out, making up for the sleep he had missed committing multiple felonies the night before. I let him sleep. Breakfast consisted of cold chicken and warm Coke. If nothing else, this battle with Gerrard was ruining my diet.

I peeped out the windows, did some calisthenics on the living room floor while Matt Lauer interviewed a writer with a bad haircut, and took a shower. But I never stopped thinking about what Gerrard's reaction would be to Eddie's arrest. The idea was to make it look like Eddie had gotten information from Toby Miller before I got to the warehouse that night. Gerrard was supposed to think Toby had gotten away with Hall's drugs and money after the murder on the river and that Toby told Eddie where the stuff was before Eddie killed him. That's why we chose the city where Toby was killed to make the deposits in Eddie's name. The general idea was to convince Gerrard that Eddie deposited the money the day before in New Orleans, drove to Dothan, had the funds transferred to an offshore numbered account, and then went home to Birmingham, where he stashed the cocaine in a self-storage unit for a rainy day. Putting the map of Gerrard's property and the explosives in Eddie's garage was more or less an afterthought to make it look as though Eddie had contemplated killing Gerrard to avoid being hunted down. I originally asked Sam for the dynamite to blow the River's Womb—maybe with Eddie inside, if I could manage it—but, fortunately, that screwy idea gave way to the plan that Joey and I concocted at Susan's farmhouse. It was a pretty good plan, but it hadn't exactly uncomplicated my life. As I told Joey, either we were out of the woods, or we were in deeper than we had been when we started.

A few minutes after ten, I got tired of worrying alone and woke up Joey. He was wide awake by the time I made two steps into his room. I said, "I've been awake for three hours."

Joey said, "Go away."

"Get up. It's time to start thinking about how to handle this mess if Gerrard doesn't call." Joey just looked at me. I said, "And I'm tired of worrying alone."

Joey rubbed his eyes with the palms of both hands. "What've we got for breakfast?"

"I had cold chicken. I saved a can of sardines for you."

"Thanks a lot. I'm gonna take a shower. I'll be out in ten minutes. We're going to town to eat." Joey got out of bed, walked past me, and shuffled down the hall in his boxers. I went into the living room and looked out at the river.

Everyone says he'll be ready in ten minutes. Joey actually was. He came out with wet hair, fresh clothes, and a disposition that went with his empty stomach. In town, we found a cholesterol fest at a small diner, then headed out to Susan's to see how she was faring under the watchful eye of Sam's armed men.

They were gone. Susan answered the door herself. "Good morning."

I said, "Where are Sam's men?"

"I sent them away this morning to get some sleep. They were here all night."

Joey said, "Anything eventful happen? I mean, after somebody tried to blow you up and all."

Susan laughed. "Not much. Just some pickup drove halfway across the dam about midnight. Whoever it was just sat there for a couple of minutes, turned around, and drove away."

I said, "That's weird. The same thing happened to me at the lake house a couple of days after Hall's funeral. I was sitting in the woods watching the house—"

Joey said, "You were what?"

"Watching the house."

Joey said, "Who was in it?"

I said, "Uh, no one. I was watching to see if someone, uh . . ."

"That's interesting, Tom. So you've also experienced someone turning around in your driveway. Of course, Susan wasn't hiding in the bushes watching her own empty house when it happened to her, but"—Joey was smiling—"I probably wouldn't tell that story to a lot of people, Tom."

I said, "Kiss my ass," and both Joey and Susan started laughing.

We had just gotten settled into the living room when the phone rang, and Susan went to answer it. She came back. "Tom, it's for you. It's your father."

I walked into the kitchen and picked up the receiver from the top of Susan's desk. "Hello, Sam."

Sam didn't bother with greetings. He said, "Mike Gerrard just called here looking for you."

"Where are you? At the mill?"

"No. I stayed home today."

"What'd he want?"

"Gerrard? He said he wants you to call him before the day's out. What's going on?"

"I'll tell you later if it works. Everything looks good now." I said, "Did you see the news last night?"

Sam said, "Yeah, I saw it. Looks like one of your problems in Birmingham took care of itself. That should help some."

"That was the general idea."

"What do you mean 'that was the idea'?"

"Nothing. I can't talk about it right now. If everything works out, I'll come by tomorrow and fill you in." I asked, "Did Gerrard leave a number?"

Sam said, "Yeah," and gave it to me.

I went back in the living room. "Guess what." No one guessed. "Gerrard just called my parents' house looking for me."

Joey said, "Well, that beats a bullet in the head. If he's calling, he's got something to say."

I said, "Yeah, but I don't." I stood there waiting for someone to say something that would make me feel better, but there wasn't much to say. I walked back to Susan's little built-in desk and dialed Gerrard's number. An older man—maybe the one who served us lunch at Gerrard's house—answered and then went to fetch his boss. Most of a minute passed before Gerrard picked up the line.

"This is Tom McInnes. I understand you want to talk with me. You know, I've still got seven days left. I don't have time—" Gerrard interrupted. I was bullshitting, and he wasn't interested.

He said, "I will be in Coopers Bend tomorrow by ten A.M. Meet me at the Bassmaster Inn. Do not ask for me at the desk or anywhere else. Come directly to room one-oh-two. We need to talk face-to-face."

I said, "I'm not crazy about—"

Gerrard cut me off again. "If you are not in front of room one-oh-two by five minutes after ten, you and your secretary will be dead before nightfall." Then he hung up.

The next morning, I didn't want to look anxious, but I didn't want to die either. I pulled into the parking lot of the Bassmaster Inn ten minutes early. Room 102 was on the back of the building. I followed the drive around and pointed the Blazer at a parking space just outside the room. A heavyset man in jeans and a windbreaker waved me away and pointed to a space twenty feet away. I parked and looked around. Four men were obvious—the guy directing traffic, a younger man leaning next to the room door, and two men in separate cars flanking either end of the back parking lot. I couldn't see anyone else, but figured there might be more. After all, I couldn't see Joey, and I knew he was watching me from somewhere nearby.

As I approached the door, the two men outside the room each gripped one of my wrists and led me inside. They spun me face first into the wall and the heavier man patted me down. He was very thorough. I've had girlfriends who didn't touch me in as many places as he did.

When he was through groping me, he said, "Okay," and Gerrard stepped through the doorway and walked past me into the room. Gerrard sat in a chair that had been pulled behind a round table covered with wood-grain contact paper. His men had arranged the cheap furniture into a kind of makeshift office. Gerrard said, "You two can step outside. Leave the door cracked." Both thugs left, and Gerrard trained his eyes on me.

The room didn't suit him. Gerrard wore a tailor-made, navy blue suit over a white shirt with French cuffs. A dark red tie separated the wings of his crisp collar with a perfectly triangular Windsor knot. The entire contents of the room had cost less than his shoes. Textured wallpaper showed through mustard paint. The bed, the dresser, and the table in front of Gerrard were all particleboard with sheets of wood-grain-look sheeting glued to the surfaces. The bedspread sported orange and yellow flowers on a cream background, and it had a hole in one corner near the foot of the bed.

I said, "Nice room."

Gerrard said, "I guess you know about Eddie." I said I did. He said, "Quite a coincidence. Eddie getting arrested with money and drugs in his house during the very week when you've been busy finding those same things."

"I haven't found anything, so far. And I'm starting to think I can't find anything because Eddie found it right after he talked to Toby Miller in New Orleans."

Gerrard didn't say anything. He was studying my face. "How do you think that happened?"

The man was working me. I realized this was where I was supposed to explain every detail of Eddie's alleged plan, like a guilty suspect trying to misdirect Columbo. I said, "I just figured Eddie got Toby to talk before I got to the warehouse. You know, Eddie wouldn't let Toby say much with me in the room. Just that he killed Hall. After Toby said that, Eddie shot him in the head. So, Toby and I didn't have time for a really meaningful conversation."

"I'm sure you feel just terrible about what's happened to Eddie, though."

"Nope. Couldn't happen to a nicer guy."

Gerrard said, "It has occurred to me that—since I'm not sure what happened here—I'd probably be better off without either you or Eddie around spreading gossip. What do you think of that idea, Tom?"

I said, "I think it might work, except for one thing." I waited. He didn't bite, so I went on. "I may not have found your cocaine, but I have found some other useful things. You know, information. Information about your shipping company—Alturo Shipping, isn't it?—and Industrial Barge. I also know about contacts in Houston and Pensacola, and everything else Zollie could give me before he left the country." I decided to throw in Zollie's name at the last second. I had told Rudy that I would protect Zollie. But now Zollie had left me to twist in the wind, and I couldn't see where I owed him a whole lot.

"That's pretty weak, Tom. Am I supposed to be worried?"

"Well, I would be if I were you. You see, I've given copies of the records and notes Zollie gave me to two attorneys in different parts of the country. If anything happens to me or to anyone else I care about, the packages are going to the FBI and the Justice Department." I said, "It may not be original, but I believe it'll work."

"I'm very disappointed, Tom. All of that can be changed in time. Zollie's limited information about my business won't protect you forever."

"I think it will."

Gerrard rose to his feet, and I noticed that he was clenching his jaw. He said, "You little prick."

"Yes, Gerrard. I thought you knew that." I thought it was funny. He didn't.

Gerrard looked at the carpet for a few seconds and worked his jaw. Then he seemed to grow calm, and he sat back down as quickly as he had stood. "Tom, I was right. You are interesting. What do you want in return for the information that you think you have?"

Mike Gerrard, scion of old steel money, was a true sociopath, and that was his genius. I was betting that he would make decisions based on outcomes, based on what benefited him most, and not based on the human emotions of loyalty or friendship or even anger. I said, "I want to be left alone, and I want someone to take the fall for Toby. Hell, Eddie killed him. It's only fair that Eddie takes credit for it."

Gerrard said, "I don't think so. I like the way things stand now. I have you implicated in the murder of Toby Miller in a New Orleans warehouse, and you have some information that makes me somewhat uncomfortable. It looks like a balanced situation to me. It looks like the basis for a good business relationship."

"I can live with the standoff, but we do not have a business relationship or any other kind of relationship. The minimum conditions are that I and my family and friends are left alone, and that I am under no obligation to you whatsoever." Just in case he wanted to argue, I tried to make it plain. I said, "I am not going to work for you, with you, or through you. Not now. Not when hell freezes over."

Gerrard examined his fingernails, then looked out the window for a few seconds. Finally, he said, "And I can live with that."

I thought jumping up and down and yelling "yippee" would be too much. Anyway I had one more problem to work out. I said, "What about Eddie? He's going to try to kill me if he can."

"Oh, he can. If Eddie wants you dead, then you're dead."

"Well, that poses another problem. The information packs are going to be released if anything happens to me. It won't matter if it's Eddie who does it, you're the one who will suffer."

Gerrard smiled. "And you."

"Yeah, and me."

Gerrard said, "Eddie is not a problem. Recent events indicate that Eddie has either become disloyal, or he has allowed himself to be manipulated to my detriment. If Eddie has become disloyal, then I have no alternative but to end my relationship with him. On the other hand, if Eddie was dumb enough to be set up—and you really were smart enough to orchestrate this thing—then he's still a liability and I still need to end my relationship with him."

"How does that help me? If Eddie's not working for you, then he's free to come after me with no one to interfere."

Gerrard smiled the same friendly smile I'd seen over lunch at his home in Mountain Brook. "Tom. When I say I am going to end the relationship, I don't mean that I'm going to ask for my ring back. Eddie Pappas has become a liability. He will no longer be bothering anyone. Eddie's been a good employee, but his life is of little value in the overall scheme of my business interests. And, Tom, no matter what you think you know about my operations, your life will be worth even less than Eddie's if you renege on our agreement or cause me any further problems." He paused and said, "Do we understand each other?"

"We understand each other."

"Good." He said, "You may leave now."

I was climbing into the Blazer when it hit me: *It's over.* It felt like the first day of summer vacation in elementary school. I picked up Joey two blocks over and headed for my parents' house.

Sam listened carefully, said, "Good work," and offered us a drink. Wow.

We left and headed for Susan's, where Joey and I kidnapped her and took her to Jimmy Carpenter's restaurant for lunch and drinks and more drinks. On the way back to the farm, I said, "Susan, we've got all but about sixty thousand of the money left. Part of it's in my office safe where you put it, and the rest is in a numbered account in Jamaica. I want you to have two hundred thousand."

Susan had been looking out the window and laughing to herself. She stopped. "Tom, I'm sure you mean well, but I don't want your brother's drug money." I tried to interrupt. She said, "Shut up, Tom. This is a wonderful afternoon. You're going to screw it up if you keep talking."

I shut up.

Susan asked us to stay over at the farm, but we still had to drop off Sam's Blazer and go back to the lake house and pack before we could head for Mobile, where I wanted to get an early start the next morning making arrangements to get the rest of the money out of my safe and into a nice safe bank in the Bahamas. As quickly as I could arrange it, Kelly and Christy were each going to get big chunks of the money and so was Joey, and Loutie Blue would get her twenty thousand.

Joey followed me in his rental car while I drove the Blazer to my parents' house, then he waited outside while I spent some time talking with Mom. Finally, we headed back out to the lake house to pack and make phone calls to Loutie Blue and Kelly. More than two hours after dropping Susan off at the farm, Joey and I headed for Mobile in the rental car. Joey still drove like a cop, which is to say he showed total disregard for speed limits and the laws of physics. When we pulled onto the white gravel drive at my beach house, he had shaved thirty minutes off my best time.

As he came to a stop, I said, "Joey, we've got a lot of money, and you're going to be quite a bit richer in a couple of weeks."

Joey said, "That's all I ever wanted to be."

"Look, I don't know how I'm ever going to thank you for what you've done. You put your life on the line for me more than once during the last couple of weeks."

Joey said, "You aren't gonna kiss me on the mouth now, are you?"

I didn't think I heard him right at first. I said, "Huh?"

Joey said, "Get the hell out of my car."

The man certainly knew how to accept gratitude. I opened the door and got out, then yanked the door back open at the last second before it slammed shut. I said, "Look," and pointed at the carport. There in the shadows was the Jeep Zollie borrowed the night he left me tied to a chair.

Joey just said, "That was nice of him." Then he seemed to think better of it and reached to pull his gun out of the glove box. As he stepped out of the car, he said, "Like I said, Tom. You're getting to be a real pain in the ass." As he walked around to my side of the car, he said, "Stay here." Then he disappeared around the beach side of the house. Twenty seconds later, he came walking back with his gun dangling from one hand. "Somebody in there all right." He was smiling.

"Who?"

"I've never seen her, but unless you know two beautiful, tall women with auburn hair and green eyes, I believe it's Christy what's-her-name from Coopers Bend."

"You're kidding."

"No shit. She's in there setting the table with silver and candles and flowers. Got the lights down low and a fire going. I don't know what you're having, but I'm pretty sure she's planning on tube steak for dinner."

I shook my head. "This is unbelievable."

Joey laughed. "You can say that again. A puny little lawyer-type like you. Must be one of those pity things you hear about on 'Oprah'." As he opened the driver's-side door, Joey said, "Go for it. It's a perfect way to end a perfect day. Hell, I think maybe I'll go see what Loutie Blue's up to. See you around, buddy." And he was gone.

chapter twenty-nine

SOMETHING SMELLED WONDERFUL. Christy was in the dining room, bending over the table in a dark green silky dress that moved in and out with every curve. I said, "Hello there," and she turned to face me.

Christy said, "I wanted to surprise you."

"You did."

"Good." She walked over to the sideboard, filled two glasses with ice, and poured Glenfiddich into both. I walked over to take the drink, and she met me halfway. "We have cold lobster, fruit salad, and an ice-cold white burgundy. Nothing's hot, so it will all keep. You can eat now, or you can have a few drinks and relax and then eat."

"I must be dreaming."

Christy smiled. "I'd say you've earned it. After everything you've been through in the last few weeks, I couldn't stand the idea of you coming home to an empty house and ordering a pizza."

"Bless you. Look, I need a shower. Give me fifteen minutes, and I'll be right down."

Upstairs, I clicked on the lamps and got undressed, tossing my keys, money, and billfold on the bed. When I dropped my pants, Sam's 9mm Browning clunked onto the floor behind me. All I needed was to get shot in the ass with my own gun and ruin Christy's plans. Christy would be disappointed. I would have cried. I pulled open the drawer in the bedside table and dropped the Browning inside. I noticed the phone was unplugged, and the thought ran through my mind that Joey must have left it unplugged days ago when he checked the beach house for phone taps. I snapped the plastic plug back into the wall jack.

The water temperature had just gotten perfect when the phone rang. Too much had happened that day to ignore the call. It could be Susan or Joey or Kelly or Loutie Blue; it could be a lot of people who deserved to have the phone answered. I walked out into the bedroom and picked up the receiver.

After I said hello, a familiar voice said, "Tom, this is Sheriff Nixon."

"Are we going to argue about the mess at the dock yesterday? Because if we are, I just don't have the energy—"

"Tom, Susan Fitzsimmons has been attacked."

"What are you talking about? I was with her until two o'clock. I ate lunch with her."

"It must have happened right after you dropped her off. Someone was waiting for her in the house. Came at her with a knife. Really cut her up."

"Is she—"

"She's alive, but she's in bad shape. I've been calling you for hours. Where have you been?"

"I just got home. How bad is she?"

"Dr. Pearson operated on her this afternoon. He says she'll be okay, but it looked bad for a while. Tom, I need to know if you've seen Christy Shores."

"Why?"

"Answer me, Tom. Christy's the one who attacked Susan."

"Bullshit. That's bullshit."

"Susan told us herself when she came out of surgery. She said Christy was screaming about Susan fucking you and getting all the money. Christy left Susan for dead, Tom."

The room swirled out of focus. Nixon was saying something else that sounded like static. The line went dead. Christy had her finger on the button in the earpiece well. She said, "Who was that?" I couldn't answer. "Tom, please tell me who was on the phone. I unplugged the phones so we wouldn't be bothered tonight. Who was it?"

I sat down on the bed and nearly lost the towel tied around my waist. I said, "Sheriff Nixon. He told me what you did to Susan Fitzsimmons, Christy."

"What are you talking about?"

"He said you attacked her with a knife."

"Tom. No. You know that's not true. Tell me you know that's not true."

"Susan's alive, Christy. She came out of surgery and told Nixon what happened." I looked up at her face. "How could you do that? Why on earth would you do that?"

Christy's face changed. Even her posture changed. She looked ready to fight. "That bitch was trying to get you and the money. I was just protecting what's mine, Tom. Don't you understand? You're smart. Hall always called you that—the smart one. We could have every-thing, Tom."

"Get the hell out of here."

"Listen, Tom. You've got to listen. I gave Hall everything. I put up with his fights and gambling and getting messed up on drugs. I put up with everything, and he said he'd look after me. Hall said he was sav-ing up so we could leave the country, but he wasn't going to make it, Tom. He wasn't going to make it. Hall made all that money, and just when it looked like we were going to make it, that fucking Bird Fitzsim-mons had to stick his nose in. Hall saw Zollie kill Bird and it messed him up. He started having nightmares, snorting coke all day long. Hall got his brain so scrambled he was running his mouth around the wrong people. He was going to blow everything. Can't you see that, Tom? Can't you? I *had* to do something. I had to, Tom. But now it can be me and you. You like me. I know you do. It could be great, Tom. Tom? Tom!"

A cool breeze wafted into the bedroom through open French doors. Outside, a charcoal sky rested on black ocean. When I spoke, my voice was weak and sounded like someone else. "What do you mean you 'had to do something'?" I looked up. Christy looked like a trapped animal. I said, "You're going to take care of me the way you took care of Hall? Is that the deal?" It all finally fell into place. I said, "You're going to screw me for the money, just like you screwed Toby Miller. Just like you got that poor, stupid sonofabitch to kill Hall so you could stop Hall from blowing everything because he finally found his conscience." I saw the small hard fist coming and grabbed Christy's wrist just before she hit me in the temple. I squeezed the small wrist bones harder than I needed to and spun her toward the door. She landed on the floor with her dress around her waist. I said, "Get out of here." Christy started to speak. I cut her off. "Every cop in Alabama's going to be looking for you by morning. See how far you can get. I've got Hall's money. See how far you can get without it."

I looked out at the ocean and glanced back just in time to catch a flurry of green dress out of the corner of my eye and stiff-arm Christy in the sternum as she made a run at me. She fell to the floor, clutching her chest. When she could talk, Christy said, "You're a big man, aren't you? A big fucking man. Why don't you just kill me? That's what you want. Why don't you go ahead and kill me?"

Christy's face was flaming red. Veins popped out on her neck and forehead, and white spittle flew from her mouth and stuck to the corners of her lips as she spoke. I said, "Christy, I'm not going to kill you because you're not worth it. I'm going to be happy just seeing you go to prison for a very long time. Now, this is as civilized as I'm going to get. I'm not going to kill you. But I have a gun in this drawer, and if you come at me again—if you do anything but get the hell out of my house and out of my sight—I'm going to shoot you in the knee and call the cops to come get you."

Angry tears streamed out of her bloodshot eyes. She opened her mouth twice as if she couldn't breathe, then stood and walked out. I followed her down the stairs and locked the door behind her. A few seconds later, her Miata peeled out of the shadows where she had hidden it so she could give me a "surprise." Christy spun gravel down the driveway and squealed onto the pavement. I walked into the dining room, turned up the lights, and poured another scotch on the rocks.

Christy's fire burned in the hearth. It was built the way Zollie taught Hall and Hall taught her. I walked upstairs and placed a call to Gerrard's number. No one answered. Next I called Spence Collins at home. This time he answered his own phone.

"Spence, this is Tom McInnes. I need to talk with Mike Gerrard."

"Call me tomorrow at the office, Tom. This is getting out of hand. I'm sorry I ever got mixed up in this thing between you and Mr. Gerrard."

"Shut up and listen, Spence. Gerrard and I made a deal this morning. He's going to leave me alone, and I'm going to leave him alone. It's complicated, but that's about it. But the deal's got to change now, Spence. The man Gerrard and I thought killed Hall didn't do it alone. Hall's girlfriend, a girl named Christy Shores, put the killer up to it."

"Look, Tom. I don't want to know this. I don't want to know about any shady deals you made with Mike Gerrard, and I sure as hell don't want to know about any killers. Like I said—"

"Please listen. Christy attacked a woman in Coopers Bend with a knife this afternoon and nearly killed her. Christy's on the run. The police need to know she was a co-conspirator in Hall's murder. The cops need to know what kind of person they're looking for, and—when she's arrested—Christy needs to go to prison for a long time, longer than an attempted murder charge will put her there."

"You're upset, Tom. Take some time to think about this."

"Give Gerrard the goddamn message, Spence."

Spence sighed into the phone. "What is it?"

"Tell him I'll stick with our agreement, but things can't stop there. Tell him I will protect him as much as I can, but something has got to be done. Christy's going to pay for my little brother, Spence. You understand? I'm going to make her pay for what happened to Hall."

"Okay. I'll tell him, Tom. I'll tell Mr. Gerrard tonight, but you better have a good story for him when he catches up to you. That is, if he waits long enough to hear one."

"Thanks. Goodbye."

Ugly, tortured snapshots of Christy and Hall and Toby and Rodney poured into my brain. I went to the bathroom to wash my face. The shower was still running. I tugged off the towel and stepped inside. The water was still hot, and I let it beat against my skull and face and neck. I found the soap and tried to scrub away the filth of the last two weeks. When the hot water was gone, I stepped out onto the bath mat and rubbed at fog on the mirror over the sink.

A small noise seemed to float in from the bedroom. I listened carefully. Nothing. Then the noise came again. *Shit. The gun.* I hit the bathroom door and charged into the dark. Someone had cut the lights. I ran to the bedside, snatched open the drawer, and frantically ran my hand around the inside searching for the Browning. It was gone. Something moved in the corner of my eye. I dropped to the floor just as a shot rang out and the bedside lamp exploded. I bolted up, rolled across the bed, and hit the screen door shoulder first. I sprinted across the deck to the railing, planted my right hand on the rail and sprung over the top as another shot split the night and splintered wood a foot from my hand. The sand came up fast, and a hot jolt of pain shot up the outside of my right ankle.

No way to run. Can't take the weight. What? Dark. Pitch black. Overcast. Get to the water. Swim out. Swim way out. She can't see me in the water. It's too dark tonight, too overcast. Move, goddamnit, move.

Hurt and naked, I hobbled for the breakers as footsteps echoed on the front steps on the other side of the house. Cold water hit my feet. I dropped facedown into the foam, crawled into the surf, and began pushing out to sea with both hands and my one good foot. After fifty feet, I looked back at the beach. Nothing moved. Thirty more feet. I scanned the water between my little spot in the Gulf and the shoreline. Still nothing. Minutes passed. A shape, dark against the sand, seemed to float back and forth between the house and the surf, before turning and heading away to the north. I turned south and began to swim, first in a slow, quiet dog paddle, then with stronger strokes that sent waves of pain through my ankle and leg. A hundred yards down the beach, nothing moved on the sand around my neighbor's Cape Cod that sat huddled between two grassy dunes. The downstairs lights were on.

The pain grew stronger as I moved toward shore. Thirty feet out, the bottom came up and bumped against my knees. With my left foot planted in the sandy bottom, I eased up and slowly tried shifting weight to my right foot. Searing pain dropped me back into the water. *Shit.* I planted my foot again and looked up. Christy stood two yards in front of me, pointing Sam's Browning 9mm at my face. Wet hair was plastered against her skull. Dark makeup ran from her eyes and made jagged black streaks across her cheeks and lips, and the soaked green silk dress looked black and clung to her breasts and thighs.

She said, "Stand up."

"I can't. I broke my ankle."

"You're breaking my heart. Get up. I'm going to shoot you in the knee the way you said you'd do to me. Then I'm going to shoot your dick off. Then I'm going to put a bullet right through the middle of your brain."

I planted both hands in the sand to push up. Christy moved closer. She kept coming as I got my good foot under me. She was about three feet away now. Christy wanted a close-up view when the bullets went in. *What the hell.* I shoved the pieces of my broken foot into the sand and shot forward with every ounce of strength left in my freezing legs. I heard a loud crack and felt a hot coal pass through my right calf as we both crashed into the surf. I could feel her trying to get her hand free, to turn the gun and put a bullet in my stomach. I found her wrists, spun behind her, and pulled her under in a bear hug, trying with all my strength to crush her rib cage and hold her head under the waves.

The rest seems like a dream or a half-forgotten movie. I remember being very cold. I remember lying on the sand as frigid waves licked at my feet. I remember seeing Christy's dark body undulating in the surf. I remember thinking how small and limp she looked just before everything went black.

N OT AGAIN. IT FELT like I was tied to another chair. Fuzzy shapes crossed back and forth in front of a bright rectangle, and muffled voices floated through the room. This time I didn't drift back off.

"Tom. Tom? I think he's coming out of it. Tom! Can you hear me?"

I squeezed my eyes shut and opened them again, and Nixon's predatory black features came into focus. I said, "Get out of my face."

Nixon actually laughed. "He's fine, Sam. Just as big a prick as he ever was."

I looked down. Sam stood at the foot of the bed where Nixon had joined him. Kelly was asleep in a green vinyl chair. I said, "I think I killed Christy."

Nixon said, "Yeah, Tom. We think you did too. Your neighbor heard the shot that went through your leg there and called the police. They found you lying buck naked in a decent-sized pool of blood. Christy was facedown in the water about ten feet away."

I asked, "What's going to happen now?"

Sam said, "Nothing for you to worry about. Sheriff Nixon searched Christy's cabin last night before we drove down. Found the knife she used on Susan Fitzsimmons hidden out in a little potting shed. When we got here, they told us Christy had powder burns on her hands, and the cops are out at the beach right now with a metal detector trying to find the gun. Everybody knows it was self-defense." I looked down, and Sam said, "Tom, I know it's rough, you know, killing a woman. But you did the right thing. You've done the right thing throughout this whole mess." He turned and looked out the window. "Nixon agrees with me. Nobody else could have done what you've done here, son."

That had not been easy for Sam, and I didn't know what to say. Fortunately, only a few seconds of uncomfortable silence passed before a pretty young nurse pushed open the door and said, "Okay, everybody out. We've got a tired patient here. He needs rest, and it's time for a shot." Kelly woke up and stretched her arms into the air. The nurse said, "Come on, honey. You too. Your boyfriend'll still be here tomorrow."

Kelly stood up and smiled, then walked over and kissed me on the forehead. She looked at the nurse and said, "He's not my boyfriend. He's my friend." Kelly squeezed my hand and followed Sam and Nixon out the door.

My nurse pushed the door closed and came back to the bed-side. She reached into her uniform pocket and took out a bottle of yellowish liquid, a syringe, and a packet of alcohol swabs. She pulled liquid into the syringe from the bottle, dropped the bottle back in-side her pocket, and laid the syringe on top of the white covers next to my hip. As she tore open the swabs, she said, "I have a message for you."

I asked, "From who?"

She began to rub down the inside of my elbow with alcohol. "Mr. Gerrard wants to know if it's over."

"What?"

"I'm just a messenger. Mr. Gerrard wants to know if the girl's death ends it. He said you would understand. He wants to know if you're still going to the police about the girl, or if it's over now that she's dead." As she spoke, she lifted the syringe from the bed and held it near my arm while she thumped for a vein.

I said, "Yeah, okay. Tell him it's over. The deal's good. If he lives up to his end, then I'll live up to mine."

"He'll be pleased to hear that, Mr. McInnes. I think he likes you."

"Great." I said, "Now I can die happy."

The nurse returned the syringe to her pocket without giving me the shot. As she turned to leave, she smiled and said, "Not today."